Raves for ... Extraordinary New Novel of Family Love and Courage

"SUE MILLER'S *FAMILY PICTURES* IS TRUE TO ITS TITLE; READING IT IS LIKE FLIPPING THROUGH A FAMILY ALBUM, drawn deep into recollections that cut across time....The writing is so engrossing and the scenes so immediate that a reader feels like a participant in the family's complex history."
—*San Francisco Chronicle*

❖

"MILLER MAKES US FEEL, INTIMATELY...Her ambitious and complex story touches a major nerve."
—*Glamour*

❖

"*FAMILY PICTURES* IS EVEN MORE CONVINCING FICTION THAN MILLER'S ACCLAIMED BESTSELLER *THE GOOD MOTHER*; the author leaves very few stones unturned in this comprehensive familial portrait....A complex, deeply believable story about the intricate bonds between children and their parents."
—*Parenting*

❖

"AN ALBUM FULL OF FAMILY TRIUMPHS AND TRAGEDIES...Miller's is a disciplined, stunning performance, one that cannot fail to make a lasting impression on anyone who reads *Family Pictures* with an open heart."
—*The Atlanta Journal*

"ENGROSSING...HARD TO PUT DOWN....Each major character is beautifully drawn....Those Eberhardts upon whom the author turns her gaze are firmly imprinted on our consciousness. Their multiple perspectives are utilized to great advantage—we understand them, care for them, forgive them their trespasses more thoroughly than they can forgive themselves."
—*The Detroit News*

"INTIMATE...The currents of anger, pain and tenderness she describes are convincing."
—*Mirabella*

"STRIKINGLY RENDERED. With a photographer's eye, Miller distills the details that allow a reader to see her characters in their surroundings and furthermore to know what it is to be any one of them at a particular instant."
—*Chicago Sun-Times*

"A BIG, WONDERFUL, DEEPLY ABSORBING NOVEL THAT RETAINS THE VIVID DOMESTIC FOCUS OF *THE GOOD MOTHER* WHILE SPIRALING FAR BEYOND IT."
—*Newsweek*

Also by Sue Miller

INVENTING THE ABBOTTS
THE GOOD MOTHER

FAMILY PICTURES

A NOVEL

SUE MILLER

HarperPaperbacks
A Division of HarperCollinsPublishers

HarperPaperbacks   *A Division of* HarperCollins*Publishers*
10 East 53rd Street, New York, N.Y. 10022

A hardcover edition of this book was published in 1990 by Harper & Row, Publishers, Inc.

Cover illustration by Aristedes Ruiz

First HarperPaperbacks printing: May 1991

Printed in the United States of America

HarperPaperbacks and colophon are trademarks of HarperCollins*Publishers*

10 9 8 7 6 5 4 3 2 1

*For my father, James Hastings Nichols,
who helped me believe in my dreams*

and always, for Doug

I want to thank the John Simon Guggenheim Memorial Foundation for its generous support during the final stages of work on this novel.

Contents

PART

ONE

1

IT'S my brother Mack's birthday. He's fourteen. We're all sitting at the table in the dining room. The curtains are drawn, though you can see the glint of summer evening light through the cracks. When my mother rounds the corner from the kitchen with the glowing cake, we burst into ragged song.

Heaped next to Mack's place on the table are his opened presents—odd homemade things from me and my younger sisters; but a nice sweater my mother gave him on behalf of my other brother, and three Roy Orbison forty-fives from my older sister, Liddie. You can also see the neck of the guitar my parents have bought him, leaning against the table's edge. It seems to me that color rises to Mack's face as we sing to him, though perhaps it's just the soft light from the candles that makes him look this way—young, and suddenly sweet and shy. When my eyes meet his, I'm embarrassed; I feel a catch in my voice.

The moment we've finished the song, Mack leans forward and blows the candles out. In the silent twilit aftermath of our applause, my other brother—my autistic brother, Randall—speaks. "Happy birthday, dear Mackie," he says.

We are all silent, and then Liddie, the oldest, laughs. "My God!" she says. "Did you hear him? My God!"

"I wouldn't get excited, Lydia," my father says. "That's about his annual quota of words, isn't it?" And my mother's face, which has turned in astonishment to her younger son in the dim light, instantly drops. My father changes the subject; someone gets up to pull back the curtains on the windows, to let what's left of the daylight in.

This is the way I remember it. But I'm wrong.

My mother tells me he never spoke after the age of four or so. My sister Liddie says it's *her* memory, her story, one she told me much later. I've appropriated it, she says, the way I do with everything in our family's history. I've changed it to suit myself—made myself older, an observer, when in reality I was an infant when it happened, and Mary and Sarah weren't even born.

And yet. And yet it seems as clear to me as a picture I might have taken. I could swear this was exactly what happened.

But that's the way it is in a family, isn't it? The stories get passed around, polished, embellished. Liddie's version or Mack's version changes as it becomes my version. And when I tell them, it's not just that the events are different but that they all mean something different too. Something I want them to mean. Or need them to. And of course, there's also the factor of time. Of how your perspective, your way of telling the story—of seeing it—changes as time passes. As you change.

Now, for example, I see that we must always have known, my younger sisters and I, that we hadn't been wanted or planned, that there was something complicated and painful for our parents in our very existence. But what we would have said then was just that there were too many of us, too many children in our family. So this might be one place to start my version of our story: how we felt about ourselves, in our world, where every house spilled kids into the Chicago street.

Most of them spilled two or three, though. Four was a little excessive. Five absurd. And there were six of us. Six meant something different, a special case in some way. Catholic. Or a man who couldn't keep his hands off his wife. A neurotic breeder of a woman. People would ask, *"Six* of you?" and *yes* never seemed a sufficient answer. Occasionally I would say of myself and my younger sisters, "Well, we're the extras," passing along one of our father's nicknames for us without understanding it—as though it might answer the question. And sometimes it seemed to. "Oh!" the questioner would say. "Yes."

Certainly even then we thought of the family as neatly divided down the middle. The first three, Macklin, Lydia, and Randall, were the special ones. Even those names, we thought, showed greater imagination, greater involvement on our parents' part, than ours did: Nina, Mary, Sarah. Clearly by that time they had run out of gas.

But we didn't necessarily connect any of this with our father's nicknames for us. These were embarrassing not because of what they meant—which none of us stopped to consider then anyway—but because they existed at all. Not because they pointed to some quality we shared, but because they pointed to us. He called us "the unexpected guests," or "the surprise party." He would lower his book and watch us as we passed his study door, the three of us always together. Under his high, narrow forehead, his blue eyes had the trick that eyes in certain portraits or photographs do, of seeming to follow you while actually remaining steady, unmoving. "There they go, the extras," he'd say. Or, "Ah, the fleet's in. The Nina, the Pint-sized, the Santa Maria." We were "the little pitchers of health," "the coup de grace," "the last straws." We complained and laughed and whined about it, we told our mother, but it only made him worse.

"Pay no attention to him," Mother said when she was in a good mood. But when she was in the dumps, her mouth went tight. She would turn away from him quickly in anger. She'd pick up again whatever she was drinking—cold, milky coffee, flat beer, an inch or two of something brown and sticky in the bottom of a glass. "I don't know why you imagine they're never going to understand you," she said once to him. "Someday, out of the blue, you know, they will."

"And then what, Lainey?" he asked. And when she didn't answer, he said, "The truth shall set you free."

But there was no moment out of the blue, no revelation. It didn't happen that way. And though I did feel a strange sense, a sense that ran through my childhood, of being yoked to my sisters, of having some meaning as a group that had nothing to do with who I was alone or intended to be—still, what my father said remained as meaningless, as much a part of unexamined family habit, as when my mother called one of us "honeybunch" or "sweetie pie." Who would dream of asking what these meant, literally? In fact, it wasn't until years later, long after I already knew the sad story of how we got here, that I realized what the nicknames referred to, that I understood he'd been joking about it with us since we were small. Affectionately, ruefully, he'd dared to make fun of the awful way we'd come into the world, the way he'd felt about us before we were people. And we'd heard only the affection, paid attention only to his tone. "Ah, the unexpected blessings," he'd say mockingly, tenderly. "Let's count them: one, two, three."

No, in my version of our story, it was always my mother—boozy, or jittery from too much coffee—who made us feel strange when we were small. It was her intense loving that frightened us, her desperate quick embraces, her sudden anger, her "internal combustion engine," my father called it—a set of mysterious, private emotions which ruled her. You could never tell in what direction she'd suddenly veer.

My father, tall and sober and steady, would listen to me, to all of us. In spite of the teasing, the sense of mockery in much of what he said, he seemed reliably connected to the world of events in a way our mother didn't, then or later. He knew the names of stars, of galaxies; he knew what berries you could eat and which were poisonous. It was he who explained to me, with a little chart he sketched on a paper napkin, the Mendelian laws, which dictated that probably one of Impy's kittens—like her—would have no tail, two would have half tails, and one would have a tail the length of any other cat's. Because he was a doctor, it was he who sat at the edge of the bed when one of us felt sick, who touched our foreheads for the heat of fever, who looked for white blisters on our throats or the toss of red splotches on our bodies. His hands were cool and dry.

But that changes over time too. He moved out for a while when I was twelve, and for me, after that, his magic seemed to vanish. This was partly because, though he sometimes had Mack or Liddie over alone, when I went I was always invited with my two younger sisters. At that time I was eager to be thought of as different from them, more grown up, and this didn't seem fair to me. It was true that the first few times we visited were like an adventure. His new apartment was clean and bare. I had never seen such rooms, uncluttered by what I'd always understood to be the necessary, the normal, furniture of family life. There was a bunk bed and a fold-out couch in the extra bedroom, so we could all sleep together, a treat for us. For dinner he usually fixed us what he called his "spécialité de l'appartement," runny omelets crammed with mysterious flavors he wouldn't tell us the names of, but which we all loved.

But then, very quickly really, it got boring. We began to find things to grouse about to each other.

We never had exactly the books or drawing things or dress-ups we wanted; we couldn't get any real projects going because he wanted it all picked up before we went to bed. And strangest of all, the teasing seemed awful, embarrassing, without the others there—without Mother—to hear it, to be amused or offended. Three wasn't enough for my father. His gifts required an audience, a larger house.

He seemed to feel it too. He often phrased his invitations in the negative. "I don't suppose you'd like to come over and keep an old man company," he'd say. "I guess you're probably too busy to have dinner tonight." And as time went on, he asked us less and less. And what I felt about this shift, I realized after a while, was pure relief—relief that my father, whom I'd loved more dearly than anyone in my family, seemed to have forgotten us, "the extras."

I can remember that moment, the moment when I knew that, sharply and clearly. It was summer. I had been sent by my mother to get my brother Mack from Steinway's drugstore, where he liked to hang around. I was walking down Fifty-seventh Street toward the university, running my hand along the top of a dusty, squared-off privet hedge; and all of a sudden, here was my father, walking toward me on the other side of the street. He was alone, moving fast. He had his jacket off, hooked on a finger over one shoulder, and his tie was dancing out to the side. I stopped to watch him, and I nearly called out. But at the last minute I decided not to.

He did look over as he hurtled along—he glanced quickly my way. But nothing about me stopped his moving eyes or slowed his motion. He kept walking; he passed by me on his side of the street. I turned to watch him striding away, the swing of his jacket across his back, the lilting alternation of his legs in blue-striped seersucker; and what I felt was gladness that he hadn't really seen me, that I'd not had to talk to him. That he hadn't even recognized his daughter in this adolescent girl on the street.

Part of what shapes the story for me is that my father is a psychiatrist. Now that psychiatrists are defrocked weekly in *New Yorker* cartoons, it's difficult to recall what this once meant, how seriously men like him were taken. But when I was growing up in the fifties and early sixties, he was a sort of shaman in our world. My friends used to worry that he could read their minds, and often they were silent in his presence. Grownups too reacted oddly to him. They were too respectful, even defensive, as though he could see through them, as though he knew their weaknesses at a glance. "Now, I know this will sound compulsive," they'd say, after telling an anecdote or recounting a dream. Or, "I suppose you think I've got some sort of Oedipus complex."

More important to what happened in our family, though, was the way my father felt about his work. He loved it. He believed in it with a pure fervor bordering on the religious. I heard him speak often of the excited feeling he'd had while training of being in a profession that was truly on the verge of understanding how the mind worked. And he was as uncomfortable with those who backed away from the implications of Freudian teachings as a priest would have been about revising what was inconvenient or painful in the Church's pronouncements for a parishioner's comfort.

But he wasn't rigid or unkind in his approach to patients. On the contrary, his work brought out his most generous, gentle qualities. He had an office downtown, an office I went to as a special treat every time I had to see the dentist, who worked only a few blocks away. My teeth were "a tragedy," my mother said, and each time I went, I had to have at least one filling, usually two or three. After the slow grinding of the drill, the long tortured probing at what seemed to me like the place where all pain started, I would walk the two blocks to my father's building, rolling the silver bits around in my mouth, surreptitiously picking them out. Sometimes I stopped in the lobby and splashed water from the fountain onto my face before I took the elevator up, hoping he wouldn't be able to tell I'd been crying again in the dentist's chair. He liked me, he liked all of us, to be brave.

I would wait in the room outside my father's office, pretending to read *Life* and *Look* and *National Geographic*, staring at the disasters, at the photographs of inexpressive victims, phlegmatic witnesses. This seemed the mark of the adult to me, the blankness on these faces as bodies were carried past. I could hear his patient's voice—not the words but the dreamy murmur—through the frosted glass pane of my father's office door; and occasionally, too, my father's voice, clear, gentle, with a short question that set the murmur going again. When the patient was leaving—pulling on his coat and hat in the waiting room—I would carefully avert my red, sore eyes from his curious ones.

My father always took a few minutes before he came out, and when I saw him, I always burst into tears, even though I knew he didn't like it. He would hold me silently for a moment, not speaking, not comforting me except by his touch. And then he would tell me what treat he had been saving for me, as though I *had* been brave: a sundae, a special painting at the Art Institute he wanted me to see, a pretty doll just right for me at Carson Pirie Scott. His voice at those moments was always tender, and I remember the sense I had that I was getting something meant for someone else, that the special tone was connected to the office, to the patient who'd just left, to my father's professional life.

By the time we got home, my crying would have become a joke; he would say something about it in his usual mocking voice at the table for the amusement of the others, and I would have to laugh too. But I would remember his tenderness in his office, as though it were a quality that resided there; I would remember the soft murmur of his voice alternating with his patient's. Later I used to wonder why it was so difficult for him to bear the pain of his family when he was so forgiving of the pain of his patients. I've sometimes thought that if he'd had a different profession, maybe everything would have been different, too, in our lives.

It's especially hard for me to imagine what he must have thought when he discovered he had a son with what he believed at the time was a psychogenic illness. Wasn't there sometimes a bitter pull to his handsome face as he surveyed Mary and Sarah and me, just before he called us "the little pitchers of health"?

This was the way it had worked, I thought: My parents had made their family, they had had the requisite three pretty children, they'd bought a house on a street in Chicago where other young couples were buying houses in the years after the war. My father's career was flourishing, they loved each other.

And then it all went haywire.

Randall sat in their midst, more beautiful than the first two, but immobile. At two, he still didn't walk. He didn't speak except when whole sentences, out of context, dropped from his mouth, as though someone invisible were using him as a ventriloquist's dummy. He seemed possessed, my mother has said. Enchanted. Under a spell.

Sometime in the process of Randall's diagnosis—he was variably and at different times thought to be deaf, retarded, autistic, and schizophrenic—my mother got pregnant with me, as though she thought another child would break the spell. Mary followed a year later, and then Sarah a year and a half after that. From the start we knew what was expected of us. We were to be normal, happy. We were to make up for Randall's illness, Liddie's resentment, Mack's wild struggles. Sometimes, looking at us, my mother's eyes would fill with tears. "Oh, my perfect babies," she'd say, and swoop down on whoever was closest to fold her up against her broad, strong body.

For my parents, and for Lydia and Mack, deciding what Randall's illness meant and figuring out what to feel and do about it became lifelong preoccupations. Mostly it meant they struggled with each other, since they all disagreed about him. For us, though, for Mary and Sarah and me, Randall was a given. He was just there, silent and for the most part lost in his inner world. Sometimes he was in the way, but sometimes he was useful to us: he was the troll under the bridge, he was the baby in the carriage, he was the bogeyman, the prince, the father.

When we were older, teenagers, we occasionally called our siblings and our parents "the Giants." "What were the Giants up to today?" we asked each other, wanting only to know the mood in the house. We poked into their lives, talked about them, theorized. No one really had time or energy for us, the extras, so everything we knew we found out for ourselves. Shamelessly we opened letters, read diaries, eavesdropped on arguments, lovemaking. Unapologetically we used them, used the drama of their lives and their pain, as our primer. We appropriated everything.

Somehow, though, my sisters broke away from

all of this early on. They made their own lives, free and clear. And actually for a long time it seemed I had too. It's only more recently that I have wanted to think about it all again, to make sense of it once more—in a different way—for myself.

Why? Because I dwell too much in the past, my mother would say. Let it go. She's something of an expert in this, having shed several lives like useless old skins. In this latest one we all call her Lainey—except for Mack, who says he can't bring himself to it.

Liddie says my problem is just that I know too much about everyone in the family, that they all think of me as sympathetic and pour out all their secrets to me. "They don't notice till a whole lot later, cherub—if they ever notice at all—that you never tell yours back, do you?" She was a little drunk when she said that to me, so we both just laughed. But it's true. Once, actually, I was sitting in a mirrored restaurant, listening to my sister Mary, and I kept seeing reflections of my face, maybe ten of them—all so anguished, so sympathetic, that it shocked me: I was aware of feeling almost nothing at the moment. I was just watching Mary's mouth and thinking about what time I had to meet Will, my husband. I think it's that reflex in my face, the sympathy that rises to my features sometimes without my feeling it, that makes me a good photographer. People look at me and they believe that I understand, I care. Then they don't mind so much if I take a few shots. I've passed some human test. Sometimes it isn't until much later that I weep, if I do. Sometimes when I'm developing a picture, then it finally seems real, whatever's happening—a fire, a funeral, an eviction, all that suffering.

In any case, I don't think I would have wanted to look so carefully back if I hadn't gone home to visit a few years ago. It was the late summer of 1983, and it was not a good time between me and my first husband. I'd gone to Chicago as much to get away from him and us together as to see anyone in my family. I ended up staying almost three months. I was also waiting to hear about a grant, and looking back on this now, I think that I had devised some magic rules governing all of it: If I won the money, it would be a sign that I was meant to have a life alone, and I'd leave Will for good. If I didn't get it, it meant the opposite, and I'd go back to New York. That's what I thought at the start of my visit. By the end of it, my life *had* changed—but for an entirely different set of reasons.

My parents themselves had finally been divorced a year before my visit, and I was staying with my mother in her new apartment. The guest room, the room she gave to me, was still full of unpacked boxes and trunks. "It's all family stuff," she said. "In another world, it would have sat in funny places around the house till we both died, and then you girls would have come and divided it all up. Now it'll just sit here, I guess. You're welcome to anything you'd like. I haven't the moral fiber even to look at it." This was like her. A quality other people would have character-ized as energy or strength—or even curiosity—had a purely moral element for my mother.

And so each morning I woke among the boxes that held my past, my family's past. My mother had a job now, and she was usually gone by the time I got up. Often I began my day idly flipping through the ar-tifacts of all our lives.

In the evenings she and I sat around together drinking beer or tea and talking. She talked a good deal about my father, about their marriage and our childhood. It was as though the divorce had set her free to acknowledge all the problems that had plagued them in their younger life. She never spoke angrily. My father's very name, *David,* seemed to make her voice soften, and she talked of him, of them both, of all of us, as though we were dear relatives who'd gone together through some natural disaster— a shipwreck, a tornado—and barely survived.

Her job was painting sets for a theater designer who was well known in Chicago. She smelled of turpentine and soap when she arrived home, and her cuticles were permanently stained, her fingers slightly tinted, as she gripped her glass. Early in my stay, it was usually hot in her apartment, and we would sit out on her balcony and watch the twilight thicken, the car headlights coming on down below under the wide dark trees on Hyde Park Boulevard. The colors slowly bled from both of us as the light left, until I was, like my mother, just a grayish shadow on the deep porch, and only our voices—remembering, reinventing the past—had any color or depth. Over the months, I came to feel that these talks, this remembering, were somehow connected to the point of my being there at all.

"How shall we work this?" she asked after dinner one night. "You ought to spend some time at your father's too, I suppose."

"I've been seeing Dad," I said. "I'm having dinner with them Friday."

She had her back to me—she was pouring us beers—so I couldn't tell whether this news startled her. I felt foolish that I hadn't said anything to her before, but I simply hadn't been able to figure out how to bring it up. I watched her back. She was wearing jeans and a T-shirt, and from this angle, if you didn't look at her elbows, she looked as though she were in her twenties. She'd gotten thinner in her fifties, she took better care of herself now. She poured the beer slowly, in stages, for a few long moments. "How did he seem to you?" she asked. She turned then and leaned against the counter, raising her glass. "Tony suits him, doesn't she? I'm glad they're getting married."

I didn't want to answer her question, so I said, "Why don't you two just call each other up and talk? He asked me the same thing about you."

When they had finally decided to separate again, several years before, my father had moved out to an apartment. But then, within a year or so, he moved again, into the home of an old family friend, Tony—Antoinette—Baker. She lived halfway down the block from the house we'd grown up in—the house Lainey was then trying to sell. They were planning on getting married.

The first time I'd gone over there, it wasn't just my father, but Tony too, who had asked how my mother was doing, each when the other was out of the room.

"We're having fun," I said. "It's like having a roommate again." I said this to Tony, maybe in part to make her feel bad, to make her remember that she'd once been good friends with my mother.

"What about this man she's working for?" Tony asked. Her voice was lowered so my father wouldn't overhear her. "Anything happening there?"

"Terry?" I asked, incredulous. Had she never met him? Was she blind?

"Well, I guess I just hoped."

"Tony, he's gay. And besides, I don't think Lainey's interested right now."

"Everyone's always interested," Tony said firmly. She was beautiful still, at around sixty. Small, exquisitely formed. Her hair was the same dense halo around her head, white now where it had once been a glittery gold. I wondered if I should tell her everyone was not always interested. That I, for example, couldn't have been less interested at the moment. Instead I changed the subject, and we began to talk about her children, whom I'd grown up with.

My father was even more straightforward when we were alone. "Your mother's by herself too much. I worry about her," he said. "Don't you know any men she could go out with?"

I stared at him, trying to register my disapproval. Then I said, "Why don't I fix her up with Will? He's available." His face seemed to pinch in. I went on, recklessly. "The only problems are that he's twenty-five years younger than she is, he lives in New York, and he's on the rebound."

There was a long silence, and my father looked shamefaced. "All right," he said gently. He took off his glasses and polished them. When he put them back on, he smiled his modest smile and said, "Well, Freud teaches us we're all, always, on the rebound anyway."

I laughed with him. Then I stopped and said, "You mustn't talk that way about Mother to me again."

"I know," he said. "I'm sorry."

The night I went over for dinner, I showed my father and Tony some of the pictures I'd been taking. They were studies of children I'd made in the playground near the apartment Will and I lived in. It was a mean playground, asphalt and busted swings, the ground in the corners and under the one grimy linden littered with glass and the occasional syringe. The children were mean in the same sense too—roughly dressed, foul-mouthed, sometimes scabbed with impetigo. But their play was not so different from what I remembered from my own childhood. In many of the photographs, I'd been experimenting with a technique that results in a central sharp image around which the background appears to swirl in dizzying motion. I liked it because it recalled the way life felt to me when I was young, when you focus on what's important to you so clearly that everything else swims out of your consciousness.

My father took a long time looking at the pictures. His eyesight was already pretty bad then, and he had to hold them at a certain angle to see them. One by one he moved them around in front of what was his narrow tunnel of vision. Finally he said he didn't like them much. "They're very riveting, and they do get your attention." He gestured. "But it's all really a gimmick, isn't it?"

I felt stung. My face must have changed, because Tony was watching me and she suddenly began talking, picking up first one picture, then another, trying to decide which was her favorite.

I waited until she was through. Then I said to my father, "You might be right. It might just be a gimmick. But you have to be willing to try gimmicks. It's how you learn technique. That's all technique is, finally, anyway: gimmick. Gimmick perfected."

A few days later, my father called me to ask to look at the pictures again, so I got them out and brought them over. Again he went through the odd business of waving them back and forth in front of his face. Then he set them down, arranged them neatly in a stack, and apologized. He said that actually he thought they were good, very good. He said he had realized almost right away that his first response had been bizarre, based on some unconscious associations. He'd been lying in bed after I left that night, feeling uncomfortable about his remarks to me, when he remembered. And then he told me this story. His story.

My father is walking home, toward the IC down Fifty-seventh Street. Let's put him in a seersucker suit—the same one I saw him in years later, when he didn't see me—because it's summer again, the Fourth of July actually, and because he's just been seeing patients. Not his everyday, ambulatory patients—those he sees downtown—but his hospitalized ones, those more deeply confused, those gone beyond understanding that the doctor might not come today because it's a national holiday.

It's 1950, patriotism is still fashionable, and he notices the occasional flag hanging off someone's front porch, draped out an apartment window. From time to time one of them billows dramatically in the breeze coming off the lake. My father's suit flaps too, flaps against his legs. The jacket flutters behind him as he strides along, moving fast, bent forward slightly from the waist in his hurry. He's a tall man, dark-haired and too serious-looking. My mother has said that when she met him, he looked so sober it was her impulse to want to make him smile, laugh. He still looks that way eight years later. He invites the attention of women with his apparent gravity, though he himself is cool and witty.

He's hurrying because he's promised my mother, his wife—Lainey—that he'll be back in time for the Fourth of July parade and block party. All three of his children will be in the parade, Liddie and Mack marching with tiny flags distributed by the teenage girls who've organized everything. And the baby, Randall, aged nearly two, who has been chosen to ride in a carriage at the head with a two-year-old girl from the block, king and queen of the whole affair.

Lainey told him about this several nights earlier. Told him while they drank beers in the kitchen and did the dishes. It was hot, and she'd changed into a sheer cotton nightgown after they'd put the children to bed. She was laughing as she described the delegation of self-important teenagers who wanted to borrow her youngest child. "It was like a Nobel Prize committee," she said. "It took them about five minutes of hemming and hawing to get around to their announcement." They had made crowns and scepters, which they showed Lainey, as though that would convince her if all else failed. "Good Lord, these projects," she said, and set the clean plate she'd been drying down on top of the others. "All I did at that age was follow my brothers around, hoping somehow I'd figure out how to be a boy."

"Clearly you had no luck there," he had said, looking over at her.

Now he turns the corner onto Harper Avenue, and first hears, then sees, through the tunneled light under the dense elms, the parade meandering toward him. Ahead of it, circling on their bikes like wheelbound birds of prey, are boys, teenage boys, braying to each other, their faces masked in contempt for this girlish civic enterprise. The sidewalks by the square, where the parade will end, are thick with people waiting, and my father begins to push his way through them. He sees the two elderly Chase sisters parked in lawn chairs by the curb so they won't miss anything. He's in the crowd now, looking for Lainey. His hand brushes across Harold Baker's shoulder. "Seen my wife?" he asks. Harold gestures vaguely behind him. David moves slowly along the sidewalk, and then he sees her, leaning against the wooden rail at the edge of the square. She's talking, holding a cigarette; her hair is barretted severely back. She looks like a big, strong girl. The crowd is dense around her: people have brought guests, adults he doesn't know, visiting relatives. He's waving to Lainey, but she doesn't see him. She throws her head back and laughs.

There's a press forward now, as the front of the parade reaches the square. David finds himself, too, pushed and pushing toward the curb, still looking more at Lainey than at the children—but turning now, just turning—when a voice at his left and behind him rises, resonant with concern, with diagnostic inclination: "What on earth is wrong with that child?"

And as my father's face swings to look at the approaching parade, he knows—the sudden fist of his heart in his chest hits it home—that the voice is speaking of Randall, that he will see him now, emperor of the parade, stripped of the illusions of normalcy they've spun for him.

As he looks, it seems the other children, the parade itself, the adults watching, all swirl and blur, are only color, motion, like the background in a photograph. Dead in the middle, motionless in the carriage he shares with his tiny queen, sits Randall, unseeing, inert, his sequined, glittering cardboard crown perched square on his head. His queen, a frail wriggling blonde, is chewing on hers. She's turned backward, squirming to see the big costumed girls pushing the carriage and the grownups cheering as their children march by. My father watches them pass, watches the messy little girl, her chin streaked with drooled paint. He sees her speak, point with a tiny finger. Randall, perfect king, rides on, looking neither left nor right; and the pubescent baby-sitters—now yanking at the queen to keep her seated—let their eyes fall on him with nearly maternal pride. My father stares, appalled, at the motionless, joyless lump that is his child, frozen in the blur of life around him. Over and over, his brain asks, "What's wrong with that child? What's wrong with that child?"

"It was the first time I let myself think that there *was* something wrong with Randall," he said to me as he stacked and restacked the photographs. "And what I remember most vividly is the relief, the letting go of all the denial."

I could hear Tony in the kitchen, the water running, the radio playing softly. They'd agreed, apparently, that he should talk to me alone about this. We sat in Tony's handsome living room, full of bright colors and carefully chosen objects: an Eskimo-looking clay mask hanging on the wall, the Portuguese tiles around the fireplace, a cherry-red woolen shawl carefully placed along the back of the couch. My mother had had no such gift. Preoccupied, exhausted, she'd let the house happen around her. She seemed never to notice that the slipcovers were worn, that a lampshade had a scorch mark. Even now her apartment looked unplanned and shabby.

"But hadn't you noticed it before about him?" I asked. "I mean, Mother said he was strange from the start."

He nodded quickly. "Well, of course that was true. He was slow in every way, and sometimes we thought he couldn't hear, he seemed so locked away. But then he'd speak—a whole sentence—and we'd think, Well, he's just doing it at his own pace. We didn't want to seem to be pushy parents, you see. We'd mention Einstein, who was famous for not speaking until he was three. We talked about perfectionism, children who waited and waited and then just magically did something impeccably. It seemed possible. His first word was 'umbrella,' for God's sake." There was a kind of happy wonder stamped on my father's face. He was still sharply handsome, his taut skin nearly unlined. "Perfectly enunciated. 'Umbrella.'" He shook his head at the memory.

We sat in silence for a moment. Tony said something to herself, or perhaps to the radio. My mother had this habit too. I'd hear her voice somewhere in the apartment when I knew there was no one with her. It startled me in both of them.

"In all honesty, the thing is, we were both awfully

busy. We couldn't afford any help then, and your mother had her hands full—the ironing alone took her almost a day a week, wedged in around the children's needs. And I was . . . very happy in my work, very occupied. So we were both probably relieved that he was so quiet. So good, you might say. In some ways, I must confess, I saw him as being like me. Liddie and Mack had been such surprises to me, so lively, so vigorous. And Randall was . . . what? You could have said *hesitant, inwardturning.* He seemed perhaps more the child I should have had. And the pediatrician kept assuring your mother that we'd been spoiled by the precocity of the other two, that Randall was still within the normal range."

"So what difference did this . . . revelation make?"

"Oh, probably not too much, practically speaking. I mention it mostly by way of apologizing to you for my response to your pictures." He focused on me briefly with his intense, pale eyes. Then looked away. "It *is* true that over the next year we began to push for tests. But we might have done that anyway as he got older. It's just that, from that moment on, I had the conviction that there was something wrong with him. And that changed my life. And eventually, of course, your mother's."

"It would."

He nodded sadly, acknowledging, it seemed to me, what there was of blame in this. "I hadn't thought of it in a long time, but I kept a journal that year. It was the only way I knew to cope with it. I'd always kept a professional journal—notes on each patient at the end of the hour, that kind of thing. But this was more a sort of personal journal. Though in essence it was like the professional journal. But slightly larger-scaled, and all about him, about your brother. And it started because of that moment, there's no doubt of that."

He stood and crossed to the mantelpiece, picked up a book lying there. "I got it out yesterday. Tony helped me find it." He flipped a few pages, frowning down at it. Then he looked over at me. "I thought you might be interested in looking at it. It's nothing I'm proud of, but it's part of what happened."

"Oh, I would be," I said.

He paused a moment, holding it. It was old, a liverish red worn almost to pink at its edges. "I'd like it back when you're done," he said.

I nodded. "Of course," I said, and then he handed it over.

When Tony came back in, she brought us both Irish coffee, with homemade whipped cream, I noted. Somehow this made me happy for my father. We talked about their plans for the wedding, about which of their children might be able to come. They'd heard from Sarah, my youngest sister—and, I suspect, my father's favorite—that she couldn't make it, that the country band she played fiddle with had gigs lined up in Washington and Oregon straight through the next couple of months.

When I got home that night, home to my mother's apartment, I opened the book and looked quickly through it. Page after page was filled with my father's neat, rhythmic handwriting in black ink, fading now to a yellowy brown. I got under the covers then and began to read. The journal started with a list my father had made on July 6, two days after the parade, a list of things my brother had never done. Never asked for the name of anything, never pointed, never hugged, never fed himself, never gone up or down stairs, never said *mama* or *dada*. On and on, everything a two-year-old might have been expected to do.

And then the list of his accomplishments. Tapping his mouth, unfurling his fingers over and over, rocking for half an hour at a time, spinning objects with great dexterity. Once he said, "Lucky Strike means fine tobacco." His favorite toys: rubber bands, a bathroom plug chain, string. His favorite object was a red blanket. He liked to lie underneath it and hum.

In all of this my father never noted his own response to Randall, his feelings about this baby my mother once told me was undeniably the prettiest of her children. Just over and over the initial *R*, and then the observation.

The tests began in October, usually several a month. My father recorded them all. There were tests at first for his vision, his hearing, for the possibility of motor problems. All negative. Then tests for neurological problems. Again normal, as far as they could tell. Throughout, my father makes notes on what they think, what they say to each other: "October 4: L. sure it's neurological. Some damage, she thinks. Maybe that long wait, the nurses telling her not to push because the Dr. wasn't there yet?" "October 12: L. said he jerked his head today when a car outside backfired. A distant pop, she said, and he started slightly, eyes widening. Clearly not deaf." "November 2: R. alone in the backyard. I set him on the grass, then timed him. For an hour he didn't move, except to swing his head after his hand, to laugh when the trains went by."

Throughout, too, terse notes of other events in their lives. In January: "L. tells me she's pregnant. How? I ask. These things happen, she says. I suggest terminating it; L. unresponsive. She's happy, so I pretend to be too, though I'm uncomfortable with something so clearly compensatory." In February: "All three children in bed with croup. L. moving from one to another, and in between violently ill because of pregnancy. My going to work seems self-indulgent."

Then the psychiatric evaluations and interviews begin and seemingly go on for months. My father's notes are more cryptic here. *F.* is the doctor, and clearly my father feels he knows what he's doing. Various references are made, abbreviated, to the standard wisdom in these situations, to Bettelheim's point of view. What's most evident, though, is that slowly Randall as the patient disappears and my mother becomes the focus of the journal. "L. reluctant to consider psychogenic options. Weepy. Denies there's any possibility she rejected him, even subconsciously. But we've hit dead ends everywhere else, I tell her. And F. is the finest in this field. We owe it to R. to pursue this. She consents, but I'm sure the issue's far from resolved." In April: "L. broke down last night. Wants to know why no one is helping R., why they keep talking to her about her feelings instead of training him, teaching him. It's difficult for me to try to explain the psychiatric perspective, needless to say. I start, and she's instantly defensive: 'I wanted this baby. No one can tell me I didn't. I love him. I wanted him.' Her fatigue with this new pregnancy isn't helpful either."

The sorry year progresses, with a palpable distance growing between my parents. My mother's pregnancy with me is clearly a difficult one, and the intermittent interviews, the long waits between for the system to respond, all push my parents farther and farther apart. Slowly the pattern emerges: a medical system that can't, won't, provide answers about Randall that don't implicate my mother; my mother desperately insistent that he's the one who needs help, not her; my father implicitly a part of the system that's making the accusations, that's saying she's the one who caused the disease.

And more and more this image of my mother: exhausted, angry, difficult, drinking too much. Everyone's adversary.

As summer approaches and the last trimester of my mother's pregnancy, she becomes obsessed, apparently, with polio. It's easy enough to imagine. Predictions call for an epidemic year, and the heat starts early. Down the block an older child is hospitalized. My mother begins boiling dishes, she buys glass straws. She takes Liddie and Mack out of school ahead of time, and she won't let them leave the house to play with other children.

It has been recommended by now that she go into therapy, that she discuss with a professional her ambivalence about having Randall. It has been recommended that Randall be institutionalized when he's old enough, in order to separate him from her destructive emotions. She's having back trouble, she has a heat rash between her breasts and the raised shelf of her belly, her feet have swollen to shapeless lumps.

"L. seems lost to reason in this polio thing. In anger over the irrationality of it, I accuse her of trying to prove something about R., about herself as a mother, by this compulsive need to keep the others safe. Everything quickly out of hand. I make the mistake of labeling R. autistic, I say we know what causes it, that she has to come to grips with it. She tries to hit me. I hold her. L., weeping, 'Don't dare to say *we* to me! We! We! I am not your patient. I am your wife.' "

In July, three days after this entry, I am born. The note is: "We have another little girl. Not named yet. Seemingly healthy. Peaceful day at home. Penny manages the children smoothly. I'm trying to arrange for her to stay on until Mother Green gets here. R. speaks at breakfast: 'Quaker Puffed Wheat. Shot from guns.' "

Sometimes as a child, because I didn't understand its nature, its embattled origins, I felt confused by my mother's intense love for Randall. It seemed so different from her love for the rest of us. And it made me suspicious of her love for me, even when she was most affectionate, because I felt that it was false; that the moment it was put in the balance with her love for Randall, it would be found wanting.

I remember one summer afternoon. I was ten, I was working on a project on the dining room table, coloring in the intricate patterns on some Elizabethan dresses I'd copied from the *Encyclopaedia Britannica*. Randall was in the living room, sitting in a patch of sunlight with his Slinky, lifting the end again and again and watching it fall, almost humming as he did it. My mother was in the kitchen, making a cake. It was Mack's birthday. She called out, "Nina, come in here and look at this. It's turning out beautifully!"

I finished coloring in the red flower on a skirt. My pencil was labeled *vermilion*, and I remember saying the word to myself out loud as I set it down. I had never heard that word before. I looked quickly at Randall before I left the room, but he hadn't noticed Lainey's voice. He was watching the Slinky undulate metallically in the sun.

"Lookee here, Neen," Lainey said as I walked in. She held the cake decorator in her hand and stepped back from the kitchen table. A cigarette dangled from her mouth. It was hot in the kitchen because the oven had been on, and she wore a sleeveless blouse and shorts. Her feet were bare, her toenails painted red. The back door was open, and I could hear my sisters' voices in the yard, the splash of water in their plastic pool. I looked at the cake. It was a series of concentric circles, like a bull's-eye—pinkish-red, yellow, blue, green. In the middle, it said *Mack 15*.

"Pretty snazzy, wouldn't you say?" Mother asked. She put her arm around me and I could feel her big soft breasts and belly squish against my own body. I wanted to turn into that flesh, to be cuddled, but I held myself back, I thought of the boniness of my body as a kind of reproof to that possibility.

"It's pretty," I agreed.

"Think Mack'll like it?" she asked.

"Uh hunh," I said.

My mother released me. "It's going to be lovely," she said, stabbing her cigarette out. "I love all you children's birthdays. I think of each of you as a baby—you were all such lovely babies—and it brings back those happy times."

Then Lainey pushed a couple of the pastel-filled frosting bowls toward me and said, "Now, *someone* or other is going to have to clean these up."

Together we sat down at the kitchen table and began to scrape the bowls with our fingers. "Don't tell a soul," my mother said, "or we'll have every Marey and Sarey in town in here with us."

My fingertips slowly stained a bruised-looking color I couldn't lick off. Lainey sang the song about the sow and the three little pigs through twice, the second time laughing so hard with me that her snorts became real and uncontrollable.

"Ig, Mom," I said, and stuck my finger in the green bowl.

"Ig yourself, my baby pig," she said. Her lips were the same purplish brown as my fingers, darker than the lipstick she wore when she and my father went out.

"Your mouth is all purple," I said. "You look nutty."

My mother stuck her dark tongue out at me, and we both laughed again.

When I went back into the dining room, Randall stood over the table, letting little pieces of torn paper flutter to its surface from his hand. It took me a few seconds to realize what the brightly colored confetti was. Then I ran at him, grunting with rage. I grabbed his arms and swung him from the table. Though he was nearly as big as Mack, he was uncoordinated, floppy and awkward, and he didn't resist me. I slapped his face as hard as I could. His head snapped back. He bared his teeth and laughed soundlessly.

"You bad! Bad! Bad!" I shrieked, out of control. I slapped him again, and then again; but Randall shut his eyes and continued his silent laughing. Sometimes he could go on for hours like that once he'd started. I was lost in fury, lost in hitting him, in wanting to hurt him. As he staggered backward I pursued him, punching him on the face and chest and shrieking at him.

Suddenly my mother's hands grabbed me, flung me away. Then reached out and stung like electricity across my cheek and mouth. She seemed huge. Randall stood behind her, still laughing. I held my face where it felt torn.

"You are not to hit him!" she said. She was panting; her face was white, her mouth still bruised dark red from the frosting treat we'd shared in secret. "Not ever, you understand?"

I covered my face. Then she was holding me. "Oh, Nina," she said. "Oh, I'm sorry."

Randall sat down on the couch, rocking, laughing out loud now. I watched him as my mother held me. She had started to cry, but I had stopped even wanting to, as if by magic, the moment she touched me. Now I blurred my eyes and held my breath and let my dizziness pull me far away from them both—from my crazy brother, who wouldn't stop laughing; and from my mother, who seemed to be taking comfort from the body I'd left behind me as I swam forward to a safer place, a place where I couldn't feel or see them, where the world rocked rhythmically with my own dark pulse.

*   *   *

While I was in Chicago, I went with Tony and my father to a party, an open house of the kind I remembered from my youth. Then, I would have been making the rounds with an hors d'oeuvres tray or drifting around the edges of the grownup groups, happily eavesdropping, made invisible by my age. There was such a child at this party, wearing a frilly, old-fashioned dress with a bow at the back of the waist, a dress very like the ones I'd had to put on then to help. "I know you," I wanted to say. "I know what you're thinking."

Now I was expected to account for myself, and I dutifully did. I spent a long time talking to a woman who'd been a classmate of Liddie's. "I always wondered what happened to girls like her," this woman finally said.

"What do you mean?" I asked, offended on Liddie's behalf. "What do you mean, *like her?*"

"Oh, you know," she said. She shrugged and looked embarrassed, as though only at this moment realizing I might not share her assessment of Liddie. "Girls who come into it all so early."

"Oh. Sexy girls," I said. "I wouldn't worry about them," and I turned away from her.

Across the room I could see Tony giving me a signal, pointing to her watch, then raising a hand, fingers spread, to show me she wanted to leave in five minutes. I signaled back, enthusiastically, and then realized that an elderly woman between me and Tony thought I was waving to her. Her hand up, echoing my gesture, she approached me, an expectant smile lifting her face. I smiled back.

"You must forgive me, dear. I don't remember you."

"Oh, not at all," I said. "I'm Nina Eberhardt."

"Nina. Such a pretty, old-fashioned name. I hope you don't mind my saying that."

"No; I'm glad you think so."

"And I'm Alice Curtin. Charles's wife. My only claim to fame."

I'd heard of Charles Curtin. A professor at the law school. "Well, that's not an insignificant claim, you know."

"Oh, yes, I do know that. I know it well. Now, what are you eating?" We were standing in front of the dining room table, which was laden with platters of food. "Those little caviar things? Fish eggs, I call them. You've got one stuck, just right there," she said, and tapped her front tooth.

I swiveled my tongue in my mouth and smiled at her. "Better?"

She nodded. "What pretty teeth you have, dear. Be grateful. I've a mouth full of porcelain, entirely artificial. Everything in here but the kitchen sink, I always say." She bent over the table, frowning, then gave up and turned back to me. "Now, tell me what you do. I know you do something. All you clever young girls do."

"I'm a photographer."

"I knew it. How smart of you. That must be fascinating work, poking your camera where the rest of us daren't go. Or do you do portraits, that sort of thing?"

"No, I'm more the nosy kind, as you say. News, and photographic essays." I shrugged.

"Nosy!" she objected. "I never said it." She laughed. "But it must be quite interesting. I can definitely see the appeal of that kind of thing. Eberhardt," she said abruptly. "Isn't your husband the young man in all the trouble?"

"No. Not that I know of. Actually his name isn't Eberhardt. And he doesn't live here. I grew up on Harper Avenue, but I—we—live in New York now."

"Oh, Harper. Then you know the Masurs."

"Very well."

"So your father is . . . now tell me his name."

"David Eberhardt. He's here somewhere, actually." I looked around and glimpsed Tony's aureole of white-gold hair, saw that she was near the door, holding her coat.

"David Eberhardt. Jiggle my memory. What does he do?"

"He's a psychiatrist. And he used to teach at the medical school." I started to move back, to murmur something about having to go.

And then the light dawned behind her eyes. "Oh, yes!" she said. "Now I remember the story. You were the family with that tragic young retarded boy."

She was so forthright that all I could say was, "Yes, that's right."

"My dear, I'm so sorry. How hard that must all have been."

I made some fuzzy remarks about how young I'd been, about how happy we'd all been then, and began to back away, excusing myself, bumping against the people around me as I made my way toward the door.

When I told my mother about it, she didn't respond at first. I couldn't see her face. She was bent over the table, setting it. My sister Mary and her husband were coming for dinner. "Doesn't that seem preposterous to you?" I pushed. "It's been twenty or twenty-five years. And we've all had our own completely separate lives. And accomplishments. And scandals, even. And what we're still famous for is Randall."

She didn't turn her head or look at me. Her voice was matter-of-fact. "No," she said. "No, to me that doesn't seem preposterous at all."

2 LAINEY had cried out in her sleep just seconds before the telephone rang. She had been dreaming, and in her dream one of her sons—it was hard to tell whether it was Randall or Macklin—was drowning. Her arms and legs were like those we own so often in dreams, heavy stumps disconnected from her will. They wouldn't lift to save him. She had to watch, frozen, as he gently sank—she could somehow see him floating down to the glowing pebbles at the bottom of the stream. His eyes, his mouth and nostrils, were wide with terror. They leaked iridescent bubbles, which rose to the silvered undersurface of the clear brown water. For a moment, in her sleep, the diminished bell of the distant telephone became that sound, the sound of the shiny bubbles slowly rising; and then she woke, she was out of bed, sprinting down the dark hallway to stop the noise before it roused the children or David.

It was her father at the end of the line, clearing his throat, apologizing for waking her. Even before she caught her breath she began to reassure him, falling into the familial habit of politeness. Then she checked herself: here she was, standing in her pajamas in the dark in David's study, her bare feet sticky on the nighttime cool of the wooden floor, the breathing sounds of the silent house around her. Why had he called now? "What's wrong?" she asked abruptly.

"It's Mother," he said, and coughed gently, repeatedly, a nervous tic. Then: "She's had a heart attack."

"And?" Her voice rose in wild impatience. "How is she now?"

"I'm afraid it's not good." He paused. "She's gone, Lainey."

"Gone? Dead? You mean?"

"Yes," he said quietly.

Lainey's voice was harsh, her answer pure reflex, like a quick retaliatory slap. "No she isn't," she said.

He was silent a moment, then answered gently, "Yes, she is."

Lainey couldn't answer. Her heart believed, she could feel it like a knuckle pressed into her throat; but she had no response. Finally she said, "I just can't understand." She stopped. "This doesn't seem true." She felt dizzy, and she touched David's desk for the sense of something solid in the whirling dark.

"I know, dear. I'm the same way." Her father's voice was kind and professional. It made her remember abruptly how much grief, how much pain and misery, he'd had to help people through in his life. He was a minister, an expert at condolence. "I keep waiting for her to walk in the kitchen here and ask me what I'm doing up at this hour."

She shut her eyes then in the dark and saw his tired face, the empty shiny kitchen, with even the last few snack dishes of the day rinsed and set by the sink on the old linoleum counter, the steady groan of the ancient refrigerator the only sound in the quiet house. "Are you *alone?*" she whispered. Somehow this was more horrible, easier to focus on, than her mother's having died.

"Yes, for now. I called Sam, and he's coming, and Paul. I couldn't reach Pete. But I'm sure I'll get him tomorrow, and then he'll be on his way too." These were Lainey's older brothers, scattered with their families around the Northeast. Lainey, in Chicago, lived the farthest from her parents.

"And I'll come too, don't you think?" Nothing was clear to her.

"It'd be wonderful if you could, Elaine."

"Of course I will," she said with sudden conviction. And then everything wheeled back into place for her in the dark; she was all right. There were steps to be taken, plans to be made. This was what her mother's death would mean for a while. She knew she could manage this. She found the chair, reached for the lamp chain. The light fell in a bright yellow pool on David's desk—on the choked ashtray, the stack of notes in his finicky, even script, the wire tray full of pencils, odd coins, a letter opener, a favorite Little Lulu comic the kids made him read aloud every few weeks, so old and worn the pages curled.

"I'll be a few days getting there," she said. Facing her on the desk was a framed photograph of the two older children, taken when Mack was a baby. She squinted her eyes nearly shut against it. "I'll have to arrange for the children." Randall swam into her mind, then the little ones, Nina and Mary.

"I understand, darling. Just come when you can."

"How did it happen?" He didn't answer right away. "Do you mind talking about it?"

"No, no," he said. "It's perfectly all right." And slowly he told his sad story—her mother's collapse, the ambulance, the way she looked afterward. Her skin was gray, he said. Grayish. As he was talking, his voice changed, and Lainey could tell he'd been through it several times before. Perhaps he'd even called her mother's sisters before he called her, maybe a few of her close friends. Some of the phrases seemed practiced and automatic. She could hear the distance he'd already achieved from them.

Lainey couldn't imagine her mother the way he spoke of her. *Her* mother was small, plump, pink. She smelled of rose water and was incapable of inactivity, except for a ritual nap after lunch, after which she often said, as though she'd had a cool drink of water, "My, that was refreshing."

"I think she didn't suffer," he said. "Except maybe the fear of those first few minutes. I thank God for that."

"Yes," said Lainey. "Yes, that's good." There was a silence on the line. Then she asked, "Will there be a service? When will that be?" She was reaching for a pencil. She felt a slow surge of energy: the will to organize, to be efficient.

"A memorial service, I think. She wanted to be cremated." He cleared his throat several times. "So we can wait a little. Just whenever you can get here." He paused. "I haven't really thought all these things through yet." His voice sounded suddenly exhausted, desolate, and there rose in her the impulse to give, to enfold, to offer herself, her instinctive response to need or weakness.

"Oh, Father, don't worry about any of it. We'll all help, when we're there. These arrangements should be the last of your concerns right now. There's plenty of time for that once we get there."

"Yes."

"And we'll be there soon." He didn't answer. "Can you sleep, do you think?"

"I suspect. Eventually. I'm very tired."

They talked hesitantly for a while more, politely sharing their disbelief, estranged already by her mother's absence, by the lack of the third voice, quick and warm on the line.

For Lainey was like her father: thoughtful, earnest. They shared too a kind of spiritual ambition: to be good, to be kind, to be giving. This had made their relations difficult—in a strange sense, competitive. They had often argued passionately during Lainey's adolescence, when her nose for hypocrisy was keenest, when her father suddenly seemed to her riddled with petty flaws.

Her father had found an outlet for his ambition in his work, but Lainey still drove herself in every aspect of her life and was defeated over and over, too easily exhausted. When she was young her father had tried to curb her ambition, had tried to influence her not to take herself so seriously: partly for her sake, because he understood how like him she was, how costly and difficult her ambition would be; and partly because she was a girl and he thought such an ambition inappropriate in her, even presumptuous. He wanted her to be like her mother, quick and lively, but pliant, a good wife to some ambitious man.

Now they spoke with some awkwardness of train schedules, of the details of Lainey's coming east. Each was glad for this business between them, and having separated themselves with it, they were able at last to say good night.

"And I hope you can get a little sleep," Lainey said.

"Thank you, Elaine. I think I will now." The line went dead. She held the receiver until it buzzed in her ear. Then she hung up.

She looked at the pad she'd been writing on, making what she thought of as orderly notes as her father spoke. Scrawled on it were the words *dead, DEAD, gray, service Saturday?? train schedule*. It shocked her. She had a moment of revulsion at this vision of the way her unbidden mind worked. She tore the sheet off, ripped it into small pieces, and threw it away.

Now she made another list, a list of her children's names: *Lydia, Macklin, Randall, Nina, Mary*. She sat and stared at it. Then she began to note the chores she would have to do on their behalf before she left. Retta was coming to iron in two days, and that took care of school clothes, David's work clothes. But they'd all need socks and underwear. She'd have to do a few loads of wash. And she'd need to get a day-time sitter for the little girls, someone who'd be willing to be in charge of Randall too, once he got dropped off. They could just have cereal for breakfast, and David could manage that; but she'd have to pick up sandwich things for easy lunches, and perhaps a week's worth of dinners. She needed to check the freezer, then, and she'd have to do a big shopping. She blocked out five days' meals and began to make a grocery list from that.

She tried not to think of her mother; she had too much to do right now. Perhaps on the train she could relax into grief and memory. She had a quick image of herself, rocking gently to the train's sideways rhythm, alone—smoking, perhaps weeping. It felt nearly erotic in the sudden pleasure it brought her, and she suppressed it instantly. She opened David's drawer—he kept a carton of Camels there—and extracted a pack. She tore off the cellophane, pulled out a cigarette, and lit it. Sitting in the swirl of smoke that slowly twisted and plumed above the desk lamp, she finished her list. Then she leaned back and swung the chair around to the window. Day was beginning off in the east, over the lake. She knew it in the dimming light of the stars, in the beginning of what might be green in the leaves of the mulberry tree that filled the space over their small city yard. The window was open and the air smelled fresh and she could hear from somewhere in the square the cheerful repeated cry of a bird. The night riser of his world, she thought. Around her in the house was the deep silence of her children's sleep, a silence full of their stirrings, their dreaming, their soft breathing, as the stillness of a forest is full of a kind of noise.

Abruptly Lainey thought of her mother; she saw

her waking terrified in her bed, reaching for Father. Her throat ached with a sudden pity for her in that moment, the same pity she felt for her own children when they woke in terror in the night. "Mother," she whispered, but what she was seeing was a child. She closed her eyes tight and remembered the Scripture: *Except ye become as a little child, ye shall not enter the kingdom of heaven.* For a moment, then, Lainey was so aware of the words, of the wish for her mother to be safe, that it was not so much as though she were praying as that she had become the prayer.

Then the heat of the cigarette burning in her fingers pulled her back. She swallowed and swung the chair around. She pushed the cigarette out in David's full ashtray and got up. She stepped into the wide hallway at the top of the stairs and noiselessly padded around the circle of nicked, scarred doors opening onto it. Only Randall's door was shut, hooked from the outside against his nighttime meanderings. The other children lay sleeping, humped or hurled out in abandon, visible in the dim light falling from the study into the hall. Mary, the baby, who had a summer cold, was snoring gently as a cat on her back in her crib, her tiny curled hand shot out between the slats. Lainey felt distant from them all, transformed by the event that had so far happened only to her. Though she wasn't aware of her sorrow yet, a part of her had withdrawn from the children already. How amazing that they slept on! that they couldn't somehow feel her absence, the coolness with which she looked at them. They were, for the moment, only lists of things to do, these willful, beautiful babies of hers.

At the door to her own bedroom Lainey paused too. David was turned to the wall, away from her rumpled side of the bed, away from her as she stood in the doorway. Her faint shadow fell jaggedly across the wrinkled sheet that covered him. He stirred slightly, as if he could somehow feel its touch; and at the same moment, Lainey was aware of the beginning of the nausea of morning sickness, so tentative it wouldn't have wakened her, she wouldn't have known she was having it if she were sleeping still. She was only three weeks late; the nausea had been with her for just a few days, and she hadn't yet told David. He would never forgive her for her carelessness—he'd been angry enough about Nina and Mary—and she wanted to hold on to the few shreds of goodwill left between them for as long as she could.

She wanted to wake him now, to tell him what had happened to her, to her mother. To ask for his help. But her uncomfortable awareness of the secret she was keeping from him stopped her.

Pushing that under, she thought of herself as *sparing* him for a few hours more. Besides, she reasoned, later today his turn would come. She would go away; he would be in charge. And she would become, in some last, final sense, once more her mother's daughter. In her confusion she thought of this, too, as a kind of betrayal of him. It made her recall, suddenly, the summers early in their marriage, when they took the children east and visited her parents at their shore house. They usually stayed for only a few weeks, but even in that short time David grew irritated at her attachment to her family, particularly to her mother. In the evenings, she and Lainey usually sat together around the big table in the kitchen, sewing as they talked about her brothers' marriages, about her aunts, about the series of family gatherings that Lainey, far away in Chicago, had been absent from. Lainey could feel how her love of this gossip, of these old familiar stories, pushed David out. He would withdraw to the guest cottage alone, and she would slowly feel the pull of his absence shaming her for staying on. Often by the time she left, though, he was already asleep in the bed, which smelled faintly of mildew. Then she in turn would be angry at him. Why couldn't he join her? Why in every case did she have to give up what was dear to her to be with him? The dark trip out to the cottage over the bumpy path seemed emblematic of this. She could remember turning once at the screen door to look back through the stand of elms at the glow of the windows in her parents' house—like a fire flickering through the shifting trees. She had felt a desolate sense of exile and loss then. She'd had to remind herself that it was precisely because of David's exacting nature that she'd fallen in love with him. But there were several of those early summers when they hardly made love at all, and Lainey knew this was connected in David's mind with the presence of her mother, though later he'd come to admire and perhaps even love her.

She turned away, went down the hall, and descended the back stairway, narrow and pitch black, to the kitchen. She shut the door slowly, carefully, and stepped across the linoleum floor. Effortlessly her hand found the light switch. With its sharp click, the tiny lamp over the table brought the room to life.

The old-fashioned kitchen was immense. In the low wattage of the lamp, its corners were still deep in shadow. For years David had wanted to have it done over, but Lainey resisted. The idea of putting up with workmen trooping in and out, even for only a month or two, was intolerable. They had compromised on new appliances, and so next to the white-painted Hoosier cabinet sat a nearly brand-new stove, enameled an odd mustard color—the label had called it Harvest Gold. And in the butler's pantry, an immense refrigerator quietly hummed.

The walls were hung with the children's drawings and paintings, bright blobs of running colors, which Lainey loved; and with newspaper and magazine clippings and photographs of Lainey's heroes: Joseph Welch in a prim bow tie, Adlai Stevenson resting his worn-out shoes on a table in front of him during his losing campaign.

David had hung a photograph of Freud up with them—the famous portrait—but its piercing stare had frightened Nina. When she noticed it, she would cover her own eyes and say, *"No, man!"*—would sometimes even whimper. When Lainey had found another picture of Freud, in an old copy of *Life*—a slightly overexposed photograph of him with his wife in a garden—she had substituted it. David didn't notice for a few days. But then one evening she caught him staring at it. Freud looked puzzled in the photo. He was frowning into the sun in front of some rosebushes. His wife's hand rested on his shoulder like a claim, though she held her body a little distance from him. And you could see a confusion of shadows in the space between them: flowers, or perhaps another shrub.

David had turned to her. "Well, Lainey, quite a reach you've got. You've managed to domesticate even Freud."

"We needed a more domestic Freud," she said, with willed obliviousness to his tone. "The other one scared Nina."

"Ah!" he had said. "No, this one wouldn't." And he left the room.

Now Lainey turned on one of the stove's burners to start some coffee. The kettle clashed across the metal grid. She was careless of the noise she made down here. This was where she brought Randall when he woke at night, which happened once or twice a week. The children were used to hearing in their sleep the distant, muted noises of their mother and their crazy brother as they led their separate peculiar kitchen life.

While the water heated, she went to the hall, opened the door to the dirty-laundry closet, and filled the basket. The clothes smelled of her sweaty children, and she felt a kind of animal pleasure as she bent into them and scooped them up. Before she lugged the basket to the basement door, she fished out a pair of David's socks for her cold feet.

The dirt floor smelled earthy and wet. Even in winter, each time she descended these hopelessly tilting stairs, the odor made Lainey think of the beginnings of life, of things growing. Now, inexplicably she thought, *Mother,* and then remembered. She had found her mother down here folding laundry one day during her long visit after Randall's birth; she had shooed Lainey upstairs to rest. Lainey recalled her laughing face, her mock irritation, the indolent pleasure of her own slow shuffle back to bed. Her mother had stayed for a month that time, and Lainey had often lingered in bed until noon with Randall—her easiest, prettiest baby—reading, sleeping, nursing him. As the baby's mouth pulled steadily on her breast, she could hear from below her through the walls, through the serpentine old heating ducts, Liddie and Mack's voices, and sometimes her mother's laughter. Hunched over the laundry basket, she felt the pressure of tears starting, but she wouldn't allow them now. There was too much to do. "We won't have that, thanks," she whispered to herself as she tossed the white things into a heap.

Upstairs, the coffee was ready. She lighted another cigarette and sat down at the table to have a cup. She couldn't remember when she'd last sat like this, alone, in silence in the night. Only the steady hum of the refrigerator and the distant slosh of the washing machine in the basement—mechanical songs—kept her company. She felt for a moment, in spite of all that was pressing in on her, a deep sense of luxury, a kind of pleasure. Sometimes she sat like this with Randall in the night, smoking and drinking coffee, not talking; but always he was there, her idiot child, her dearest child in some ways, drawing or playing with one of his "toys"—the silver-balled chain of the bathtub plug, a piece of string, sometimes just his hands. Every now and then Lainey would look at his blank perfect beauty and feel a pang; what had she kept him home for if she wasn't going to help him? Then she would rouse herself, she would try to engage him in a game or go through a picture book with him, saying the names of things over and over out loud.

But more often they just sat together, taking, Lainey hoped, a kind of comfort from each other.

Occasionally David would come down, waked by their kitchen noises—Randall's tuneless humming, Lainey's clattering dishes—and they would start again the argument that had run under their lives together since they had found out what was wrong with Randall.

There'd been a repeat of this only a few nights before. It had been raining gently when they went to bed, a steady, comforting noise. But sometime in the early-morning hours, Lainey woke to a wild clap of thunder that seemed to reach into her rib cage and set her heart racing. She thought of Randall before she was fully conscious. She got up quickly and unlocked the door to his room. He was kneeling on his bed, his eyes huge, his hands covering his ears, his breathing irregular. She had led him slowly to the kitchen, crooning reassurance, praying he wouldn't start yelling until the door was shut behind them. She set his blocks out on the table and put his favorite record—Danny Kaye singing the sound track from *Hans Christian Andersen*—on the portable player. When the thunder roared outside, she sang along loudly with the foolish lyrics to cover its noise. "Thumbelina, Thumbelina, tiny little thing . . ."

Suddenly the door had opened and David stood there, looking somehow self-contained and handsome, even in his bathrobe.

"Oh." Lainey's hands involuntarily flew up to touch her messy hair, then fell again. "I'm sorry we woke you," she said.

"Don't be silly." He shut the door behind him and crossed to the table. He sat down next to Randall, opposite her. "I'm sorry *he* woke *you.*"

"Oh." She shrugged. "Well. The thunder."

"Yes. The thunder," he said, looking at Randall. His son lay on his extended arm on the table, setting a red block carefully next to a blue one. A little strand of drool ran from his mouth to the tabletop. He hadn't noticed his father. "And if not the thunder, what? An ambulance. A train. A dog barking, five blocks away. We all know the list."

Lainey sat, feeling ugly and sullen. "I don't want to start it tonight," she said finally. "I haven't the energy."

"No. You're right," he said. "You're right, of course." He watched Randall for a minute. "May I have a cigarette?" he asked.

She pushed the pack over to him. He took one, tapped it on the table, put it in his mouth. The noisy flare of the match caught Randall's attention, and he sat up and watched as David lighted his cigarette. David held the match out so he could see it, let it burn down for a few seconds. "Fire," Lainey whispered, almost unconsciously; and then David blew it out.

They sat together in silence, all three of them, for a few minutes. "When's the last time he spoke?" David asked.

Lainey shook her head. "No," she said firmly. She tried to smile at him.

"Look, it's just that this would be a good time. He'll be six, Lainey. There are places that will take him at six. Fine places. The Orthogenic School, for one. He'd be right around the corner."

She shook her head again. "I'm not willing to talk about it. I'm not going to send him away. He's mine. He's *ours.* He belongs with us."

David reached out toward the ashtray, and she pushed it to him. She was aware of the scratchy, corny music in the background.

He waited a minute. Then he said, "Lainey, I'm not blaming you." His voice had become gentle. She thought abruptly of his professional life and shifted in her chair. "There's no one to blame. But even if there's nothing . . . problematic here—at home—he needs . . ." He looked down. "He needs more help than this."

"He has help. I help him. His school helps him."

His face tightened momentarily, in disgust or contempt, and Lainey felt a quick anger.

"What's wrong with Randall's school? Precisely what's wrong with it? Those people are trained too."

David looked at her and shook his head. "We've been over and over this. They only work part-time, and they only work at the cognitive level. A residence would treat him night and day, essentially. And it could really get at . . . the roots of the problem."

"I work with him night and day," she said shrilly.

Now David smiled and spread his hands to take it all in—the messy kitchen, Randall in his chewed pajamas, lining up his blocks in the same predictable rows he'd been using for what seemed like years, over and over, lost; and Lainey, her hair still matted from sleep, her robe stained, Lainey with her coffee, her cigarettes, her hopeless fatigue, and her love for Randall.

"Lainey." He leaned forward. His voice was urgent. "What I do hold you responsible for, the only way I do blame you, is for compounding the effect, when other people, people trained to work with kids like this, could help Randall. And you deny him that. I blame you only for that."

"That's all?" she asked brightly, bitterly, and inhaled on her cigarette.

"Lainey . . ."

There had been another loud clap of thunder then, and Randall jumped, made a frightened noise a little like the miaow of a cat. David leaned back and turned away. He looked out toward the window, where the night was black and drizzles of rain falling from the roof fell in silver-dotted lines caught in the kitchen's light. In the droop of his shoulders and the pull forward of his neck, Lainey could read his exhaustion, his aging, and she felt a pang of guilt for her contribution to it.

He turned back to her. "Who is this helping, Lainey?" he pleaded. "What good is it, except to make you feel more . . . *Christly* or something? And to make the rest of us miserable?"

Now Lainey waved her hand at the memory, as though it would clear out like the cigarette smoke around her. She stood and took her cup to the sink, crossed to the pantry, where the clean laundry was rough-folded, and began to pull out the clothes she would leave sprinkled and rolled for Retta to iron when she came.

When David came downstairs at six-thirty, steeling himself against the irritation he always felt at finding Lainey and Randall shut into their sloppy, silent, nicotine-smelling world, he found the table set. The kitchen smelled of bleach, bacon, coffee. Though Lainey hadn't dressed yet, she'd brushed her hair, she'd washed her face to wake herself up. When he opened the door and she turned to him and smiled—almost in embarrassment that such order should be so unexpected in their lives—she looked like a teenager, neat and pretty in her flowered pajamas. He felt a sudden stab of longing for her, for the girl she'd once been.

"My father called in the night," she said, as though in response to whatever she read on his face. "Mother died. Of a heart attack." She was still smiling.

"Oh, Lainey," he said. His hands lifted toward her.

But she turned slightly from him. Her eyes slid away from his. To David, for a moment, her blank face looked strangely like Randall's. "I'm fine," she said. "I haven't even cried yet. And it's funny. I just . . . Well." She shrugged. "Can you help with the children this morning? And then I've got to make some arrangements. I'll need your help. I'm going to go home. To Father." While she was speaking he had crossed to her and put his arm around her in spite of her odd posture. But her body didn't yield or respond—she kept talking—and after a moment he let his arm fall. He stepped back from her, he went to the stove and poured himself a cup of coffee. Above them they could hear the children's voices rising in volume. Mary began to call for Lainey.

Leaning against the front of the stove, David asked her, and she told him, how it had happened, what time her father had called, how he had seemed. The slight, embarrassed smile flitted on and off her face, as though she were one of the children having to talk of a bodily function. As she spoke of her father, her eyes reddened and she turned away.

When she finished, they stood opposite each other, looking at each other for a long moment. Then each became aware that Mary was now shrieking steadily, that Randall had begun thumping in his bed.

David set his cup down. "I'll head up and get Randall and check on the older two, if you want to do *them.*" He nodded at the ceiling, a gesture meant to indicate the babies, Nina and Mary.

She started to cross to the pantry. "Just send them down here, if they don't have messy dipes," she said. "I'll change both of them after breakfast."

At the stairs, he turned back. "Lainey, this . . . this isn't good. It isn't good for you, holding all this in." Then, as if it had just occurred to him: "Why didn't you wake me?"

She shrugged. "I had so much to *do,*" she said. He watched her for a moment as she brought the pitcher of orange juice to the table and set it down. Suddenly he noticed the old pair of his own socks on her feet. For some reason, this, more than anything, made his heart ache for her, for their distance from each other.

David was still upstairs with Randall when Lainey told the other children. Of course, Nina and Mary, perched at the wooden table in their high chairs, didn't really have a response; and Mack bent over his plate so Lainey couldn't see his face. But Liddie's expression turned instantly grave. At nine, she had a keen sense for drama, and she knew this was a moment she could rise to.

"What did she die of?" Liddie asked. She was slender and fair, unexpectedly, with a smattering of small freckles like spilled cinnamon across the bridge of her nose and her cheeks. All the other children were dark, like Lainey and David.

"She had a heart attack, honey. She was old, and her heart wasn't good. It just gave out." Lainey leaned against the stove, as David had earlier, and drew on her cigarette. The children sat around the white wooden table across from her. There were two unoccupied places set, one for David and one for Randall. None for Lainey. She never sat down at breakfast, never ate until she'd gotten everyone else fed, until David and the older children had gone off to work and school. Then, as she cleared the table, she scooped the crusts, the rinds of bacon, the dribbles of jelly off their plates and ate them, washing them down with milky cold coffee. "Mother's rations," she had called it in embarrassment once when David caught her at it; but the truth was, she liked it better than the heavy meals she made for them. Mary began banging on the table with her spoon, and Lainey automatically picked up the skillet, crossed to her, and lifted more scrambled eggs onto her plate.

"I'm so sad for Grampa," Liddie said piously. "Now he's all alone." Her voice mournfully caressed the last syllable.

"We'll all have to write him extra letters and be especially loving to him," Lainey said. There was a silence, except for the clicking of their spoons on the plastic breakfast plates and their eating noises. Lainey poured herself more coffee, thinking only how easy this had been, how matter-of-fact, how *unknowing*, the children were. She turned to the counter and began to fold the underwear and socks she'd lugged up from the basement.

Then Nina, who'd been sitting silently, pushing her eggs slowly and carefully into her mouth, stopped. She lowered her head nearly to the table to try to see Mack's face, which was still bent away from all of them. "Mackie's sad?" she asked. Lainey turned quickly to look.

Mack reached out his hand, as if to push their attention away. He turned his head to the wall.

"Mackie's sad?" Nina repeated.

Now Mack lifted his face. It was reddened, ago-nized, glistening with tears. "Don't you *care*, Mom?" he cried. "Doesn't anybody care?"

In three quick steps, Lainey crossed to the table. She knelt by his chair and turned it to her. It scuddered loudly on the linoleum. "Oh, honey, of course I do," she said. Her arms reached up, encircled him, and he leaned forward, sobbing, onto her shoulder. Lainey's heart seemed to tighten unbearably in her chest, to squeeze even her throat. She felt the sudden sweet release of her own tears. From somewhere far behind her she could hear Nina persevering: "Mackie's sad? Mommy's sad?" and Mary crowing with strange nervous laughter to hear the big people crying. Lainey held Mack tight in gratitude and sorrow and thought how often her children did this for her—released her to herself.

For perhaps a minute she and Mackie wept, holding each other. Then he pulled away, sniffling. She fished into her pajama pocket for a handkerchief and blew her nose. Liddie had begun to explain to Nina in a falsely grownup voice that Mackie and Mommy were sad but they'd be better soon.

Nina changed her chant: "Mommy's better soon? Mackie's better soon?"

Now Mack wiped his face on his sleeve and turned away from Lainey. "Use your napkin," she murmured to him, and he reached obediently for it.

"Mommy's better soon?" Nina asked again.

Lainey stood up, feeling stiff, as though she'd been kneeling for a long time. "Yes, Neen." She cupped the little girl's silken skull with her hand. "Mackie and I are sad because we miss Gram."

"I miss her too, Mom," Liddie said defensively.

"I know, Lid," Lainey said.

Mack's body spun toward his sister. "Then why are you eating?" he accused. "You ate your whole breakfast, just like it didn't even matter to you. Everyone's *eating* around here," he protested to Lainey. "That's what bothers me."

"I only ate one helping," Liddie said. Her face had gone white in shame.

"I eat a *all* up," Nina volunteered, hoping for praise.

"Ee ee ee," Mary echoed, bouncing herself rhythmically with each squeal.

"It's all right to eat, Mack," Lainey said. She could hear David and Randall starting to come downstairs, and she wiped her face again and turned to fix their plates.

"It makes me sick," Mack persisted. He pushed his plate away.

"Well, *you* don't have to eat if you don't want to," Lainey said gently.

"And *she* makes me sick. She pretends to be so upset, and then she eats and eats." His voice rose; he was near tears again. "She's a big pig."

"Mack." Lainey turned and frowned at him.

Randall stepped into the kitchen and shambled stiffly to his place, looking at no one, an awkward little machine. Lainey took his plate to him and set it down. She lifted his hand to his spoon and helped him grip it. The others all watched attentively, even Mary. Sometimes this moment didn't work, something in it didn't satisfy Randall's sense of how things should be, and he threw food, or hit Lainey, or just sat and screamed in protest. But this morning he was obedient. He scooped at the eggs, lifted the spoon to his mouth.

Suddenly Mack cried out, "Ugh!" as though Randall's betrayal were the last straw. He flung his body back in his chair.

"Mack," Lainey said. She hurried around the table and knelt by his chair again. He had turned to face the wall at her approach, so she was talking to his thin, wiry back. "Mack, Randall has to eat. Life goes on, sweetie. We have to eat." She touched his back, but he arched away and she let her hand drop. "Grandma would want us to eat, and be happy, and remember her with pleasure, remember the good things. And you know what I remember, Mack?" She waited a moment, but he made no response. "I remember how Grandma loved to cook, loved to fix special treats. And whenever anyone was upset, that was her way, to fix something good to eat, something comforting." There was silence in the room, except for Randall, who was obliviously shoveling food into his mouth.

Lainey was intensely aware of David behind her, getting himself coffee, watching, listening. "I understand that you might feel too upset now, Mackie, to eat. But it's fine for Randall or Liddie or any of the others to want to. You shouldn't blame them for that. And it will be perfectly all right for you to eat when you feel hungry again. And later on, maybe at school, if you feel like laughing and having fun, even, that's all right too. Grandma wouldn't want our life to stop because she died. She wants us all to go on and be happy." She felt perilously close to tears again herself. "Mack," she said in a pleading voice.

David spoke from behind her. "It's like in your book, Mack, when the loyal subjects say, 'The king is dead, long live the king.' Remember that?"

After a pause, Mack's head slowly bobbed.

Lainey had felt her body relax when she heard David's voice. Now she stood up and stepped back from the table. She watched them all, feeling far away from them, a stranger.

"It's the same thing with us when someone dies. Someone we love and admire. We have to grieve, we have to mourn. But our loyalty is to life. Life needs us, and we need to go on. Being happy and well and whole and strong is part of our loyalty to life, but also partly how we honor the dead.''

Lainey had turned and was watching Randall. He'd stopped eating as David spoke and was slowly rocking his spoon from side to side a few inches from his eyes, his head swaying steadily back and forth with the motion of the light's repeated trip across the spoon's gleaming surface. She had a quick memory of the silver bubbles leaking from his face—Mack's face?—in her dream. Somehow, Lainey felt, what David was saying wasn't quite the same thing she'd been trying to tell Mack.

3

LAINEY stood at the kitchen window in her father's house, her hands in the soapy dishwater. She was watching her brothers outside whack the brightly colored balls over her parents' neat lawn. It was late in the afternoon, and they were playing croquet, casting long black shadows across the grass. Lainey's father and her sister-in-law, Myra, had driven to church to see about flowers for the service the next day. Lainey was finishing the lunch dishes. The sound of her brothers' laughter washed in through the screen with the odor of the rusty metal and the smell of the sweet damp grass. They were happy to be together, she realized, in spite of their mother's death. All they needed to feel like boys again was to return to their parents' house, to each other.

She leaned forward to look at Paul, who had tucked his beer bottle in his hip pocket to take his shot. He shifted his weight slightly, and the bright orange ball leapt away from his feet. Suddenly, as though he felt her gaze on him, he turned to the house. Shielding his eyes from the sun, he looked for a long moment into the shadows where she was. Then he called, "Come out, Lainey!"

Pete turned his head too, and Sam looked up, befuddled in the sunlight, trying to find her. "And bring more beers," Sam yelled.

"In a minute," she called back, and bent again over the tepid water.

It wasn't, she thought, that they were callous, or indifferent to their sorrow either. It was just as David had described it to Mack: their pleasure in life, in being together, was like a form of grieving; their laughter could turn in a matter of seconds to tears. Such a thing had happened last night at dinner. As Lainey and Myra were setting the table, using the chipped, second-best china, with ivy leaves twining around the edges, Lainey could hear her brothers talking in the living room, that deep rumble you could nearly feel through the floor, and then the loud bursts of laughter, Sam's rising clearest above the others. Even as they took their places around the table, they were joking together about the hierarchy in seating arrangements—which place was whose, what that meant. Laughing, they pulled out the old Windsor chairs and sat down. Then a silence fell, the old chairs creaked and sighed as they shifted their weight. Lainey's father cleared his throat and began a grace. "O Lord," he said quietly, in that intimate normal voice he always used in prayer at home. "Comfort us all in our loss tonight. Give us the strength, the courage, to believe she is with You, to remember, even in our sorrow, the joyous promise of our eternal home." He paused, and his breathing faltered. Lainey heard around the table their shuddering inhalations, their snuffling. When her father spoke again, his voice was softer. "We are grateful to you for having brought us all together again, as a family, to grieve the one who is no longer among us." There was a long silence. "Bless this food to our use, and us to Thy service." His voice had broken with the *amen,* and Lainey had kept her head bowed an extra moment to give him, to give all of them, a chance to recover before she looked at their faces. But when she lifted her head, it was they who were looking at her, waiting, she could see, for her tears. She had felt ashamed then of her dry eyes and was aware of a sense of disjuncture, the sense she had now, too, looking out, of being different from them.

In part it was the chores, she thought. From the

moment she walked in the door, there had been things crying out to be done—crying out to be done by her and her sister-in-law Myra, the two women. And the chores were the same as at home. Food, clothing, schedules. They were in charge now. Now that her mother was dead. Watching her brothers playing on the green lawn, she suddenly envied them their freedom, what seemed their youth. She and Myra were like two old women among them. Like turtles, Lainey thought, dragging *home* with them wherever they went. She felt her own stiffness, her own unbending hard shell as she moved around doing her mother's chores—now her chores.

She set the last dish in the drainer and let the water out of the sink. She dried her hands. She had taken her engagement and wedding rings off and set them in a chipped blue saucer on the windowsill. Now she slipped them back on and paused for a moment to look at her hands. They were large, big-knuckled, and Lainey wasn't particularly good with them. She had learned as a girl to knit, to sew, and she'd enjoyed those activities later, mostly as a way to keep her mother company; but she rarely did that kind of work on her own. Nothing she made ever turned out quite the way she'd envisioned it. After years of pulling the lumpy, misshapen sweaters over her children's heads, of wearing dresses that pinched at the armholes, that hung as unevenly as flags at the hemline, she'd simply given up. She fisted her hands. She looked at the faint yellowing, like faded bruises, on her smoking fingers, and suddenly she felt ungainly, slothful, as she had so often in her mother's presence as a girl. Her mother, of course, had never been without some project for her hands, and her involvement with this work had given her a wise, almost abstracted air when you talked with her. David had once told Lainey that there were moments when her mother had affected him the way his analyst had, because of that slightly preoccupied, remote quality to her as she sat and listened. "You think you can tell her anything," he said. Lainey had wondered then what David might have said to her mother about their private life, about their marriage, that he had never articulated to her.

She opened the refrigerator. Her brothers had made a beer run earlier in the day, and the dark bottles were stashed everywhere in and around the dozen or so chicken and tuna casseroles, coffee cakes, jellied salads, and cookie tins that jammed the shelves. These offerings had been sitting all over the kitchen and dining room when Lainey arrived, brought by the women of the parish. Lainey and Myra hadn't had to cook yet, though they'd all been here two days. Lainey extracted four bottles, one for herself too, and slammed the heavy door shut with her foot. A little wind of cold air puffed out and lifted the sweaty hair from her face. The bottles burned cold against her flesh, wet through her shirt. She stepped across the kitchen and grabbed the opener from where Pete had left it on the counter. Then she crossed the back porch and went out into the yard.

A rich meadowy odor rose from the lawn. It had rained steadily all morning and into the early afternoon. Now the sun was lifting a faint smoke up through the grass, as though there were a fire burning somewhere deep in the earth. The flowers in her mother's garden were bent over from the weight of the jeweled water on their blossoms.

The house sat on a hill overlooking unused fields choked with devil's paintbrush and daisies, with stiff blue lupine. Below her, at the foot of the driveway, Lainey could see her nephews, Sam's sons, riding bikes. Patty, her niece, was apparently a traffic guard or a policewoman. When her arm went up, they stopped in a noisy swirl of gravel.

"A mirage," Sam cried when he saw her. "A walking oa-sis." He fell to his knees and grabbed his throat. The other two stopped playing and applauded her approach. Sam was the oldest. He had been drinking steadily since he arrived, though he never seemed quite drunk. Lainey couldn't tell—she hadn't spent more than a few hours at a time with him in years—whether this was out of habit or grief. Sam was a school psychologist. He worked with adolescents. And in spite of his paunch and his thinning hair, he seemed to Lainey now more oddly like an adolescent himself than he'd ever been in his youth.

Myra was his wife. Lainey noticed that she had an air of patient, amused tolerance with Sam; as though he were one of the children. And he called her "Mommy." When Sam had first embraced Lainey in the driveway outside the house the afternoon she arrived, he'd murmured, "Mommy and the kids are here too," gesturing behind him; and for a fraction of a second, Lainey felt a shock of confusion. But when she looked up behind him, it was, of course, Myra's big frame that loomed vague as a ghost behind the rusty screening of the back door.

Now Sam called for a time-out from the game, and they moved to the Adirondack chairs that sat weathering at the edge of the flat lawn. Lainey looked around at her big sweating brothers. They were barefoot, and the cuffs of their pants were darkened and greened from the wet grass. Pete was telling them an anecdote about their mother, about how she'd barely bothered to get angry one time when she'd caught him sneaking in at dawn. He began to describe her as he'd encountered her in the hallway—groggy with sleep but nonetheless amused at his efforts to pretend he was up early, strolling around the house for pleasure. Lainey thought abruptly of her own impatience as a mother, of the countless times she'd lost her temper with her children, the times she'd slapped them or wept, the terror she could sometimes see convulsing their faces at her enraged approach. She felt a shame like nausea sweep through her. How had her mother done it? "Galoots," she had good-naturedly called Lainey's brothers. "Hooligans." When they bothered her, she'd swipe at the air around her to make them disappear as though they were so many irritating flies. "Out of my sight, you great hooligans," she'd say in the midst of one of the endless string of chores that occupied her. "Out of my kitchen." "Out of my garden." Her mother had been at her most flirtatious and charming with them as they got older. It was clear she took pleasure in being a small pretty woman among the big admiring men she'd made.

Sometimes, as a child, Lainey had felt lost in her family. Outsize too, like her brothers, she had no femininity as they'd all learned to define it from their mother's delicacy. Her legs were varicosed with purplish bruises, and behind them a fading history of older wounds in pale green and yellow—things she'd bumped into, stumbled over, fallen on, dropped on herself. Her nails were chewed down to where the flesh was rosy and insubstantial, a veil drawn over her blood. It made others wince to look at her hands. For years her neck seemed disproportionately long, and she had the air of having to think consciously about how to carry her head on it. And she had no sense of humor. Her brothers would tease her lightly, affectionately, and she would only stare, flushed and thickwitted. In bed at night she thought of light, charming answers.

When she was small, she was allowed to "carouse," as her mother called it, with her brothers, and these were the childhood memories that brought

Lainey the most pleasure. Her brothers guaranteed her popularity. She was part of baseball games, allowed as many strikes as it took till she connected. They took her ice-skating, one of them holding each of her mittened hands, pulling her along at dizzying speed as they raced past her wobbling friends around the edge of the flooded town common. She went swimming with them at the quarry, where no other girls went, and they all thoughtlessly jumped around naked in front of her. They taught her to drive the car before she was twelve. One of her brothers' great pleasures was to sit in the back seat, all three of them, with their feet dangling over the edge of the front, and direct their sister through the quiet streets of Pawtucket, past the houses of girls they admired. Sometimes one of them would rest his feet on her head. She wore her heavy crown with pride as she concentrated fiercely on shifting, steering, braking. When ordered to, she would honk the foggy bass of the horn at someone they recognized. Once, coming home from one of these jaunts, she had driven partially through the back wall of the garage, forgetting for a moment where the brake was. Pete had taken the blame with their father, had endured the punishment—made worse because their father suspected he must have been drinking to do such a thing.

But then, slowly, Lainey had felt the jaws of her destiny close around her. Her mother was its agent, its enforcer, though it seemed to Lainey that there was sometimes a note of compassionate apology as she laid down the new rules. No longer could Lainey go out with the boys at night—they were going places "not suitable" for her. She couldn't wear pants. Ladies didn't. She couldn't play in the empty lot with the neighborhood children anymore. And it was Lainey herself who realized she didn't want to go to the quarry again, she didn't want to see the startling white of those clefted buttocks, the dangle of brownish flesh in front amid the fur. Slowly all of that part of her childhood began to seem impossible, a distant dream, something that had happened to another version of herself, in another place and another time.

She began a series of lessons: deportment, dancing, piano, bridge. And she began to impose on herself a private religious discipline, stricter than anything her father or Mrs. Dana, her Sunday school teacher, would have dreamed of. Every evening, alone in her room, she examined her behavior of the day for hypocrisy or pride. She had small painful penances for these sins: pebbles in her shoes, ordered numbers of pricks with a straight pin. To rid herself of earthly desires, she gave away her favorite doll and a cloisonné brooch that Aunt Lalie had brought her from China. Occasionally she hit herself across the thighs with a wire hanger. It was during this period that she dreamed of training for the ministry, but her father spoke mockingly of this ambition on her part, and she slowly realized there was something of overweening pride in it, and something almost comical to others. No, it was Paul who was encouraged in this direction, Paul whom both parents defined as having the ability to have a vocation—this in spite of his only average grades and his relentless and passionate interest in what her parents called "the gals." And Lainey had made accepting this a part of her discipline, a punishment for prideful thoughts.

Now, telling his tale, Pete's voice cracked. He broke off and shook his head. "Some lady," he said. "Some lady." Sam wiped at his eyes.

They all sat in an awkward silence for a moment. To end it, Lainey said, "It looks like the guy with the yellow ball is having his troubles today." They looked over at the grass. The jots of bright blue and orange winked near the far end of the court. The yellow ball was at half court, near the almost invisible middle wicket.

"Yeah, that's mine," Pete said. "It's the beer talking."

"No, no, no, no. Don't *let* the beer talk," Sam said earnestly. "You talk to the beer, the beer does not talk to you."

Paul stood up and stretched. "Okay, enough palaver," he said, looking down at the rest of them. He was the leanest, the trimmest, of Lainey's brothers. "This jawing is just a strategy—I see it now—to avoid getting thoroughly trounced. C'mon, up. I want to win this and get it over with."

Moving more slowly, the two bigger men heaved themselves out of the deep chairs. "Lainey, gonna play?" Sam asked.

"I don't know," she said. "Have you got room?"

"Of course there's room," Sam said. "The only question is how to bring you in. Maybe should we all start over?" he asked the others.

"No, let's give her some free shots to catch up," Pete said. "Say . . . five of them?"

"That seems like a lot," Lainey said. She was lifting the red ball from the bottom of the channel in the croquet stand.

"What the hay," Sam said. "You're a girl, right?"

He and Pete laughed.

Lainey felt a surge of disproportionate rage, as though she were an adolescent again. "The hell with you," she said. But they all laughed now. She walked away from them. She set her ball a mallet's length from the starting post and began to play through. Fueled by her anger, she played well, stroking the ball with careless assurance and power.

She reached the center of the court with four shots still to spare. As she drove through the middle wicket, her ball rolled toward Pete's, coming to rest against it with a gentle *tock!* She stepped up to the balls, nestled like strange bright eggs, and looked at them a moment. Then she lifted her sandaled foot, set it down on her own red ball, and swung as hard as she could against it. The yellow ball shot out, spun quickly across the flat lawn, then rolled twenty feet or so down the incline toward the driveway. There was an abrupt silence behind Lainey. Then Sam said, "Good Lord! Killer croquet!"

"Gee, Lainey, what'd I ever do to you?" Pete asked. He sounded genuinely plaintive.

Lainey didn't answer. With careful, grim pleasure, she aimed for the next wicket. The ball rolled steadily but came to rest just in front of it. She heard Sam ask, "How many shots she got left?" and Paul answer, "I make it two." He always knew. He was the only one who ever really cared how things were done. They used to joke that he read Hoyle for pleasure in his free time. Hunched over the wicket, Lainey shot through.

Now she could move on to the double wickets at the end of the court, but Paul's ball lay over to the right of them. She turned and aimed at it. Behind her, her brothers were watching. The balls collided with such force that the blue one jumped and landed more than a foot from hers. Lainey walked over, picked her ball up and set it next to Paul's, then repeated her powerful swing against the red ball under her foot. Paul's ball spun away from her toward the house, disappearing into the rhododendron bushes under the dining room windows.

Lainey had no idea now how many shots she had left, whether she had any. She felt a pure anger at all of them, an anger somehow connected with her mother's death and somehow exciting in its viciousness. In two shots she hit Sam's ball. It too she drove downhill toward the driveway. It sailed out over a bump and rolled on past Pete's, coming to rest nearly where the children were bicycling. They stopped for a moment and looked up at the grownups, suddenly brought back from their invented world by this tiny bright missive from another.

Lainey stood and looked up and down the court. She was panting slightly from effort and the excitement of her anger. Her red ball was the only spot of color on the smooth green expanse of lawn. The men were clustered, silent, behind her.

Suddenly she had a sense of deep defeat, a sense of her own foolishness. She let her mallet fall—let them pick it up, let them pick it all up—and, without looking back at any of them, walked toward the house. She heard one of them say, "For Christ's sweet sake?" in perplexity, and then another, in an undertone, something she couldn't understand.

Lainey walked on, into the dark shadow of the house. Inside, she was blinded by the contrast with the sunlight, but she fumblingly made her way to the stairs, past the worn elegant furniture, the marble bust of Homer, the tea service on the hall table, all the familiar hand-me-downs or gifts from her parents' parishes, set on display over and over in the series of homes that weren't really theirs. Up one carpeted flight in the still house, rising away from the easy boys. She felt her fatigue, her pregnancy, like the weight of age, though she was the youngest. *It isn't fair,* she thought, for a moment almost believing in the relevance of the protest. Then the second flight, to the attic, the bare chipped stairs below her becoming slowly visible as her eyes adjusted.

The attic room was small and stuffy, though the single window was propped open with a short board. The sun was streaming in, and dust motes swam slowly in the hot light. Her brothers' voices rose from the lawn, a dim murmur. She heard laughter explode, then die.

Her mother had used this as a sewing room. The sewing machine was still set up, the old-fashioned treadle kind her mother preferred. There was a dress form standing in the corner, small and bosomy. Its curves were shaped of a padded gray muslin stretched over a wire frame. The frame hung below the muslin like a kind of narrow, abbreviated hoop skirt. Against the wall, a long rectangular mirror rested in a wooden stand on the floor. It was swung up now at an odd angle so that it reflected only the blank surface of the ceiling. It looked like a blind eye. Lainey stepped over to it and swung the mirror down. She met herself, for a moment rocking wildly in the motion of the glass, tall and dark and somber in the dusty yellow light. She stood and waited as her reflection stilled. Then she stared back for a long minute at the surprisingly young-looking, strong-looking image, as though she were seeing a stranger. She was shocked by the vibrancy her coloring gave her. She felt so washed out, so pale, it was hard to remember that the world saw her this other way.

Suddenly she reached to her chest and began to unbutton her shirt, watching her big hands moving in the mirror. When she was finished, she dropped her arms, then wiggled out of the shirt. It fell with a whisper to the floor. Moving quickly, she unhooked her brassiere, let it slide forward off her arms. She fumbled with the side buttons on her shorts, pushed them down with her underpants, and awkwardly, hurriedly, stepped out of them both. Last she bent over and unbuckled her sandals. Wildly, as though they were hurting her, she kicked them off. They bounced across the floor and landed, yawning, several feet from each other against the wall. Now she stood looking at herself naked in the mirror. Her hips were wide, her abdomen streaked with silver, her pubic hair a dark thick flag below it. Her big breasts hung, already slightly swollen with her pregnancy, the nipples so elongated by nursing that they looked like two of Mary's stubby fingers pointing downward. Lainey stepped even closer to the mirror, stared at her face, then at the used-up flesh of her body. She lifted one breast, let it flop. Then she saw again, in the mirror, in the corner behind her, the dress form, small and neat, its little cluster of straight pins glinting like a brooch at this distance on its bosom. She felt the impulse to weep clutch her throat, and she looked away. She turned and crossed to the unmade rollaway bed. She lay down on its rumpled, coarse sheets. In the rush of air caused by her motion, the dust motes stirred frantically, danced golden and thick in the sunlight falling across the bed.

The waxy light lay in a warming rectangle over her body. Lainey felt the stirring of some inchoate desire. She held her breasts, trying to conjure an image that would focus this yearning. *David,* she thought; and then, when her mind stayed blank, blank as the uptilted mirror: *Mother.*

The next morning, Lainey stood in front of the mirror again, carefully pinning on her hat, a scrap of dark straw with a veil. She was wearing the same heavy green silk suit she'd worn on the train. She noticed there was a grease stain the size of a half-dollar in the front near the hem—probably something spilled on the ride from Chicago. Well, there was nothing to be done about that. She adjusted her veil to cover the upper half of her face. At each corner, where four strands of the veil came together, there was a tiny mesh rectangle, and the blur this network established across her vision gave her a strange sense of distance from the reflection in the mirror. The suit was stretched slightly across her belly, and she pulled her stomach in, turned first one way and then another. When she had walked down the aisle in the train on her way to her private berth, she had slowly become aware of the unfamiliar, sexually appraising stare of two or three businessmen. She had at first felt a rising, a quickening in her; and then abruptly remembered the baby that was responsible for her newly rounded figure, her plumped flesh. It was a miracle David hadn't noticed, she thought, or perhaps just a symptom of how little he noticed her at all anymore. But then she recalled how wonderful he had been as she got ready to go. He had canceled several afternoon patients to be with the children so she could pack, had gently kissed her as the taxi waited out on the street. "I'll call," he had said, and he touched her elbow. She could only be grateful.

Below her now she could hear her brothers gathering outside in the driveway, the crunching sound of their shoes on gravel, the opening and slamming of car doors, their voices calling back and forth. One of Sam's children was whining somewhere below in the house, and she heard Myra answer sharply, "I said *no*. I said no once earlier, and I meant it." Lainey tilted back, checked her seams, picked up her purse, and went downstairs.

In the car on the way to church, she and Paul and Pete were silent. Their father had gone ahead in his own car to be sure everything was all right. Myra and Sam and the children were driving behind them.

Each of them sat against a car door, smoking, staring out into the woods that flickered quickly past. There were still a few rhododendrons and mountain laurels blossoming in the deep shade. Lainey thought of the thousand Sundays from their past, all the mornings when they had to be forced up from their thick adolescent sleep, prodded into the costumes of middle age it was customary to wear to church or formal events. Then, however, their mother would have been at the wheel, chattering steadily to them to get them ready for conversation, civility, their father's interested congregation. Now Paul was driving. Lainey looked over at him. He was her favorite brother. His hands gripping the steering wheel were white, prettier than her own. She looked at his face. Under his eyes and running from his nostrils to the corners of his mouth were the beginnings of the lines of age. The same marks of having lived, having suffered, that seemed so unremarkable to Lainey on her own face seemed unwarranted on Paul's. Cruel. She deliberately blurred her vision to erase them. He felt her gaze, looked over at her and smiled. "I'll be glad when this part's over," he said.

"Me too," she answered.

As they came into town, Lainey could feel herself stiffen in readiness. The white wooden church stood with its doors flung open at the head of the town green. The green itself was completely encircled in cars, parked legally and illegally, some tilted with two wheels up on the lawn. As they passed the church, Lainey looked over. People were mingling on the stairs in the sunlight, or slowly shuffling in. Beyond them she could see the dim, chaste interior, briefly she could hear the organ's gentle rhythm, like the cool breathing noise of the building itself. She felt a sinking, a resistance to the role she would have to play.

Paul drove a block or so past the green and parked. As they started to walk back to the church, Pete bent toward Lainey, touching her elbow. Softly he chanted: "Manu*fact*ure your sobriety, *re*surrect your piety. Time to get set for . . . the Lord, strong and miety." Lainey smiled. He had recited this regularly as they got out of the car on Sundays; and their mother had always said, "Hush, you child in adult's clothing," and sometimes swatted him lightly across his bottom if she was close enough.

Most of the congregation that had gathered in little groups on the steps and in the narthex fell back from them slightly as they entered. Lainey was grateful. There would be enough polite commiseration with strangers at the tea afterward. But in the back of the chapel, waiting for them, were her mother's sisters, Margaret and Eulalia. They were both short, pretty women, like her mother, though Margaret wore eyebrow pencil and a rigid blue permanent in her hair. It was Aunt Lalie, childless and scatterbrained, who had been closer to Lainey's mother. She began to weep when she saw them, and Lainey crossed to embrace her. "Now, I wasn't going to cry," she said into Lainey's ear. "But then I saw you, my dear." Her voice was deep and warm, like Lainey's mother's. She stepped back and looked searchingly into Lainey's face. "Isn't it awful?" she said. Lainey nodded, and turned to Margaret.

As soon as she could, Lainey broke away and walked quickly, alone, down the aisle of the church, leaving her brothers and Myra to accompany the two older women. She went directly to the pew at the front on the right, slid in, and bowed her head, as if in intense prayer. Even when her brothers filed in and sat down next to her, she didn't look up, and so they didn't speak to her. It was only when the organ stopped its gentle murmur, paused, and then began the pealing processional, that she lifted her head.

The room was full, perhaps three hundred people, and the sound of their rising was like a great roar. Her father and the assistant pastor filed in, and each stood in front of a wooden bench behind the pulpit. The assistant pastor raised his arms toward them. He intoned: "I am the resurrection and the life, saith the

Lord; he that believeth in me, though he were dead, yet shall he live: and whosoever liveth and believeth in me shall never die." Lainey's throat clotted. The assistant pastor was a young man. His voice was hopeful and strong. "I know that my redeemer liveth, and that he shall stand at the latter day upon the earth: and though this body be destroyed, yet shall I see God: whom I shall see for myself, and mine eyes shall behold, and not as a stranger."

His voice changed; lowered. "We brought nothing into this world, and it is certain we can carry nothing out. The Lord gave, and the Lord hath taken away; blessed be the name of the Lord." Their "Amen" was like a moan from the congregation, and they sat down.

While the assistant read from the Scriptures all the promises of a bright life after this one, Lainey stared ahead of her, through the clear glass windows, at the ferns and lupines moving in and out of the sunlight with the breeze. The church was austere and simple, not like the imitation-Gothic church she attended in Chicago. The windows were clear, the walls white, the floor a painted gray.

Between the Scriptures and the hymns, several of Lainey's mother's friends rose to speak of her, talking of her energy, her compassion, her activities on behalf of others. Lainey felt a kind of jealousy of their knowledge, a competitive resistance to their way of knowing her mother that made it hard for her to listen to what they said. One of the women broke down partway through her eulogy, and her husband came forward and finished reading it at her side.

Near the end of the service, Lainey's father stood up and came forward behind the pulpit. He was going to do the Twenty-third Psalm. He had wanted to do this. Lainey closed her eyes, and like the afterimage of what we see in bright light, she saw him as he'd been through those countless Sundays of her childhood and adolescence: rising above her in his robes like some magnificent bird, transformed into a spiritual being untouchable and pure, even his voice changed, his elocution a tribute to years of training and to what Lainey then felt was his direct link to God.

Now he began the old beautiful words, and with their rhythm, Lainey felt her readiness to let herself be touched, comforted. But almost instantly she found that his elocution disturbed her. His words were too smooth, too professional. She felt a quick, hateful anger for her father. She remembered Mack crying out, "Doesn't anybody care? Don't you *care*, Mom?" and she felt that same indignant confusion. Next to her, Sam had begun to weep, and she turned to look at him. She met the dry-eyed stare of his two boys beyond him, looking also. She had a sense then, before she turned quickly away, of how strange she must seem to them, so held in she couldn't even cry for her own mother. Maybe if her children were here too, she thought; and she let herself remember the release of tears they had worked for her when she told them the news.

The last hymn was "Guide Me, O Thou Great Jehovah," one of her mother's favorites. Lainey had a terrible voice, unmusical and sharp, and she usually pitched herself an octave below the sopranos to submerge it. She could never hear her own voice separate from the congregation's, and now she felt particularly lost in the ringing sound that surrounded her. She was still thinking in a distracted way of her children, of the way they had looked around the kitchen table when David spoke to them of life and death. On the third verse, though, as the sopranos rose sharply on the words "Feed me till I want no more," she had a sudden clear image of her mother in that same kitchen on Harper Avenue, the first morning Lainey had ventured downstairs after Randall's birth. It had been late, almost lunchtime, and Lainey was as hungry as a child. When she stepped into the room, her mother was bent over the stove, a spatula in her hand, lifting a cookie from the sheet that sat cooling on the burners. The kitchen smelled of butter and lemon and cinnamon. Her mother turned and lifted her face when she heard Lainey. "My dear!" she had said, in her quick, thrilling voice, and her face shone with joy to see her daughter.

"Feed me ti-ll I want no more," the sopranos were singing. Lainey heard her own voice break below theirs. She sat down and covered her face with her hands. She heard the assistant pastor say the benediction. She was aware of a low keening noise coming from her chest, and then Sam's arm was around her, and she leaned blindly into his big embrace.

When the recessional began, his arm helped to lift her, to move her out of the pew. She didn't want to go. On her own, she would have sat there not moving, holding on to the image of her mother, to the sound of that warm voice in her ear. Sam kept his arm around her as she stumbled slowly down the aisle to where the doors had been swung open again on the town green. As they crossed the threshold and the sun struck her face, she had to shut her eyes against its glimmering light, refracted and intensified through her tears. In the orange darkness behind her lids she saw her children's faces, sliding like motes across her vision.

But now they all looked strangely like Randall, and their mouths opened to her like hungry birds, and she blinked her eyes quickly to blind herself to them for just a moment more, as they began to call her, call her back to them.

4 AT least twice in the night David had waked to hear Lainey with the new baby, Sarah—the scratchy, chickenlike cries of hunger diminishing quickly to faint grunting and smacking as Lainey found the infant's mouth with her breast in the dark. The last time there was a gassy pale light in the bedroom, and he tented himself in the dim must under the covers to find his way back to sleep.

It seemed much later when he heard the children, their thumping and yelling through the house. Lainey was gone. He sensed the cold on her side of the bed—she'd been up for a while. And then he remembered: it was Christmas. Lainey had come home early from the hospital just for this. Everyone had advised against it, including David. Sarah was only three days old, and Lainey was still in a pained daze of postpartum exhaustion and excitement, her body still nearly as swollen as before she'd given birth. He opened his eyes and looked up at the ceiling. A calcimined patch curled down directly over the bed.

He'd gone to the hospital to get Lainey the evening before, and they'd driven back slowly through a thick wet snow that had started to fall while they were checking the baby out. The wipers pushed steadily against it, and mushy triangles formed at the corners of the windshield. Lainey had shuffled painfully down the long, slushy path to the house. When she came into the front hallway, he could sense the older children's fright and alarm at seeing her—hunched as though to protect her insides from the slightest motion, her skin a bleached white, her hair lank and unwashed. They'd sat silent, their faces rapt in the candlelight, as she read the Christmas passage from Luke—a holiday custom. But he felt their attentiveness was born as much of fear as of interest in the story, and it reminded him again of his anger about this last careless pregnancy, his anger at her for what he saw as a kind of reckless, oblivious disregard of all the strains the family was already under.

He'd said nothing to her, of course. And then they'd each had all the chores of Christmas Eve to occupy and separate them; they'd both collapsed into exhausted sleep at the same time, curled away from each other in their bed. If they could just get through this long day without tears, without recriminations, David thought, tomorrow life would resume. Retta would come and stay for a week or so to help out, he'd go back to work. And he and Lainey would find a way to get by. They always did.

By the time he had dressed and gone downstairs, she had organized everything for the long ritual day. The dining room table was set for breakfast. He could smell a sweet baking odor, and coffee and bacon. He went directly to the dark basement to stoke the furnace. The coals still glared white-hot in the middle of the old cast-iron monster that squatted in the heart of the front room, and he took a primitive satisfaction in this: it had been a bitterly cold night. He shoveled for a few minutes, blanketing the glowing coals with black, thinking of himself as feeding a hungry force. He enjoyed everything about this ritual—the heavy lift of the old shovel, its gritty clang on the cement floor, the oily smell of coke, the kiss of heat on his face as he bent toward the open door.

When he came back up into the kitchen, Lainey was standing with drooped shoulders at the stove, wearing her red wool bathrobe, her socks and slippers. Her body was held awkwardly, her discomfort in it visible, but she looked up at him with a childish, dazzled excitement lighting her face. Her hair was pushed back carelessly, trapped by a bobby pin. "Oh, David!" she said. "Merry Christmas."

"Merry Christmas to you," he answered. In some nearly imperceptible way, she seemed to lift her body toward him, and in response he rested his hand for a moment on her back.

He poured himself coffee. She had turned quickly back to what she was doing, and for a moment he watched her. "Was it a tough night?" he asked finally, willing his voice to concern.

"*Three* feedings," she said gratefully. "That's what you get for having such a tiny one. The balance evens up after that easy birth."

"I thought I heard you a couple of times," he answered. The coffee burned in his mouth. "What can I do now?"

"You might check Sarah. I put her in the carriage in the dining room."

He started out of the room.

"And I want everyone sort of spiffed up before breakfast," she said. "Teeth brushed, bathrobes, slippers."

"Will do," he said, as he rounded the corner into the dining room.

He leaned over the carriage to look at the new baby. She was lying silent near the tall windows, in a square of dusty sunlight. She was covered with the threadbare quilt that all the children had slept under as infants, made by Lainey's mother for Liddie years ago. Her mouth was working in her sleep, and she gave a little shuddering sigh as David bent over her. He'd seen her eyes open only once, in the hospital. Most of the time, except for feedings, she was still deep in her infant sleep. Her skin was yellow and wrinkled, and her head was misshapen, with oily-looking spikes of black hair. At supper the night before, when Lainey was out of the room, the children had agreed she was the ugliest baby they'd ever seen. They'd refused to listen to David when he told them they'd all looked the same way, perhaps—in certain cases—worse.

Now he turned to the living room, to where they were gathered around the presents, noisy and still oblivious of him. Randall cruised the edges of the room, moving fast, humming and swinging his head as though he wanted to dizzy himself, to cut himself off from the noise of the others. The light in the room was dusky because the tree blocked the big front window, but someone had plugged the Christmas tree cord in, and the bubblers and bright ornaments sparkled.

"Merry Christmas to the cherubim and seraphim," David announced; and then suddenly he was surrounded by them. They bumped against each other, they all talked at once. Joking, efficient, David took charge. He sent the older children up to get their bathrobes, to brush their teeth, to bring slippers back for everyone.

As he led Randall to the first-floor lavatory, Mary on his hip, David could hear water running in the kitchen, could hear Lainey singing, slightly off key, *"Arise,* shine, for thy light is come."

In her carriage, the baby began to cry.

"Now, this is the way we should begin every day," David said, crumbling his coffee cake. "A grand gathering in the dining room, *en famille,* the good china, the three-course breakfast, everyone groomed to the gills. . . ."

"What's anfaneel?" Mack asked.

"En famille. It's French. 'In the family.' Means everyone all together."

Lainey smiled benignly and drew on her cigarette. *"Très amusant,"* she said. "Maybe when the kitchen staff return." She wasn't eating. Even on Christmas she couldn't eat until she'd made herself jittery with five or six cups of coffee.

"I can't stand it when adults talk French," Liddie said. "It's so unfair."

"Mmm. It is a little . . . almost sneaky, isn't it?" Lainey said. "Well, we won't do it again."

"Maybe, just maybe, I got the chemistry set," Mack said. "There's one box that looks just about the right size, and it kind of sounded like it."

Liddie heaved herself dramatically back in her chair, revulsed. "That is so disgusting, that poking around."

"Lydia?" David touched her arm while Mack babbled on cheerfully to Lainey. "Just for today, let's let it go. Let sleeping dogs lie. Let the barbarian hordes descend, good manners be damned." He had tried for a light tone, but her face showed him he'd failed.

"More," Mary announced.

Wounded, Liddie pulled her arm away from David's hand. She turned quickly to Mary. "More what?" she asked loudly, almost in falsetto.

"More what?" Nina echoed.

The children began picking things up, holding them out to Mary. Delighted by the attention, she smiled, showing her tiny grayish scalloped teeth, and shook her head *no* to everything.

"Say it. Say what you want, baby," Liddie cried. "You can talk, you can. Sticky bun? Want sticky bun?" Liddie held up her roll and took an exaggerated bite. "Mmm. Yum, yum." She rubbed her stomach.

David leaned toward Mack. "Did you by any chance check my packages too?" he asked.

Mack paused a moment to gauge the tone of this remark. Then he smiled, delighted, and shook his head.

"Drat. Then I won't know until I open them if they're what I wanted."

"What did you want, Dad?" Mack asked. Sugar crumbs sat in the corners of his mouth.

"Too late now," Lainey said. "Should've asked him weeks ago." The baby crowed suddenly, and she reached over to the handle of the carriage, began to jiggle it gently. There was a rusty snicker, then silence.

Mary frowned down at the carriage from her high chair. "More bacon," she said tragically and clearly. Lainey put another piece of bacon on her plate. Mary picked it up and began to chew with her mouth open, making a sucking sound with each tight swivel of her jaw.

"Michael Rosenberg got one for his birthday," Mack was saying. "And he mixed certain stuff together—it says all how in the directions—and he made this stink. This stink like *peee-uuuu.*" He held his nose, grinning.

Randall pushed back from the table, crooning under his breath. He got up and moved toward the living room, calmed by food and slower now than earlier. Lainey turned for a moment to watch him.

David raised his cup. This china had been Lainey's mother's, shipped to them by her father a few months after her death. David liked the way it felt, its lightness, the touch of the thin rim against his lip. There were no such treasures coming down from his family.

"What's the point of that?" Liddie asked.

"Of what?"

"Of making a stink? Why doesn't he make something useful?"

"Dummy, that's not what chemistry sets are for. They're for learning about what happens when you mix certain things."

"Oh, yeah? Why don't you just mix dinner, then? You'd learn the same stuff. And that would be useful."

"Not everything has to be useful," Mack said, after a long silence.

"Right, Lid," David said. He set down his cup. "What would you do about, let's say, painting. Art. Or your lovely music. Some things aren't meant to be useful. They're meant to give pleasure."

Lydia looked offended. "Pleasure can be useful too, you know." She had finished her cake and was licking her fingers carefully.

"Ah. An interesting thought," David said.

"Pleasure *is* useful," Lainey said. She held her cigarette in her mouth as she spread butter on Nina's coffee cake. "I absolutely agree with Liddie. Like grace notes in music. Unexpected, wonderful things like that. They make life *possible,* and what could be more useful than that?"

The sun lay over the table, and Mary leaned back now in her high chair to stare at the flash of yellow light reflected off Lainey's knife, dancing on the ceiling.

"But if pleasure is useful," David said, "then Mack's stink must be useful too. It pleases him, no?"

"Yeah!" Mack yelled.

Liddie's face pinched. Betrayed. She turned to her brother. "Well, if all you're going to do is make a stink, I, for one, hope you don't get it."

He jutted his jaw forward at her. "Then I hope you don't get what you want."

"Macklin." Lainey spoke wearily.

"Well, she said the same thing to me. You heard her."

"I don't want either of you—either of you—starting this business this morning." Her voice sounded suddenly teary. "Please. It's Christmas. Let's just have a lovely day. As Daddy says, *en famille.*"

"Ugh!" said Liddie.

There was a light tinkling *pock* from the living room. Lainey spun around in her chair. "What was that?"

Randall moved out from beside the tree. He was shuffling across the mountain of presents, oblivious.

"I think an or-na-ment," Nina answered carefully, proud to pronounce such a long word.

"Oh, heavenly days," Lainey said. The baby creaked. Lainey looked at David, then quickly away, down the table at her children. "Let's see. Mack, darling. Are you done? Can you go in there and just"— her voice rose with a frantic edge—"just keep him away from that stuff till we get there?"

"Why do I always have to?"

"Liddie will help clear."

"And me," Nina said. "I can help."

"And Nina." Lainey smiled abruptly at the little girl. "That's so nice of you, Nina. Thank you, sweetie."

Mack got up from the table. "Well, if I'm in there, I'm going to have to feel the presents." He was grinning diabolically.

"*Mack,*" Liddie said. She looked around at both parents, counting on them to be responsible at last.

"How can I not?" Mack called back.

"It's all right, Lid," David said.

Lainey poured herself another cup of coffee. "Would you like some more, David?" She held up the pot.

"I'll come get it." He headed around the table, holding his cup.

"Should I start now?" Liddie asked. Only Nina and Mary were still eating, soberly and methodically.

"Give us another lovely moment or two of peace, darling," Lainey said, and lifted her china cup.

*   *   *

It was while they were at their busiest—Lainey nursing Sarah, David making a new pot of coffee, helping Liddie and Nina to clear and load the dishes—that Mack, who was barefoot, who hadn't been able to find his slippers anywhere, stepped on a piece of the broken ornament and sliced his foot open.

"Oh, good Lord!" Lainey cried when he held it up to her. Her nipple pulled out of the baby's mouth. Mack stared at it, the long pink glistening thing, and took a step backward. "No, no. Don't move! Don't move!" She didn't seem to know what to do. The baby began to cry, and she held it out as though to give it to Mack, then realized what she was doing and gave him instead the clean diaper she had draped over her shoulder.

"Put this on it, wrap this on it tight. Oh Lord. David!" she shouted. She got up, one breast hanging out of her bathrobe, dribbling milk down her front. She shuffled awkwardly a few steps toward the kitchen, then suddenly spun and began to shriek, "What are you *doing* in your bare feet?" She swatted at Mack's head, but he had crouched over his foot and she missed him. Her face was blotched with quick anger. "Where are your slippers?" she wailed. "Didn't I tell you to put some slippers on?"

When David came around the corner, he couldn't for a moment understand why he'd been called, what he was supposed to see. He thought Mack had done something to the wailing baby, that that was why Lainey was standing over him, holding Sarah awkwardly and yelling. But then he saw the staining diaper Mack was wrapping around his foot, he saw his son's face, white and frightened; and he bent down to find out what had to be done.

In the car, David had Mack rest his foot on the dashboard and push down hard on one of the clean diapers they'd brought with them. It was bitterly cold, more like a deep January day than December, and the wet snow that had been falling the night before when David drove Lainey home had frozen into a hard, glittery crust on everything. The thin flannel pajamas slid up Mack's skinny, bluish calves, and David winced for his son's bare flesh. He hadn't thought to bring a coat for him. Their breath in the car plumed and frosted the windshield with jungle shapes.

"Is it going to hurt?" Mack asked after a few minutes.

"They usually give you a little local anesthesia. The stitching does feel odd. It pulls, and it's uncomfortable. But it's not what you're afraid of, no."

"Will you stay with me?"

David looked at Mack. He looked much younger in his fright. Younger, even, than Randall. "Yes."

The streets were empty of life, all the stores and restaurants on Fifty-seventh Street shuttered and closed, the sidewalks unshoveled, pristine. The sky was an unflinching blue, though, and the sun bounced off the endless snow with a cold, wide beauty that David was suddenly aware of taking pleasure in, even now. He felt liberated, released from the long, stuffy day at home with the new baby, from the endless Christmas celebration Lainey insisted on. He realized, abruptly, that part of the reason he'd been angry at Lainey for coming home early was that he'd been looking forward to a Christmas without her, without her rigid insistence on certain ordered ways of doing things. And now he had escaped, he and Mack. He looked over at the frightened boy. He wanted to comfort him somehow, to share a little of his own sense of release. He inhaled deeply and began to sing: "Let every good fellow now join in a song: *Vive la compagnie!*"

The emergency room lot was nearly empty. David

parked close to the door and carried Mack across the little shoveled path. The boy was heavy, but his tensed muscles and the corded wiriness everywhere in his body made him easy to carry. How different from Randall, David thought. He frequently had to carry Randall, but his younger son's flesh was flaccid and dense, even though he was as slender as Mack. David took a satisfaction, a pride, in the way Mack felt in his arms, as though he were half carrying himself.

The admitting nurse was on the phone. She seemed to understand with a cursory glance that this was nothing serious. Carelessly she shoved some forms across at David. He sat in the waiting room with Mack's foot elevated on his lap and filled them out. They were the only people in the ugly room, and the plastic-covered chrome chairs, the empty gleaming ashtray stands, were pushed neatly back against the walls, as though waiting for a party to begin. Someone had looped a glittery paper chain around two of the walls at eye level, and it added to the air of failed festivity. The nurse finally emerged from her station and led them down the hall to a tiny cubicle, glaringly lighted. David set Mack on the gurney and unwrapped his foot for her.

She bent over and squinted. "Oh, not too bad," she said. "That's a real relief. I'll set you up here. Do you think you can keep the bleeding slowed?" David nodded. "We'll get to you ASAP." She turned to the stainless-steel counter and reached under it for gauze and a bottle of something. "We're on skeleton staff today, though, and we've just had an accident come in. Two of them, actually. So it might be a while." Her speech was slow. She sounded just slightly southern. Downstate, maybe. Or Kentucky. She flipped the bottle over once, twice. Then she turned and began to clean Mack's foot with a wet gauze pad. "Okay?" She smiled at Mack down the length of his body. She was middle-aged, with pouchy flesh. A redhead. The frames of her glasses were red too, crusted with jewels.

David watched his son's face enlarge in pain as she swabbed vigorously: his eyes and nostrils widened, he clutched his striped bathrobe across his narrow chest. Behind David, far down the corridor, there was a shout, and then distant footsteps, running.

The nurse looked up and frowned. Then she turned back to Macklin. "Boy, you are brave," she said, stroking the bleeding cut. "A lot of grownups, even, flip their lids when you clean a cut like this. Not you, though, huh?"

"No," Mack said weakly, obediently.

She wet a fresh piece of gauze and worked a minute more. Mack sucked his breath in sharply and closed his eyes. Then she patted Mack's shin and said gently, "I'm done now, honey." Her tone when she turned to David was businesslike. "Okay, you can see that that started it up a little again. I want you to just keep this clean gauze on it"—she showed a stack of the squares to David—"and squeeze it for a while. It should slow right down. But if you have any problems, come and get me."

"It's okay, I'm a physician," David said. He took a brief pleasure in the lift in her face.

"Oh, great!" she said. "Okay, then, Doctor. Well, as I say, it's probably going to be . . . oh"—she raised her freckled arm and looked at her watch—"maybe even an hour or more." She turned and smiled at Mack. "But we'll be back, honey, as soon as we can. Get you home to those presents, right?" She disappeared before Mack had finished nodding.

David sat down at the foot of the gurney. He held the gauze with a steady pressure. "Merry Christmas," he said gently after a moment. "When we get this bleeding stopped, I'll have to call and see how everyone's doing at home. And let them know you're going to live."

Mack lay still awhile. Then he asked abruptly, "Do you think they'll open the presents without us?"

"I'm pretty sure not. Your mother always likes Christmas to be just the same. I bet they'll wait."

"They'll cook dinner, probably," Mack said after a silence.

"Using your chemistry set."

Mack laughed. Then his face shifted. *"Is* it a chemistry set?"

"If I tell you, it won't be a surprise."

Mack looked defeated.

"But if you want me to tell you, I will. You can choose."

Mack's eyes swung away, around the bare, ugly room. Then he looked at David. "Do you think you *should* tell me?" he asked earnestly.

David shook his head. *"You* have to decide."

"It's too hard for me to decide. You decide."

"No. I don't think that will work."

"Why?" Mack's voice was whiny. "Why won't it?"

David shrugged. "I can't win if I decide. Either way you'll be mad at me. If I say yes and tell you, you'll be mad that I did, that I ruined the surprise of it—and that's part of the fun, don't you think? But if I don't tell you, you'll be mad and you'll feel that really you do want to know. So. You decide."

They sat quietly. David found himself wishing for a cigarette. He patted his various pockets with his free hand, but he hadn't brought any with him.

"What do you think they're doing now?"

David squinted. "Let's see. Probably . . . probably everyone's getting dressed. Lydia's got her third costume on and it's still not right, so she's gone back up to try again."

Mack grinned. His big second teeth were lop-sided in his mouth.

"Randall's is perfect. Delicious. He's chewing away at his cuff and wishing your mother allowed ketchup on clothes."

Mack laughed.

"Your mother hates the way she looks." He made his voice as dramatic as Lainey's. *"Simply* despises it. 'This frumpy dress, the only thing that fits. It's mon-strous. Oh, who cares? Who cares about me?' She brushes her hair. 'This rat's nest. But who's going to look at me anyway?' "

David's eyes were on Mack's eager face as he con-tinued. "Nina and Mary are helping each other. It's a disaster. Everything they're wearing is inside out or upside down. Not only are their shoes on all the wrong feet, but each of them is wearing one of her own and one of the other's."

"Yeah," Mack said.

"And they're buttoned up crooked. They've got both legs coming out one leg hole so they can barely walk, their socks are bunched down in their heels, and their bows are undone in back."

Mack snorted and giggled, watching his father. After a moment he said, "You didn't do Sarah."

"Ah, Sarah!" David said. "How could I forget? Sarah. Our little last straw. Sarah is wearing the most gorgeous, glorious, brand-new, spanking-clean *dia-per* you ever saw. She doesn't care that her hair looks glued to her head, she doesn't care that her skin is yellow, that there are lumps and bumps all over her skull. She prances, she twirls, she curtsies on her wob-bly yellow sticks, our Sarah."

Mack looked suddenly uncomfortable. "That one's dumb, Dad," he said.

David saw that he'd gone too far. That something

in his description of the baby, or in his tone, perhaps, had frightened Mack.

"No doubt," he said, trying to keep his voice light. "But that's why we like it."

Mack lay still. David listened to the muffled noises of disaster down the hall. He was aware, abruptly, of feeling real pleasure in being so close to this old familiar world, pleasure in the sounds of its drama, its life. He remembered his rotation in the emergency room during his internship, he remembered the sense of moving beyond everything ordinary in life—the giving over of dailiness, of personality, to the needs and the demands of the moment.

"But what do you think they're *doing?*" Mack asked.

"I don't think they'll open the presents without us, Mack," David said gently.

Mack swung his head impatiently back and forth on the pillow. It made David intensely aware, abruptly, of how far apart his feelings were from his son's.

"They might be doing the dishes," David suggested after a moment.

Mack watched him.

"Or maybe they're singing carols."

"Yeah. I bet they're singing carols." Mack smiled. His eyes rounded, imagining it. "I bet they are."

David changed hands on the gauze pad. "I bet they're singing 'Silent Night,' " David said. And after a minute he began to sing it, softly, pitched a little too high. When he was finished, he started "Joy to the World," lower this time. And for a while he sang to Mack, doing all the verses he could remember to "Deck the Halls," to "God Rest Ye, Merry Gentlemen," to "Away in a Manger." His throat began to ache pleasantly.

"Do 'On the First Day of Christmas,' " Mack said.

"All right. You start."

In a thin voice, high and pure as an angel's, Mack began to sing: "On the first day of Christmas, my true love gave to me . . ." David joined in, harmonizing: "A partridge in a pear tree."

As Mack went through the song, David tried to sing with him, missing half of it but doing better and better as they went along. They finished with a prolonged ritardando, very loudly, and David swung his arm out in a theatrical gesture. In the little wake of silence after their last full note, David heard again, from far down the hall, the thump, the raised voices, of something going very wrong. Then quiet.

Mack seemed to have sung himself into a peaceable state. He looked dazed and dreamy, like a much smaller child ready for a nap. For a while they sat without talking. Then David stood up. He opened the gauze pad and looked at the shriveled white papery edges of the cut. "You look cured," he told dreamy Mack. "I think I'll go call your mother. Be sure everything at home is all right."

Mack nodded.

At the door, David turned. "If someone comes, tell them you're not an orphan. Insist that you've got a father who'll be right back."

Mack smiled wanly. "Dad," he protested.

Lainey answered the telephone. Her voice was quick with concern.

David told her it would be a while. "Is everyone behaving herself? And him?"

"It's all a little aimless." She sounded tired, suddenly. "But they're all right. How's Macklin doing with it? How're you?"

"Oh, we're having a fine time, actually. A kind of Christmas Day adventure."

There was a long silence. Then she said, sourly, "Well, bully for you."

David felt a wave of intense anger. He had an impulse to hurl something ugly back at her—to remind her she could still be resting in the hospital, to bring up again the accident of Sarah's birth. But he kept his voice calm. He said, "Mack wants to know whether you're opening the presents without him."

"Oh, tell him of course not." She'd brought her voice under control too. "Tell him we wouldn't dream of it."

"Good," David said. "Well, we'll see you when we see you, then."

"Fine," she said coolly. "We'll be here."

As he emerged from the wooden booth, the nurse called to him from the front desk. He went over to her. She was holding a telephone receiver against her shoulder. She'd taken off her white cap, and her flattened red hair looked artificial, strange, wiglike. "I just wanted you to know that someone will be there in a minute."

"Good," he said. "Have things calmed down a little, then?"

"Well, in a manner of speaking. One patient's up in surgery. And . . ." Her mouth twisted painfully, as though she'd tasted lemon. "We lost the other one."

"Oh. I'm so sorry."

"Yeah. A kid too. Twenty-two years old." Her voice roughened, and she stopped for a moment and pressed her lips together. She shook her head. "Can you imagine? On Christmas? On their way to some family get-together, probably." She heard something from the receiver and lifted it to her mouth, her ear. "Yes?" she said. "Is this the Novicki residence? Does Dennis Novicki live here?" David was watching her intently. She put her hand to her forehead and turned away from him. "Well, is your mother home?" she asked.

David walked away, down the empty corridor. "Honey, can you get your mother, please?" he heard her saying.

David stood in the doorway to Mack's cubicle and looked at his son, sleeping. He was tall for an eight-year-old, but he looked tiny in the middle of the adult-sized gurney. There were football helmets of different colors on his pajamas. The bottoms of his feet were dirty, except for a wide white circle around his cut. David felt a sudden wash of powerful gratitude for his health, for the sweet domestic size of his accident. He crossed to Mack and touched the boy's arm.

Mack's eyelids rose instantly. His dark eyes swam unseeing for a moment, then focused on his father.

"Hi," David said.

Mack licked his lips. "Hi," he answered. "I wasn't asleep."

"I never dreamed you were."

Mack lay still. Then he said in a tiny voice, "Are they opening the presents?"

"No," David answered. "They're going to wait for us."

After a minute Mack frowned. "But how much longer is it going to take?"

"The nurse said pretty quick."

Mack looked intently at his father for a moment. Then he said, "Dad, how come you just can't do stitches and stuff? How come we always have to go to Dr. Peabody or come to the hospital?"

"You know I'm not that kind of doctor."

"But you know how, don't you?"

"Yes; I was trained to know how to do those things. But there'd be a couple of problems if I practiced on you." David moved Mack's feet over carefully and pulled himself up onto the end of the gurney again. "One: I'm a little rusty, since psychiatry is a rather different specialty. I'm not sure how well I'd do. Two: there are all kinds of new techniques and medicines that I haven't kept up with. That I don't know about. And three: it's really not a good idea to do medicine on your own family. In fact, there are actually rules against it."

"Because why?"

"Because, mostly, it's hard to be good professionally with someone you know very well, and love, and are worried about. You'd be too nervous. You might sew their foot to their *knee,* for example."

"Dad!" Mack wanted to be serious.

"No; it's just better not to."

David watched Mack. He lay quiet, tensed, thinking. "Is *that* why you don't cure Randall?" he said suddenly.

David inhaled quickly, slowly let his breath out. "Ah. Well, that's a complicated one also."

"But that's why? Because of those rules?"

"Well, yes. Partly. Of course. Randall is my son, just as you are, and it wouldn't be a good idea. But also, I'm not trained, really, in the kind of medicine that Randall needs. He has a disease that only a few people really know how to treat, and even then the treatment lots of times doesn't work. But in any case, it's not my kind of psychiatry." David wished again for a cigarette. Uselessly, he checked the same pockets he'd checked before.

Mack turned on his side, tucked his palm under his cheek. He was frowning again, working hard at something. "If I grow up and become a doctor . . . if I become a psychiatrist"—he looked up at his father—"the *right* kind: will they *still* not let me cure Randall?"

"Oh, Mack." David reached out and laid his hand on his son's skinny leg.

"What? Will they or won't they?"

"There are just too many answers to that question."

"But what are they? That's what I want to know."

David felt a helpless confusion that made him momentarily angry. "Well, first of all, I don't think you should be thinking of your grownup life in terms of Randall. Your mother and I are in charge of Randall. You should just be thinking about you, about what it is that you want to be, best of anything you could choose from. Not thinking about rescuing your brother. Or anything like that."

"But I *do* want to be a doctor." The skin on Mack's forehead tightened in his seriousness.

"Well, fine. That's fine, then," David said. He could hear the irritation in his own voice. "If it's really your choice."

"It is."

They were silent, not looking at each other, both unhappy with their agreement.

When the doctor came in, David slid off the gurney. He was a young man, and he looked tired. He was wearing surgical greens, with the mask dangling, like a child's bib, on his chest. He shook David's hand and introduced himself. When he turned to Mack, his voice rose in false cheerfulness. "Well, young man, what have we here?"

He made bright small talk to Mack as he looked at his foot, as he set up the tools of his trade on the end of the gurney. David noticed a brown thumbprint of blood on the shoulder of his green shirt. He was bent forward, readying the needle where Mack couldn't see it. "You'll just feel a prick," he said to Mack as he lifted the boy's foot.

As soon as they got outside again, Mack began to cry. "You said it wouldn't hurt," he moaned. David was carrying him, wrapped in a blanket he'd borrowed from the nurse, and Mack hid his face in it against his father's chest. "It did hurt. It hurt a lot."

"I'm sorry, Mack." David was aware of the coolness in his tone. "Sometimes the cure seems worse than the disease, I know. But I don't think it was that bad." David walked carefully, holding his son. Their shadows on the snow were bluish now, and his steps crunched loudly on the frozen crust. He had to set Mack on the hood of the car to open the door, and when he turned back to him, the boy was wiping his face with the back of his hand. "I'm freezing," he said. His voice was thickened, but he'd gained control of himself. David felt a quick pulse of guilt: his lack of sympathy had exacted this of Mack.

"I know," he said. "Let's wrap you tighter." He tucked the blanket close around Mack's chest and set him in the car on the passenger side. When he slid in behind the wheel and looked over at his son, he saw that Mack's eyes were reddened and his teeth had begun to chatter. David started the engine.

They didn't talk for a few minutes. The car's tires bit loudly on the rutted snow in the street. The Midway was a vast blank tundra. Then Mack said, "I wish this didn't have to happen on Christmas."

"What day would have been better?"

"Any day."

They passed a solitary walker, a man carrying a big package wrapped in green paper.

"In my experience, no day is great for an accident," David said. "It always stinks."

"But if it happened on a schoolday, I could get to stay home."

"Ah. There is that." David smiled. After a moment he said, "If it happened on a trash day, you wouldn't have to take out the cans."

Mack tilted his head back against the seat and

looked over at David. "Yeah. If it happened on a Wednesday, I wouldn't have to have my piano lesson."

They made a long list of better days for an accident, and by the time they turned onto Harper Avenue, Mack had forgotten his pain.

Lainey opened the door for them, still in her bathrobe. But David saw at once that she'd washed her hair, that she'd put on lipstick and rouge, and he felt grateful for her effort. The house smelled of cooking spices, of evergreen.

"Hi," he said. "I've brought a Christmas present for you."

She clapped her hands and squealed. "Oooh, just what I always wanted. A Mackie-boy."

Macklin was smiling in embarrassed pleasure as David carried him into the living room. Lainey followed, and when he'd set Mack down, she bent over him, shifted his foot this way and that, exclaiming about his bandage, about his bravery. She pulled the pillows out and tucked them all around Mack to make him more comfortable.

In the hallway, David shed his coat. Then he went back to the kitchen to find a cigarette, to fix himself a drink. He could hear Lainey talking to Mack, and the high-pitched, excited murmur of his son telling her all about it. Then she was in the hall, calling upstairs to summon the girls and Randall.

David came back and sat down in the living room. The girls were dressed, dancing around, talking to Mack and David. Lainey had gone to find paper and pencils to make thank-you lists as they opened the presents.

When they were finally set, Lainey declared that Mack got to be first, because he was the one who'd had to go to the hospital. Mack blushed and then asked for the package that he'd checked on earlier.

Liddie, who delivered the presents on Christmas, found it and brought it to him. It was from David and Lainey. Mack pulled the shiny red paper back quickly, violently, and when he saw that it was a chemistry set, his face opened in sober, shy pleasure. He looked up at each of his parents. "This is exactly what I wanted," he said. "This is the happiest day of my life."

David was moved by this, unexpectedly, and had to look away.

One by one they opened their gifts, showing each to the rest of the family, in the custom Lainey insisted on. Each child slowly accumulated a pile of treasures—a big gift from David and Lainey, and then many smaller ones, from David's parents and Lainey's father, and from all the aunts and uncles and cousins, mostly on Lainey's side.

Liddie unwrapped Randall's gifts for him. David and Lainey had given him an outsize gyroscope. Liddie set it spinning and held it out before him. It seemed to David that Randall smiled, watching it, though he quickly went back to a coiled ribbon he'd pulled from the heap of tissue and trash, breathily singing his pleasure as he twirled it.

The children's gifts to each other were small, inexpensive treasures: a little net bag of gold-foil-covered chocolate coins, a squirting flower ring, a tiny book whose pages you flipped rapidly to see the images move.

"Nothing from Sarah this year," Lainey said after they'd finished. "She just didn't have time to get organized."

She had been up, in and out of the room a dozen times, checking on the progress of the meal in the kitchen. David watched her moving slowly around, bending over one child and another as they unwrapped something, calling out across the room, "Did you write that down? From Grandpa? From Auntie Lalie?"

Her face, which had been puffy late in her pregnancy, had thinned dramatically over the last few days, he noticed. She looked years younger than she had when he took her to the hospital.

When they were finished, Lainey stood again and moved slowly around the room, turning on all the lights. Suddenly the windows were black, the day was over. She went back to the kitchen to finish preparing the meal. David helped the children pick up the torn paper, the boxes, the ribbons, the name labels. They took turns stomping them down in the big cardboard carton Nina's tricycle had come in—David lifted each child in and out.

In the dining room, Sarah began to cry. It started slowly, the intermittent dry calls of hunger. But no one came, and within a few minutes, the carriage was trembling with her desperation. David went to the kitchen door. Lainey's face was red from exertion, from the steamy fragrant heat of the kitchen.

"Your newest is calling you," he said.

She slammed the lid down on the big kettle and spun to the sink. "She'll have to wait, then," she said. He stood watching her. "Oh, can't you do it, David!" she burst out. "You can see I've got my hands full."

As he turned into the dining room, she called out, her voice suddenly remorseful, "Just rock her for five minutes. Or change her. I'll be ready to feed her by then, I think."

Sarah had kicked her quilt off. The upheld wrinkled pads of her feet felt ice cold to David's fingers. He lifted her and wrapped the quilt around her legs. Her sobbing diminished, and she curled into a tiny boneless crescent against his chest. Then he realized that she was wet—soaked really—and probably cold on account of that too. She began an earnest rooting against him with her head as he carried her toward the stairs.

"Not me, little girl," he whispered. "Not me."

He mounted the stairs carefully and went down the hall to the room Lainey had fixed for Sarah, full of the chipped, worn infant furniture Mary had barely finished with. He laid the baby gently down on the changing table. Her chuckering complaints shifted up; she squawked. When he pulled off her rubber pants, the ammonia odor of urine almost brought tears to his eyes. Carefully he unlatched one pin on the soggy diaper, then the other. He lowered it, then stood up straight: down its center was a vibrant streak of blood. For a moment he thought she was hurt; and then that it must be Mack's diaper, that somehow Lainey must have pinned one of the diapers they'd used as a bandage back on the baby. But then almost immediately he remembered. He remembered it with his other daughters: the sweet-sad bleeding from deep inside, caused by Lainey's hormones, the hint in infancy of what would come later. He felt a quickening tenderness for the ugly little girl lying under his hands. Gently he slid the diaper out from under her.

The cold air had struck her like a new insult, and she was shrieking now, a high, piercing noise. David moved quickly, rubbing Vaseline onto her narrow, pinched bottom, powdering her, pulling a dry double diaper under her. He watched her face, closed tight as a fist. A single adult-sized tear snaked down from under her lashless, blue-veined eyelid, landed in the delicate furred cup of her tiny ear. He wrapped her again in the worn quilt and cradled her in his arms on the changing table, his hands cupping her tiny skull. Her crying slowly stilled. He lifted her then, her swaddled body tilted up along his forearms, her head in his hands so he could look at her. She shivered once, a convulsion of her whole body, and then she frowned. With great effort she slowly opened her eyes. Their deep, unseeing navy blue questioned

David's face intently for a long moment, and he stared back at her. *Sarah*. She was utterly still in her concentration. Then she closed her eyelids slowly, as though they were unbearably heavy.

David folded her carefully against his chest. Immediately she began the purposeful pushing with her head again. She made little ticks and grunts of hungry life as he carried her back downstairs. When he gave her to Lainey in the kitchen, her desperation increased. She cried out and struggled until Lainey got her to the living room and sat down to nurse her. David stood in the doorway and watched for a moment the desperate swinging of the tiny head, the grabbing mouth as Lainey opened her nightgown. When the baby's lips closed on her, Lainey smiled; and then Sarah's cheeks began to pulse rapidly with the sucking motion, she snorted and choked and swallowed. "She has enough determination for someone twice her size, doesn't she?" Lainey asked. She stroked the baby's lumpy head with her free hand.

"She does," David agreed.

When everything was ready in the dining room, David called to the children from the foot of the stairs. They trailed down from their rooms, Mack hopped in from the living room, and suddenly they were all there, the dining room was noisy and wild with life.

As Lainey was putting Sarah back into her carriage, David bent to help Randall into his chair. They straightened simultaneously and caught each other's eye. Lainey pushed her shiny, swinging hair back from her face and smiled, an apologetic shy smile that made her suddenly pretty and young again.

"Well," David said, moving to his place at the head of the table. "God bless us, every one."

There was a second of silence, and then Mack said, "Was that grace? Can we begin?"

"No," Lainey said. "That was Dickens. We're

going to do the Doxology.'' This too was part of custom on Sundays and holidays, a leftover, like all the other customs, from Lainey's life in her family. ''Liddie, will you pitch us?''

Liddie hummed, and they began, tentatively: ''Praise God from whom all blessings flow . . .''

Even Nina knew the words, David saw. Her lips were moving, though he couldn't hear her baby voice. ''Praise him all creatures here below.'' David came in at full volume: ''Praise him above, ye heavenly host. Praise Father, Son, and Holy Ghost.'' Mack made his voice quiver with fear on these last two words, as he always did; and he and Nina were laughing through the *amen*.

5

DAVID had slept with a number of women when he was in college and medical school, but it wasn't until the first year of the war, when he was working in a VA hospital in San Francisco, that he had a sense of himself sexually. The city, which had seemed a sleepy town when David arrived, changed nearly overnight with the declaration of war. Suddenly it was flooded with women, women who in another life would have been saving themselves for the right man. Here, they were glad to give themselves away. The very air seemed charged, and David moved through it in a state of nearly constant sexual excitement.

He became aware of women's flesh, its texture and its smell, the way they exposed it or hid it. He could guess what a woman would be like in bed—how she would use herself—from the way she moved her mouth as they introduced themselves to each other, the way she held herself or touched the flesh on her own arms or face as they talked. What they talked about didn't matter. It was always the same anyway—where they were from, what they were doing in San Francisco, how this band compared with the one in this hotel or that joint a week before.

He thought of these women as unclaimed, as living *out of time,* in some sense. Their lodgings, the beds he slept in with them, were always temporary: hotel rooms, boardinghouses, cramped apartments they shared with other women. Often there were photographs sitting on their nightstands of lovers or husbands now overseas in Bataan or North Africa, but their faces seemed to have nothing to do with the urgent grappling they smiled down on.

David was startled once to wake up and find himself staring into the sober brown eyes of a child, perhaps around two years old, who was standing up in a playpenlike bed next to the one David was sleeping in—a child who had presumably been there the night before too, when David and the woman who was now gently snoring behind him had pushed at each other drunkenly for what seemed like hours, making wild, animal noises. He felt called back, momentarily, to a world he'd allowed himself—or willed himself—to forget about.

It was during this period of his life, too, that David began to be interested in psychiatry. In medical school, it had seemed so much voodoo to him, pure mumbo jumbo. But in San Francisco, his patients were more and more fresh from the war, traumatized by it, by their injuries, by the deaths of friends. Often they were referred to psychiatry in addition to whatever medical treatment was required. And slowly it began to seem to David that those wounds were the deeper ones, that psychiatry was the more important form of healing. He came to think of his own work with his patients' bodies as simple, mere tinkering, like a mechanic working on a car. He went to Dr. Erdrich, who ran the psych ward, and asked for recommendations about what to read.

The old man seemed amused at this autodidactic approach, but he jotted down the names of five or six books in a hurried, foreign-looking script. When David came home from being with some woman, he often sat up and read one of them for several hours. His hands turning the pages smelled of sex, and in his mind everything about those days merged together, everything seemed erotically charged and exciting: the slanted light in the hilly white city, the lectures and cases he was reading, the brassy energy of the music he danced to in hotels and jazz joints, the intense, serious nature of the games he played with various women's bodies.

He tired of it, finally; or he tired of this version of himself. When he went to Chicago to start his psychiatric residency, some balance seemed to restore itself to his life. In the analysis he began, he came to see that the energy that had fueled his desire in San Francisco was connected to the energy that had made him choose psychiatry—and that both had their source in his desperate need to break away from the net of family obligation and duty in which he'd felt completely trapped. In the year before he met Lainey, he slept with two more women, but he didn't feel again as driven, as out of control, as he had for a while in San Francisco.

And so he was willing, if not glad, to go as slowly as Lainey wanted, though they'd been lovers for months before they married. And he was comfortable with what seemed her reticence, her deep passivity. Sometimes, though, in the early days of their shy, orderly lovemaking, he would remember something he'd done with some stranger in San Francisco, some acrobatic position they had wound up in, and he would be filled with hungry yearning for a wilder passion.

But he loved Lainey, and so he adjusted, he got used to her. And after Liddie's birth, making love with her came to have another kind of power for him entirely, a power that moved him sometimes, over the years, to tears. It was only after she'd given birth that Lainey was able to come, and only then that he realized that she hadn't been able to before. But in addition, the sense of everything her broad, strong body was going through as she had the children, as she nursed them—that, and the intense feeling she brought to their lovemaking—stirred him deeply in a way he wouldn't have guessed himself capable of.

The first time David pushed gently into her after she'd had Liddie, she was silent, staring up at him intently; and he felt certain she was thinking, as he was, of how her body had split wide, too, in giving birth. Afterward, as he lay next to her, she began to talk. "I just feel so open to you, for you," she whispered. He was holding her breast, feeling her blood tremble under the soft flesh. "Open to have the baby, open to nurse her, and now open to take you back in me again and again." He turned and put his mouth over her closer nipple. He felt almost immediately the rush of sweetish milk against his tongue—and in his hand, the warm drops flowing in sympathy from her other breast. He pulled her body to him in a burst of feeling. She moaned and pressed his head tightly against her breasts, her opened thighs gripped his waist. "I feel so used, David, so happy," she cried. "I want you to use me. Use me all up."

She told him later that sex with him felt nearly holy to her now, that she thought of it in words that came to her with doubled potency from religion, words like *riven, cleft.* She said that even in church she was sometimes swept with desire; she had to lower her head when they read aloud the words of Scripture: flesh, blood.

David had met Marie Lomassi a few times, but he hadn't really noticed her until the week after the new psychiatric residents came in that summer—the summer of 1956—vulnerable young men with new neckties, new haircuts. David was sitting in the little darkened observation room with Marie, who was the head nurse on the ward, and three of these frightened young men, watching a fourth through the two-way mirror as he did his first patient intake. It wasn't going well.

The patient was an old man, violent, paranoid, and confused. He was moving rapidly around the room, stopping only to yell abuse at the seated resident, Dr. McGill. His wild shouts made the speaker mounted on the wall in the observation room crackle with static. McGill's voice was lost behind it, an ineffectual murmur. He was a slender blond man, and he nervously tapped his pencil on the clipboard while he waited for the patient to calm down. There was the creak of chairs in the observation room as the other residents shifted and moved in sympathetic discomfort.

"He's got to take charge." It was Miss Lomassi. David turned. She had leaned forward; her frowning face was inches from David's. In the semidark of the room she looked very young. Her breath smelled of something sweet and butterscotchy.

"Let's let him play it out," David said. He turned back. He was nervous on McGill's account too. And he felt responsible for his dilemma, since he was in charge of preparing the residents for this first intake, and he knew very well he hadn't prepared McGill for anything like this. The old man continued to shriek: "You're so smart, you fuck! You fuck! I'll kill you all, you fuckers! You think you know it all, you're so smart." He tore at his hair, then at his shirt. The resident sat, his lips moving in useless, inaudible phrases. They could see a looping, brown-stained undershirt under the shredded cotton of the patient's shirt. They watched for three or four more minutes. "Doctor?" he heard Miss Lomassi say. David shook his head *no*.

Finally the man began to circle the room, yelling, kicking at the walls. He seemed to be looking for something. He picked up a chair and held it out toward the resident as though he were an animal trainer and the resident a wild beast. "You think you can? You think you can? You fuck! You dead fuck! You're all dead! I'll kill you all. . . ."

Miss Lomassi had stood up. She was by the door. "Doctor?" she asked again, impatience in her voice. It was a formality. Before David said *all right*, she had yanked the door open, and seconds later she appeared in the intake room. The resident looked up at her with a mixture of startled shame and relief. For a moment she just stood there, leaning against the wall—pretty, small, dark, and a little plump in her white uniform. The patient had swung to her when she entered. Now he slowly moved the chair in her direction and began yelling again.

Her voice was shockingly loud on the speaker, loud and calm. It pierced through the string of profanities. "Put the chair down," she brayed. "Put the chair down. Now." The man fell silent and lowered the chair. He stood looking at her. Miss Lomassi stepped forward, began speaking in a quieter tone, but her voice was still firm, it still had a hard edge. She had put her hand on the man's shoulder, and David could see the soiled cotton pull under her fingers' white grip. She was telling the man he needed to calm down, they were going to help him, they needed to ask him a few questions. Slowly the man seemed to collapse inward. He looked at the chair with a sense of recognition and lowered himself into it. Sitting there with his stricken expression, he seemed suddenly only what he was, a bewildered, confused old man. Miss Lomassi knelt by him and continued to talk, her hands always touching him—his shoulder, his knuckled dirty fingers.

By the end of the intake, he was sitting next to her at the square table in the center of the room, weeping occasionally and trying to answer the questions the resident was feeding to the nurse. She'd repeat each one to the old man as though translating from a foreign language, and he'd struggle to puzzle the answers through with her: where did he live? did he live alone? when had he last been home? had he been seeing a doctor? had he been drinking? taking any medication?

When they had finished and started to walk him out the door to the ward, he had another moment of panic, but Miss Lomassi put her arm around him and he relaxed against her. As they shuffled down the long hallway, David and the other residents emerged from the observation room. McGill was walking behind the head nurse and the patient, shifting his clipboard from hand to hand. David could smell the ripe odor of the old man as they passed, and he wondered at Miss Lomassi, whose head was bent, touching him.

At the nursing station, Miss Lomassi asked another nurse to settle the man into the ward. Then she walked back to where David and the residents were clustered. For a few moments they stood together as a group, talking about the admission, how tough it had been. "We wouldn't expect a first admission—any admission, actually—to be so difficult," David said. "But we arranged it that way." He smiled at McGill, and his voice was gentle. "Humility makes you receptive to learning."

The group laughed in nervous relief. Then David turned to Miss Lomassi. In an impersonal voice, a teaching voice, he said to her, "And I've been wanting to tell you how much I think we can learn from you, from the nursing staff, about how to manage patients."

"Thank you, Dr. Eberhardt," she said. She shrugged. "I think you get an instinct for it, probably." Though she was speaking to David, she too was actually addressing the residents. "In the end, I think you can just tell when a patient would be more comfortable with someone really taking charge of him. It's just something that you feel . . . well . . . almost in your bones." She laughed, and he thought for a moment of her flesh, the bones moving under it.

The group of residents slowly broke up, but David stood by the nursing station for a few more minutes. He began to ask Miss Lomassi about herself, about when she'd come to the hospital, about where she'd worked before, where she'd trained. He was barely listening to her answers. Instead he looked at her mouth and hands, whose short, stubby fingers were in constant motion. As she spoke, a wispy loop of black hair, pulled loose from under her cap, slowly fell forward toward her cheek. Without thinking, David reached up and started to tuck it back.

She stepped away from him, as though his touch carried a current. Her cheeks were burning, her eyes had widened. "I can manage that, Doctor," she said. Then she smiled at him, a slow, radiant smile. "Thank you very much," she said. And she turned and went into the nursing station.

David was shocked at himself, and through the last activities of the day—a supervision, a closing round with the other residents—he kept thinking of the way his own hand had looked rising toward Miss Lomassi's face.

He would do nothing about it, he told himself. He resolved this at least partly because of his feelings for Lainey—at odd moments they could still sweep him with a hard rush of love, and this was enough to keep him hopeful for both of them. Sometimes what triggered it was as simple as a gesture, an expression on her face: the intensity with which she focused on one of the children, speaking, or the way she pulled her legs under her when she sat in her favorite chair in the living room. But sometimes, too, it was a more elaborate circumstance, a chance event. There had been a day this past winter that worked this magic. On an impulse they had called a baby-sitter for the four youngest children and had taken Mack and Lydia ice-skating at the Midway. Lainey had learned to skate in her youth and was better at it than David. Once or twice she glided away from him and the children, and as David watched her quickly stroking across the gray ice in her old blue coat, lacing her way through the crowd, her legs pumping rapidly, her red scarf flapping brightly like a banner behind her, he felt an unselfish, surprised joy that she could still look so alive, so free.

The day had been dark and cold, overcast. Several times they went with one or the other child into the wooden shed against the embankment to warm themselves by the stove. The last time, David and Lainey went in together and sat side by side on one of the long, narrow benches along the walls. It was steamy and noisy in the crowded low building. Children yelled and ran around in their loosened skates for the pleasure of the resonant thudding sound they made on the scarred wooden floor. Lainey said something to him, and David had to lean close to her to hear her speak. She smelled of the fire, of wet wool, and her cheeks were fevered splotches of color. He had a sudden vision of her goodness, of the way she must have been as a girl—a tomboy, innocent and strong. He wanted to hold her, to protect her. For days afterward he lived on that tenderness.

But it was more than this that made him hesitate to do anything about Marie Lomassi. For David's youth had been made difficult by his father's chronic infidelities to his mother, and it was one of his deepest assumptions about himself that he would not repeat this pattern.

*　　　*　　　*

David had grown up in a small mill town in southern New Hampshire. His father was a pharmacist. He owned the town drugstore, one of a series of shops housed in a wooden building with a wide arcade across the front. All through high school and during vacations in college and medical school, David had worked in the drugstore alongside his mother, selling pills and ointments and phosphates, looking out at the distortions in the passing life of the town through the huge dusty jars of colored water that sat in the drugstore window. In college he had often skipped classes for several days when his mother was working on an inventory, to go home and help her. Even much later in his life, he dreamed of the store once or twice a year—of its smell, of the clink of cheap metal spoons on the marble counter. His hands in these dreams reached up to adjust a display, to count the boxes of rose-scented soap, and when he woke he would wonder at the distance he'd traveled from that world; and sometimes for a few moments in his sleep haze, he'd feel an almost friendly nostalgia for the remembered objects, for the medicinally perfumed air.

David's father drank too much. There was a special room behind the pharmacy section of the drugstore, where he shut himself in with the door locked unless there was a customer who needed a prescription filled. Then David or his mother pressed a doorbell-shaped button by the cash register—you could hear its muffled ring out back—and after a few minutes David's father would emerge, smelling of peppermint. He was a tall, stout man with gray hair, which he slicked into an elaborate, foolish pompadour. He always wore a white smock, a bow tie. Though he rarely spoke to his wife or son, he was unfailingly polite to customers—unctuous, David thought. It seemed to him as a boy, and then as a young man, that the customers found his father contemptible. Sometimes he thought he saw a smirk or a lifted lip as the older man asked in his oily voice what he could do for them today.

Once when he rang, his father came out of the back room and started to mix a prescription with a streak of dark lipstick smeared across his forehead.

David had stepped close to him. "You've got something on your face," he whispered. His back was to the customer, an old man David hated for his shameless nosiness, a Mr. Walkeley.

"Don't bother me now," his father murmured irritably. He was bent forward over the counter, the red brand presented to anyone in the store who cared to look.

"You've got something," David said again. He was unable to bring himself to explain to his father what it was. "It's all over your forehead."

David's father reached up and rubbed his forehead. Some of the lipstick disappeared. "Satisfied?" he asked, turning to David. David smelled Brylcreem, his father's minty breath, and behind it the complicated sour richness of liquor.

When he started back to the cash register, he glanced at Mr. Walkeley. He was smiling; and for a moment David thought he saw on the old man's face an expression of eager, contemptuous amusement. His heart burned with hatred for his father and for the town he lived in.

It was David's mother who actually ran the drugstore, which was open six days a week from eight-thirty until seven. She was a small, silent woman with pinched features and thin hair, and David could remember only a few conversations with her that didn't have to do with the store.

She was never openly critical of him, never discussed his life with him, but when she didn't want him to do something he was talking about—to go out for the football team, to buy a car, to date a particular girl—she would say softly, "I'm very surprised to hear you say that." And David would almost always reconsider.

She had spoken those words, or nearly those words, years later, when he told her he was going into psychiatry. She had wanted him to be an internist, a general practitioner, the kind of doctor she was acquainted with, the kind of doctor whose prescriptions her husband had filled for years in the drugstore. She said she was surprised to hear of David's change of heart.

He told her he was sorry she felt this way but that his decision had been made. It had been made, in fact, nearly a year before, during the time he was in San Francisco, but David hadn't been able to confront her with it then. Finally, well after his residency had begun, he'd made a special trip home from Chicago to bring her the news.

They were having dinner together at the big dining room table, and for a while after he spoke, David didn't eat anything. He was afraid that if he lifted his hands to his knife and fork, she would see how badly they were trembling. He sat with them in his lap and looked out through the curtains at the street, blurred and whitened through the net mesh. From in here, the houses across the way looked like those in old, sunstruck photographs. The only noise in the room was the ticking of the hall clock and the sound of his mother chewing and swallowing. His father was out "on business," business that he no longer even bothered to name.

David had been in analysis for several months. He'd been reading his way through Freud. Now he was thinking about his hands. He realized abruptly that their trembling was a symptom, a sign of his fear of his mother, the anger at her that he'd been coming back to again and again in his analysis. And he felt, suddenly, a sweep of painful gratitude, like the momentary awareness of the presence of grace, which was so intense it caused him to bow his head: gratitude for his accidental entry into this new knowledge, this understanding that had let him see the ways his mother's long-suffering silent goodness had trapped and paralyzed him. When he raised his head again, he felt that he had achieved some new kind of compassion and pity for her. He was able to speak. He asked her about her arthritis, and then about the high school kid she'd hired to help her. He lifted his hands and began to eat.

It was a moment David never forgot. It moved him from being only keenly interested in the ideas involved in psychiatry to understanding in some deep, emotional way how they could work. It made him a believer.

The moment when he touched Marie Lomassi's hair had for David some of that same powerful sense of revelation. In its aftermath, he felt as though a part of himself was waking up, some thick anesthesia painfully dissolving: suddenly he saw and felt what was there, what he had known since San Francisco was in himself, what he had refused to look at all around him.

In 1947, Lainey and David had stopped one hot summer night by a small square on a street near their apartment. They had Mack and Liddie in the carriage, trying to lull them to sleep with its motion. They leaned against the low wood fence that ran along the sidewalk at the edge of the square, smoking and taking turns gently jiggling the carriage; and they watched the children of the street playing wildly, unsupervised, on the worn grass, until the rectangle of light above them, like a window to the sky, darkened and adult voices from up the street, pitched high and set rhythmically to carry over distance and the squall of the children's games, began to call them in.

About six months later, they bought their house, in this square, on this street. They couldn't really afford it, even though it was cheaper than comparable houses in Hyde Park because the train tracks ran right behind it. But when Lainey saw the advertisement she remembered the square, she remembered that summer night; and she asked David if they could just go and look at it, just once.

They left the children with a friend and met the agent at his office on Fifty-seventh Street. When the agent walked them through, David could feel Lainey's eagerness. The rooms were large, with high ceilings and carved woodwork. There were five bedrooms on the second floor, enough for each of the children and a study besides for David. The family that owned the house had heavy drapes on the windows, dark furniture, dark wallpaper, dark rugs. But Lainey kept murmuring about the colors they could paint it, about how little work it would take to lighten it up.

To David the house looked too much like the one he'd grown up in—cheerless, airless, crammed with possessions. But when Lainey turned to him on the walk home and asked what he thought, he tried to believe in her version of things. She had stopped him with a gloved hand on his arm. Their breath made clouds between them. She was two months pregnant with Randall. Her blue coat was pulled tight across her belly already, and she hadn't buttoned the bottom two buttons.

"I think we should go ahead," he said.

Her face lifted in excitement. "We should buy it?"

"Yes," he said.

She had stepped forward then, to embrace him, he thought. He was tensed, a little embarrassed to show such affection in this public place. One hand lifted to take his hat from his head, the other to encircle her. He felt the bulge of her rounded belly against his abdomen, he bent to kiss her cheek. But then her arms tightened muscularly around him, and he felt his weight rock forward. She was lifting him! His feet left the ground, and she twirled him fully around before she let him down, before they stood panting and laughing, looking at each other with pleasure.

They moved in in March. With the first warm day a few months later, several young mothers appeared parked on blankets on the grass in the square. Lainey, who was still painfully shy sometimes, barely needed to exert herself to get to know people. She just opened the front door and stepped out with Mack and Liddie into her new life. That first day she moved from blanket to blanket like a bee among flowers; and when David came home that night, she reported on their neighbors to him. There was Jane Gordon, whose husband worked downtown at the Art Institute and who had three kids, the youngest Liddie's age. There was Tony Baker, with a little boy just Mack's age and a baby born only a month or so ago. And over the next days, weeks, there were new names: the Lees, the Rosenbergs, the Murphys, the Masurs.

Within days they were all calling on each other—for coffee, for lunch, for drinks in the late afternoon: women with cigarettes tucked in their shirt pockets, babies on their hips, toddlers in tow. They left older children at home to run their own universe—to set up elaborate pecking orders, violent vendettas, to rifle through drawers and medicine chests in search of the answers to formless questions—while their mothers smoked and drank and talked. They talked about their children, about their husbands, their pregnancies, about the election, about the Kinsey Report, about wallpaper. Like Lainey, most of the other women had one or two little ones, and more than half were in varying stages of pregnancy. They treated their fecundity as a sort of combined blessing and practical joke, and Lainey felt relaxed among them.

David quickly came to anticipate that several times a week he'd arrive home to see a note from Lainey on the newel post, telling him at whose house he could find her. He'd walk across the square, down the block, and be greeted by the meandering children, the other couples, the pitcher of martinis or the g&t's or the bottle of bourbon set on the coffee table. Later he would think of those years as the happiest period of his life. And these would be his children's earliest memories—of playing with other children in their houses as it got dark, of being fed pickup meals while the grownups laughed and talked; of being dragged home by their parents in the twilight that rang with the shouts of older children still at play. Or of curling up in strange beds with other children of the street, and then being carried home half asleep late at night through the silent dark, their parents smelling of *party*, different from their daytime smell, and the grownups' muted calls to each other—*good night, good night*—a kind of lullaby.

By the time Randall was four or so, the group was most often at David and Lainey's house, because he wouldn't sleep in strange places, because he had to have things happen in a certain, predictable way. Often they fed one of the pickup dinners to a group of six or eight children and almost as many adults. But by then this social life had become a necessity for them and they were its hub, made animated and energetic by their need not to be alone together, by their need to turn away from the increasing difficulty of their married life.

Lainey in particular would rise to these occasions, moving smoothly through the myriad steps of getting the odd meal on the table, of keeping everyone's glass full, of keeping the conversations, the arguments, the games going. She was capable of a desperate flirtatiousness within the group. Once she called Lew Rosenberg back with the promise of a strip-tease if he'd stay another half hour. While the record played through a scratchy version of "Love for Sale," she slowly and seductively removed her belt, extracted by degrees a wadded Kleenex out of her pocket and threw it carelessly over her shoulder, draped herself in an afghan her mother had knitted and walked in and out of it, and finally, doing a bump and grind, unhooked her necklace and tossed it backward into a corner of the dining room.

It was only a few days after he'd lifted Miss Lomassi's hair gently off her cheek that David realized for the first time what had developed for the others along with all that hard-drinking conviviality. They were at the Masurs' house, and David had stayed on after Lainey and a few other wives had gone home to get the children to bed. It was a Tuesday evening, and there was a sense that they needed to break up soon—everyone had work the next day. But no one really wanted to go. There was a small group of them sitting around the living room, talking desultorily, telling political jokes, gossiping. Someone had met Stevenson's ex-wife, knew some interesting details about the marriage. David picked up his glass, which had only a swallow of gin left. He got up and went back to the kitchen. Tony Baker was there, talking with Erica Masur. "Where's Freddy?" David said. "I want another martini."

Tony looked up quickly. "I'll fix you one," she said. "I make a mean one myself."

"No insult intended, but I'll just find Freddy."

David went back to the dining room, the front hall, looked once more in the living room, to see if

Freddy had returned from the bathroom, or wherever. He returned to the kitchen. "No sign of him," he said to Tony. "You'll have to do."

She was already pouring gin into the glass pitcher Freddy used for what he called his "potion." "I told you, I'm good," she said.

"Ah! It's not that I don't believe you. It's just that it's one of the things I look forward to when we're here." He turned to Erica, who was starting back out to the front of the house. "Think he's upstairs?" he asked her.

Erica shook her head quickly, almost frantically, it seemed to David, and was gone.

"David," Tony said in a low voice, and stopped. He turned to her. "What?"

She looked at him. Her face was sober and girlish under the aureole of gold that was her hair. She went back to her task. "Freddy's just not here," she said flatly. She measured a capful of vermouth into the pitcher. "Let it go, will you?"

But about half an hour later, Freddy was there again, a tall, skinny man with a horsey face. There was no sense of question among the group about his absence, no sense of mystery. They simply folded back up around him. It seemed to David suddenly that this had happened before—with Freddy, with others—and that he had been careful not to notice it. When David said good night, Freddy was laughing in the kitchen with Maurey Lee. He raised his martini glass in farewell.

That Friday night there was a slightly larger gathering, a party Lainey had planned ahead of time, at their house. She was gay and argumentative, as she frequently was among the group. David was sober, watchful. Sometime a few hours after the party had started, Jane Gordon, whom David had always thought of as fat and not very interesting, left alone. A few minutes later, Freddy left too.

David asked Tony to dance. He liked dancing with her. She'd been a professional dancer, actually, with a modern-dance company in New York before she married Harold. She was small and held herself so that you were always aware of her spine. The slightest touch on her back made her shift direction. They were the only dancers for the moment, alone in the dining room except for Freya Rosenberg, who was sorting through records in the corner by the piano.

"I've got a question for you," David said, softly enough so that Freya couldn't hear him over the music.

"Shoot."

"How many other affairs besides Freddy and Jane . . ." He leaned away from her, and she had to tip her head back to see him. "Am I guessing right? How many are there? Going on now, I mean."

"You honestly didn't know before the other night?"

"I didn't."

She shook her head and laughed. "Lainey, of course, is the original sweet, hysterical naive, but I thought you, surely you, old sexy David . . ." She trailed off as he spun her rapidly backward under the arch of their arms, then in close again.

"So how many?"

"Well, *I've* been known to indulge." She laughed again, a little breathlessly this time, and looked up at him.

"Ah!" He was truly surprised. She and Harold were a good couple, fond, funny together, sarcastic to each other in a way David, who was almost always careful of Lainey's feelings, was jealous of.

He held her out, away from him, and looked at her. She was very fair, with white skin. Her nostrils and eyelids were always a little pinkish, as though she had a cold. He found it sexy. "And Harold knows?" he asked. "They all know? *We*"—he bowed slightly—"all know?"

"Harold does know, yes. And I think some of the rest of us. Though I've been a careful girl." She made her lips prim for a moment, batted her eyes. Then her voice changed, and she said softly, "Erica Masur does not know. Does not know anything. Does not wish to know. She's like Lainey."

"There's nothing for Lainey to know," he said.

"Of course not," she said, and grinned at him. She moved closer and they danced. David felt the soft fleece of her hair against his chin. He turned his head slightly so that it brushed his lips. Hank Gordon had drifted back from the living room and stood by Freya, talking to her. "So it's okay by Harold?" David asked, after a minute.

She looked up at him, amused. "You're a nosy bastard, aren't you?"

"Well, it's like any party game. You like to know the rules."

"The rules!" She laughed. "Well, here's rule one: what's sauce for the goose is sauce for the gander."

"Ah!" he said.

"Ah," she echoed. Hank and Freya were dancing now, and David had moved Tony gradually away from them, toward the corner of the room. She looked at him. Her face was suddenly serious. He had to bend down slightly to hear her. "But I'm not sure, darling David, that I'm a person who could have stayed married if it hadn't been *okay by* Harold." Then she smiled. "If he hadn't been my kind of gander."

He didn't answer, but he felt his penis stiffening, and to hide this from her, he twirled her out abruptly, away from him. The music was rising to its conclusion—David remembered how in San Francisco the band would stand at this point, the horns blaring, unmuted. He turned Tony around three, four times, and then they stood, startled slightly by the end of the brassy noise, several feet from each other.

"God, you're a discreet man," she said abruptly. "Why *are* you so discreet?"

He lifted his shoulders. "This is a kind of revelation, Tony."

"Well, make use of it, darling," she said carelessly. And she walked away from him, her spine straight.

David wandered around the edges of the party. Harold Baker was telling a joke, the punch line of which was "Chop Suez," and Lainey's laughter rang loudly above the others. He thought about the group, about their marriages. It all made a kind of sense to him. They were the children of struggling middle-class parents or stuffy upper-class ones. They'd all had those moments of freedom during the war, they'd all married young, and then they'd moved to this community, drawn by the university, by the promise of something different, a kind of intellectual freedom, maybe a slightly bohemian life. And they *had* remade their lives here, reinvented them—the things they thought about, talked about; the way they raised their children, the way they entertained. Why not their marriages? He was in the kitchen, and he could see Freddy and Erica Masur in the dining room, framed by the doorway. They were talking seriously to each other, both frowning; and then smiling suddenly in agreement, Freddy showing his long horsey teeth. He touched Erica's shoulder. A marriage.

Why not his marriage?

He was holding a drink, and he had to set the glass down, his hands were suddenly shaking so hard. He turned away from the rising noise around him and looked out the dark window over the kitchen sink.

Why not his marriage? Why not this relief? This way out?

And then almost instantly he felt the *no*, the *no* of Lainey, of her version of life, of her understanding of their marriage. The *no* of the children. The *no* of the strange powerful bond between them on account of Randall and all that was unresolved because of it.

He thought of her near-hysterical gaiety at parties, of the endless passionate arguing that was undoubtedly at base the same sexual energy that drove Jane or Tony to have affairs. *Toujours la chose génitale.* He bowed his head, smiling. He thought of her naïveté, the nearly blasphemous association she made between their sex life and her religious feeling. From the other room, he heard her whooping, slightly false social laugh. He was flooded, suddenly, with tender protectiveness for her. She seemed so fragile, so vulnerable. It was impossible to risk exposing her to the others, to their ridicule or amusement—to their eager smiles—in the way he would if he accepted what had clearly been Tony's invitation.

He fixed himself another drink, and then another, but he seemed unable to pass into the oblivious state he would have liked. The party was winding down anyway. He emptied a few overflowing ashtrays; he noticed a circle of spilled liquid on the kitchen floor; he watched Tony leave on Harold's arm. He'd avoided her after their dance, and she hadn't said good night to him. He got involved in a long discussion with Freddy, who suggested they each buy the other's house and rent them back to each other. "It's an idea of great genius," Freddy said. "Great genius. The tax benefits are extraordinary." When David persisted in treating it as a joke, Freddy insisted he was serious, he'd worked out the figures, he'd show them to David cold sober.

Hank and Jane Gordon were the last to go. They

sat in the dim living room—only one light was on—
and Hank told a long and confusing story about how
he was being passed over at work because the woman
directly under him was somehow related to the man
directly over him.

After they left, David and Lainey went back into
the living room together and, in a practiced, familiar
rhythm, began to gather up glasses. "He's a terrible
bore, isn't he?" David said.

"Oh, *I* don't know," Lainey said. "Tonight he
told me this absolutely wacky story, fascinating in a
perfectly dreadful way." She stopped, frowning, to recall it. Her pronunciation was exaggerated, drunk.
"He had some *ancient* relative, a great-great-great-
aunt or something, who had a conversion experience
when she was four, at the hands of Jonathan Edwards.
He seemed to see this as some kind of pedigree. Isn't
it nauseating?" She was holding four glasses on as
many fingers, and abruptly one slid off, landed in a
darkening pool on the couch. "Oh!" she cried out,
and leaned against the wall, closing her eyes.

David set his own glasses down. He stepped in
front of her. "I prescribe many aspirin," he said, lifting the glasses from her hands. "Immediate bed rest
and many aspirin. I'll finish down here."

"Truly?" she said. She watched him for a moment.

"I'm wide awake," he said. "I'd just as soon."

She sighed. "Well, I won't argue." She came
slowly to him, brushed her cheek against his, and
then turned quickly toward the stairs. Her rhythm up
was heavy and lumbering. "Thank you," she called
down formally from the second landing, like a child
reminded of her manners.

"Fine," he said, and took one collection to the
kitchen.

In the middle of gathering glasses, emptying ashtrays, David thought of Tony with her delicate nostrils and her wild hair. He thought of Marie Lomassi, dark and plump in her white uniform. He felt the pull of his cock, hardening. He thought of Lainey in another world, when they were trying to get her pregnant with Randall; for the first time in years, he thought of a lover he'd had early in his San Francisco years—Marjorie Evans.

Marjorie had been the wife of one of David's patients, and David had believed for a while that he was in love with her. He had thought they needed to do something, something honorable and brave and painful, about their affair; but every time he broached this with her she would laugh and recross her legs, or have another drink. She drank a good deal, mostly bourbon, and she had very long legs, which were in constant motion, like nervous hands. Making love, David could feel them stirring the air around his head and back, and sometimes they held him in an animal clutch, like monkey's legs. He remembered telling her once that they owed her husband at least the truth, and she had answered that he might be the single most naive person she'd ever met. There was nothing unfriendly in her tone. "Let me tell you something, honey," she had said. Her makeup had rubbed off in their lovemaking, and her lips were puffy. She had balanced a glass on her chest, and now she was moving it in circles that left a gleaming slick over her breasts. "As soon as Wayne gets better, I'm taking him back to Portland. In Portland, I'm a member of PEO. I belong to the Methodist Church. I volunteer at the county hospital. Everyone likes me. They like Wayne. We have a marriage, honey. A good marriage. We're going to live happily ever after, and what happens between you and me has nothing to do with that."

David had sat down. Now he turned off the light and unzipped his pants. Alone in the smoky darkened living room, he pumped himself, violently, quickly. When he was done, he felt no real relief, just a kind of jaded relaxation. He sat on the couch listening to his heart rate return to normal.

After a while he turned the light back on. His limp penis was curved sideways across his pants front, leaving a glistening slug's trail on the cloth. The house seemed airless. The nicked coffee tables and the mantel were still littered with glasses, spilled ash, crumbs. The room looked bare and unwelcoming. They'd had to remove the rug and the curtains, because Randall had stained one and torn the others. He felt a sense of desolation seize him. He rose and, with still-sticky hands, began again to collect the glasses.

The next morning was gray and overcast. The leaves on the silver maple sat motionless and green outside the window when David woke. Lainey moaned when he got out of bed, and turned away.

He shut their door quietly behind him. In the hall, the other doors yawned open and half open. He could hear at least some of the children downstairs. He unlocked Randall's door. The boy looked up; he smiled sweetly at something just beyond David's shoulder.

"Good morning, old chum," David said, and bent to clear the sleep crusts from Randall's eyes. Randall tossed his head like an impatient animal at his father's touch. Efficiently, singing, David moved him through his toileting, got him dressed, got him down the stairs.

Liddie, her hair in curlers, was already on the telephone in the hall, lying across the bench in her nightie. Her feet stuck out past the newel post, white and dirty. "No, not the red one," she said. "It's a kind of orangey, with all those little tiny buttons, you know what I mean?"

David stroked the bottom of one foot as he went by.

She jerked up. "Daddy!" she complained.

"I'll need your help. Mom's sleeping in," he told her.

In the kitchen, Mack sat at the table. Sarah, in her high chair, was picking carefully at the Cheerios someone had sprinkled out onto the tray for her. Mack was slumped, reading *Mad* magazine. David greeted them and sat Randall down in his chair.

Sarah's face opened in a huge smile, showing her few baby teeth. "Daddy," she said blissfully. Mack looked up from her to David. *"Daddy,"* he imitated.

Moving quickly, David fixed Randall a bowl of cereal, poured him orange juice, helped him start.

"Who's eaten what?" he asked Mack.

No answer. He knocked lightly on Mack's skull and then, for pleasure, rubbed his hands over the soft bristles of his crew cut. "Who's up, who's down?" David asked. "Who's eaten? Do eggs make sense?"

"Eggs—ugh!—do not make sense. Everyone's done but the grownups."

"Is this all Sarah's had, though? Chickadee feed for our little chickadee?"

"It's all she likes, Dad," Mack said defensively.

Liddie swept into the room. "That made me mad, Dads." Her eyebrows were pulled into fierce arches by the metallic curlers. She was yanking a sweater on over her nightie.

"What?" he asked, sprinkling more Cheerios for Sarah.

"I was talking on the phone and you interrupted me. You never allow us to do that."

"Well, it wasn't so much me as life, Liddie, that interrupted you, and that's permissible." He'd crossed to the sink and started to make a pot of coffee.

"I knew you'd say something like that." She

scooped up a Cheerio of Sarah's, and then, when Sarah did nothing, another. Sarah whimpered, then drew herself up and said, "No!"

"*No,*" Mack imitated. "*No, no, no, no, no.*"

Sarah watched him, then said again, grinning, "No!" But he'd turned back to his magazine and was lost.

David set the coffeepot on the stove and turned to Liddie. "Find Mary and Nina for me," he said. "I'd like them to be dressed." He began to list instructions for her and Mack.

By the time Lainey came down, the little girls were all dressed and out in the yard. Lainey had a hangover, so David offered to drive Randall to his speech therapist. At the last minute, on impulse, he called to the girls and told them he'd take them to the Tot Lot while Randall had his lesson.

They walked ahead of him out to the car, Nina and Mary chattering, and Sarah struggling to keep up with them. Randall shuffled silently, obliviously, next to David. His hand in David's was damp; David thought of it as trusting. He felt a sudden sense of calm, of contentment—a sense of how dear to him these children were, the three little girls he hadn't wanted and the son he would wish away if he had the power. He reminded himself that these feelings were pure sentimentality, that on another day the girls might be whining, Randall might be screaming, struggling, and he'd feel another way. Randall saw the car and mooed joyously. He let go of David's hand and began to run toward it.

David and the girls had the Tot Lot to themselves. Gradually the smooth gray above them crumpled into clouds. Blue appeared behind them, and then the occasional glinting light of the sun. David pushed all three girls on the swing for a while; he ran around the edge of the whirligig while they shrieked and laughed. Then abruptly he felt a dizzy fatigue, there was a metallic taste at the back of his throat. He crossed the dirty sand to one of the slatted benches set on concrete and sat down. He could feel his blood pulsing thinly with last night's alcohol.

The Tot Lot had filled slowly. By now there were fifteen or twenty mothers and children milling around. David closed his eyes and pretended to sleep in the warmth of the sun. Someone sat down on the bench with him, but he didn't open his eyes.

Suddenly he felt a stinging lash across his face. His lids jerked up. Mary stood in front of him, and he saw that he was holding the girls' sweaters and jacket, that Mary had swung them carelessly into his lap. He raised his hand to his mouth, where a zipper or button must have caught him.

"We don't need those, Daddy," she said.

In his pain, David's eyes had filled. Mary saw the change in his face and took a step backward. She looked frightened. "Nina *said,*" she defended herself. And then she ran away.

"Cute," the woman on the bench with him said. There was a professional appraising tone to her voice. "Yours?"

"Yes," he said. He looked at her. Nobody's mother. She was teenaged, an angry blistering acne scarring her face. She held a movie magazine open on her lap.

"I'm baby-sitting, myself," she said. "My sister's kids. Those two."

Now David had to follow her pointing finger to the group of children by the slide. "Ah, yes."

She waited.

"Cute," he said.

The girl sighed. "I don't know how she does it," she said.

He didn't answer.

"I mean, all day, every day."

"No," David said.

"But at least they grow up in the end and move away."

When he didn't answer, she lifted her magazine. David settled back again and closed his eyes. He ran his tongue over his lip. It felt puffy.

"But then it just begins all over again—you know what I mean?"

David opened his eyes. "Yes, I suppose I do." He was trying to keep the irritation out of his voice.

The girl was frowning. "I just hope I don't settle for that."

After a moment he said, "You want something better."

"Of course. Didn't you? When you were young?"

"I can't remember," he said. He closed his eyes again and listened to her turn a page. Someone walked by, singing a tuneless song: ". . . but my real name is Mis-ter Earl."

When he rose to go, the girl looked up. She smiled. "It was nice talking to you," she said.

David saw that without the acne, she might be pretty. He felt a sudden tender pity for her. "Yes," he said. "Nice talking to you too."

The Tot Lot was crowded now. It rang with wails and excited cries. He had to cross nearly all the way over to Nina and Mary and Sarah before he got their attention. But they came running over to him quickly and followed him out the open gates, down Fifty-seventh. Just as they got to the car, though, they heard—then turned and saw, approaching from the other direction—a Good Humor truck.

"Ice cream," Nina said reverently. She turned to David. "Can we? Please, please, Daddy?" She was taking tiny jumps in her excitement.

Mary immediately began to echo her.

David had barely said okay when they squealed and started to run toward the truck.

David picked Sarah up and they walked back the half block to where the other two were standing, the first ones in line. The truck had pulled to the curb in front of the Tot Lot, its chimes ringing out "Pop Goes the Weasel!" As soon as David was close enough to hear her, Nina started begging for various special treats whose pictures dotted the truck's side in fading decals, but David was firm. They all had to have the same thing, because they needed to hurry and pick up Randall. And he would choose it so they wouldn't have to have a long discussion. She consented to an ice cream bar. David stood at the window and asked the man for three, paid him the three dimes. He unwrapped all of them for the girls and handed them out.

They walked slowly back down the sidewalk ahead of him, the two younger ones weaving a little, they were so intensely concentrated on the ice cream. They had stopped talking entirely, and now they drifted away from each other, as though each wished to be solitary in her pleasure. Nina reached the car first and stood leaning against it, carefully angling her wooden stick so the ice cream wouldn't drip on her.

David looked at his watch, imagined Randall standing with his tutor in the foyer of her apartment building, waiting for them. He had slowed down to Sarah's pace, and she was barely moving. Ice cream dripped steadily onto the front of her pink coveralls.

"Come on, Sarey Berry," he said. "Let's *walk* a little here." He took several long strides ahead of her to set an example.

She looked up, took a few obedient, jerky running steps, and the ice cream dropped off her stick into the dirt. By the time David reached her, she had squatted and started to raise it in her hand to her mouth. It was coated with grit.

David grabbed her wrist—it was tiny in his hand—and shook it. The ice cream plopped again to the ground. He lifted her up, away from it, and began to explain to her as he carried her toward the car. But her eyes had rounded immediately in disbelief, her lower lip jutted, and now she began to cry. The two other girls looked up as he approached, and kept on eating. David had begun a chant of explanation— about the dirt, about how bad it was for Sarah—but the little girl wasn't listening. And when she saw Nina's ice cream and Mary's, her body arced away from his in rage and she shrieked wildly.

"Poor Sarah," Nina said with exaggerated pity. "She doesn't understand."

"Right," David said. "When she's as big as you, she will."

"Poor Sarah," Mary echoed, and she took the last bite of her ice cream bar.

Sarah, hearing the sympathy, wailed louder, collapsed huddled against David's chest.

"Yeah," Nina said. "When she's big, then we can explain *everything.*"

David was enfolding Sarah. He felt her sticky hands on his neck, the hiccuping sobs that racked her body. Now she wailed again with so inconsolable a sorrow that it seemed she'd been born understanding pain.

David felt some deep answering grief in himself, some accumulation of his own misery. He turned his face away from the eyes of the other two girls. Gently he held his smallest, his most unknowing child. "Oh, Sarah, my love," he murmured, holding tightly to her tiny, compact body, comforting her for this little loss—but thinking of all the loss, all the inescapable sorrow and loss that would visit her, that would visit all of them, over and over in life.

The following Monday, before his first private patient arrived, David called Marie Lomassi on the ward at the hospital and asked her to meet him late that afternoon for a drink. His hands, he noted with mild amusement, were trembling slightly as he dialed the numbers.

Through the few months he slept with Marie, they met in a dark basement apartment she shared with another nurse. The first time she brought him there, she poured each of them a glass of syrupy sherry and disappeared into the bathroom. David sat on a worn sofa for a few minutes, sipping at the awful drink. Then he got up and paced through the three odd rooms of the apartment. There was a doll on the neatly made narrow bed in the room Marie had indicated was hers, a large doll with a wide ruffled skirt made of ribbons the color of the satin edging on Randall's blanket. A doll. David felt heartsick, laughable. He wondered if there was a way he could leave without insulting Marie.

But he didn't leave. He drank the sherry, he followed Marie to her room and watched her move the doll from the bed. And when he lay down next to her and felt the shocking push of her strong young body against his own, he was struck with such a sense of grief, of loss, along with his intense desire, that his eyes filled with tears. And though Marie Lomassi was much smaller than he was, though she was startled by his emotion, still she held him as you would a little child, until his breathing grew regular again. Until, with some embarrassment, they could begin.

6

NINA and her younger sisters were sitting in the third-floor bedroom. Nina was looking out at the snow, her forehead pressed against the cold glass. An early snow—it was only December tenth—but it was sticking, piling up thick and fast, a blanket on their neighbors' garage roof, a narrow vein of white on every uplifted black branch of the wet mulberry tree below her. On the other side of the wide plain of the railroad tracks it flew over and over, like a plague of moths, through the circles of light glaring in a bright row from the Illinois Central Hospital roof.

"There's nothing to do," Mary said. Her voice was whiny. She was lying on her bed, across the narrow strip of bare painted floor from Nina's. "Pineapple beds" the girls called them, because sitting on top of each of the four wooden posts there was a carved stylized pineapple. Mack called them grenades.

Nina turned back into the room, where everything looked suddenly worn and messy. She felt intensely aware of the brownish water stains on the striped wallpaper, of the burned spots on the lampshade, of the piles of clean clothes waiting to be put away, of the nicked, ugly furniture. They were trapped up here, trapped because it was the night of Mother's annual big party, and everyone on the first floor was busy getting ready. The invitations had said from seven to nine, only it always lasted later, and they got to sit on the stairs and watch. But it wouldn't begin for an hour yet, and they'd been sent up here to get them out of the way.

Mary and Sarah were looking over at her expectantly. Nina felt a band of irritation squeeze her insides at their dependence, but she tried to ignore it. She said, "We could do The Movies." This was a game she'd invented the summer before. It was really just spying, looking in the lighted windows of their neighbors after dark. But there was something special about the difference between the coolish twilight where she and her sisters stood clustered on those summer evenings and the hot lighted world of the houses they peered into, which thrilled them.

Once, in a drenching gray rain, they'd watched a man in the first-floor apartment across the square pull a splinter from his wife's bare toe, an ordinary act. But the scene in the kitchen had seemed to Nina as potent and magical as the diorama of the doctor with his patient on display at the Museum of Science and Industry—the man and woman were so nearly motionless, so concentrated and intent, she on her pain, he on the needle he probed with. And Nina had felt so utterly separate from them, so shut out, shivering in the cold rain, standing on the rocking garbage can she'd pulled up under the window. She was startled to see a drop of bright blood roll down into the crack between the woman's toes, startled at this evidence that the figures were real. When the man finished, he held the toe and squeezed it. Then, looking intently at the woman's face, he slowly lifted her foot to his mouth and began to lick it. Nina and her sisters had laughed so hard at this that they had to jump down from the window and huddle against the grimy wall in the downpour so they wouldn't be noticed. And when they climbed back up, just a minute or two afterward, the couple was gone from the room. Nina felt almost as if she had imagined it all.

Now she had a quick vision of the way things would look spying in from the snowy world—the bright boxes of yellow light, with silent figures mouthing silent words, everyday life made mysterious and magical because they would be looking at it from the white outside.

"Let's," she said firmly. She didn't wait for them to agree, just got up and started out of the room. More often than not this worked; Mary and Sarah followed without arguing. This time too. As Nina started down the stairs, she heard Mary's excited voice rise behind her, planning it, telling Sarah which houses they ought to try.

Then Mack's voice called from behind the closed door of his room, across the third-floor landing from theirs. He said, "Hold it, you guys."

Mary called back, "What for? You're not the boss." Nina had stopped halfway down the stairs. She was watching Mack's door. Hanging on the center raised panel was a wooden plaque with a picture of Rodin's *The Thinker*. Under it were the words GENIUS AT WORK.

They could hear Mack coming toward the door. "Oh, oh, oh, wat iss ziss I hear?" he was saying. Suddenly he yanked the door open. "I em nott zee boss?" He grabbed Mary by her sweater. "Says who, mein liddle pippensqueeker?"

"Cut it out, Mackie." She squirmed against his grip. Suddenly, without warning, he let her go. She staggered back, slammed against the stair rail with a hard noise. Tears instantly filled her eyes. "You did that on purpose," she said. "I'm telling."

"Try another one," he said in his own voice. He grinned and shut the door, hard.

Mary's face had twisted up in her effort not to cry. Sarah kicked Mack's door. Nobody home. "You're a dummy, Mack," she yelled. Sarah could say whatever she wanted. She was the baby.

A diabolical laugh floated out.

"I even like Randall better than you," Sarah called up loudly as she started down after Nina.

"Sarah!" Nina was genuinely shocked.

"Well, it's the truth," Sarah said. "I do." But her voice was small. She was frightened she'd said it.

When Mary reached the foot of the attic stairs, she turned and shouted up, "Mack is an idiot!" and slammed the door shut. You could hear little chips of paint fall.

After a moment, their father's voice rose, accusatory, from the first floor. "Who's that slamming doors?"

They were silent, making scared faces at one another, half grinning too.

"Whoever it is, cut it out. Take it out on each other, if you must." His footsteps went back into the living room. They looked at each other. Nina laughed. It was so exactly the opposite of what their mother would say.

They waited a minute and then went down to the front hall and began the struggle with stiff woolen leggings, with coats, with the mittens on strings that jammed up in your sleeves. Nina could see down the hall to the kitchen, where Liddie moved back and forth. She and mother were talking. Dishes clattered. Liddie had gone away to college the fall before last, and now when she came home it was as though she brought her own weather into the house. The arguing, the bitterness between their parents, which silenced the rest of them and made them feel ashamed, had no effect on her. Mother said she was like "a breath of fresh air," and that seemed literally true to Nina. Her long curly blond hair blew back in knotted streamers when she moved. Her short dresses swung against her body. She was light and quick. Even her speaking voice had a musical sound—and Mother never laughed more than when Liddie was working by her side. Daddy called Liddie "the escapee," but it seemed to Nina he must have called her this before she left too, that he was talking about some quality Liddie had—had always had—of belonging more to the world out there than to their family.

Later, when they were ready for bed, Mother was going to let Liddie bring them up a tray of party food: the tiniest sandwiches, miniature hot dogs—it seemed weird for grownups—and they'd sit in Daddy's study and Liddie would sing for them or tell them a story while they dressed their Barbie dolls, all three the same, from Grampa Green. ("Original," Daddy had said when Sarah unwrapped the second one. And when Nina unwrapped the third, Mother said to him, "Not a word from you, please. I mean it. He's an old man, he's all alone, and it's amazing he even manages to get presents to them. Not one word, *s'il vous plaît!*")

Sarah had begun to whimper. "I can't *do* this, Neen." She had her red rubber boots partway on, but they wouldn't pull up over the heels of her shoes.

Nina bent in front of her sister. "Push," she said, gripping the top of one of the boots. Sarah did, holding Nina's shoulders for support, but the boot wouldn't budge. "The goddamn thing," Nina said. It made her want to hit something.

Sarah sniggered.

"Liddie!" Nina yelled. "Come and help us with these boots. We can't."

Liddie called back from the kitchen, "Just stamp. I'm busy," as though she were one of the adults.

Sarah shouted, "Mine are bendy. Stamps don't work."

And then their father came out from the living room. "May I be of assistance?" He bowed from the waist slightly, unsmiling—a butler, a tall, slender prince. He was wearing his suit pants and a striped shirt with a tie, but he hadn't put his jacket on yet.

"Yeah. Me," Sarah said. She sat down on the

floor and held her feet up. Her boots were sticking off at clown angles.

David bent over, gripped one of them and pushed. Randall came into the doorway behind him, waiting. He looked like Mack, Nina thought, but his face was dreamy, smooth somehow, as though you'd taken Mack's face and wiped off all his intelligence and personality. As Nina watched him, he began inserting his fingers one by one deep into his mouth. She looked away. Once she'd seen him make himself gag doing this.

David pushed, and Sarah slid back to the wall. "Brace yourself, pet," he said. Sarah lay flat and set her hands over her head against the baseboard. Nina's father pushed again. "Are these new shoes with old boots?" he asked.

"Yeah," Sarah said. "They're from last year."

"I thought I recognized a syndrome," he said. He held Sarah's foot between his thighs and eased the boot from side to side. Slowly it slid on. "Other one," he commanded, and she lifted her other foot. She looked dazed and distracted, lying on her back, like a baby being changed. Like Randall, Nina thought. Sarah's leg collapsed against their father's thighs. "Help me, Sarah," he said, a little irritated. And he yanked her knee into stiffness.

When he finished with Sarah, he lifted her up and turned to Mary, who was standing behind him. Nina's boots had gone on easily. She was just waiting for the others. "I'd like nothing better than to join you girls," Daddy was saying. "The well-packed snowball was once a specialty of mine."

"We're not having a snowball fight," Mary said. Nina had been looking out at the snow, but she turned and made a hard face at Mary. The Movies were a secret. Nina wasn't sure why this had to be. Some of it was just to make it more exciting, more dramatic. But in some way, too, it seemed to Nina a revenge against her parents for all that they kept secret from her, for everything she couldn't understand about their lives.

But their father hadn't noticed anything. He was tying Mary's scarf under her chin. "That was in my youth, though," he said. "Before I became burdened with all you children, all thousand and twelve of you."

Sarah laughed and swung her loose mitten against his back. "There's only six," she said.

"Isn't that what I said?" he asked. Then he crossed to the front door. He opened it, and they all stood silent before the transformation of their ordinary world. Their father said, "Ah, the winter landscape, urban version." His voice was light, mocking as ever, but to Nina, his face looked sad and yearning.

As she stepped past him, she said, "You could come, Dads."

He turned to her. "I wish I could. But your brother and I"—he gestured back to where Randall still stood, eating his hand—"have a date in the bathroom. You'll have to have fun for me, you three." And he shut the door behind them.

They stood on the front porch in silence. The snow was just a feeling, an invisible wet touch that made you blink your eyes, except where light tipped down from the windows onto it and gave it sudden swirling substance. The square was made new by the whiteness, by the gentle grayish light that was like a flat lid above them. The houses seemed small and bright, pretty toys lighted up, so many secret stories shut against the whited wind. They went down the stairs, into it.

When Nina walked, her boots made a crunching sound biting the snow, a sound that seemed locked inside the hood of her snowsuit along with the racket of her breathing, and the *whoosh*—she was sure she could hear it—of her blood pulsing in her ears. They turned down the narrow path between their house and the Hayakawas', next door. Nina led the way.

They often spied on the Hayakawas. They were the most mysterious of their neighbors. Their children were off in college now, but even when they lived at home, they had never come out after school, they had never talked more than to say hello, they had never smiled except for the most fleeting, insincere grimaces of politeness. Mother had explained their isolation: they had been put in American prison camps during the Second World War. "To our eternal shame," Mother said in the voice that didn't allow argument. Nina and her sisters always hoped they would uncover the wonderful secret life that must lie under the blank polite exterior—to be put in prison! wouldn't that make you strange?—but the Hayakawas led a scrupulously ordinary existence.

The girls climbed laboriously up the Hayakawas' slippery bulkhead door. They braced their boots on the outsize hinges so they wouldn't slide down, and watched Mr. Hayakawa at the kitchen table. He was alone, reading the paper.

Sarah was too short to have a good grip on the windowsill. When she let go, she dropped to her hands and knees and slid down the tilted door. At the bottom, she rolled over on her back in the snow and lay there looking up at the gray sky, her mouth open to catch the wet flakes, while Nina and Mary continued to spy. When Mrs. Hayakawa came into the room, Mr. Hayakawa didn't even look up, and neither one seemed to speak to the other. A page of the newspaper lifted and turned, a big wing closing. Mrs. Hayakawa was at the sink with her back to them. Nothing. After a few more minutes, Mary squatted and skied down the bulkhead to Sarah. "Let's go," she whispered loudly. "They're no good. They never are."

But Nina stood a minute more before she came down to her sisters; watched him turn another page, still drawn by the mystery of the way the Hayakawas lived, by the silence and peace between them.

They tried a few more houses around the square, but there was nothing much happening. In a few of them, television sets were on, and there was something strange about the flickering blue light, about the blank stupidity on people's faces while they watched, which the girls laughed at for a moment; but her sisters were beginning to be bored, Nina could tell.

When they passed the Graysons', though, they could faintly hear music pulsing through the walls of the house. They sneaked up onto the front porch. Inside, Deirdre Grayson, who was about Mack's age, stood facing a hall mirror, singing silently with the music. When the song stopped, she moved even closer to the mirror and looked at herself. She pushed her nose first to one side and then the other, examining the flesh that hid in the crack by the curve of each nostril. Then she slowly lifted her arms behind her head. Her hair bent over them like a soft fabric. She turned her head one way, then another. She let her hair fall. Then she leaned toward the mirror until her lips touched the icy glass. "Look!" Mary whispered.

"She is really weird," Nina agreed. But she was uncomfortable. Alone in the bathroom, she'd done the same thing many times. She'd tried to imagine the cool, even pressure of the silvered glass as the touch of someone's lips. Once she'd forgotten to wipe the damp print of her mouth off the mirror, and Mackie, who was next in the bathroom, had made fun of her.

Turning, Nina saw three adult figures walking across the square toward their house. Guests. They shuffled like skaters on the snow, their identities lost in their winter shapelessness. They were talking, but their voices were muffled by the weather.

Nina gasped, to make it more exciting, and told her sisters to run quickly—quickly!—down the Graysons' front steps. The girls squatted low behind a hydrangea bush, the snow hissing on the papery dryness of the leftover blossoms. They watched the front door open, the guests disappear into the yellow light of their hall. Then the girls made their way along the neighbors' front hedges to their own walk. They ran, crouching and awkward, until they were under the window at the side of the living room. There, Mary and Nina hoisted Sarah, her slick rubber feet in their mittened hands. She wobbled and clung to them, but finally she stood up, grabbing at the slippery sill, spilling crumbling light sheets of wet snow into Nina's upheld face. They waited. "It's the Gordons," she whispered. Her voice was hard to hear. The hood of Nina's woolen snowsuit scratched over her ears. "They're coming over here!" Her legs seemed about to give. "No, now they're sitting down, and Lid's bringing in some stuff for them. She's got her fancy dress on, that blue one." Then she cried abruptly, "Down! Down!" She was squatting even as they lowered her, and Mary lost her balance and sat hard on the ground. Sarah staggered, almost falling on top of her. They laughed at each other. "They were almost *there!*" Sarah whispered excitedly.

They stayed outside—trying the kitchen windows from the back porch, creeping onto the front porch when the coast was clear—until there were ten or fifteen guests in the house, until they were wet and cold. Then they went up and rang the bell.

Their father's face lifted with pleasure at the sight of them. "More beautiful ladies!" he said. "Come in, come in, my unexpected guests," and they danced into the front hall, stamping their boots and jumping up and down to knock the snow off. David helped them get out of their gear, chatting with them as though they had been invited too, about the snow, about the people who'd already arrived.

Stripped down to inside clothes, Nina skated on the wood floor in sock feet, hoping one of the grown-ups would notice her. She knew she looked prettier when her coloring was high—otherwise she was too dark, too somber. But no one did. They stood and sat in clusters of two or three, talking too loudly, everyone holding a glass, most of them smoking. The inside air was hot and still, and the women's perfume made it exciting. She heard Mrs. Gordon's laugh in the kitchen with her mother. Mr. Gordon was out here, hunched over a bowl of nuts, talking to a woman Nina didn't know, a pretty round-faced woman with her hair twisted elaborately and pinned at the back of her head. Nina watched Mr. Gordon's fingers working over the bowl, picking out just the cashews. If Nina did such a thing, her mother would cry out in disgust.

Liddie came into the living room, brushing against Nina. "Move, bunny rabbit." The air she stirred smelled of flowers behind her. She set down a tray with crackers and cheese. Mrs. Bennett grabbed her arm and started asking her questions about school. Liddie picked up a cracker. She began to talk in her beautiful voice. She was going to transfer, she explained, transfer to Julliard. Nina knew by now that this would make Mrs. Bennett listen to Liddie for a while. It made everyone listen. It was, as Liddie put it, "quite the achievement." Nina moved over closer to Mr. Gordon.

"It's all a question of style," the woman with him was saying. "JFK had it, but *this* guy. I can't bear it. 'Wang wang wang,' when he talks," she said, making her voice come out through her nose.

Nina reached over and took two cashews, popped them quickly into her mouth. Mr. Gordon leaned forward and spread his hand over the bowl again. "Oh, come on, Judy," he was saying. "Those are hardly the relevant criticisms. And finally he just may prove to be the better man."

"Who cares?" the woman said, shrugging her shoulders. Nina turned to watch her intently. "*I* know . . ." She flattened her hand on her bosom. "You know; everyone knows: the world turns on sex appeal. That's the course of history. And this guy . . ." She shook her head vigorously. "He just ain't got that swing. I mean, those ears."

Mr. Gordon laughed. "You can't make your sexual response the basis for your politics." And he began to scold her, while she smoked and smiled at him.

The saltiness turned liquid in Nina's mouth, but she held the cashews there, not chewing for a while. She was wondering if *swing* was a kind of dirty word. Then she was thinking of President Kennedy's funeral. They had stayed home from school to watch it, all of them silent in the living room, and her mother had cried when she saw the frisky horse with no rider, the empty boots turned backward.

Suddenly her father's hands were on her shoulders. He whirled her around, back to the hall. "Ah ah ah ah ah," he was saying into her ear. "I spotted you." She tilted into his warm body as she walked ahead of him. At the foot of the stairs, he smacked her behind lightly. "Now skedaddle, madame. I sent your gang of thuggees on ahead. You remember the deal."

Up two steps, Nina turned—she was just as tall as he was from up here, as though she were a grownup—and reached over to his shoulders. "Dads?" she began. She was starting to lean her weight against him, but she saw irritation tighten his face, and she rocked back.

"Neens?" he answered. But then the bell rang.

He went to the door, and Nina clung to the newel post and watched him greeting the Bakers, who lived down the street. Mrs. Baker's hair rose around her head like glittery mesh. Melting flakes of snow were trapped in it; they caught the light and shone like jewels. After Dr. Baker went into the living room, Nina's father reached up and started to brush them away, but Mrs. Baker stepped back and turned quickly to Nina. "How are you, Nina?" she asked. Her cheeks and nose were pink from the cold. "Have you tried the snow yet? It's good packing."

"I know," Nina answered. Mrs. Baker smiled at her and then followed her husband into the living room.

When Nina's father came back and stood in front of her again, he seemed distracted. Nina knew he was going to try to send her on her way. She lurched against him to get his attention. "Daddy, how come I always have to be treated like Mary and Sarah? I'm much more mature than they are. I could help, like Liddie does."

He looked thoughtful, and for a moment she imagined she might have a chance. "Please," she said. But then she was aware, instantly, both that that had come out whiny, which he hated, and that he was listening to something in the noise behind him anyway, not considering her request at all. She hung her weight against him, petulant.

"No, sweetie," he said firmly. "A deal is a deal."

"A deal!" she said contemptuously. "I hate all deals. It wasn't any deal. Ma just told us."

"Howsomever," he said. He took her hands and lifted them, pushed her weight back onto her own feet. "If there were going to be briefs and charges and countercharges, they should have been filed before this, wouldn't you say?" He was smiling at Nina now, and she saw that she'd never really had a chance.

"And I should point out to you that Liddie's been helping all day, that getting to be a hostess is connected to that. Whereas you've been out playing until nearly this very moment."

Nina felt the heat of shame. And he was right, that's what made it worse. *Playing.* She hated Mary and Sarah. She hated herself.

He smiled gently at her. "Now," he said. "I want to see you flouncing up, please. Your inimitable disgusted flounce."

Nina turned and slowly mounted the stairs, keeping her back as straight as she could.

"Nina," he called when she was at the second landing. She turned. "Maybe next year," he said in a private voice meant to make her feel better.

"Oh, boy!" she accused, and tears roughened her voice. "Next year." She ran up.

"Nina," he called again. She stopped and looked down at him.

He smiled his slight, intimate smile. "It was, as always, a pleat and a treasure to talk with you."

When Liddie came up with the plate of food, they were all in their nightgowns, in the study. Liddie had arranged the food carefully, as though they were important guests. In the center were little hot dogs, wrapped in the toasted dough that Mother whacked, raw and swelling white, out of cardboard tubes. Stuck through them were toothpicks in every color, a prickly rainbow. Around this was a circle of black olives, then one of green, then the hot pink of radishes cut like flowers, then Ritz crackers spread with a bright orange cheese. Liddie set it down on the table by the couch.

"Mother wants to know have you said your prayers." She rolled her eyes, and they all laughed at their mother, even though Mary and Sarah still believed such things as that God was in every bird, every insect, in Randall as well as in someone like Martin Luther King.

"Yes," Nina lied. It was partly true. She had sat still and quiet when Mary had done hers. She had watched her sister's brow furrow, her fingers clench, as though you could get to God isometrically. But Nina didn't pray anymore.

She had until recently. She had prayed for years that Randall would get well so her parents would stop fighting—not even a selfish prayer!—but it had done no good. And when she had heard that the president was shot, she had prayed he would live, and instead he had died. Hopeless and angry, she was attending confirmation classes now only because her mother insisted. They all had to be confirmed. After that they could choose whether or not to go to church. Nina knew already she would never go again. Even now during the services she just mouthed the confessions, the prayers, occasionally tearful at the isolation she felt in the rumble of voices all around her, her only consolation her shining integrity.

"Would you like the report from below?" Liddie asked, squishing in among them on the raggedy couch. It was ripped all along what Sarah called "one sleeve," an afternoon's project of Randall's. He'd swallowed some of the cloth, and Mother had yelled at Mack, who was supposed to be in charge, that she could never get a minute's time off, never.

"Look at it this way," Daddy had said when she had told him that evening. "Now you don't have to worry about getting him to eat dinner."

They were all in the kitchen, standing around or sitting at the table, and it was as though the room itself took a breath in, waiting for Mother's response. Her face was still a moment, thoughtful, and then she laughed. And then they were all laughing. "All right," she said. She was looking at their father in a way that seemed to shut them all out. "My master of the silver lining."

He had raised his glass to her. "My mistress of the dark cloud," he said, and drank.

"Oh, it's true, I know it's true," she had answered, as their laughter died down.

Now Nina pushed in next to Liddie. She smelled good; she always did.

"The scene is: Dad's flirting with all the ladies, or they're all flirting with him, as usual. And Mother is arguing about politics with Mr. Gordon."

"Why does Ma always argue?" Mary asked earnestly.

It was true, Nina knew. Their mother didn't know how not to fight. She couldn't take a joke, their father said. Everything mattered to her. And she fought with everyone, not just at home. She was always writing to her congressman, her senator, her alderman. She'd left one church and joined another because she got in a fight with the ministers over what was truly Christian. She'd embarrassed Nina at school by fighting at the PTA about whether the children should be divided into labeled reading groups. Nina had been an eagle then, the top group, and she had liked it. She'd been humiliated when her teacher said their groups couldn't have names anymore because "some parents"—and here she'd raised her arched penciled eyebrows right at Nina—had "raised a ruckus." Sometimes when Mother didn't approve of what you'd done, she'd bring the whole weight of her personality down on you. She'd say she was "deeply ashamed" if you made fun of a classmate; "shocked beyond words" if you made a racial remark. If she caught you in a lie, even a white lie, she was capable of weeping over it.

"What else can Mother do?" Liddie answered.

"It's just the way she is. Now, what would you like, a song or a story?"

"A story," Nina said quickly. Nina hated to listen to Liddie sing. Not that her voice wasn't pretty. It was, Nina knew it was. But it wasn't Liddie who sang. Somehow she changed, she became another person behind the music. Her voice was adult, foreign. Her posture changed, and she held her head alert, like a weapon. Her nostrils got bigger too, which made Nina most uncomfortable of all.

"No, a song," Mary said.

"A song, a song," Sarah cried. And then reached forward for a cracker.

Nina felt betrayed. She watched Sarah pop the cracker in her mouth and start to chew. In this moment, Nina realized that her youngest sister was prettier than she was, than Mary was too. She felt a shimmer of hateful envy for her.

"Okay, okay," Liddie said. "Here goes." Then she paused. "Are you ready?" she teased. "Are you set?"

"Yes—we—are—ready!" Sarah yelled, bouncing on each word.

Liddie laughed, and Nina, sitting so close to her, felt her breath. It was warm, and a little winy. It smelled a bit the way Mother's did, but different, Nina thought.

"Okay. Really. Here goes," Liddie said. She took a deep breath in. And then it happened: her face changed. Nina looked down quickly at her own hands, trying to think of the beautiful full voice, of the foreign words, as coming from somewhere else, from a record.

When she was finished, they sat for a moment in silence on the chewed sofa.

"What were those words saying?" Sarah asked.

"Mmm. Let's see." Liddie frowned. "It's actually sort of foolish. It's this very polite woman singing, saying thank you over and over, to this guy, her lover. She says she's miserable when she's apart from him, thanks. She used to drink to freedom, and he blessed the goddamned drink, thanks. And now she's so blessed, she sinks on his heart. Thanks thanks thanks."

"That's too polite for me," Sarah said.

"Well, that's life," Liddie answered. "In Strauss's version anyway." Now she stood up, leaving a gap among them on the couch, a cool patch on Nina's side. "I'm heading down," she said. "You want me to help you get this stuff to the landing?"

"Yes. Help us," Sarah said, sliding off the couch.

The front stairs dropped from the second-floor hall for five steps, then had a landing, turned, and dropped for a second five steps to another landing, then turned and descended sideways into the front hall. There was a carved wooden panel along the side of this last flight, which faced the front door. It was the first thing you saw on entering the house. It had a bench worked into it, which was usually littered with the children's stuff. As soon as you came in, you could tell who else was home by the books, the jackets, that lay on it. Tonight it was heaped with the coats of the guests.

On a party night, the girls were allowed to come down as far as the first landing from the top to watch, that was the rule. If they came down farther or bothered their parents in any way, straight to bed.

It took them two trips to assemble everything they needed on this landing. Liddie set their party plate in a corner a little distance away from the blankets and pillows and dolls. Then she said good night, and the three of them made what their mother called *nests* and settled in to watch the grownups below. From their allowed spot, the arched doorways off the front hall into the long living room and the dining room gave them a funny angle on the action. The grownups' bodies were slightly foreshortened, the tops of their heads, which otherwise the children never saw, their most distinctive characteristics. They moved on and off stage as they appeared and then disappeared into the invisible corners of the softly lit rooms.

They could see Liddie below. She was standing in the doorway with her back to them, talking to someone deeper in the living room. In a corner of the dining room, Mrs. Gordon and Mr. Hess were dancing, smooth and close. Sometimes she pulled her head back to smile or say something.

"The hell you say," someone said loudly in the living room, and the room burst with laughter. Their mother crossed into the hallway below them, back to the kitchen. Her lips were moving. She was talking to herself. Ugh, Nina thought. Embarrassing.

Someone else was speaking: ". . . and I said, For Christ's sake, this is Chicago—we *are* integrated."

After a while their mother was back, holding a tray of glasses that fizzed. They couldn't hear her, and then suddenly she was arguing again. "I'm sorry," she said in an unsorry voice. "That means-to-an-end stuff is crap. Crap," she said. Her neck corded with feeling. The tray was tilted slightly now, and someone took it from her hands. Someone else laughed.

Nina and Mary giggled too, a little scared. Their mother.

Just when they were most comfortable, Mack came down the stairs. He pretended not to see them. He stepped on Nina's back and Mary's butt. "Oh, God," he said, dancing on them in his heavy desert boots. "I must be going crazy. The ground is moving. It's an earthquake; it's . . . it's the end of the world!" They squealed and protested and grabbed at his ankles, but he laughed at them and whirled away. He took the remaining short flights of stairs in one jump each. When he got downstairs and was putting on his jacket, Mary threw two olive pits at him.

He went to the living room doorway to say good night. It transformed him, having to talk to the adults. He stood there awkwardly, his body hunched and nodding, as though their questions were snowballs he was avoiding. Someone asked him about college, and his voice cracked nervously with his answer.

As he backed away from the doorway, their mother came out and stood in the hallway with him. "Have you *seen* this snow?" Her voice was shrill. She gestured at the front door. "Who's driving?" Hectic color lit her face, and she looked young to Nina suddenly. Like a person, not just their mother. They couldn't hear Mack's answer, and then Mother said. "Okay. But no later, not a second later, than one o'clock."

"Got it," he said, and opened the door.

"But where are your boots?" Mother cried, stepping after him.

"*Mom*," he said, and shut the door quickly behind him.

Their mother yanked the door back open. "One o'clock," she yelled. "Or your name is mud."

Nina drowsed for a while. At one point their father, going in or out of the living room, spotted them. He came and sat for a moment on the landing and rubbed their backs. His hands were strong and cool on Nina, and she felt perfectly happy. "My nest of vipers," he said before he left.

Then Nina dreamed she was at the party too, but invisible, just watching, moving freely among the dancing, laughing couples. She was wearing some clothes from her Barbie doll, which miraculously fit her. But then they began to shrink, to change back to their real size, and as they did, Nina lost her magic, she became visible. Everyone turned to stare at her. She lurched awake. Her mouth was cottony. She sat up and ate some of the food from the tray Liddie had set in a corner of the landing.

At some point Liddie and some of the adults Nina didn't know very well must have left. She saw that the remaining group were the grownups she had been spying on all her life, her parents' oldest friends. The talk was louder, drunker, than before, and mostly incomprehensible—therapy, mortgages, work. Mrs. Baker, who'd been a dancer once, came into the little open space between the dining room and the living room and demonstrated exercises to improve your flexibility and prevent back pain, while the invisible people in the living room whooped and applauded.

Their mother's voice got loud again from the living room. She was interrupting someone quieter. "Well, it wasn't a disease with the ancient Greeks. We just *say* it's a disease. We say almost everything is a disease. But that's not a fact; it's a judgment. Why don't we just say it's not. Let's just say it's not. What happens then?"

She stood in the doorway now, stopped on her way to the kitchen with a bottle in each hand, gripping their necks as though she were about to juggle them. "Oh, happiness," she said contemptuously. "We all know being heterosexual is the perfect guarantee of *that*, of course." She disappeared back into the kitchen. In a minute Nina's father appeared and started to follow her, but she came back below them, a different bottle in her hand; and then they were talking intensely, arguing—you could tell by their faces, pushed like threats at each other, though you couldn't hear them.

"Don't . . ." Mother said shrilly, and yanked her elbow out of their father's hand. Suddenly Dr. Baker was there, touching Mother's back, talking to her. She turned and said into his face, "I'd adore it," in another voice entirely. She held the bottle to their father without even looking at him again, so he had to take it. Then she and Dr. Baker moved in a smooth way, not dancing but getting ready to, into the dining room.

By now Nina had lost all sense of what the time was. Sarah and Mary had fallen asleep for good, and she was herself groggy from cigarette smoke and being up so late.

Below, their father appeared, with Mrs. Baker. He was facing her, holding her wrist. He led her into the front part of the hallway. His voice was very private, as though they were telling secrets. "A little moment, a nice little *tête-à-tête*," he said, stumbling slightly as he stepped backward. Nina thought he was saying *tit,* and she eased herself up slightly. Mrs. Baker laughed and let their father pull her forward to the bench. They sat, perched awkwardly on the heaped-up coats. Nina's father's voice murmured gently, tenderly. All Nina could see through the railings were their heads and shoulders. Her father's head was bent toward Mrs. Baker. His face seemed to have been opened, made young, as he talked to her. Then he leaned closer, and his face was lost behind the spun gold that frizzed around her head. He was kissing her!

Nina lay still and felt Mary's breath hot on her shoulder and neck. It seemed to her that her heart was slowly crumpling like tinfoil into something small and hard and shiny in her chest.

For a long time their father was bent in toward Mrs. Baker. His head made slow movements, adjustments. His arm had slid around her, he shifted her slightly this way and that. A faint moan rose from one of them.

Then Mrs. Baker pulled her head back. Nina could see her father's face again. His mouth was open, and he looked sleepy. Suddenly Mrs. Baker stood up. She stepped across the hall to the door, then turned around. "We can't do this anymore, David," she said, looking across at him. But Nina could see her face; it was as pink as it had been when she'd just come in from the cold, and she was smiling tenderly. Nina's father said something she couldn't hear, and Mrs. Baker stepped forward as though she would touch him. "That was so long ago," she said in a pleading voice.

And then Nina saw her mother, almost at the same moment Mrs. Baker did. There was a quick motion in the hall, one that seemed to connect her mother and Mrs. Baker but left them standing just as they had been. Her father must have seen it too, for he turned, a second or two later, to see where it had started.

And there was Nina's mother, standing so still, a sudden burst of laughter like a wall behind her. They all seemed frozen, looking back and forth at each other. Then Nina's mother said in a trembly voice, "Pay *me* no mind," and she went back quickly to the kitchen.

Nina's father got up. Coats and scarves slid to the floor. He looked stupidly down at them. He didn't seem to know what to do. He turned toward Mrs. Baker; he raised his hands and seemed to say something. She nodded, and he followed Nina's mother out to the kitchen. Mrs. Baker turned and looked out the window in the front door. She was hugging herself.

Nina lay still as a mouse. She was listening, through the din, for her parents, for the familiar, almost reassuring sound of their arguing. Mrs. Baker, standing so still in the front hall looking out at the snow, seemed to be listening too. But all you could hear were the music and the loud voices in the living room.

Then Mrs. Baker spun around and began moving quickly in the hall, digging under the coats, kicking at the boots. Nina saw her face, popping red, glazed with tears. She angrily slung a long scarf in two different directions around her head, flattening her halo of hair, transforming herself utterly. She threw a coat on over her shoulders, and then, carrying her boots, she left the house, abruptly, silently.

Nina waited. It seemed she might have slept. The Gordons came into the hall, put on coats, and left. There was quieter conversation, only one couple moving in the darkened dining room to music. Then she heard her father's voice, almost natural, joking, in the living room. She sat up, rigid. Mary's head hit the blanketed landing with a little *whump!* but she didn't wake, just puckered her face for a moment. Her father was saying good night; it seemed he was leaving. Yes, he was "called out," he said.

He came into the hall and with what seemed to Nina like one continuous motion lifted his coat from the hook on the wall and swung the front door open. He stepped quickly out into the night, pulling the door carefully shut behind him.

And that was that. He shut the door and he was gone. Nina remembered wanting to call to him just before the door shut, she remembered she'd had something she needed to say, though she couldn't recollect later what it was. But she was as frozen as we are in dreams when we need to do something but we don't know what. And then she lay down again, she lay very still on the landing, thinking her father would come back, he must come back; someone needed to carry her sleeping sisters to their beds.

Sometime much later her mother bent and

waked her. Her face was puffy, her voice was gentle, terrible in its tenderness. She was already scooping up Sarah, and Mack stood behind her, with Mary flopped like an oversize doll on his shoulder. Nina didn't ask any questions. She got up and followed Mack up the attic stairs, pausing twice behind him when he staggered a little under Mary's weight.

She sat on her pineapple bed and watched Mack lower Mary gently onto hers. He was transformed, his face in the dark was smooth and scary: a different person from the carefree, mean Mack who had walked across their nest and bodies a few hours earlier. He touched her head before he left too, and it was this gesture, more than anything else, that made Nina understand her father was gone for good, that made her cry when she curled up under the cold covers.

And though later, of course, Nina saw the apartment her father got for himself—though she sometimes even spent the night—still, when she thought of him during those years he lived away from them, the picture she had in her mind was of her father wandering alone in a world made immense and blank by the snow, a little dark shadow in the distance against a whited ground, looking in at the bright lights that made the other lives, even her life, seem so dramatic, so full of mysterious meaning.

7

MACK sat in his pajamas in the living room, staring at the television. Randall was kneeling on the floor in front of the set, but he wasn't watching Wile E. Coyote fall off cliffs, get smacked by trucks, scorched by dynamite. Instead he was playing with a toy Nina had invented for him a few days before, a string tied onto a stick. He bobbed the stick up and down, up and down, and imitated with his head the swaying dip and catch of the string behind it.

The house was silent except for the explosions and screams on the TV. The little girls had locked themselves in upstairs because Mack had been mean to them. He was in charge, baby-sitting. His father had been gone for almost five months, and his mother was out, doing the weekly grocery shopping.

Mack knew he was going to get it when she came home. One of the little girls was bound to tell. His mother would yell at him, or cry, or say she needed to be able to count on him. Or just look more tired.

She had looked awful this morning.

Randall had waked in the night. Mack had heard him through the air duct that snaked up behind the walls. He was rocking on his mattress, chanting, the steady *whump* of his head on plaster a gentle shudder in the house. After a few minutes, their mother's muted voice, more tender than it ever was in daily life, rose into Mack's room too. Slowly the rocking, the strange singing, stopped. Then her voice sank away, and Mack knew they'd gone to the kitchen, where his mother would drink coffee or bourbon, depending on some decision she made about the hour; and the two of them would sit together at the table, doing a puzzle, or drawing, or—if she was too tired—just staring idly with a similar blankness until the house came to life.

Mack had lain there a long time, listening to the house's odd night noises. Then he was touching himself, getting hard. He tried to think about Sharon Fine, who'd been his girlfriend until she moved away a few months earlier. They had spent the last few nights before she left dry-humping on the back seat of his mother's car, and the memory of that—of the smell of the car's interior, the touch of Sharon's flesh, the hard rise of her pubic bone as he pushed and rubbed against it—usually worked to rouse him. But tonight it was difficult to recall Sharon, to recall how she'd looked or felt. It seemed as if she'd been gone forever. Instead he had a sudden image of his younger sisters' bodies, the shocking bald V, deeply split, under the slope of their bellies. They sometimes played a game they called Bumping Bottoms in Nina and Mary's room, and Mack had watched them occasionally from the dark of the hallway outside. They kept their dresses on but had their underpants off, and they'd jump around, laughing and screaming and lifting their skirts to that sudden vision, trying to press against each other.

He'd begun to stroke himself to a regular rhythm, when out of the blue he thought of Randall—Randall with his pants down, whimpering, pulling at his penis violently—the purpled thing, half erect, flopping from side to side. Mack stopped. It made it all seem too weird. He rolled over on his side.

But he couldn't stop thinking about it—about screwing, about girls. And then he remembered the last time he'd gone over to his father's. Liddie had been there too, home for spring break. When they arrived, his father was standing in the hallway saying goodbye to a woman, a woman much younger than his mother, a woman wearing black, all black. Black stockings, a black skirt, a black turtleneck shirt. Her hair was black too, and her eyes were dark, circled with black pencil. Only her skin was a bled white, shocking in contrast to everything else. She'd left a few minutes after Mack and Liddie came in, but Mack had watched his father in the hall with her. He saw his father's hand, white and spread out—it looked strangely like a starfish to Mack—rest on the woman's black breast a moment.

During the meal at his father's, Liddie had been gay, she'd talked with almost frantic energy about her school. She told anecdotes about the house too, about their mother, all in a mocking tone that made Mack uneasy; but he was glad to have her making noise, because he had nothing to say. As Liddie and his father laughed together at the table, Mack felt like an outsider, like a child forced to sit with parents whose concerns, whose interests, are incomprehensible to him.

His father drove them home. Liddie sat with him in the front seat and moved the dial quickly from station to station. Just as they turned onto Harper Avenue, Mack's father asked, "What did you think of Beth?" For a second Mack couldn't imagine who his father was talking about. Beth? Who was Beth?

Liddie answered. "She seemed okay. I mean, she was there for about two seconds, Dads."

"Uhmmm," their father said. "And you, Mack?" His head lifted to see Mack in the rearview mirror.

"What does it matter what I think?" Mack asked furiously.

"I'm just curious." The car moved down the dark street, past Al's house, the Rosenbergs', the Murphys', all the families that lived together. Mack was aware, suddenly, of holding his breath, the way he had as a child when they drove past cemeteries.

At the square, his father pulled over and cut the engine. He turned, with his hand along the back of the seat, and faced Mack. His smooth, handsome face was kind and concerned. "You seem angry. Have anything you want to say?" he asked.

Liddie looked over at Mack too.

Mack slid to the door. "Are you going to marry her?"

His father laughed. "What a question!" he said.

"Ask me then," Mack said, opening the door. "Ask me when you decide to marry her." He stepped out and slammed the door.

No one was awake in the house, and Liddie didn't come inside for another ten or fifteen minutes. As he roamed frantically through its quiet, Mack knew they were sitting in the dark car, his father and sister, and talking about him—as though he were the crazy one, as though he were disturbed.

Mack had hit Nina in the back, partly because he could see that she was expecting it.

His mother had had to wake him to be in charge this morning. It was ten-thirty, and he'd been drifting in and out of a deep, dream-filled sleep for what felt like hours when she bent over him. He opened his eyes and stared blankly up at her for a moment. Her voice was gentle and loving in a way Mack could hardly stand anymore—he was seventeen—and he'd barked, *"Okay.* I'm not deaf," as though she'd been screaming at him.

When he came downstairs, his hair still rumpled from sleep, his face scarred with the print of the folds on his pillow, the little girls were launched into their day, a swirl of projects usually organized by Nina and bought hook, line, and sinker by the younger two.

They ignored him. That was fine with Mack. Being in charge mostly meant making sure Randall didn't hurt himself or wreck anything, but even so, Mack felt burdened by it, resentful. It seemed directly connected to his father's departure, to that absence it appeared he felt more acutely than anyone else.

While he grumpily ate Cheerios and cleaned up after himself, he paid no attention to the noise of the girls in the dining room—someone thumping away on the piano, squeals, arguments about what came next in some dance they were creating. But he leaned in when he was about to turn the TV on and told them to quiet down.

They did for a few minutes. Slowly, though, they forgot about him and got noisier again. This time Mack yelled. "Shut up! We're watching in here." Randall didn't look up, but the girls piped down. Briefly.

The third time, he went in. "Did you hear me?" he asked. There was pure meanness in his voice. He could feel how nearly out of control he was. The two littler ones froze and watched him with stupid, scared faces, but Nina had been playing the piano, and in defiance, she kept on. She wasn't even looking his way, but her fingers made mistakes, her back was arched in readiness, and he could see on her face that she knew he was going to hit her. His punch made a noise that opened her mouth, that sounded like a burp when it came out.

When his mother came home, Mack made the long trip out to the curb three times to get the groceries. By the time he was back with the last load, Mary and Sarah were in the kitchen with her, and he knew by the excitement in their faces when they looked over at him that they'd told. His mother was lifting the food out of sacks on the kitchen table, sorting it into piles. She didn't meet his eye.

He opened a bag of Hydrox cookies and took a handful. "Am I off?" he asked her, his mouth full.

"Yes. Randall's in the living room?" she asked.

"Yeah. He's watching TV."

"Well, that's it, then," she said. Now she looked wearily at Mack. He stared back defiantly, and she looked away, began pulling more groceries out of the bags. She wasn't going to say anything. It seemed worse. Once recently, she had actually spanked him, wailing, "What am I going to *do* about you? What am I going to do?" Mack didn't know how to react, and so he had laughed at the ineffectuality of the blows through his chinos and all the junk in his back pockets. He was taller than his mother too, and that had made it somehow more comical, more awful. When he laughed, she had turned away sharply, making a strange, guttural cry.

"What time is Dad coming?" he asked her now, trying to get her attention, wanting her to get mad, to care about him, to get it over with.

"I don't know. You made that arrangement," she reminded him. "Here, Maresy, put this stuff on the shelf in the pantry." She shoved a brightly colored collection of canned goods over to his sister.

"One," he answered himself.

"One o'clock?" she asked.

"Yeah."

"Well, you should try to eat before then. That's hard work."

Mack and his father were going to take down the storm windows and put the screens on. It was April, and for several weeks now he'd been free of the night-time chore of starting the furnace.

"What's for lunch?"

"You mean, besides cookies?"

"Yeah," he said. He took a few more.

"I don't know yet. Soup, I guess. Soup and English muffins, let's say." She crossed to the counter with an armful of baking things—flour, cornmeal, sugar, bags of chocolate chips.

"What kind of soup?"

"What would you like?"

"I don't know."

"Cream of mushroom, then," she said, returning.

"Ugh," he said.

"Oh, Mack!" she cried, and slammed the boxes of Bisquick and cake mix together. The girls watched, little teasing smiles animating their faces. He was asking for it.

"Yeah?" he said.

Her face tightened, then relaxed. She shook her head. "Nothing. Absolutely nothing. I'll call you when lunch is ready."

"I don't know if I'll be hungry," he said.

"Lovey, it makes not one bit of difference to me whether you're hungry or not," she said. Her voice was trembling.

"Thanks a *lot,*" he said, genuinely wounded, and left the room.

His father came promptly at one but spent a long time shut in the kitchen with his mother before he called Mack down. His father would be the one talking to him, then. Mack lay on his bed and stared at the sloping attic ceiling. He could imagine what his mother was saying: "I'm at my wit's end." She would be smoking, drinking coffee. "I'm at the end of my rope." "I can't do a thing with him." They were the phrases his grandmother had used long ago, only with her they were a kind of joke, because she wasn't ever at her wit's end. Mack's mother often was, especially since his father had moved out.

His father's voice called up from the second floor. "Mack!"

He got up from his unmade bed and crossed to open the door. "Yeah?"

"I'm ready to roll with these screens. You all set?"

"Yeah," Mack said. He came down the stairs two at a time.

It was mild and damp outside, everything the monotonous faded gray-brown of an early midwest spring. Their noises were magnified in the still, wet air. Mack helped his father set up the big wooden extension ladder in the backyard. They rested it just below Mack's third-floor window. Then he went back into the house—upstairs, into his own room again. The air felt stale after the heavy moisture outside.

His father was at the window, his head and shoulders floating there like a nightmare. Mack opened the inside window, pushed the stiffened hooks holding the storm window out of their eyes, tapped the frame out. Now he leaned forward, gripped the heavy storm window, and pushed up, taking most of its weight on his extended arms as they lifted it together off the prongs over the window frame. He had the thought, suddenly, that if he pushed out now on the window, his father would fall backward to the ground and die.

"Okay, I've got it," his father said. He gripped the storm window, swung it carefully to one side of the ladder, and started slowly down. He held the window angled awkwardly out, away from the ladder.

Mack watched him from above, the top of his head getting smaller and smaller. He looked at the whitish patch on his father's head where the hair had thinned and his skull showed. You couldn't see this in everyday life, and Mack hadn't realized how much hair he had lost back there.

His father came up more quickly, carrying one of the screens. Together they hooked it on the prongs over the window. Then, as his father started down again, Mack turned the rusted wing nuts on the screen's latches.

Mack went back down through the house. His mother was flopped on the living room couch, reading, and the girls were at the dining room table with Randall, hard at work with crayons and paper. Outside, he helped his father move the ladder to the next window. Then he climbed back up the stairs, this time into Nina and Mary's room. Their beds were still unmade too, and the wrinkled sheets exuded their sweet, sweaty smell. Mack crossed to the window and waited until his father appeared on the other side of the glass again, and then they went once more through their slow routine.

As he and his father worked their way around the house, Mack made this trip over and over. He was in every room of the house for a while, and in the long waits while his father went up and down the ladder— he didn't want Mack doing this; it was too dangerous—Mack looked around him, as he almost never did. The girls' rooms both looked the same, every surface littered with dolls, drawings, incompleted projects and activities. Their beds were all a rumple of sheets, like his own, and there were dishes scattered here and there, waiting to be carried down to the kitchen. Liddie's room was the only neat one in the house, just as it was when she was home. Her bed was crisply made, her clothes put away. Tacked on her wall were magazine photographs of her heroes— James Dean, Maria Callas, Marlon Brando.

Randall's room was nearly bare. His bed was a mattress on the floor, to prevent momentum when he rocked at night. There was one shelf of his odd "toys," no curtains, no pillows. The wallpaper was peeled in long strips where he'd gone wild. On the mattress, neatly spread out, was the red blanket he'd had for years. When you sat for him, the only way to get him to sleep was to cover him entirely with it and tuck it in tightly on all four sides around him. Sometimes his erection stuck up like a tent pole in the middle of the blanket and made the little girls giggle if they were helping.

Mack didn't really look at his mother's room, just waited by the windows for his father. He knew exactly what was here anyway, exactly the way the bottles, the combs, the silver-backed brush and mirror, the few pieces of family jewelry, were spread out on her dresser; exactly what pictures dotted the walls—his grandparents, his uncles' children, his sisters and himself and Randall at various stages of growth. He even knew what clothes were hanging in her closet and what they smelled like, for it was in the back of her closet, on some useless shelves, that he had hidden as a little boy when he wanted her to come seeking him, to hold him. And everything was the same as it had been in his childhood, as though from some early stage on she hadn't had the energy to buy things or change things, to try to make things nice. She had even kept the big bed she and his father used to sleep in together. The unused pillows were neatly stacked on his side, as though she was hoping he might come back any night.

As they moved from window to window, Mack had a sense of being neither in nor out, but somehow both places at once; a sense of being with his father but seeing him half the time only through a glass, crazily. He felt preoccupied, weird. His arms ached from the weight of the storms, his fingers were stiff from turning the rusted wing nuts. He was dreamy and confused and nearly dizzy from the work; and so, even though he'd warned himself earlier to get ready, even though he'd known it was coming sometime, he was startled when his father turned to him and said: "Let's take a break before we put these away, Mack. I want to talk to you." They were outside. His father sat down on the back-porch stairs.

Mack didn't answer. He stepped away from his father and picked up a few stones, started chucking them at the train embankment.

His father spoke to his back. "Your mother tells me you've been hard on the kiddies."

Mack aimed carefully and *plock*ed the stone off the trunk of the silver maple.

"Well?"

There was an edge of impatience in his father's voice. Mack smiled. "They're hard on me."

"They're half your age."

"Yeah, but there's three of them. If you add them together, they're twice my age."

"Let's stick to the matter at hand, shall we?"

Mack was silent. He aimed now at the rail along the top of the embankment.

"Would you like to tell me what happened?"

"No. I wouldn't *like to.*"

"Well then, *will you please* tell me what happened?"

Mack threw again at the rail. "I was trying to watch TV."

"And?"

"And they kept making noise."

"And?"

"And I told them to stop, and they didn't, so I hit Nina."

"Why Nina?"

Mack hit the swing set this time. "She was the one playing the piano. She's the biggest. She gives me a pain."

"Stop throwing those stones!"

Mack stopped, frozen.

"And get over here."

He turned and walked over by his father. He

stood a few feet in front of him, looking down. He wished his father would stand up. He didn't like this angle, this vision of his thinning hair, his gleaming skull under it.

"Now look, son. Everyone around here's under a lot of strain right now. No one has a lot of resilience. The edges are frayed."

"That's not my fault," Mack said.

"No, it's not. Quite the opposite, I know. But you have a choice about how to respond to that. You can make it better, or you can make it worse. It's up to you really. And I'd like you to think about it. To think hard about it. That choice." There was a long pause.

"Somehow, Mack . . ." His father stopped. Then started again. He had made his voice gentle and reasonable. "You're the oldest one home now, Mack. The way you handle things sets an example for the rest. I'd like you to be asking a bit more of yourself."

All of a sudden, Mack felt he might cry. When he finally spoke, his voice was high-pitched. He sounded like a little boy. "How would you know what I'm asking of myself?" He meant this, but he was gratified, too, to see the way his father's face looked, suddenly soft and sorrowful.

"I can't know," his father said gently. "I can't know unless you talk to me about it."

"I can't talk to *you* about it."

His father looked down at where his hands dangled useless between his knees. Then up at Mack again. "Well, would you like to talk to someone else?"

Mack looked away sharply. He knew what was coming. "What do you mean?"

"I could arrange for you to see someone—a psychiatrist whose business it is to make it easy for adolescents to talk about what's bothering them." Mack stood motionless, looking off through the misty air at the row of empty backyards—the Frawleys', the Gordons', Mrs. Dodge's. "It strikes me that it might be helpful to you to have such a person in your life, to help you understand why you lose control of yourself."

"I don't lose control."

"Well, what would you call it, then?"

Mack spun and looked directly at his father. "I make the wrong *choice.*"

His father's face changed; closed, suddenly. "Perhaps you need to get control of that, then," he said.

His father was angry, but he wouldn't say so. It drove Mack nuts. His mother at least knew she was mad when she was. She yelled, she hit. She even threw stuff sometimes. His father just talked.

Now he was saying, "It'd be one thing, Mack, if you were like Randall, if there were something wrong with you. But you're not. You know very well what's going on around here, how difficult a time it is for everyone. But you persist in this kind of unhelpful—"

Mack couldn't stand this. "But I am like Randall!" he cried. He began to rock from foot to foot in front of his father, his head swinging, an ecstatic smile on his face. He cried out, "I am like Randall! I'm just like him. See? I *am* Randall." He began to chant rhythmically, "I am Randall, I am Randall."

For a moment his father sat speechless. He was tongue-tied, this imitation was so perfect, so unexpectedly cruel. Then he stood up. "That is enough!" he shouted.

But Mack couldn't stop, though his face was fearful now. Maybe his father would hit him. But his father just stood there, watching Mack dance. Then at the dining room window he saw the girls, attracted by his father's loud voice. They were staring at him too, they could tell instantly who he was imitating, and their mouths made O's of surprise. Mack danced a minute more. Then he slowed, stopped. He turned away from all of them. He wanted to *do* something; he wanted something awful, something violent, to happen.

After a moment his father said to him softly, "I just don't know what to say to you, Macklin."

"Then don't *say* anything," Mack said furiously. His father sat down again, but Mack continued to stand. A few raindrops had started to fall. The girls, all but Nina, drifted back into the darkness of the house. A train ratcheted by, screaming.

Mack knew his father would say something. He always had something to say. Mack stood waiting, as tense as Nina at the piano when she was expecting him to hit her this morning. His eyes slid to his father and caught him staring back, his face full of helplessness. Mack looked quickly away.

When his father got up without speaking and began to carry one of the storm windows down the open bulkhead into the basement, Mack felt as shocked, as uncertain of what to do next, as he had the night his father moved out.

Late that afternoon, Mack sat watching TV again. It was pouring outside—silver sheets of rain sliding down the window—and nearly dark. The table was set for dinner, and the smell of roast beef permeated the air. There was the sound of conversation, of music on the radio from the kitchen. Sarah came to the living room doorway, gripped it, and swung in and out for a moment. Then she broke free and ran over to the couch, where Mack was sitting. She landed on her knees the first time, then flipped over and was sitting next to him.

"What's on?" she said.

"I don't know. This is just ending."

They watched the ads silently. Wonder Bread. Spic and Span. Phillips' Milk of Magnesia.

"What's regularity?" Sarah asked.

"When you're regular. You know, not weird."

She looked at him a moment, weighing it. She was the prettiest of the three little girls. She had big, steady brown eyes, which rested on him now, trying to read him. "Not the truth," she said sternly.

He shrugged, took a pillow, and swung it into her lap. Her legs and upper body folded together around it. Then she relaxed, and they watched again. It was a news program. Sarah left the pillow on her lap.

After a minute she said, "I didn't tell."

"Didn't tell what?"

"I didn't tell on you."

He looked at her. She held the pillow and watched the screen, unblinking. "Who cares?" Mack said, and relaxed in his corner. "It doesn't even matter."

The program was about Vietnam. *Anguished*, the announcer called it. His voice was deep, serious; it boomed evenly on about protests against the government. Suddenly there was a fire on the screen and people standing around watching it. In the flames you could see a shape, motionless. The cutout of a body. But no, the announcer was saying it was a person, a Buddhist monk. He was immolating himself, the announcer said.

"What's immolating?" Sarah asked.

"Burn," Mack answered, watching the flames, the still figure, the people not doing anything about it.

"Eeeuu," Sarah said. She was almost leaning on Mack.

"No kidding," he answered. Sarah lifted her hand and started twirling a strand of hair. Without looking at her, Mack reached over and gently pulled her arm down. How would it feel, he wondered, to care so much about something that you'd be willing to die for it? No: not to die necessarily; but to have pain. The worst pain, the pain of burning. The flame was guttering, dwindling now around the blackened monk, but he hadn't moved. The picture cut away. Still photos of the country's leader, his wife.

Mack was remembering the time when Randall burned himself. They were having a huge bonfire. Three or four of them—the bigger boys on the block—had worked for hours raking the pile of leaves together. Mr. Rosenberg was in charge. All the mothers gave them bags of marshmallows. They didn't start until after dark, and the flames rose fragrant and magical and made the children's faces look as though they were glowing from within. Randall had put his hand right in, before anyone could stop him. He took it out almost immediately, but he didn't cry or scream or anything. If Mack and Liddie hadn't seen it, no one would have known until later—until they saw the raw flesh, the blisters—that it had happened. When Mack asked his father about it afterward, his father said that Randall *did* feel the pain at one level. But that his psychological makeup meant that he'd retreated from his body, from reality, so that he didn't react as we did.

Maybe the Buddhists retreated like that, Mack thought. He felt Sarah's hot weight on his arm, her head and shoulders resting against him. They watched.

Mack told his mother he didn't know what time he'd be home, and went up the street to Al's house. Together they walked through the rain down Fifty-seventh Street to Steinway's. Tucker Franklin was meeting them there. They didn't much like Tucker—not even girls liked him, although he might have been the best-looking boy in class. But his clothes were too expensive, he smiled too much: he was slimy. Still, he was one of the few boys who had his own car, so they went out with him a lot.

Mack's friends were all sixteen or seventeen. They all had their licenses. Sometimes on Saturday nights all they did was drive, carloads of them. They drove all over the city. Someone would have heard of a place downtown where they had good fried shrimp to take out. They'd drive there, pass the greasy cartons and the little cups of hot sauce back and forth in the car. Someone else heard that if you went down by the planetarium parking lot and just walked around, you could watch people doing it in their cars. You could tell which ones to look at, too, because the cars rocked a little with the fucking motion. They drove to girls' houses, to parties they heard about in South Shore or the North Side. Someone knew about a place that sold beer with no ID, a bar in the ghetto that served anyone. They crashed slumber parties, they dropped in where someone's girlfriend was baby-sitting. They had music on the radio, they yelled out the windows at girls walking in threes and fours, at other cars full of boys.

They were all good boys. They were all applying to college. They were all on teams, they made A's and B's, they sometimes had girlfriends. But what they liked to do most of all on Saturday night was drive around. When Mack was dating Sharon Fine, he had missed it. He had felt left out when Al or Terry or Soletski had talked about what they'd done without him.

Tonight they sat for a long time in the booths by the windows at Steinway's, drinking Cokes and waiting for someone good to walk by. But the steady drizzle meant there wasn't much life on the street. A group of three girls came in and sat with them awhile, pushed into a tangled, exciting intimacy because the booth was meant for only four people. But they were pre-freshmen, too young, and when they asked the boys to come to a party they knew about, the boys were suddenly contemptuous and mean to them, and they left.

Finally they went with Tucker to a party in South Shore; but they didn't stay long. Too many girls they didn't know. They stopped on the way back at a drive-in on Stony Island for hamburgers and French fries. Then they dropped into the Tropical Hut to see if anyone they knew was there, but the witch in pancake makeup who ran the place gave them a hard time. "Are you going to order anything, boys?" she asked about twenty times. "If you're not going to order anything, you'll have to leave."

Now it was nearly eleven. There was nothing to do. Mack felt the kind of restlessness that once or twice recently had gotten him into a fight. They were driving along the Midway—the wide grassy band dividing Hyde Park from Woodlawn—on the wrong side, the Woodlawn side, when Tucker remembered that Kathy Wood lived over here. They made noises, crude remarks. Mack held his fists in front of his chest and said in falsetto, "Kathy Wood. You bet she would!"

Kathy Wood had huge breasts. She wore tight sweaters so that everyone could see them. But even though everyone talked about her—about her tits—no one ever asked her out. She wasn't pretty, she wore too much makeup, she was too quiet, and her breasts were too big, freakishly big. It would be like taking out a spass. You wouldn't do it.

Now Tucker was saying she had a crush on him, that she had written him a note a couple of weeks earlier. He said he bet he could get her to show them her tits. A dollar each.

They sat in the car while Tucker ran up the long, glistening walk and rang her bell. After a moment, the door opened and he disappeared. He was gone awhile, and they got restless. Terry needed to pee.

Mack began a narrative describing what was happening between Tucker and Kathy, in a syrupy French accent borrowed from Charles Boyer. Terry got out of the car, finally, and disappeared around the side of Kathy's house.

When the door opened, Mack stopped talking. He watched Tucker come back down the walk. Tucker was smiling. They rolled down the windows and looked out into the light rain at him.

He leaned against the car. "C'mon," he said. "I think this will work out. She's alone."

This, it turned out, was not quite the case. She was baby-sitting for a younger sister, who was asleep upstairs, and when they all came stomping in—wiping the wet off their feet with clumsy thuds, talking loudly—she was nervous, she kept telling them to keep it quiet. She led them downstairs through the regular part of the basement—a washer and dryer, stacks of paint cans, a huge cast-iron furnace like the one Mack tended at home—to a rec room with one fluorescent bulb floating in a metal reflector above the Ping-Pong table. The other half of the room slid away into darkness.

Mack was restless and excited. Something was going to happen! He began to sort through a stack of forty-fives in the darkest corner of the room, squinting over each label, pretending not to listen to Tucker working on Kathy. ("Listen, we all talk about you all the time. No joke. Half the guys in the junior class are crazy to take you out. I'm not kidding.")

Mack put on a few records. Soletski and Terry had started to play Ping-Pong. Al began hitting a punching bag in rhythm to the music. There was enough noise so that you couldn't really hear Tucker except when a record stopped. He was sitting next to Kathy on the couch, talking to her earnestly and sincerely. Abruptly, though, he came over to Mack. He remembered he might have some beers in the trunk, and he asked Mack if he'd go out and check. "I'd go myself, but . . ." He gestured behind him. "You know."

"Your servant, your humble servant," Mack said, backing away toward the door and bowing to Tucker over and over.

It was black and wet outside. The rain had softened, and the air smelled clean. For a moment Mack had the impulse to leave, just to walk home alone in the wet spring night. He stood for a long time under the little overhang by the front door, thinking about it. Then he walked out to Tucker's car. Rolled into corners of the trunk, just as Tucker thought, were seven Black Labels. Mack gathered them up awkwardly and slammed the trunk shut on the empty, echoing street. He felt around in the glove compartment and found a church key. He went back into the house, down to the ugly basement.

Tucker was dancing with Kathy now, his hands working her back. She seemed lost in pleasure, but when she saw Mack hand the first beer can to Al, she jerked away from Tucker. "Oh, my God!" she said. "Oh, you guys! God, you've got to remember to take the cans with you when you go. Oh, if my parents thought I'd been drinking . . . Oh, my God." Mack saw that she wasn't wearing the layer of makeup she usually had on in school. It made her look younger, more normal. He turned away from her and gave a can to Soletski.

Tucker had followed her. He folded his arms around her again, talking all the while. "What do you think we are, idiots? No one will ever know. Don't worry about it. C'mon. No one's leaving anything behind."

They danced some more. When the record stopped, Mack put another one on quickly. He selected a stack of them, all slow ones. After three or four songs, Tucker and Kathy stayed locked together even on the breaks while the next record dropped. Mack was watching from the couch, sipping his tepid beer slowly. Tucker's hands had begun to slide up and down Kathy's sides, along her waist and breasts. Mack had a little hard-on, watching. In the break after "You Belong to Me," before the next record dropped, he could hear Tucker asking Kathy to unhook her bra. "I just want to feel you without this thing," he said. His hand was resting on her tight blue sweater where the strip of her bra cut visibly into the flesh of her back. "C'mon. I mean, what will it hurt? I won't try to touch them, I promise. I just want to feel you."

She seemed to be objecting, but coyly, flirtatiously; and then the music started up again. When Kathy had her back to Mack, Tucker grinned at him over her shoulder. But his lips never stopped moving by her ear.

All the boys were grinning now. They didn't meet each other's eyes, and everyone was busy doing something, but they were all grinning. And each time the record stopped, there was a frozen kind of attentiveness in the air while they tried to hear Tucker's murmuring voice.

Tucker and Kathy had been dancing for half an hour or so, when suddenly he said loudly, "How bout cutting that light, you guys?"

Kathy was smiling, her eyes shut.

She'd agreed to something! Mack felt a pitiless contempt for her. He got up and reached for the light pull.

But Soletski was playing Ping-Pong with Al now, and he said he wanted to go to twenty-one. Mack didn't want to seem too eager anyway, and so he sat back down and waited through two more records. They all listened to the music, to the *pock* of the ball, and smiled crazily at each other. Finally it was Soletski who turned the light off. He came and sat next to Mack on the couch.

It still wasn't completely dark. The door to the other part of the basement was open, and there was a bare bulb lighting that space. A strange parallelogram of light fell into the rec room. Mack could see Tucker and Kathy, but not Al, who was somewhere in the back of the room, in the dark. Terry had come over to the couch now too. Tucker slowly moved Kathy to just outside the slice of light. After a few minutes, she reached up behind her—her elbows looked like wings—and fumbling through her sweater, she unhooked her bra. Tucker's hands lifted to her sides, pulled at the sweater from there, trying to release her breasts. Finally you could see the *boing* of one as it flopped out under the soft wool, even bigger than it was in the bra. Tucker said "Oh!" so loudly you could hear him over the music. He flattened Kathy against his chest and arched against her.

On the couch they all sat, staring. Tucker danced with her a long while. Mack changed the stack twice. In the end Tucker had stopped moving his feet. He was just swaying. He had Kathy turned with her side to them. They could all see his busy hands sliding along the covered breast. Mack could hear Tucker talking, telling her how good she felt. Mack wanted to touch himself, but he was embarrassed to. The music stopped and started, over and over, and they all watched Tucker's hand, and the band of white skin that slowly widened between her pants and her sweater.

Kathy was holding tight around Tucker's neck now. Her hips moved slowly against him. Tucker's hand slid under the edge of the sweater. They watched her gut suck in, heard her inhale. His hand moved up. You could see it under the sweater resting on her breast, squeezing, letting go. Mack tried to imagine what it must feel like. Sharon Fine hadn't let him go this far. Tucker's hand was moving faster now; it was as though he were milking her tit. The sweater had pushed up on his arm, and Mack saw glimpses of the breast, huge and fat and white—bluish, almost—sliding around under his fingers.

Then Tucker just pushed the sweater up—he just did it!—and there it was. Mack stared at the nipple. Tucker's hand came back to it, quickly, but very gently now. He was letting them see. Soletski made a noise, and then the music stopped again. They could hear Tucker's voice, muffled behind her arms. "C'mon, sure. Let me look." She murmured. "Oh, please. C'mon. I know they're so great. Just let me look." But she was holding tight, as though she'd never let go.

Mack was frantically adding two or three records to the stack, starting the machine all over, looking back and forth as much as he could at Tucker's fingers and the fat white thing pushing out between them.

When the music set them in motion, Tucker's fingers began again. He pulled the nipple out, made it longer. "Jesus!" Terry whispered. It was as though Tucker heard this. He began doing stunts. He held the nipple at them, wiggled it back and forth, poked his finger far into its pinkish tip. He pretended to squirt it in their direction. They couldn't believe it. Mack ached. He could feel Soletski or Terry moving, the rhythm of the couch. Tucker was really talking now: "Oh, come on. Yeah. Yeah. Come on. Just let us look. These guys too. They're my friends. They want to see. Nah. No one'll tell. Just for one second."

And then her head pulled back, she turned to the three of them on the couch. She actually sort of smiled at them, as though she were a person, as though they might be expected to like her. Then, as she buried her head against Tucker's shoulder, she turned her body away from him, open to them. One of Tucker's hands held her head down on his shoulder, the other moved across her exposed chest, lifted both breasts.

Suddenly she spun back against him, embraced him again. Tucker began kissing her, holding her butt and nearly lifting her up as he jerked into her. Her breasts squished flat. Mack couldn't see them anymore. He realized that his mouth was open, his throat dry. Then there was no music, and he could hear the breathing in the room.

After a few moments Tucker straightened up a little, pulled her sweater down. He lifted his hands and loosened her arms from around his neck. He stepped away from her, into the light.

She squinted at him and then looked over to the couch. It was as though she had just waked from a nap; it reminded Mack of his sisters. Her eyes were puffy, her hair frazzled. Her sweater was ruckled strangely above her breasts, on account of the pushed-up bra.

"Well, ah," Tucker said. His voice was loud and casual. "I guess we better go now." He was backing up.

"You don't have to," she said. "My parents won't be home till real late."

"Yeah, but I have a—uh—" He looked at his watch. "A twelve-thirty curfew."

The guys on the couch were getting up. They edged ahead of Tucker to the open door. Al emerged from the darkness. No one was talking but Tucker. "I'd like to stay. I'd really like to, Kathy. But—" He spread his hands. "I got this curfew." His grin was dopey, helpless.

Mack was at the door. He looked back once at Kathy's face in the funny light. Ahead of him he heard Soletski and Terry running up the stairs. They were starting to laugh. Al pushed from behind him and followed them. As Mack started up, Tucker was coming out the rec room door, almost walking backward. Kathy followed him. Tucker was close to laughter; Mack could hear it in his voice.

"But listen," he was saying. "I'll see you in school Monday, right?"

Mack was nearly running now too, but he stopped at the top of the stairs to look down once more. Kathy's face was lifted up at them; she understood now what had happened. If they stayed they could watch her cry. Tucker was actually pushing past Mack, his voice cracking. "Thanks a lot," he said, he brayed, and snorts of laughter erupted from him as he ran for the front door, open to the wet black night.

Mack was the last one out. He ran too, but not fast enough. Before he was outside he could hear her crying start in the basement, an involuntary sharp wail, as though she were in pain, as though she had burned herself.

In the car they were noisy—laughing, talking about her boobs, about how bitchin' cool Tucker was. Mack got in and they peeled out, the tires squealing. He looked back at the open front door. For a moment he felt bad that he hadn't shut it behind him. It wasn't a safe neighborhood, and she might not come up from the basement for a while.

The radio was on; they were all talking at once. Everyone got his wallet out, and they began an elaborate, laughing exchange of ones, fives, to pay Tucker off. "Want to know the best part?" Tucker asked as they drove down Fifty-ninth Street. "The best part is, *we left the beer cans!*" They were hysterical, Mack too, laughing, whumping each other till they cried.

Tucker did have a curfew, it turned out. He dropped Mack and Al at Blackstone, and they walked home, hardly speaking, suddenly. The water-weighted air floated in garish clouds under the high streetlamps. No one else was on the street.

"Did you feel sorry for her?" Mack asked after a minute. Al was his best friend.

"Kind of. Not right then. But afterward. Tucker is . . ." His voice trailed off.

"Yeah," Mack said. "He's an asshole. But we did it too—you know what I mean?"

"Well, it's not the same, though," Al said.

"I don't know. We watched, didn't we? Maybe we're worse, actually. We paid him money to do it for us."

"Yeah, but it's not." Al was shaking his head. "It's not the same." They were almost at Harper Avenue.

"Well, maybe not," Mack said. "Listen, are you hungry or anything? Want to go back to the Tropical Hut?"

"Nah," Al said. "What? Are you?"

"I don't know," Mack said. "I just don't feel like . . ." He raised his shoulders. "I don't know. You're not hungry?"

"No. And I got to get home anyway. There's not enough time. My deadline's one. We'd barely get there and I'd have to . . ."

"Yeah," Mack said.

"I would otherwise."

"Yeah," Mack said, and raised his hand slightly at his hip as he turned into the square.

Al stood watching him for a few seconds. Then he called out, "It's not the same, Mack." Mack kept walking.

The houses were dark around the square, except for the Graysons' porch light. There was a glow from the rear of Mack's house, though. The kitchen. Mack went down the side walk to the backyard to see who was awake.

His mother, alone tonight, was sitting at the table, reading under the wall lamp. The light over her head made her dark hair look white. Next to her, cigarette smoke rose straight, then cirrussed in some little wind. She was wearing her old red bathrobe. She was utterly still, as she never was during the day. Mack felt like a spy, as though he were seeing something private, something it was wrong to look at. This was how she looked when she thought she was alone, when she thought no one was watching her. She turned a page, reached for the cigarette and pulled on it, sat in the cloud she released.

All of a sudden her head lifted, she swung it to look at the kitchen doorway. She must hear something, Mack thought. Then, after a few seconds, she slowly turned to the window: she was staring straight out to where he stood in the side yard, though he was sure she couldn't see him. But Mack felt as though they were looking right into each other's hearts, as though there were no glass between them. Mack felt somehow that she'd been watching him with this deep gaze all night, that she had known, had always known, what he was doing. Without blaming him, she saw who he was, how he was. His throat ached.

Her head bent down again. In a moment she turned the page. Some part of him wanted to call out to her.

He backed up slowly, his eyes steady on her still form. He stopped when he touched the fence. For a minute he stood leaning against it. He felt a sense of desperation, of trapped yearning for something nameless, something he couldn't have guessed at. Then he turned and climbed the fence, dropped silently onto the weedy embankment, and scrambled up.

It was a different world up here, with strange bluish lights high overhead. His childhood was full of myths about this world. About live rails, attempted suicides. Maimings. There were ten or twelve sets of tracks going north and south on the wide rise. Mack walked south for a while, not looking at the dark houses, at the familiar backyards of the street. He picked up a couple of rocks. He threw one across the shiny rails, trying to skip it over them as though they were still water.

Behind him, far away, he heard a train. He turned and saw the distant headlight growing larger three tracks over. He stepped back, out of the way, to the edge of the embankment. The wild metal shriek came closer, screamed down at him. It was probably the last of the scheduled commuter trains from downtown, the noisiest of the trains that ran past their house.

Suddenly it was there. The wind of its passing slapped against Mack; the noise was all around him. The wide yellow squares of light flipped by, dizzyingly fast. He saw one set of head and shoulders in the first car through the glass; none in the second. His arm was cocked. As the last car screamed past, he threw it forward with all his strength, and the stone rocketed into the glass, splintering it, multiplying light into the car.

8

NINA was playing the piano, forced to do thirty minutes directly before her lesson, because her mother had discovered she'd practiced only twice this week. The metronome nagged, and she arched her fingers and worked through her piece mechanically and softly. It was the *Moonlight* Sonata. Normally she played it emotionally, giving it a feverish, melodramatic quality. Sometimes she could bring herself to tears this way, and this weeping—over Beethoven, over beauty—made her feel purified, lifted her out of everything she thought of as ordinary and difficult in her life.

Today, though, she wasn't even listening to how it sounded. She paid no attention, either, to the noise of her sisters at play with the other children on the square—their shouts filtered through the dusty, paint-dotted screen in the dining room. Today she was eavesdropping, trying to hear what Retta and her mother were saying in the kitchen. A moment ago she had heard Retta tell her mother she had bought a gun.

Lainey's voice had been instantly anguished. "A gun!" she cried. Then she paused, and when she spoke again, it was a lament. "A gun, Retta. Oh, why?" Through their voices came the thump of the iron. It was Retta's laundry day, and the house smelled of heated cloth and bleach.

"For company," Retta answered. She was never intimidated by Lainey's sorrow. "Jus to keep me company."

Lainey's voice went up and down for a while—Nina could hear only a phrase or two—and Retta answered her. Nina started playing a scale so she wouldn't have to think about the music. No one would ever notice anyway. It was so hypocritical—her mother just wanted the practice time. She never even listened to what Nina was playing. This was because Liddie had the musical gifts; everyone knew it. Nina had wanted lessons at first, and even now she loved the music. But no one encouraged her, no one wanted to hear it, because they were used to Liddie's real ability. When her father asked about her lessons, which he did sometimes—especially if he'd recently made out a check to her teacher—his question was, "Still thumping away on the old pianner, Nina?" And she would have to answer as though she, too, knew how foolish it was: "Yep."

Recently Mary also had been discovered to have a gift—Mary, whom Nina had always seen as simply an echo to her own voice, the agent of her imagination. Now she was enrolled in advanced science classes, and Nina had begun to be scared about herself. How was she ever to be special, to be great, without some gift too?

She heard her mother say sharply and clearly, "Are you telling me that gun is in this house?"

"Don't get all bothered," Retta said. "I've got it put away. Ain't nobody goin' to find that gun."

"I don't like it, Retta. What if one of the children . . . ?"

"I told you don't worry. Now don't worry."

There was silence for a moment. Probably her mother was smoking, blowing twin streams from her nostrils. Sometimes she let thick sheets of smoke rise from her mouth and enter her nose. Nina and her sisters called that *waves*. When their mother did it, they said she was *making waves*. "And how!" Liddie said when they used this term in front of her.

"Besides," Nina's mother said suddenly, "what's the point?"

"The point is"—and Retta smacked the iron down for emphasis—"*let* somebody try takin' my money off me again."

"Oh, Retta, you wouldn't be capable of such a thing. Shooting someone?"

"You bet I would," Retta said.

"I don't believe it," Nina's mother said quickly.

"You don't need to," Retta said. "But the next time some boy so high on drugs he don't know *what* he's doin' says, 'Gimme your money,' *he's* gonna believe."

"Oh, Retta, you're breaking my heart."

"Girl, your heart is bound to be broken. You want to believe the world is not a bad place, and the world is a bad place, so your heart is gonna *be* broke. Time and time again. I can't be sorry for you."

Retta often spoke this way to Lainey. She was the only one who did, and Nina always felt a little frightened by it. But Lainey never got angry, never fought with Retta about this tone, as she would have if one of the children had tried it. "I'm here to tell you," Retta would pronounce, and Lainey would listen to her tell whatever it was. Listen with what seemed like respect and curiosity. "Time you grew up," she'd tell Lainey if she expressed disbelief about something Retta felt was plainly the bitter truth. And almost all Retta's truths were bitter.

But Nina sensed that Retta admired her mother too. She defended her to the children. "That woman," she'd say, and shake her head in awe. Lainey often napped during the days when Retta was in the house, and if they made too much noise, Retta was on them like a fury, bursting without knocking into Nina and Mary's room or a playroom they'd made in the basement. She was a skinny woman, with yellowy-brown skin and a pronounced underbite that made her look angry anyway, and when she frowned at them and scolded, she was just plain ugly. "Here, don't you know your mother been up all night with that Randall? And you makin' all this noise? Well, don't."

At their house Retta wore strange costumes to work in—stained dresses, or shirts that didn't fit. She rolled her stockings down like thick anklets and slipped into big men's shoes. But she wasn't just their Retta. She arrived a different person, wearing a suit usually, an elegant veiled hat. And Nina had once seen her moving slowly down Fifty-seventh Street, her high heels giving her walk a gentle sashay. She was smoking a lazy cigarette and looking like a movie star, if Negroes could be movie stars. Nina had remembered her full name then, so amazing on the Christmas card envelope where she'd seen it that she'd had to ask her mother, "Who the heck is this—Florette De-Lacey?"

But the truth was, Retta didn't need to scold them very often anymore. The girls were careful of their mother since their father had left. They'd been frightened into it, for it had been awful, especially at first.

In the days right after their father moved out, whatever semblance of order their lives had had collapsed completely. Lainey functioned only around Randall. The rest of them were left to fend for themselves. They would go in to wake Lainey when they got home from school. Her eyes would be swollen from weeping, her voice thick. "What time is it?" she'd ask. And if it wasn't close to Randall's drop-off time, she'd burrow deeper into the covers, into her misery. "Look, why don't you chickadees get a little money from my purse and head to the store for a snack. Whatever you like this time. And bring me some coffee. Hills Brothers drip grind. Be sure it says drip. It's no good to me unless it's good and drippy."

Directing them to her purse, her white arm would rise from under the covers in the shade-drawn twilight of her room and point, vaguely, away, away.

At first they took only what they needed, and they tried to buy things they thought of as healthy—hot dogs, Velveeta, frozen pot pies, or TV dinners. But when they realized that she didn't care, she didn't even notice what they were doing, their purchases changed. They would take five dollars, ten dollars, and buy whatever they wanted—Sara Lee cream cheese cakes, big bags of Fritos, Twinkies, bottles of Coke—things she would never have allowed in the house. For three days running at one point, Mary ate nothing but Choco-mallows, and Lainey didn't even know it. Months later, Nina found a coffee cake they'd hidden in the playroom, blackened and pulsing with the motion of greedy ants. Her rush of nausea seemed connected to the memory of that frightening time, and she threw the pan into the darkest corner of the basement in revulsion.

It was Mack who finally took charge, Mack who was changed because of all this. His meanness lost its gaiety and took on a purposive quality. He began to tell them when to fix meals, what to buy. He made them cook and clean up. Once, he grabbed Mary and started to choke her. She thought it was a game and began to scream and struggle, laughing in his grip. But then he stopped and held out the dingy beads of dirt and sweat that had rubbed off in his hands. "See that?" he said. "It's disgusting. Tonight you take a bath."

Nina remembered once coming downstairs—he'd yelled up to her room, told her to get to the kitchen and fix hamburgers—and hearing his voice in the second-floor hallway. It was so gentle, so persuasive, that for a moment she thought it was her father talking, her father as she'd heard him only every now and then—with patients, or when one of them was hurt. But when she looked, it was Mack, tall and skinny, slouched in the doorway of their mother's darkened room. He was telling her she needed to get up, Randall would be back soon. "And we've got dinner going for you," he said, as gently as a lover.

And somehow, it seemed as though all alone he did it. He woke her up, he brought her back to life. And though her withdrawal had lasted only a few weeks, it had the endless, fascinating, and repetitive quality of nightmare when Nina recollected it.

That part was over; but for months longer they would wake several times a week to a new noise in the house—their mother, talking on the telephone in their father's study, her voice strident, hysterical, a series of obscene accusations about their father and other women. Nina sometimes wept to hear her use the same words the boys used at school—*fuck, screw, asshole*—words Nina understood only in the most general sense: they were dirty, they were bad.

Once, just once, their father's voice was there in the night too, summoned by—what?—their mother's threats, her rage? He was shouting back at her, the same words. He yelled the names of people he'd slept with, people he'd *fucked*. Some of them Nina didn't know, but some were mothers on the block. He said Mr. Rosenberg and Mr. Masur had slept with other people too. When her mother started to cry, he told her she was just pretending she hadn't known, he told her she must have known. "You *willed* yourself not to see it, the same way you've willed everything else around here, all this goddamned perfection. The whole thing was a lie," Nina heard him say. "The pretty family with the pretty autistic boy and all the perfect children. All to make you feel all right about yourself." His voice thrilled with meanness. Nina was standing outside her bedroom, on the third-floor landing. She had thought, when she first heard his voice, that she'd go down and make them stop.

"Oh, liar! liar! liar!" Mother shrieked. "It's you—you who believe in perfection, who want everyone perfect, everyone cured, fixed with your . . . psychiatric crap. Fix yourself, then! Make yourself able to love. To love where everything isn't perfect."

Suddenly Mack was on the dark landing with Nina, white and flat as a cutout figure in his pj's. "What are you doing out here?" he whispered sharply.

He answered himself: "You're listening in." His voice was disgusted. He came over to her and pushed her toward her room, a sharp push, like punching her. "Get back in there, or you'll be sorry."

Nina ran and shut her door, and then the voices were just energy below her, alternating for what seemed like hours in their jubilant viciousness.

A few months later, Nina had asked Mack if these stories were true, if their father had had love affairs with other women. It was after Lainey was better and the scary part was over. Mack said he didn't know about before, but there were sometimes women now at their father's apartment.

"What are they like?" Nina was standing in the doorway to Mack's room. He was working at his desk, doing math. The sheets were full of numbers and funny symbols she couldn't believe she would ever understand. He looked up.

"What do you mean, what are they like? What a dumb question. You mean, are they like zebras, are they like gargoyles, are they . . . ?"

"I mean, are they like . . . Mums?"

"They're women." He shrugged. "They have tits and stuff like that. Is that like *Mums?* Is that what you want to know?"

Nina wasn't sure what she wanted to know. She

turned to go back to her room. "It doesn't matter," she said.

But it did matter. It did. Because Nina had always imagined that her parents might divorce each other. And then what she had dreamed of, she realized, was that Mother and Randall would move out, and the rest of them would live together in peace—a peace Nina would radiate in the house. The fighting would all be over, and *she* would take care of everyone. So there was some sense in which these *other women* had usurped her place as much as they'd usurped Lainey's; and Nina's heart was hardened against her father because of it. Since he had moved out, she felt, for the first time, a sense of being female, of being like her mother. Sometimes, traipsing around with oblivious Mary and Sarah in the days just after he'd gone, stuffing herself with sugary treats from the store, she would think of her mother weeping in her darkened room, and she would yearn for the right to that same extravagant grief.

But then their mother got better. Like someone recovering from a fever, she appeared downstairs, pale, thinner, in her bathrobe, and they began to have real meals again. Slowly she came back to them in other ways too. And when she was finally able to yell at them once more, to be indignant over their sloth, their self-satisfaction, their unkindness, when they could catch each other's eye and make faces about her, when she became someone they didn't have to feel pity for any longer, then they all relaxed and became again who they were too. Only Mack seemed unable to return to them in that old, reckless way. But maybe he was just getting older, Nina thought. Maybe it didn't really have anything to do with what had happened.

And what seemed especially strange was that now that their father was gone, there *was* a kind of peace and freedom in the house. This new mood was different from what Nina had imagined they could have if their mother had left. There was still deep disorder like a stain everywhere. Mother still stayed up half the night and slept at odd hours during the day. And there were no rules. Mack drifted in and out of the house, focused on his own increasingly mysterious world. The girls were free to construct their own universe in the attic bedroom, in the playhouse in the basement, outside with the other kids on the block. But they all seemed to want this freedom, this giddy chaos. They all consented to a mutual relinquishment of the standards that seemed to have worn their mother down so. They ate standing up in the kitchen or on the couch in front of the TV. They were allowed to take trays up to their rooms. In any corner of the house you could find bowls encrusted with stiff specks of what had been soup or cereal, plates flecked with crumbs, glasses with hardened circles of milk or juice in the bottom.

The dining room, the room Nina sat in now to practice, was the worst. They almost never used it for meals anymore. Instead the table was permanently laden with homework or projects: paper dolls, Mack's cartoons, posters for school events, Lainey's correspondence about autism and retardation. The nights before Retta came, Lainey would sweep down on the children, would rush through the rest of the house, picking things up. But the dining room, with its welter of ongoing activities, its piles of everyone's belongings, its finger-smudged wallpaper, was impossible. Even Retta said so. She vacuumed it, twice a year she washed the windows, but otherwise she said she wouldn't touch it with a ten-foot pole. Even now Nina's fingertips were slightly blackened from the gummed dust that had accumulated on the piano keys.

They were embarrassed by the mess in front of others—a friend of Mary's had wrinkled her nose as she came in the door and said, "Your house *smells* funny"—but the truth was, Lainey and the children loved this disorder. There was an element in it of defiance, of naughtiness. Once Nina had watched Mack pick up his plate as he started to leave the living room, then stop and deliberately set it down again. And it stayed there until the night before Retta came.

About six months after their father moved out, Lainey hired a graduate student to help with Randall—she said she was too old to be toileting a fifteen-year-old boy—and now that Bob got Randall up and off to his ride in the morning, she often slept through breakfast. This meant that she had more energy for them. She sat with them in the evenings, helping with homework, reading, fixing snacks. Sometimes she played Ping-Pong in the basement with them, or Monopoly. She frequently won at Monopoly, and there was a hard glee in her voice that seemed out of character as she announced her exorbitant rents. Her properties were littered with hotels and houses. And she had a strange patter she kept up, remembered insults and threats from games she'd played in childhood with her older brothers. "Okay, short-pants," she'd say to her daughters. "Prepare to meet your Maker." Sarah often got teary and refused to play with her.

Liddie was the only one who objected to this new regime. She came home from summer school, dropped both bags at the door to the living room, and announced, "My God, this place is a wreck."

A dull red burned up from their mother's neck. "Retta's coming tomorrow," she said quickly, apologetically.

"Not a moment too soon," Liddie said.

*   *   *

It was in hope of hearing more about her older sister that Nina had started to listen to Retta and her mother. They had been talking about Liddie, Liddie and her new boyfriend, earlier, when Nina was fixing herself a snack. She'd stood in the pantry, staring into the refrigerator, pretending to choose, and heard Lainey say, "She's been home—what?—a week? ten days? Where'd she find him so quick? That's what I'd like to know. I barely had a minute to talk to her, and now she's off, and Lord knows what they're up to."

Retta said, "Wasn't her findin' him. She be puttin' it out, like a smell she got. That's what happens, at that age. Don't tell me you can't remember."

"But I don't even know his last name," Lainey said. " 'This is Gregory.' Gregory what? Gregory who?"

Nina reached in for anything, an orange.

"His *last name*," Retta said, and laughed, a spike of contemptuous sound.

Lainey laughed too, just for a minute. "Still," she said then. "I worry about her."

"Go ahead," Retta answered. "All you want."

Nina came into the kitchen from the pantry and saw her mother arch her dark brows at Retta to be quiet about this.

Retta made a face. "Who you kiddin?" she said, and grinned at Nina.

Now Nina started the *Moonlight* Sonata again. She was thinking of Liddie. She had waked in the night because she'd heard something funny outside. Whispers, voices. She lay still. Mary's asthmatic breathing whirred from across the narrow space between their beds. Then Nina heard another sound, a deep gurgling from the open window, like the motion of slow water, but human. She sat up in bed. When Mary didn't stir, she folded the covers back and went to the window. Below her she could see the mulberry

arched dark and thick over the yard. Partly underneath its branches was the Frawleys' garage. And on
the roof where they climbed to hide sometimes when
they played Sardines, there were two bodies tangled
up, white against its tar-paper top through the leaves.
Nina could see the man's butt moving slowly back and
forth, his flesh almost iridescent. His legs must have
been in pants still, they disappeared below the thigh
and became roof, leaves. Under him was Liddie; Nina
could tell by her pale hair and light skirt. They were
fanned out around her. She made a shape like the
angel print you left in snow. Her wide-flung legs bicy-
cled slowly in the air, stopping, backing up, racing
again. And somehow, although she was the one who
was pinned down, the one who looked cleft by the
knife shape that must have been Gregory, it was she
who was swimming free, whose movements seemed
wild and glad through the trembling black mulberry
leaves. Nina's hand slid between her thighs, pushed
the hard welted seam of her cotton pajamas into her
crotch as she watched.

She sat still on the window seat a long time. She
sat until they lay quiet side by side, until they separated, until they climbed down from the roof. Until
she heard the faint sounds of Liddie below on the second floor, the hum of water in the buried pipes as she
washed herself.

When she woke this morning, Nina wasn't sure
it had happened; it seemed so much like a dream she
might have had. But when she put her pajamas in the
dirty-clothes closet, there was Liddie's pale blue skirt,
crumpled in a heap. Nina lifted it up and looked at
it. Across the back were smeared reddish stains, the
blood of the mulberries Liddie had been lying on.

"Has it been half an hour, Neens?" her mother
called.

"How should I know? You were supposed to keep track."

Her mother appeared in the doorway. "Well, we'd better say so," she said. "It's time to get going anyway."

Nina stopped playing. She caught the upright swinging arm of the metronome and hooked it under its catch. As she turned on the seat, she said, "I want to change, though, Mums." They would drive right past Steinway's, where the high school kids sat in booths drinking cherry Cokes and staring out at everyone who passed.

Exasperation pinched Lainey's face. "Why? You look perfectly all right. This is just a piano lesson, after all. Look at me." And she gestured down at herself, at her canvas skirt, her sandals, her old shirt.

Nina stared at her. "So what?" she said.

Her mother looked at her a moment, seeming to measure something. Then she relented; Nina could see it in her face a second before she spoke. "All right. *Hurry,* though," and she went back into the kitchen to smoke a last cigarette with Retta.

Upstairs, in spite of the heat of the day, Nina put on a mint-green angora cardigan she'd bought with her allowance, put it on backward, and laboriously buttoned it down the back. In the second-floor bathroom she leaned toward the mirror and whitened her lips with a color called Pale Flesh. Then she drew a line in black on her upper eyelids, making a little tail, just as Liddie had taught her, at the outer corner of each eye.

When she came into the kitchen, her mother looked at her, then leaned forward and stubbed out her cigarette. She was frowning. Nina's stomach tightened.

"Lookin good," Retta said quickly, as though to stop Nina's mother before she could start.

Inner heat pushed blood into Nina's cheeks. "Thanks," she said, without being able to meet Retta's eyes.

Her mother turned away quickly and said nothing.

9

THE benches were warm under Lainey's legs, the worn, dry wood felt soft. She sat on the top row and leaned back onto the iron pipe that formed the frame for the stands. It was cool against her neck. Mary sat down next to her, unexpectedly close, and Lainey was conscious of a pleased rush of affection that released her from the irritation she'd been feeling for her daughter. She had arranged to have the afternoon off—Bob, the student she had hired to take care of Randall, was going to take him for a long walk after school—and she had planned to come to Mack's baseball game alone. At the last minute, though, Mary begged to come with her, and Lainey relented. But Mary had taken so long to get ready that they'd missed several innings.

Mack's team was behind three to two, one of the kids standing around had told them before they climbed to their seats. Now they watched together as the first batter from Mack's team, then the second, came up, friends of Mack's who just this year had started looking like men instead of tall boys. But Lainey had trouble concentrating on the game. She was still too aware of the teenagers around her, listening to their conversations with a kind of abstract and benevolent distance. "What it is with me," she heard a girl standing behind her say, "is that they have to be bigger than I am, and there's only three boys in the tenth grade who are. So naturally I'm interested in juniors or seniors." Mary had turned around to watch this girl as she spoke. When she swung back, she looked over at Lainey.

"*Mother,*" she said.

"What?"

Mary said nothing, but her pretty face was stern. She was frowning downward.

"What is it?" Lainey asked. She followed Mary's eyes to her own lap, to where she had rucked her skirt up between her legs to feel the sun on her thighs. She was about to dismiss Mary's fussiness, but then she looked at her daughter's long legs, flat as planks in jeans, and she realized how immense, how grotesque, her own wide thighs must seem to Mary—white, and where they pushed against the hot bench, slightly stippled from within. Lainey's mother, neat and trim, had never offered her the possibility of disgust at her sexuality; but in the presence of that delicate woman, Lainey had sometimes felt some of Mary's revulsion at her own size, her own fleshiness—like an overlarge set of clothes she was forced to wear until she grew into it. Now, with a strange sense of pity for her daughter, she pulled the skirt back down over her knees.

A third and then a fourth batter had come up, and there were two men on base. Suddenly Lainey saw something familiar in the player standing near home plate, a tall slender man with big-boned shoulders. "Oh, here's Mack, Mary," Lainey cried.

"Shh, *Mom,*" Mary said, though when Lainey spoke she looked over to where Mack stood just outside the batter's box, tapping his cleats with the bat. He seemed oblivious of the crowd, of them.

"All *right*, Macklin," Lainey yelled. He didn't look up.

Mary grinned into the air, embarrassed.

Mack took his stance, his legs bent, his arms taut as he held the bat high over his right shoulder, twirling it in smaller and smaller circles. He had the perfect body for baseball, Lainey thought. Lean, but shapely and muscled. He looked so competent physically, in a way Lainey had never felt herself to be. His bat stilled as the pitch came in. Then it dropped. A ball. Mack relaxed, stood up, stepped out of the batter's box.

He was facing the stands now, and for a moment his eyes met hers. A slight smile flickered over his face. To Lainey, for that second, he was David. She was breathless and bent her head. When she looked up, he was back in the batter's box, tensed again. The uniform showed his long calves, his muscled buttocks, to advantage. How strange it was, Lainey thought, that there were so many uniforms for men, so many ways for them to be anonymously handsome, glamorously part of something: some team, the army, the navy. Even medicine: those gods in white coats. There was a point floating at the edge of expression, some observation about this aspect of men's lives, that she wanted to make, to make to Mary. She touched the girl's shoulder and Mary leaned toward her. "Isn't it interesting, honey," she began, "how wonderful men look—" But then Mack uncoiled violently with a sharp crack, the ball sprang straight up, the catcher rose in a quick spiral, throwing off his mask, dancing, looking skyward.

"Oh, goddammit! Goddammit!" Mary cried. She was half standing. "He's got it." And the ball dropped in a plumb line into the catcher's fat glove.

Mack flung the bat down in disgust. They watched him walk back to U-High's bench, kicking at the ground.

"Wonder if he's doing okay today," Lainey said.

Below her, a girl with preposterously teased hair, a lacquered bubble on her head, looked back. "He had a hit. A double, I think."

The boy next to her, without turning, said, "Yeah, a double, and he walked."

"Thanks," Lainey said.

Through the next half inning, Mary sat restlessly. "I hate it when the other team's up," she said to Lainey. "You just don't know anyone. It's so goddamn boring."

"I wish you wouldn't swear so much, Maresy," Lainey said softly.

There was a pinched silence. "Everyone else does it," Mary said finally.

Lainey made her voice light. "Why on earth would I want you to be like everyone else?"

Mary had no answer, but the line of her shoulders was sullen. She turned her body slightly away from Lainey. After a moment she got up. "I'm going to walk around," she said. She stepped smoothly off the edge of the stands, dropping the four feet or so to the ground. She flicked her ironed hair once and walked away.

Between batters, Lainey watched Mary moving at the edges of the groups of older kids, trying to look indifferent. Sometimes someone spoke to her; probably someone who knew Mack, Lainey thought. And then her face seemed convulsed by eagerness; color rose to it as she struggled to seem older, to be cool. How pretty she was, Lainey thought, watching her from this distance. All three little girls, really. Seemingly untroubled, sunny, doing well in school. The pitchers/pictures of health. Though part of David's nickname for them was, of course, an accusation against her—that she'd had them to prove that Randall wasn't her fault, that she could make normal babies. And she knew that was at least to some degree true. Although Nina, Nina had really been an accident. She'd had the diaphragm in, but as soon as she woke in the morning and felt a kind of dull ache inside her, she knew it had got turned, it was resting the wrong way in her, and that there might be problems.

But with Mary and Sarah she'd consciously decided to take the risk. She had thought, each of those times, that it didn't seem worth it to stop David in order to put the diaphragm in, when they hardly ever made love at all anymore. And each time, she couldn't help hoping that somehow these bright, beautiful, normal babies would mend the rent in their marriage that had begun with Randall. But they hadn't, of course. She'd been stupid to think they might. Each of them had, in fact, made it worse.

Now she was remembering one night when Sarah was still quite small, when she'd asked David, then begged him, to make love to her. He'd heaved himself up from bed as soon as it was clear she would persist, as though to get out of the range of her touch. He'd turned on the bureau lamp and found a cigarette. While he smoked, he quietly, rationally explained his position to her, as though she were one of the children asking for an exception to some rule that he could not allow. He simply couldn't feel desire for her now, he said. He thought it better not to pretend. Even getting into bed with her, lying beside her, made him feel bruised. Lainey had sat up in bed while he talked. Though she tried not to, she'd begun to weep, and her face, because she wouldn't give herself over to it, grew rubbery and red and ugly: she could see herself in the bureau mirror.

"At this point I associate it with Randall," he said. "And with your getting pregnant over and over again." He said perhaps it would get better in time. He hoped so. But he couldn't help feeling exploited sexually, tricked. How was it possible to feel any real desire under these circumstances?

She had yelled back, finally—anything to stop that calm voice!—that if he hadn't blamed her for Randall in the first place, maybe she wouldn't have felt so desperate, maybe she wouldn't have needed to have all the children.

There was a long silence in the room then. David had leaned forward to put the cigarette out, and his face was caught suddenly in the light above the open top of the lampshade. Harsh grooves leapt onto it, made him grotesque, then were erased as he leaned back into the shadows. "Well, there we have it," he said. His voice was hoarse and fatigued. "The battle lines, rather neatly drawn."

When Mack's team came up again, Lainey tried to focus her attention on the game. She lighted a cigarette and hunched forward. She cheered with the kids for each batter, and especially loudly for Bobby Soletski, a friend of Mack's. He was smaller than the other boys and homely, with a big nose that had grown much faster than the rest of his face. Lainey felt a special fondness for him. It was no use, though. Soletski struck out, and the inning ended with two men left on.

When Latin was up, Lainey lost interest again. It was boring, just as Mary had said. Lainey found herself instead watching the kids standing around on the packed dirt and scrubby grass near the bleachers. They were talking, punching each other, wrestling. This was how the boys touched the girls, via the artful half nelson, the Indian grip on the wrist. Occasionally they watched the events on the field, and the cries of enthusiasm or encouragement alternated with the pained, indignant shrieks of that other conversation.

Lainey felt a pleasant sense of her own invisibility to them, her absence as a sexual person generally. She'd let herself gain weight since David left; she'd stopped wearing makeup. She was amazed at how quickly and easily she'd given up the idea of herself as possibly attractive. There were old women on their street, and she'd found herself noticing their eccentricities, their solitary rituals, like promised pleasures. One of these women, Mrs. Dodge, had stopped her recently as she lugged a bag of groceries from the back of the car, and after the briefest pleasantries had said abruptly, "You've put on some weight, haven't you, dear?"

Lainey had smiled ruefully. "Oh, Mrs. Dodge, of course you're right."

"Oh, no, my dear! I think it looks marvelous on you. Just marvelous. It makes you look quite jolly." And she'd teetered off, a lingering smile on her face, as though she'd been welcoming Lainey into some kind of club.

Jolly, Lainey thought now, and she had to stop herself from laughing out loud at the memory of it.

Suddenly Lainey was aware that Mack was in the on-deck circle again, swinging at the air over and over. She'd been dreaming, she'd missed the beginning of this half of the inning. She leaned forward, determined to concentrate on the game again. "Come on, U-High," she cried, and clapped. She surveyed the bases. Empty. No one on.

The kid ahead of Mack hit a hard ground ball, but their shortstop was right there, flicked it over to first base neatly, and he was out.

"How many outs is that?" she asked down to the bubble-headed girl.

The girl turned. "One," she said, frowning at Lainey.

Now Mack walked over to the batter's box, performed four or five of those batter's tics, as Lainey thought of them—tapping his cleats, digging into the dirt with a sideways shimmy of his hips and legs—and then he placed himself. He fouled the first pitch down the first-base line. The next two pitches were outside, one of them clearly a ball even to Lainey's uncritical eye. But the fourth pitch seemed to rise directly toward the bat as he pulled it around. There was a sharp retort, and the ball shot straight and level between the first and second basemen. The right fielder threw it back in. Mack held, hopping, on first.

Lainey was standing with the screaming kids, clapping and yelling, glad Mary wasn't next to her to scold about her behavior. Slowly they all quieted and sat again. Lainey leaned forward, ready to watch the game more attentively.

"You must be Mack's mother," the man said. He had swung himself up on the bench next to her. Now he sat down.

"How could you tell?" she said, and laughed.

"I'm one of his teachers. Mr. Skelly. History."

Lainey looked at him. She realized she had seen him standing around with the kids behind the stands and thought he was one of them, though his neatness should have been a giveaway. And up close now, she saw that he had some gray in his hair and, smiling at her, a skein of wrinkles around his eyes. He was perhaps only seven or eight years younger than she was, one of those small, trim men that age is kind to.

"Oh, he likes you," she offered. This was true. Mack had said he was "hip," which had made the girls laugh.

Mr. Skelly smiled. "And I like him. Though he makes me angry sometimes."

He was still smiling, so she didn't foresee any danger. "Why so?" she asked. She'd turned back to the game. She didn't know this kid, the one standing, swinging. Mack had taken a big lead off first.

"Well, he won't really *work*. In class, I mean. It's all private with Mack. In class you'd never know he'd even done his homework. It's as though he doesn't want to separate himself out or make himself remarkable in any way. I've actually given up calling on him. And that's a real shame. He's a bright kid, you know.''

"I do know. I'm not his mother for nothing.'' She watched the next kid swing, miss. Mack moved back to the bag.

Mr. Skelly started again. "At first I thought maybe he lacked confidence, he was afraid to try—you know? But you just have to read a paper or two of his to know that's not it. And then look at him out here.'' He gestured.

Lainey made no response.

"Is there anything going on at home that might explain it?''

She looked at him sharply. He was frowning; his eyes were kind. The amateur shrink. "Yes and no,'' she said.

"What do you mean?''

The next kid swung, hit a hard single into left field, and Mack scampered to second. When Lainey sat down again, she turned to the teacher. "Well, the thing about home is, there's life at home. I don't want to start in, or you might think I was trying out for 'Queen for a Day.' '' She tried a charming bright smile, one that always made Bob DeGroot, the student she'd hired for Randall, beam back at her. "It's just life, that's all. And life is sometimes not easy. Don't you agree?''

"Well, sure, I understand that.'' Mr. Skelly's voice was reluctant. He wasn't charmed.

"You should, teaching history. I mean, that's history's first lesson, isn't it?'' She made her voice an announcer's, deep and loud: *"Life can't be cured.''* He looked startled. "Or that's what I learned from history,'' she said apologetically, in her own voice. "From my own history, and then also what I've read in books.'' She smiled again, nervously this time. She wished he would go away. She realized abruptly that

she *had* been worried about Mack—a kind of abstracted withdrawal in him sometimes; his bitterness
toward David; his sudden emotionality, occasionally—and that she'd consoled herself with his accomplishments, his increased sweetness to her and the
girls, when perhaps she should have probed deeper.
Cared more. "I'm sorry, Mr. Scully," she said.

"It's Skelly."

"Oh. Sorry. Again." She could feel the stupid
smile cracking her face. "But my point simply is, I
think, that being troubled, or a little neurotic anyway,
is kind of what comes of being alive. Isn't it?"

Mr. Skelly frowned.

She shrugged. "I just mean, we're all a little
crazy." She watched the game, unseeing, for a moment, then turned to Mr. Skelly again. "I think what
I'm saying is just that you don't need to worry about
Mack. Mack is strong and healthy, and he'll be okay."
Then, because she thought she might have been rude
to Mr. Skelly, because she wasn't sure Mack would be
okay, she started again. "You know, it all just de-
pends—doesn't it?—on how you think about childhood, childhood and adolescence. And I just feel that
it's a big mistake to try to separate it from things that
are . . . troubling. Or difficult."

"Well, but surely, some separation . . ."

The noise suddenly rose around her. She looked
up and saw Mack slide into third. Safe. Safe. She
smiled. When it was quiet again, she turned once
more to Mr. Skelly. "Look, don't you think it's an in-
vention of ours, this idea of childhood innocence? Of
sheltering kids and giving them this period of not having to know anything about life? Kids know anyway.
They see more than we think they do."

Lainey was aware that a couple of the kids below
her had turned around and were watching her. She
realized she'd been talking too loudly again. Mr.

Skelly had looked quickly at them, too, and then back at her.

She made her voice softer. "In my humble opinion," she said. She shook her head. "I don't know. I think what I feel is actually that they should know all along that life is tough. Why not? They're young, they can be generous, they can understand it. Or stand it anyhow." She shrugged and tried to smile once more.

"I see," he said, and nodded. She knew he was sorry he'd got her going, that he'd leave now as soon as he could.

"Anyway," she said. "Yes, there's lots going on at home. Always will be. But that's just the luck of the draw, isn't it? I mean, none of us, surely, would *volunteer* for life's little lessons, would we? And whether that explains anything anyway, whether you can say that causes anything in Mack, I'm not sure. . . ."

There was a sudden shift in the stands, everyone moving at once, and with it, from several places, cries: "Heads up!" "Heads up!" Mr. Skelly's hand lifted quickly. Lainey's head swung, she was confused, the faces turned to her, and then her leg flashed with burning pain, she heard the dull *whump!*, she cried out. Mr. Skelly bent toward her. She had doubled over the stab in her thigh, was gripping it. They were all talking at once: *Mack's mother, Eberhardt's mother.* Then there was a silence, waiting. She kept her eyes shut, grunting, a few seconds more, until she could get control of the pain. Then she opened them and looked around at the grave, questioning faces. "It's all right," she said. "I'll be okay." Surprised tears had sprung to her eyes. She sat up slowly, looked at the flesh of her thigh, reddening in an oval. Everyone started talking again; there was nervous laughter.

Then Mack's coach was there standing behind Mr. Skelly. He stepped across him and leaned over her. He was a heavy man, paunchy, with a lined, kind face. "Did it hit you?" he asked. She nodded.

"Your leg?" he asked, and sat next to her. He smelled of pipe, he smelled comforting.

"Yes," she said. "It's okay, though. I think."

He leaned over, grabbed her leg with both hands. It was a thing to him, an injury only. He held it as impersonally as a doctor might, her wide bare thigh which had bothered Mary so. He looked at it clinically. Then he turned and shouted something to the bench. One of the boys in uniform came running over, held up an ice pack. The coach took it and set it firmly on Lainey's leg. "Here you go," he said. "Now, you keep this on it." He was patting the ice pack, and his voice was reassuring and professional. "This is just the ticket. You take this home with you, okay? You keep this on till you go to bed, I promise you it'll keep the swelling down."

And Lainey, a trusting patient, felt only grateful for his wisdom. She smiled obediently back. She thanked him. She said yes. Yes, she would.

Before dinner, Lainey changed into a muumuu which had doubled as a bathrobe since she'd gotten heavier. She used the ice pack as an excuse to sit at the kitchen table and boss the children around. But they were cooperative and cheerful. Nina set the table, Mary and Sarah cleared. Mack loaded the dishwasher.

Retta had left chicken salad and rolls she'd baked that morning. Randall was hungry after his long walk with Bob, and he ate without fuss and toileted himself successfully after the meal. Everyone was so relaxed that Lainey thought the children must feel, as she did, the sense of blessing that came from Randall's sunny moods, his cooperation, what might even be his happiness.

After dinner, everyone scattered. Mack called

back the time he could be expected home, but Lainey barely listened. She was sitting with Randall in the swing on the front porch, waiting for Bob to return from the dining hall at the university and put him to bed. Randall liked the motion; he could be happy for hours out here. Lainey began to sing him a song about what he'd done that day, to the tune of "Danny Boy."

Oh, Randall boy, you went to school with Mikey.
When Mikey came, you jumped into his bus.
He drove you there, with Monica and dah dah Len.
You played with sand, with water, and with paints.

He crooned along, smiling at the air. Lainey watched him. He looked so remarkably like Mack to her—the same dark hair, the same fine, almost delicate features. Like Mack, but also like a two-year-old, uncomplicated, simple. His face was open now in pleasure, open in a way Mack's hadn't been in years, and for a moment she felt overwhelmingly the pull of her response to the sweetness in his nature. She stopped swinging in this stunned pulse of love, and Randall rocked his body forward, grunting, to get the motion going again.

Lainey invented another verse to the song, and then she sang the chorus without invented words, just changing the name. She remembered how Liddie's voice had floated down from upstairs when she was singing this in high school, pure and clear as a violin. Lainey had had a second bourbon by now; she felt the tears rise at the memory. *The Lainer's getting drunk,* she thought. Soupy, sappy. She set her glass down under the swing.

When Bob turned into the square and approached through the twilight, she stopped the swing and pointed him out to Randall. But Randall was unresponsive. He whimpered and jerked the swing forward with his body again, so she went back to swinging and watched Bob's approach. His rocking, graceless stride was so unlike any of her own children's that she felt a moment's mean pride in their collective beauty, their grace, as though she were in some sense responsible for it. She called out to Bob at the halfway point, and he called back to her and then to Randall, whose face stayed blank and enraptured with motion.

Bob came up the stairs. He stood, holding the railing and watching Randall's happy, empty face tipped up at him.

"He doesn't want to look at me," Bob said.

"No," Lainey answered. "He likes to swing too much."

Bob leaned against the post. "I meant to ask you how Mack's game went."

"They won, thank the Lord. But even more to the point, Mack had a good one. He can be so surly if he does badly, I'm always grateful for a good performance." She swung Randall in silence for a moment. Then she asked, "Were you like that?"

"I wasn't like anything. I was awful at sports. Terrible."

She nodded. "Me too. The only physical test I ever passed well was labor. I was good at having babies."

She watched him blush. He had a crush on her; Lainey knew it. She even played to his feelings a bit, saving her worst tirades for moments when he was out of the house. It was harmless enough, she thought. And after all, he—and of course Retta too—had become, in some measure, most of Lainey's social world. She no longer fit at parties, a single person, and she felt the coolness of her friends in her presence. They didn't know what to make of her life now, her conspicuous, awkward aloneness. She was, she supposed, a kind of freak in some ways. And she knew that she'd been difficult and hysterical those first few months, scary to herself and the children and probably everyone else too, with her fury at David, her drinking, her erratic rage.

Now she was embarrassed for Bob, though, and glad when he recovered himself, when he started recounting the details of his afternoon with Randall. He kept calling Randall "the big fella": "The big fella got his own shoes on." "The big fella and I walked along the lake." As he did each day, he chronicled every little achievement of Randall's as though it signaled the beginning of the end of his illness, as though each were a developmental milestone.

Lainey had to force herself to listen. She thought abruptly of how she must have sounded sometimes to David when he got home at the end of a day. Now she was the one who had to consciously hold herself back from saying to Bob, "Don't, don't tell me this stuff. I've seen everything he can do."

But she knew she should be grateful for his involvement with her son. And she was, truly she was. Though she thought Bob did too much for Randall. It was her policy, for instance, when he fussed helplessly at the table, to put his spoon in his hand and go through the motion once or twice, then leave him on his own; or when he pushed her hand to make her do something for him, to return the gesture, to lift his hand to the refrigerator door and curl her fingers outside it on the handle until he gripped it himself. But Bob would feed Randall, or open the door for him. So far, Lainey hadn't said anything. She kept hoping that Bob himself would see that it didn't help. Then she wouldn't have to correct him, which would be painful for them both.

Of course, she reminded herself, nothing she did really helped, either; nothing changed, nothing developed. It wasn't as though she'd even really "taught" Randall to open the refrigerator. But she'd taught him, at any rate, that she wouldn't do it for him. And perhaps that was something. Now she watched as Bob took Randall's hand and led him into the house. Randall was taller than he was. As they mounted the stairs inside, she could hear the kindness and energy in Bob's voice talking about the tub, about the warm water, about the bubbles Randall could have.

After they'd gone in, Lainey sat alone on the swing. The children weren't in the square tonight, but she could hear their voices down the block, calling for each other, arguing across some distance. She wanted another drink, but she knew she'd better pace herself. If nothing else, Bob's presence in the house had made her aware that she went to bed drunk too many nights, and she'd been trying lately to stay in control of that. From inside the house she could hear the tumble of Randall's bathwater. There was a motion on the porch next door. Lainey looked over. Mrs. Hayakawa was draping a small rug over the railing. She stood looking up for a moment at where the sky was still light above the darkening square, then went inside without seeing Lainey.

Lainey swung herself slowly, the ice pack burning on her leg, and watched the darkness fall.

Then Mary's voice was audible, and the girls rounded the corner into the square and straggled toward her. Mary was complaining about some unfairness on Nina's part. She seemed like a small child again. When they came up the stairs, Lainey greeted them. They were startled.

"Mummy!" Sarah said. "We didn't see you. It's like you were hiding in the dark."

Nina and Mary went into the house, still arguing, but Sarah came and sat next to Lainey. She began an account of her day, something she often did. She was still comfortable being Lainey's little girl. While she talked, she bounced the swing energetically.

Then Bob called down that Randall was ready to say good night. Lainey and Sarah came in, shutting the front door behind themselves. Lainey slowly climbed the stairs. At the top, she stood for a moment in front of the doorway to David's study, Bob's room now. "Shall I shut the door?" she asked. The girls were on the first floor. They had turned on the sound track to *My Fair Lady*. "It's awfully loud if you're trying to work."

He had looked up from the table he was sitting at. "Yes, thanks," he said, and smiled his adoring smile at her.

Lainey went to Randall's room. He was in bed, completely covered with his worn red blanket. The satin binding had frayed to gleaming tatters around its edge. He was crooning to himself. Lainey slid under the covers beside him. His face was barely visible in the pinkish twilight under here. Both of his hands were at his crotch.

Lainey lay perfectly still next to him. At one time she had talked to him under his blanket. But sometime after he'd started puberty he cried out when she had begun talking, and then, when she didn't stop right away, his face convulsed, he leaned forward and bit her on the shoulder, breaking the skin. Now he tolerated her presence as long as she didn't speak.

He breathed with his mouth open. His breath fell moist on Lainey's face under the tented covers. It smelled sweetish and minty. What would Freud say to this? she wondered. Mom as bedmate. Encouraging Oedipal feelings. Sick. But what was the difference with Randall? If he'd ever had one Oedipal feeling about her, she'd have wept for joy. But Randall lived safe from neurosis. He'd escaped Freud. Sometimes she found herself wishing, even hoping, that he'd connect his masturbating under the covers to her presence, that he'd try to touch her or look at her. But those impulses came on him autistically too. Once she'd found him alone in the backyard on a raw March day with his pants around his knees, yanking at himself and looking cold and scared. And several times, one of the girls had yelled, "He's doing it again, Mom," and she'd found him with that same dazed look, flailing away at the upright arm of his penis in the living room or the front hall, or wherever the feeling had come on him. Then she would lead him gently upstairs to privacy. Sometimes, if he resisted, she went up and brought his blanket down to him, wrapped it around him like a cloak. It calmed him down, soothed him, told him where she was taking him, and he consented, then, to go.

After five or ten minutes, Lainey kissed Randall's cheek and slid out from under the covers. Carefully she tucked his blanket back in. The room was dark, but in the hall light you could see where the walls were shredded, the paper peeled down to various depths in different places. She lowered the two crumpled shades in case he was still sleeping when the sun came up. In the doorway she looked back. His hands were working under the bedcover; it trembled and jumped. She looked away. His shelf of strange uninviting toys stood, the only object in the room besides the mattress, the bureau. Bob had arranged them carefully, in rows, as he did every night. She remembered, abruptly, the way his face had looked when she showed him Randall's room, the active revulsion in it. He, who hadn't blanched when he saw Randall, who'd moved comfortably through the mess downstairs, was as silent and shocked when she showed him this wrecked room as if she were revealing instruments of torture.

"I think you'll understand the ways his room

makes sense after you've worked with him a little,"
Lainey had said.

"Yes, of course," Bob said, but his tone had insisted *never*.

Lainey shut Randall's door and locked it.

She went downstairs, past the racket the girls
were making and into the kitchen. Her glass had been
washed and set in the rack, pristine, a chastisement
to her. Nina, probably. She crossed to the pantry for
another glass and some ice, ran a little water into it,
and then poured bourbon in until it was the honey
color she liked.

From the drawer under the sink she pulled out
a dented pot and its lid, then turned the fire on under
it. She fetched oil from the cupboard and a jar of popping corn. The kernels hit the pan like rain on a copper roof.

Sometimes Lainey went for several days fixing
meals for the children—meals bloody with meat, wet
with vegetables—but herself nibbling, eating only a
little canned soup in addition to her starchy pleasures: nuts, crackers, popcorn. Finally she'd wake one
morning and feel dizzy. She'd take extra iron pills, left
over from when Nina was anemic. She'd eat only eggs
and salads for a few days.

A minute after the popping began, Sarah appeared in the doorway. "We want some too, Mama.
Double batch!"

"Say please, at least," Lainey yelled, but she was
gone.

Lainey pulled out the big yellow bread bowl and
poured the first batch into it. Then she began another,
bigger one. When both were done, she cradled the
big bowl against her body and picked up her bourbon
with the other hand. The girls didn't notice her as she
went by. They'd lugged the hall mirror into the living
room and had it propped in front of the fireplace.

They stood in a row in front of it, practicing gestures they'd worked out to the song "Get Me to the Church on Time." Lainey grabbed her ice pack and went silently up the stairs. When she reached the second landing, she shouted, "I've got the popcorn up here if anybody wants it."

Sarah squealed and came out of the living room, but Mary called her back. "No, dummy. We've got to finish if you want to do this with us."

Then Nina stepped to the foot of the stairs and shouted in a businesslike way, "We'll be up in a few minutes, Ma."

"Fine," Lainey said. "It's all the same to me." She padded barefoot down the hall to her room. In bed, she settled back comfortably and began to read.

But when they burst in ten minutes or so later, she gladly set her book down and made room for them on the bed. Nina sat at the foot, no closer, facing Lainey, and insisted that handfuls be passed to her. But Sarah snuggled against her mother, and Mary perched cross-legged by her hip. Inspired by the song, they were talking about whether Liddie would marry Gregory. He had impressed the two little girls by walking on his hands across the square the summer before.

"I hope she does," Sarah said. "He's cruel."

"It's *cool*, stupid," Mary said. "She thought it was *cruel*," she reported to Nina contemptuously, as though Nina hadn't heard.

"What are we talking about here?" Lainey said. "Liddie barely knows this man. Besides, none of you girls should get married till you're thirty anyway. That's going to be the rule in this house. No weddings till you're almost middle-aged. Liddie especially, if she wants to do something with that voice. As well she might."

"But you weren't thirty, Ma," Sarah said.

Lainey took another handful and sighed. "You see exactly where marrying young got me. Here I sit, a fat elderly lady with so many kids she doesn't know what to do. Some days I barely get out of bed, as you may have noticed. A great slug of a woman. I was ruined by"—she raised her glass—"booze and kids and too much early passion. And your father. Who's now off pretending to be thirty again himself."

Nina was looking at her, and their eyes met. Nina didn't even smile. Lainey could make the other girls giggle and squirm when she talked like this. Their memories were short. They forgot how it had been after David left—Lainey's rage, the darkened room. But Nina's gaze was steady and knowing, her dark eyes sober.

Lainey looked at Sarah. "No. I say no. Forget it, you girls. Don't saddle yourself with just one. Play the field! I'm sure it'll be years before Liddie marries anyone."

"Daddy's a lot older than thirty," Sarah said.

"You're not kidding," Lainey answered.

"He's even got gray hairs."

"That's not the half of it, dearie. But I say, if he can get away with it, let him. If I could, I would."

"I think Liddie *will* marry Gregory," Nina said suddenly. Her voice was challenging, and she watched Lainey.

"Well, what makes you think that, Neen?"

"I think she loves him."

"Oh, love," Lainey said in a weary voice. "Sure, she may love him. But she'll love others too. Love's not so hard to find. And Liddie can find it even where it isn't. A dowser for love is Lid."

"But I think she specially loves him." Nina's voice was insistent.

Lainey stopped and looked hard at her. "What makes you say so, honey?"

Nina shrugged. She looked uncomfortable and confused. "I don't know," she said. "I just think so."

"Well, she could. She may," Lainey said. "It's just I've seen our Liddie at work before and I recognize certain elements of her style. But of course, you could be right, Neen."

Suddenly Nina got up.

"Don't go, honeybunch. You're probably right. Really. I don't mean to sound so . . . so callous. That was horrid. It really was. I offer you my apology."

Nina stopped at the door. "I'm just getting my camera."

"What?"

"I'm getting my new camera. I can't understand anything in the instructions. I want you to look at it."

"Oh, good Lord, I can't work a camera."

"But you can figure out the instructions, maybe," Nina yelled back.

"Well, bring me a towel, then," Lainey shouted. "I can't touch it with these butter fingers."

They sat in silence a minute, eating.

"Is that where that word comes from, Ma?" Mary asked.

"What word, sweetie?"

"Butterfingers. When you can't catch stuff, you know? You're . . . spassy or something? Does it mean your fingers are slippery as butter?"

"Honey, don't say *spassy*. What an awful word."

"Well, but you know what I mean," Mary said.

"Hmm. Yes, I bet that is where it comes from, actually. Only this time it's absolutely, literally true."

Nina came back, carrying the camera, a booklet of instructions, and a bath towel.

Lainey wiped her hands on the towel. David had recently given Nina the camera, a fancy new one. Nina had been taking pictures for about a year, getting better and better. This summer she was going to stay home and take a course in photography at the Art Institute. This was because she hadn't wanted to go to camp with the little girls. She'd insisted on something different for herself this year. "I'm too old for that, Mother," she said. "I can't go on doing exactly what Sarah and Mary are doing forever."

Now Lainey waggled her fingers at Nina, and Nina handed her the booklet.

Nina stepped back, stood against the bureau, and looked at them, at the room, through the viewer. Her head swung with the camera.

Lainey put the booklet down and watched Nina. After a moment she said, "Look at Nina, making us get little and unimportant in her magic lens."

Nina grinned behind the camera. "It's true. You're shrimps. A million miles away."

"Well, come back here, petunia, and show me what you don't get," Lainey said.

Nina came over and sat on the edge of the bed. She and Lainey started going through the diagrams in the booklet, locating knobs.

Mary and Sarah had begun to talk to each other about the camp, wondering what the other girls would be like, who they'd get for counselors, whether they'd be put together. Lainey looked up and reminded them that they were going the next day for the shots the camp required.

"Shots again?" Sarah cried. "We had them last year."

"Not all of them," Lainey answered. "Time for boosters."

"I can't stand it," Mary said. "The way your skin feels, so full, like it's going to explode."

"Yeah," Nina said. "And Dr. Peabody is such a liar. He says, 'This will *pinch.*' And then he jams that twelve-foot needle into your bone, practically."

"Don't talk that way, Neenee," Lainey said. "You'll scare Sarey."

"Do we have to, Mom?" Mary whined.

"Don't be boring, please," Lainey said. "Don't waste your energy complaining about something like this, something that has to be. Besides, you should be grateful. You should be saying"—she made her voice ecstatic—"Oh, shoot me, Doc, shoot me!"

The little girls looked at each other and giggled.

"No. Truly," Lainey said. "Because look at Robert Chapin." This was a young man down the street, corkscrewed helplessly into a wheelchair, pushed everywhere by a dour, fat black woman who never spoke. "When he was little, there wasn't a shot. You could die of polio. You had to worry about it all the time. In the summers, you couldn't go to the beach or even to a public place for a picnic. It was dreadful. It was so hot, and there we were, just cooped up together, getting on each other's nerves. Why, when Liddie and Mack were small, I had to keep them locked in the backyard in the summer so they wouldn't catch it. I spent hours—hours, I promise you—boiling dishes and sterilizing things the year Randall was little." Her voice caught.

Nina was watching her with a blank, unsympathetic face. "You're exaggerating, Mother," she said.

Lainey swung to look at her. She could feel the tears smarting in her eyes. "What?" she said.

Nina was instantly frightened, and it made her defiant. "You're exaggerating," she said again.

"Oh, I see. Thank you," Lainey said. Her face pulled into bitter lines. "And just how would you know this?"

The little girls sat up straighter.

Nina looked back. "I can just tell. I can tell when you exaggerate."

"Oh, can you, my sweet judge. How very helpful

to have you around, then. You can tell, can you?"
Lainey's voice was hard.

"Yes," Nina said.

"Perhaps you'd like to tell me—to tell us all—tell
us how you know so very much about it all," Lainey
said.

Mary put her hand on Nina's arm. Nina looked
at Mary. Stop it, Mary's face said. Let it go.

Lainey saw the look, saw Mary's hand. She was
suddenly deeply ashamed of herself. She closed her
eyes and listened to the frightened silence in the
room. "Lord," she said softly, and looked at them.
"I'm afraid I've had it," she said. "I'm sorry. I'm sorry,
Nina. I'll help you with your camera in the morning,
but you kidlets better skedaddle now."

Slowly the two little girls slid off the bed. "Can
we have the rest of the popcorn, Ma?" Sarah asked.

"Yes, take it," Lainey said. "Take it. Just get out
of here." And before they were at the door, she had
flicked off the bedside lamp.

Lainey lay in the dark. She rolled the last mouth-
ful of bourbon around in her mouth. She thought of
Nina's scared, defiant face. She pushed her head back
into the pillow. She rocked it back and forth. "Ugh!"
she cried out softly. "Ugh. Ugh. Ugh." Her clenched
fists struck at her thighs with each animal noise. She
tried to make herself think of a time when she had
been thoughtlessly good; innocent. When she had
liked herself.

She could not. Instead she was suddenly remembering again the year of the polio scare, when they'd
begun the tests of Randall, when he was two. She remembered David and the pediatrician, the two men
talking together in those resonant, professional tones
Lainey hated. She'd felt that she and Randall were
nearly invisible to them as they discussed his fate.

Over the months that followed, David had

seemed to Lainey to put a great distance between himself and Randall, and her too. And then in October, when they began the tests, David produced the notebook he'd been keeping since Randall's second birthday. Lainey was incredulous. It wasn't that she hadn't wondered too, hadn't made observations. In fact, some of David's observations were from her. But that he could have compiled them in this clinical way, could have looked at their beautiful little boy and noted him as *R* in a book like those he used for patient records, shocked her.

Her immediate response had been desperately sexual. She had turned to him feverishly, trying to re-engage him with herself, trying to pull him to her perspective through making love. Trying to make him love Randall again, using her body. And though mechanically everything had worked, she could feel that somehow David was absent. It increased her sense of urgency, and for weeks they made love every night, even when Lainey was exhausted.

In January, she told David she was pregnant. He was appalled. He said he could arrange an abortion. She refused. He reminded her they'd wanted only three children.

"I want *this* one," she said.

"It won't change anything," he said.

"What do you mean?" she asked. But he didn't answer, and she didn't ask again. And slowly their lovemaking stopped altogether.

Now she was remembering clearly one summer evening—it must have been only a week or two before Nina was born—when David came home from work unexpectedly early. She was sitting on the steps off the kitchen, Randy next to her. Macklin and Liddie were bickering in the yard. They'd been irritable all day, wanting to see friends, wanting to go somewhere. She had pulled them apart time and time again, had enforced extra rest periods in separate rooms, had hit out at Liddie, the older, twice. Finally she had reached some point of not caring, not seeing anymore. While she sat on the steps, they began really to fight, scratching at each other, biting, crying. Lainey simply watched, as dull and tranced as Randall next to her. She didn't hear David come up behind her, she didn't feel his presence as he stood, shocked, in the doorway. Swiftly, decisively, he stepped around her, his shoe grazing her hip slightly, and went to separate the miserable children. When he turned to look back at her, crouched, holding a squalling child huddled against his body in each arm, she saw a pure cold hatred for her flickering in his face.

It was only a day or two after this that she read the notebook he had been keeping about Randall. She hadn't planned to. She'd run out of cigarettes and gone to look in his desk drawer for an extra pack, when her hand touched something at the back of the drawer. Instantly she knew what it was. She pulled it out and opened it. The children were all napping, the house was utterly still. She sat in the desk chair with David's things laid out in front of her and went through the terrible chronicle. Only gradually did she become aware of the change in focus from Randall to her. Toward the end of the notebook, though, the pages were dotted everywhere with capital *L*'s. *L:* Lainey. *L:* herself. *L:* the patient.

Her heart felt as though it were slowly tearing in her chest. She rested her hands on her moving belly and wept silently as she read. What she was looking at, she realized, was the account of the end of her marriage.

10

THE italicized quote under Mack's airbrushed, grinning picture in the yearbook said *The Grass Is Always Greener*. Mack's first reaction when he opened the book to his page had been to worry about what his mother would say when she saw it. But it quickly became clear that she didn't have even the beginnings of an idea of what it meant. The silver leatherette yearbook sat around in the living room and kitchen for a while, and he watched her leafing through it a few times. Once, he saw Nina and Sarah sitting on the couch, holding it between them on their laps. But no one ever said anything, and slowly he lost the nervousness that had stopped his heart the first time he saw the quote. The only ones who might have understood, he realized, were his father and Liddie, and neither of them was around to look at the yearbook.

He'd started smoking marijuana sometime in the fall. Soletski had some—*reefer*, he called it. Soletski hung around the blues clubs in the ghetto—he was trying to get good at blues guitar—and he'd bought it there. For a while their smoking had an exciting quality to it, had seemed wonderfully dangerous and alien just because of its association with those places, those rhythms. The first long hit of the stale-tasting smoke would call up for Mack the dim, cigarette-clouded interior of Pepper's and that new music— pickup a cappella groups, visiting pros, bands full of old men with Delta accents so thick Mack just waited for their laughter to cue his own, helpless to understand them. The neighborhood was rough. Often they ran down the dark, littered sidewalks to the clubs, afraid of the rage their whiteness might trigger. But inside the bars a kind of country graciousness prevailed, bought by Soletski's worshipful attention to the music and their own respectful politeness and youth.

Sometimes a black woman would ask Mack or Soletsky to dance. These women were older—young women didn't seem to hang around the blues clubs—and so there wasn't any tension about it. The men sitting at the tables would call to the women and laugh as they danced with the white boys around the smoky floor. Mack, stoned, felt a kind of sexual benediction as he moved in this new way—minimal, syncopated, sexy.

At some point a little later, though, Tucker Franklin bought some grass from a friend in Winnetka. He said everyone there was smoking it. And suddenly a lot of kids had it. It was at parties. They smoked it while they drove around, they got together just to get stoned and listen to music or talk. Or to sit and stare at each other, thickheaded with revelations they couldn't find words to share.

Among those who smoked grass there was a sense of having suddenly moved light-years away from their schoolmates and their families. They felt they understood the world differently, they knew their connection to one another, to music, to nature—even in gritty Chicago. Once, on a raw January day, Mack and Al had gone stoned to the Point. The lake was a blackened roil, and the waves battering the granite blocks at the promontory seemed purposefully violent. Mack had felt intimately injured by their power. He jumped down the tiered blocks of granite, stood on the lowest level, the walls of white rising in deafening menace above him, and shrieked his rage back.

It was sometime that same month that he started going to David's apartment to smoke. He'd had the key since Christmas, when he'd found it in a white envelope with his name on it under the tree. The note explained that David wanted Mack to feel that the apartment was an alternate home, that he could go there anytime he felt like it. Mack had put the key on his ring with the others, but he didn't intend ever to use it. From the start his visits to his father had been reluctant and difficult. Somehow—irrationally, he knew—they made him feel he was betraying his mother and Randall and his sisters. He had never gone over unless his father had specifically invited him. The key, he promised himself, changed nothing.

After the first semester of his senior year, though, Mack made the honor roll. One of the privileges for seniors on the honor roll was leaving campus when they didn't have classes. As soon as Mack saw his grades and realized he'd made it, he thought of David's empty apartment, of the freedom possible there.

The first time he tried it, he went alone, feeling conspicuous and strange walking down the long, empty blocks at midday. The apartment was large, dark and elegant, but underfurnished. The stillness inside when Mack stood in the empty hallway made him uncomfortable. He heard voices outside, on the street. He went to the front of the apartment, to the glassed-in sun porch off the living room. He stood there and watched the black kids walking past, four or five of them, their voices mingling rhythmically. As Mack's eyes followed them up Kimbark, he noticed coming toward them from the other direction a tall white man in a hat, a dark overcoat. Mack's breath caught, even as he realized that the man was heavy and fair, nothing like his father.

He stood there a few minutes more, feeling the dark apartment at his back like a threatening and yet beckoning presence. Then he reasoned with himself:

His father had given him the key. He meant Mack to be here alone, to use the apartment. If his father came in while he was here, he'd look up . . . he'd look up slowly. He'd be casual. He'd say, "Oh, hi, Dad. I had a break between classes and I felt like being alone." He imagined his father's still face animating quickly with pleasure. It was what he had wanted, after all. It was what he had fucking wanted, so the hell with him. Then Mack laughed out loud, because that made no sense. "The hell with him," he said, and stepped back into the apartment from the glare of the sun room.

Mack walked aimlessly around the living room, picking up and putting down books, ashtrays. His father had bought new furniture, Danish modern. The spare pieces seemed uncomfortably small in the big, high-ceilinged rooms. He'd brought over a few things they'd had in the house too: some lamps, a framed signed letter of Freud's, a large, comfortable wing chair with worn plaid upholstery that had come from his mother's house in New Hampshire. It looked graceless and shabby next to the aerodynamic teak of the Scandinavian pieces.

In the corner by the fireplace was a small upright piano, new. This purchase of his father's had been the most puzzling to Mack. And then the lessons! Mack crossed to it. Standing, he played a few bars of "Chopsticks." The music seemed unbearably loud, and when he stopped, he felt the notes reverberate almost like an echo from the high ceiling, from the empty dark hallway leading back to the bedroom. He sat down on the bench and leafed through the music: Hanon, Czerny, "easy" sonatas of Beethoven, a book called *Classics for Beginners.* Mack was familiar with them all. They were the same exercise pieces he'd suffered with for years, that Nina had stumbled through after him. Once or twice his father had played or practiced while he was over, and the sight of him, hunched forward on the bench, frowning intently behind his glasses at the pages of notes—this had startled Mack and made him uncomfortable.

Now he stood up. On the mantel over the bare fireplace was a bunch of photographs of them, the kids. One by one, Mack examined them, as though they were people he sought to know. Most were the school portraits that everyone but Randall had to sit for annually—inane smiles, forced on your face by the photographer, who wouldn't shoot until you bared your teeth. The cumulus clouds swirled in the egg-blue fake sky behind them all. Mary particularly, with her braces—even the rubber bands visible—looked awful.

But there were also a couple of more casual photographs, taken by Nina. One was a group portrait, shot in the dining room on Harper Avenue. As he stared at it, Mack remembered the occasion: Sarah's birthday, this past December. They looked crazy in the picture, drunk. Their heads were tilted one way or another, their faces distorted by their exaggerated loud effort with the song. Sarah's embarrassed grin was idiotic. Only Liddie, who'd learned to stay beautiful while she sang, and Randall, whose mouth was just slightly open and whose face was dreamy and sweet, didn't look foolish. Mack set the photo down.

He crossed to the kitchen, off the long living room and small dining nook. There were dirty dishes in the sink, and Mack felt a vague bitter pleasure at seeing them. His father had always been the neat one, had always been after all of them to be more orderly in their habits. It was true that the dishes were rinsed, were stacked tidily, but there must have been several days' worth there.

And then it occurred to him that maybe his father had had guests, or a guest, the night before. Mack didn't want to think about it. He knew his father dated, or whatever he called it. He'd actually tried, several times, to talk to Mack about it. But it was nothing Mack wanted to have to know about. Whenever his father brought it up, Mack felt a rising, nearly physical nervousness that made him tear things—labels, paper napkins, matchbooks—or drove him to sarcasm. His father had finally seemed to catch on. He rarely spoke about it to Mack anymore.

Now Mack came out of the living room and went down the hall. He stood in the doorway of his father's bedroom. The bed was made, though casually. To Mack, the room looked cell-like and monastic. An old white-painted bureau that had held worn towels in the basement at the house was all there was besides the bed. And the bed was only a box spring and mattress in a metal frame. He thought of their rooms at home, crowded with furniture, decorated with travel posters, pictures clipped from magazines, photographs. All their beds were distinctive; they had names given them by their mother: "the Eastlake bed," "the sleigh bed," "the Amos Knowlton bed"— Mack's—an iron affair with brass knobs that rattled if you jerked off too hard. Only Randall's room was furnished this way, like his father's. It was as though his father had left his personality behind, in their house, with them.

Mack stepped across the room and opened the closet. It too was neat. Even the shoes, with their wooden trees pushed in and snapped stiff, were lined up in a row. He shut the door and turned. On top of the bureau there was a photograph. He crossed to it and picked it up. It was the baby one of him with Liddie that had once sat on his father's desk at home. They looked happy, normal.

Somehow it made Mack sad, seeing that picture taken in some other universe. Before he left the apartment, he carried it down the dark hall to the living room and set it with all the other phony shots on top of the mantel. In its place he brought back the blurry photograph Nina had done of all of them together, singing.

As he walked back to school down the icy streets, he thought of his father's face when he saw the new photograph on his bureau. He imagined a brief puzzlement, then a shrugging acceptance—his father would think he must have chosen this arrangement, chosen it and then somehow forgotten it.

That was the first arrangement Mack did. Later, when he began to use the apartment regularly with friends to get stoned, the arrangements became part of it. They never left without changing something, always something so inconspicuous Mack's father wouldn't really notice, they hoped.

At first it was just Al and Mack. They shared a fourth period free, and combined with lunch, that gave them enough time to get to David's, to smoke a joint or two, and to get back before fifth. While they smoked, they usually sat on the sun porch with the window cracked, so they wouldn't leave the smell of dope in the apartment and so Mack could watch for David. But even then, even at the start, they would change something before they left. Once, they did the dishes, laughing hysterically over what seemed beyond irony, even, in this gesture. They stole small things: Six pills from a prescription bottle. One of every pair of brown socks. An unopened box of Domino sugar, which Mack threw into a dumpster on Fifty-seventh Street. An old necktie he knew his father hardly ever wore.

Sometimes Soletski came with them. And in March and April, Mack brought Annette Stahl over four or five times. The last time, they lay together on his father's bed, tangled, imprisoned in their twisted clothes. Mack's fly was unzipped, Annie's blouse open, her bra shoved up like a thick white bandage around her throat. Mack had finally come, pressed against her leg. Afterward he wouldn't let her straighten the covers. He thought of the rumpled bedspread and the drops of drying jism as that day's arrangement.

David never said anything, never even asked Mack if he'd been there. Mack wondered, increasingly, if it was because the arrangements were so subtle that his father didn't really notice; or if his father knew very well that Mack used the apartment, that he did the arrangements, but saw the two of them as engaged in some psychological contest about it.

Finally it was Mack who felt compelled to speak of it, he wasn't sure why. He didn't say he'd been coming over, though it had been several months since he'd started to. Instead he said he "thought he might" use David's apartment, as though he were letting David know his future intentions. They were eating at Gordon's. Nina and Mary and Sarah were there too. Mack sat across the booth from David and met his cool pale eyes as he explained the rules about seniors on the honor roll. He said he got tired of being in school all day, but there was no privacy at home—his mother or Retta or Bob was always there. "I think it might be very useful to me," he said calmly.

After he'd finished talking, Mary began immediately to tell her father about how a science project of hers had won a school prize, how she might get to be in a fair "from the whole city, Daddy." Mack felt a sudden shame. He realized that he'd sounded just like her, just as though he wanted his father's approval too, for the honor roll; as though he'd wanted his father to be pleased about his off-campus privilege.

The weather warmed up slowly. One day, more

stoned than usual, Mack took Soletski into his father's room to show him the closet, the laughable neatness of it. Somehow they ended up making an arrangement of David's clothes. They buttoned his shirts shut over hangers. They chose a tie for each one and carefully wrapped it, knotted it, around each collar. They picked a jacket to drape over each pair. They argued over their decisions, criticized each other's taste, fell, laughing, on David's bed. The pants were harder, but they finally hung them from hangers, which they hooked inside the front of each shirt. Under each man shape they placed a pair of the pronged shoes.

That night his father called. He told Mack that while he welcomed Mack's using his apartment, and while he wanted to encourage him to continue to use it, he thought a ground rule perhaps needed to be— Mack smiled at the *perhaps*—that they respect each other's privacy. That just as he wouldn't have gone uninvited into Mack's room at home or poked into his belongings, Mack was not to do that in his apartment.

"Okay," Mack said agreeably.

"Doesn't that seem reasonable to you?"

"Sure," Mack said, keeping his voice as neutral as he possibly could.

But it didn't matter anyway, because after that the weather got really nice and they pretty much stopped using his father's apartment at all.

When they sent around the ticket-request form for graduation, Mack wrote 6 in the space for *Number Requested*.

Then it occurred to him that perhaps Liddie wouldn't be back from Juilliard in time. He raised his hand and asked his homeroom teacher, Mme Boutin, if he could hold on to the form until he'd checked at home.

Madame was in the last stages of pregnancy. Everything made her tired. In a weary voice she read her instructions about the tickets aloud to Mack. " 'These forms will be collected and returned by three P.M. to the business office so that the ticket order can be returned by Friday.' " She looked up at Mack and shrugged. "What am I to do? I would like to allow this most reasonable request, but I cannot. It's absurd, of course, but I simply cannot. You understand?"

Mack said he did, and when the forms were passed forward in his row, he added his to the pile.

Late that afternoon, while his mother was fixing dinner, he stood in the kitchen doorway and watched her. He was still a little stoned—he'd gone to the Point earlier and smoked a couple of joints with Al, watching the big, dirty waves slap slowly at the rock barricade. The motion had filled him with such a sense of all that was rhythmic and benign in the world that now he didn't feel any of the tension he usually felt around his mother when he was stoned—the fear that she'd notice his odd speech, or his eyes. It even occurred to him, vaguely, that in her repetitive motions, the same ones she performed day after day fixing meals, there was something as benign, as natural, as the way the waves threw themselves at the shore over and over.

"With bells on," his mother was saying. "She wouldn't miss it for the world." She smiled, slamming a pot down—again? it seemed—on the stove.

He strained. "Liddie?" he asked.

"Herself," his mother said, now crossing to the sink, reaching into it.

"So," he said, gathering all his faculties. "Six tickets was right." He felt such a sense of accomplishment at having produced this that he beamed foolishly.

She turned to him, a motion that seemed to take forever. "Six?" She frowned. "Let's see." Her fingers went up, and Mack's did too, involuntarily. Touching them, she counted. "Me, Randall, Neen, Marey and Sarey, Lid, and Dad. That's seven, sweetie. You asked for six?"

"Well, Dad's not coming, is he?"

"Honey, of course he is. Of course he most certainly is. Why wouldn't he?"

Mack stood speechless. There were a million reasons—everything in their lives was the reason—but he couldn't name one. He felt dizzy. He went and sat down at the kitchen table. Somehow this took a long while, and he had regained his composure by the time he'd accomplished it. He could see outside from here—the back door was open and all the leaves in the yard suddenly shimmered together in a long rush of wind. "It doesn't matter," he said finally.

"Oh, but, honey, it does. He'll be so hurt." His mother pulled out a chair and sat opposite him. She was holding a saucepan. "Is there anything we can do?" She was still frowning, and Mack wanted to tell her not to, he didn't want to see her face like that.

"It doesn't matter. I'll just explain it to him. I'll apologize."

"No, I mean, can't we? Maybe I could call." She looked at the wall, thinking. Several postcard reproductions of famous paintings and the old photos of Freud and Kennedy looked back. "Or you?"

"Me," he repeated. Too slow. Concentrate.

"Yes. Oh, come on, Mack. Think! There has to be a solution."

"Mom," he said, and he noticed how her face changed in response to that; it softened and lifted to him. "Mom," he said again. More of same; then a pinch of irritation.

"*What?*"

He shrugged. "What difference does it make?"

"Darling, are you being deliberately obtuse?

Daddy—must—come—to graduation. Clear? Now, shall I call school and say you made a mistake? I'm perfectly willing to. Shall I, or would you rather?'' Her forehead corrugated in worry. "I certainly don't want to embarrass you."

"No," he said. Then he said, "I thought he wouldn't come."

Suddenly he felt tearful. He felt a sense of betrayed loyalty. "I thought you . . . I was trying . . ." He couldn't talk; he felt a nameless grief.

His mother looked stricken. She set the saucepan down between them and reached for his hands. But Mack didn't want her to touch him. He leaned back in his chair. He was focusing on the yard, on the rectangle of sunlit air, on the motion of leaves.

His mother's arms were stretched across the table now, in her reach for him. "This is my fault," she said. "You poor children are all just caught in this, and now we see . . ." Abruptly she sat up and buried her face in her hands. Mack watched her, soberly. "Ah!" she cried in irritation. She lifted her head, wiped at her eyes with the back of her hand. "Lord! What self-indulgence," she said. She smiled sheepishly. "We've had enough of *that*. And you're right. Of course you were right to do what you did, under the circumstances. Oh, boo hoo," she said, and sniffed. "Have you a Kleenex, kind sir?"

"Mmm, no."

She got up, tore off a paper towel, and blew her nose, noisily. Then she spotted the saucepan on the table and picked it up. "This was for peas, if memory serves. Let me get this stuff going." She went to the sink and ran water into the saucepan. Mack was breathing evenly, thinking of the clean air going into his lungs, thinking of it as pure bubbles in his veins, thinking how he was not stoned. *Thinking clearly?* he asked himself, the voice that checked up. *You bet,* he answered. "Look," he said loudly over the running water. "I'll get an extra ticket. I'll go to the business office tomorrow." Done. Good.

She turned. She whacked a box of frozen vegetables on the edge of the porcelain sink. "I'll bet they just give you a hard time, honey." She whacked again. "Nope," she said decisively. "I'm going to call. It's only right. It's me who's confused you all. Me and Dad. We should make these arrangements, because we caused the problems. When I *think* . . ." She tore the box open, sprinkled the glittering, crystallized pellets of green into the water. Peas, he thought. Then she crumpled the box and leaned with her back against the sink, looking down at what she held in her hands as if it were her hopes, her dreams, for all their lives. "What a unholy mess we made of it." Her voice was vibrating with sorrow. "I don't know how to say how sorry I am. There should be some . . . ceremony, some ritual for this." She turned away from him, she looked out the back door. A train rocketed by, and they both froze, suspended in the noise. When it was gone, she spoke again, more softly. "In church, during the general confession, I always think of you children, of the great wrong done you. A kind of futility to confessing that to *God,* though, I guess."

She looked over at him, smiled gently. "Perhaps at some point your father and I should line you all up and say our *mea culpa*s to you."

There was a moment's silence. An abrupt clear vision of the scene she suggested came to Mack, with Randall robed as some kind of idiot pope or holy emperor, presiding over the ceremony.

"Hardly imaginable," she said suddenly.

"Cause of Randall?" he asked after a moment.

"Well, that too," she said, and laughed. "But I was thinking more of Dad." She lit a match and held it to the burner as she turned on the gas. "Dad's not big on *mea culpa*s."

"Uh," he said. "Yeah. I don't suppose he"—he felt a pang of confusion—"I don't suppose he knows that kind of Latin," he said slowly.

"Ah!" she cried out in amusement. "Precisely!" she said. She kicked up the lid to the trash bin and dropped the waxed white box in. "Can you get the gang roused?" she asked. "Dinner in maybe ten minutes?"

Mack got up, watched her a moment more in her endless traipse, and then went to find his sisters and brother.

It was about a week later that his father, at the house to pick up the three girls, asked to speak to Mack for a moment. They went outside onto the front steps while the girls yelled back and forth inside, getting ready. His father was taking them to the Fifty-seventh Street Art Fair. He told Mack that he'd be more than willing, if Mack wanted him to, to intervene with his mother so that Randall wouldn't have to come to graduation.

Mack looked over at him, sitting at the other end of the wide stair. His pale, unreadable eyes were focused intensely on Mack.

"Why wouldn't I want Randall there?"

"I'm not saying you necessarily wouldn't. It's just that he can be difficult; we all know that. And I think it should be your choice. Your mother tends to assume it's never a question."

Mack had an impulse to laugh, but he didn't. He stood up and stretched. Inside, Mary was yelling at Retta: "If I have to wear that, I'm not going to go."

"I dunno," Mack said. "I think I'd prefer it if the whole family was there."

"Well, that's fine too," said his father. "That's a

generous choice. But if you should change your mind, let me know."

"I'm not going to change my mind," Mack said flatly, and turned to go in. "Everybody's coming."

"Oh, good glory!" his mother said.

Nina looked up quickly. "What?"

They were all at breakfast except Liddie, who'd gotten in late the night before, and Randall, who'd eaten earlier with Bob and was now in the backyard, swinging. Lainey was still in her bathrobe, and she'd been sitting at the table with them, smoking luxuriantly, deeply, while she drank a second or third cup of coffee. Now she set the cup down. "I'd forgotten Randall."

"What are you talking about? I've got tickets for everyone," Mack said.

"No, what he's *wearing*," she answered in irritation. "Oh, good Lord." She stabbed the cigarette out.

"He can wear what he's got on," Mack said. "What does it matter?" Randall was wearing a school outfit, chinos and a shirt.

"I don't want him wearing what he's got on. I want him to look like everyone else." This was their mother at her worst. Her voice was strident, she was ready to be angry at anyone who crossed her. The girls had all stopped eating. They fell silent, fearful.

"Just don't do this, Mom," Mack said quietly. "I can't stand it when you do this."

"Do what?" she said. Then she caught herself. "And don't you dare speak to me that way."

"Mom, this is my graduation. I don't want you having hysterics and wrecking it. I'm sick of your having hysterics, okay? Just don't do it." His own voice had risen. The fearful faces swung to him now—his mother's too—and he checked himself. "Just tell me.

I'd like to know, what is the big deal? What do you *want* him to be wearing?"

"I want him to wear a suit, just like everyone else."

"Fine, he'll wear a suit."

"He doesn't have a suit," she shrilled.

"He can wear my suit, okay? I now have two summer suits, got it? He can wear my old suit. I will wear the suit I got for graduation, and he can wear my old suit. God!"

There was silence in the room. From outside they could hear the rhythmic squeal of the rusty swing.

"Do you think it will fit him?" Lainey asked.

"Pretty well, I think. Well enough."

Silence. "I'm sorry," she said. "I don't know what gets into me."

"Well. Just don't get like that." Mack went to the counter and turned on the radio. He leaned toward it, his back to the room. The disc jockey's voice was rapid, ebullient, giving the weather. "Seventies in the city," he chanted. "Sixties in the suburbs. Ring-a-ding, cha cha cha." Behind him, his mother was speaking to Sarah, was asking her to go up and tell Bob he'd have to dress Randall again. Mack bent over the radio and shut his eyes. He began to wish he had some marijuana to get him through this day.

When he heard Retta arriving in the front hall, it seemed like more than he could stand. He turned quickly and went up the back stairs. In the second-floor hallway, a white motion caught his eye: Liddie in her nightgown, just awake, her hair matted and wild.

"Mmm," she said. Her voice was still fogged with sleep. "It's the graduation boy."

"And it's mayhem already."

"Well." She scratched her hip through her nightgown. "It ain't what Mother does best."

"I'll say," he said, and started up to his room. Far below, he could hear Randall begin to bellow. Closer, water started to run in Liddie's tub. He shut his door and crossed to the window. Sun streamed in the angled dormer. Far across the wide tracks he could see the deep green of the treetops in Jackson Park. After that, the lake, he knew, and then the land on the other side, stretching all the way to the east coast, to where he was headed, to where he'd start his life all over, away from his crazy family. He sat down in the warm light and shut his eyes, let the sun relax and steady him. Randall's shouting was nearer now; he was in his room, Mack could tell. After a while, he got up, moving slowly. He took out his old suit and one of his white shirts. In a quick impulse of love for Randall, he hooked the new tie he'd bought around the wire neck of the hanger. He carried everything down the attic stairs. Randall's door was shut, he was yelling inside. Mack knocked and Bob called out for him to come in.

Bob and Randall were sitting together on Randall's mattress, Randall in front of Bob between the man's legs. Bob's arms were around Randall, pinning Randall's arms against his own body so he couldn't strike out. Bob was rocking their bodies together from side to side. Randall's shouts were regular as breathing.

Mack had held his brother just like this when Randall was smaller and angry about something, or terrified. He looked terrified now. His eyes moved wildly in his head, he tried to fling himself away from Bob, but he was caught in the even motion of Bob's rocking. Mack could hear Bob humming between Randall's shouts.

Mack held up the clothes. "His stuff," he said.

Bob nodded, but he didn't stop humming or rocking.

Mack hooked the hanger over the end of one of Randall's shelves and left the room, shutting the door behind him. Randall had never looked at him, never seemed aware of his presence.

Mack dressed carefully. His new suit smelled of the plastic bag it had been hanging in. It was a beige one, and he wasn't sure what socks were correct with it. It was the kind of question he would have asked his father at one time. In the end, since his shoes were dark, he wore dark socks. But he had only two ties besides the one he'd given Randall, and they both looked crummy with the suit. Then he remembered: when he'd taken the socks out of the sock drawer, he'd seen, tucked in the back, the tie he'd taken from his father's apartment earlier in the spring. He opened the drawer again and pulled it out. It was slightly rumpled, but the color seemed all right with his suit. He put it on.

He went downstairs, past the solemn poster of Che Guevara hanging in what had been his father's study. In the kitchen, Retta was bent over, loading the dishwasher, a cigarette dangling from her mouth and her face squinted up in its smoke. She slitted her eyes to look at him and then slowly stood straight. She took her cigarette out of her mouth and rested her hands on her hips. She was wearing work clothes— that looked like a man's worn flannel pajama top over a tight, pilled synthetic skirt. "Well, now, look at you," she said, and smiled. "Baby, you are lookin handsome for graduation. Why you didn't tell me you turned into a man? I might have had some use for you." Retta often joked like this with him. Never in her real clothes, though. Only when she was costumed like this, like an old woman, a servant.

Mack knew there was a kind of contempt for him in this distinction. But he still enjoyed the game. "It's too late for you. Any second I'm going to start hanging out with college girls.''

"Child, they won't even know what to do with you."

"I'll teach em."

Retta laughed. "That's all right," she said. "I believe you will."

"I'm splitting anyway, Retta. I'm supposed to be there at nine-thirty."

"All right. Everyone else upstairs?"

"Yeah. They're all getting ready."

She was following him out the hallway to the front door. "That Randall," she was saying. "He mad this morning."

"Well, they got him all dressed in the wrong clothes. Mom forgot."

"That's no good. Everything got to be just so for him. Or else you gonna hear it."

He turned on the front steps, frowning up at her in the bright sunlight. "I think he's okay now. I don't hear him anymore, anyway."

"He be fine, honey." Retta's face was kind, suddenly. "You don't be thinkin about him today. You just have fun. This your day."

From the back row of folding chairs set up in the sanctuary, Mack looked out over the audience and blurred his eyes, letting the faces, the bright dresses and jackets, of all the parents and brothers and sisters move and swim into only color, a confused daubed palette stretched out endlessly before him. Denise Daniels was delivering the valedictory, talking about the responsibilities the graduates had to the world they were entering. Her voice, in spite of its rehearsed rhythms—passages you knew had been timed over and over—rang with sincerity. It occurred to Mack as she spoke that she meant it, that all the leaders whose speeches had rung through his high school years had meant it. He had always thought they were pretending, as he would have been pretending, speaking such words. He realized now, with a kind of shock, that they had the energy to be thinking of their lives as citizens, of their place in history, of ambition. It made him think of Annie. She'd been the one, finally, who wanted to split up. And what she'd told him was that he was too cool for her. That she felt foolish, square, around him because she was so crazy about the theater, about acting. He remembered that she'd been crying when she said she didn't think she ought to go out with him anymore. "It's just every time I'm being serious about something, you make a joke, you make me laugh. But I don't want to laugh. I *am* serious. I'd like to be like you. But I'm not." And then she said, "It's just the way I am; I can't help it."

He had felt sorry for her then, for the way she was. It wasn't until he was walking home alone that he felt sorry for himself, that he realized how much he'd liked the way she was, the freedom to be serious, too, he'd sometimes felt with her. But the lights had been on at Al's house, and he'd whistled outside and Al had come down. They'd smoked some dope, they'd listened to Jefferson Airplane for a while, and he'd felt better.

"The world has changed for us since those safe childhood days," Denise was saying. "Political assassination, wars in distant lands, all seem possible in our everyday lives. We've grown up with this. We understand this, in ways maybe that you, our parents and our teachers, do not."

Suddenly, in the upturned sea of still faces, he saw motion, a rhythmic sideways motion that had all the familiarity to him of his own breathing. He squinted and saw his brother. His mother was next to Randall; she had her arm around him. The motion was a comfortable one, no trouble yet.

"Now is the moment for us," Denise was saying, "when we step into the world, with all our ambitions and our hopes for changing that world, for shaping it to us and leaving forever our footprints on its surface. We answer that call, that challenge." Randall's rhythm seemed a little connected to Denise's speech, as though she were singing to him. Mack let his eyes blur again, let the figure become part of the sea of color and form. But now he was aware, always, of the tick-tock of Randall's body. He looked away, up to where the rose window's pale radiance shone at the top of the far wall, to the medieval banners hanging in a row from the vaulted arches. But wherever he looked, that rhythm, that pulse, moved in the corner of his eye, nagged at him.

"At this moment of change for us, we say to you, our parents, our teachers"—Denise looked back for a moment at where the faculty sat, and Mack saw that her face was full of frightened gravity—"we are ready, we ask what we can do, we take up the burden gladly."

She turned, and the applause exploded loudly through the vast, chilly chapel. Mack's hands burned too, he felt unexpected tears stinging his eyes. Denise's head stayed down until she'd gotten back to her place. Then, before sitting, she looked up and nodded in acknowledgment, once. The applause welled again, rolled over her, over them all, everyone about to begin a new life. And then it stilled abruptly as the school head, Mr. Karmel, rose to begin awarding the prizes and handing out diplomas.

Outside, Mack stood looking blindly into the sun, waiting for his family. Several of the senior girls were crying and hugging each other, and here and there families were already embracing or photographing some of the graduates. But others, like him, stood separately, waiting to be claimed.

Suddenly he recognized Mary and Sarah on the steps—they seemed to spring up from under the feet of the crowd oozing its way down. They pointed at him and waved, but waited. Behind them, he saw the rest emerging, Liddie most noticeable with her tumbledown light hair. And then his eyes found his brother, and he nearly cried out at the sudden realization of how much Randall looked like him. They were all moving together toward him down the stairs, waving and greeting people they knew, and he had the strange sensation that he—not Randall—was the one up there with them. That it was himself, but himself changed, like the person you dream when you dream yourself. Happy, laughing, they made their way to him with the surrogate Mack wearing his gray suit, the tie he'd chosen with his father's gift money. Except for the haircut, the stumbling walk, it might have been him.

Then Liddie ran to where he stood motionless. She grabbed him, whirled him around in her perfumed embrace. Some of her hair swung across his lips and touched his tongue. And then they were all embracing him. His father stood back, and when everyone else was done, he shook Mack's hand. Mary grabbed his sports award—he had captained two teams, baseball and soccer, and had been voted best all-around athlete—and began to show it to Sarah, to his father. His mother was laughing and talking at the same time. Her arm was still around Randall, whose eyes were big and frightened, rolling slightly in his head.

Nina smiled at Mack, lifted her camera to her face, and disappeared behind it. Her body pivoted, got him with Liddie—he could feel the way the camera paired them—then with his father; and then he forgot about her, she was just there, and his mother was asking him questions about Denise, about the other speakers.

In a little pocket of silence his father leaned forward and frowned for a moment at the tie Mack was wearing, but Mack kept his face bland and pleasant, and his father said nothing.

Then his mother was talking to Nina, she had taken the camera. She turned to his father and spoke to him. "Would you mind, David?" she said, holding the camera out. "I want one with Nina in it too."

His father took the camera and stepped back away from them. He began directing them. They all sobered instantly. Businesslike, they began to arrange themselves. Mack put his arms around Liddie and Randall, one on each side of him. Their mother bent in a little in front of them, and Nina rested her head on Randall's shoulder. "All together, all together," their father called. "Here, you girls, squat down a bit."

He was standing facing them, one hand directing them as he watched them in the viewfinder. Mack felt the bodies press tighter around him. He was aware of their laughing light voices, the way they smelled. He was in them, of them, again; and it was his father who stood out there, who was the one looking on. He had an image, then, of what they must look like pressed together, their heads leaned in, their faces presented. A family.

"Okay, everyone," Liddie said. "On the count of three we give him the big cheese. One? Two? Three!" And they all yelled it across at their father like some sort of challenge, Mack the loudest of all. *Cheese!*

11

WHEN David opened the door, they all looked up, frozen, and he saw at once that Lainey was all right. She sat on the second stair, her face lifted toward him. The lines of blood on her forehead and one cheek looked like thicker, redder hair, hair drawn on by a child's bright crayon.

"David," she said. "You came."

And abruptly everything came to life again: Sarah, who'd evidently gone to get a wet cloth for Lainey, stepped into the front hall, saw David, and burst into loud crying. Nina moved toward him, starting to apologize; and as David shut the front door, he saw Randall huddled in the corner behind it, he was aware suddenly of the rhythmic mooing that had charged the scene with meaning from the moment he'd stepped in.

"How long has he been like this?" he said to Nina, who was standing close to him in her white nightgown.

"I don't know," she said. "Just Mom was trying to get him to go upstairs, and he pushed her, I guess." Her face was white too, and her eyes looked black and bottomless in her fear. "We didn't know right away. We were in my room."

"Get his blanket," David said. She spun back from him, ran up the stairs, her bare feet thudding on the wood.

Randall was squatting, hugging his knees and rocking a little. His eyes were nearly shut. When David touched him, they snapped open unseeingly and his fisted arm shot out at nearly the same moment. Then he hugged himself again and hunched over, and the low moans started once more.

Nina came running down the stairs and over to David. She was panting, a loud, ragged sound. He took the worn blanket she held up. He crouched and offered it to Randall, but Randall didn't seem to see it at all, his eyes didn't focus on it. They moved wildly in their sockets, and his noises grew louder. He'd had a haircut recently, David could see, and the wide bare strip of flesh above his ears and his long exposed neck made him look more vulnerable, more crazy. "Randall," David said gently. "Randall, here's your blanket."

"Sing," Lainey said. They'd fallen silent behind him, watching. He looked over at her. She was holding the towel against her head. It was smeared a brilliant red.

"Press down," David replied. "Press on the cut. Sarah, help your mother." He turned back to Randall. His mind was blank; and then from nowhere came the silly lyrics: "We are poor little lambs who have gone astray, baa, baa, baa . . ."

Lainey and the girls huddled on the stairs and listened as David sang. He moved gradually from a light whispered tone, which Randall barely seemed to hear, to full voice. When Randall finally reached for his blanket, David could see Lainey in his peripheral vision turn and bury her face in her arms.

David led Randall slowly past her and the girls, up the stairs, singing loudly now: "Gentlemen songsters off on a spree, damned from here to eternity . . ." At the top, he looked down momentarily. Nina was turned to watch their progress up, but the other two were busy, Sarah bent over Lainey, following his instructions to push.

In the second-floor hallway, he thought briefly of toileting Randall and decided to skip it. If he woke in the night, even if he wet the bed, handling that would be easier than stopping at this moment. Besides, Randall himself had already turned toward his room, and David was the follower now. Randall nearly broke into a run, the last few steps. When he reached his mattress, he handed David the red blanket, then knelt in the half darkness on his bare bed and threw himself forward awkwardly, seemingly in relief, making fluttery, eager cries. David was still singing as he bent and started to undo Randall's clothes. Calmly he stripped his son, fetched his pajamas and guided them over the inert, stiff body. Randall's eyes were shut fiercely, as though if he couldn't see it, this world would disappear. Slowly, always singing, David tucked the blanket in all around him.

He was startled, when he stood up and stepped to the doorway, to see that Lainey was there, a massive silhouette in the hall light, holding the bunched-up towel to the back of her head like a mad hat.

"What are you doing?" he whispered.

"I'm going to say good night."

He shook his head. "No. Not now. I want to look at your head now."

"I'll just be a minute. I just want to say good night." She didn't meet his eye, she was already moving past him.

"Lainey, after all this?"

She turned back and squinted into the light. "He didn't *mean* to do this!" He could see that her eyes were swollen from weeping. She shook her head. "He didn't mean it, David. And I think it's better to keep everything as close to routine as we can anyway. He expects me to say good night."

"I'll wait, then."

He stood in the doorway and watched her slide awkwardly under the covers, always holding the folded towel with one hand. The two shapes lay still, side by side, nearly the same size under the red blanket. Then he could hear Lainey's off-key voice humming "The Whiffenpoof Song"—an encore, he realized—and, after a long moment, Randall's melodic wordless crooning joining her. He felt a sudden sense of shame, as though he were watching some private, sacramental act. He turned and went down the hall, flicking off the light.

The door to what had been his study was closed. Standing uselessly in the darkened hallway, he had an odd impulse to open it, to look at what had become of his room—his *sanctum sanctorum,* Mack had called it. Instead he sat down on the top of the stairs to wait for Lainey. Below him he could see Nina, bent over, wiping up her mother's blood from the bottom steps with a cloth. Sarah's voice came from somewhere beyond his vision. A persistent tone. She'd been pushing at this, apparently: "But *weren't* you scared, Neenee?"

"Oh, for God's sake," Nina said. David watched her turn the cloth, look for a few seconds at the dark blood. Finally she countered, "Weren't *you* scared?"

"I thought she was dead," Sarah said softly, after a moment.

Nina stood up and started back to the kitchen. "Well, you weren't the only one," she said.

He looked up to see Lainey at Randall's door, locking it shut. She turned and walked toward him, not seeing him until the last second, when she nearly kicked him.

"Oh!" she cried. Then: "What are you doing?"

"I want to check your head," he said, standing up. He was on the first step down, and Lainey, in a muumuu, with her bizarre headdress, towered over him like some huge Samoan goddess. He stepped up to her.

They stood awkwardly close in the dusky light for

a moment, not quite knowing what came next. It was as though they'd just finished dancing, or were about to start. Then Lainey said, "Well, I suppose the bathroom."

"All right," he said, and followed her.

She turned on the light as she stepped ahead of him into the room. She flipped the seat down and sank onto the covered toilet, then leaned forward, resting her elbows on her knees. "God!" she said, and shook her head. "What a night. What a night*mare*. It feels like it'll never end."

He crossed to her and bent over her, put his hands on the back of her skull. "Where is it?" Her hair was still dark and thick, but he could see the springy coils of gray laced into it.

"In back there," she said, tilting down farther.

The blood was crusted brown everywhere. He straightened up. "I'll have to wash it to get a look." He got a clean washcloth out of the cupboard and stepped past her to wet it. "How did it happen? He pushed you?"

"He was confused, poor baby. Bob's been gone two days, off with some new girlfriend, and the whole schedule's shot to pieces. Last night was pretty bad, but tonight . . ." She shook her head, and the hair hanging forward swung below her. "Impossible. He was miserable all night. He wouldn't come to the table, wouldn't eat, wouldn't take a bath. He wouldn't do anything. I was trying to get him upstairs."

"And he pushed you?" David asked again. He was wiping at her scalp now. Scabs of hardened blood pulled away, then caught in her hair. He had to pick them out.

"Yes. Just *away*, you know. He just didn't want to go. And I fell exactly the wrong way, I guess."

"What did you hit?" He could see the cut now,

still oozing slightly, a clean slice about two inches long, a lump swollen under it, pushing it open.

"The newel post. Right on a corner, I think. Wham! That was it, for a minute or two."

"It must have been a little longer than that, for the girls to call me."

"Well." She was silent. "I think it was the amount of blood, honestly."

"Yes. Head wounds are like that."

"Is it okay?"

"Well, it's big." He stood back, looking down at her. "It's slowed, but it could reopen easily. I think I should take you in. Anyone responsible would give you stitches."

Her head had begun to turn from side to side. "No," she said.

"And there's a good chance that you've had a concussion."

She pushed herself up straight and looked at him. "David, I'm not going."

He sat down on the edge of the tub, facing her. After a moment he said, "You can't make it not so bad by not treating it. It's a serious wound. Someone ought to look at it."

She looked at him. Finally she smiled, a kind of mischief in her face. "Do your damnedest, Doc. I'm not going."

"I'm asking you to."

"And who will you get to stay here?"

"That's not the point. I can get someone."

"I don't want anyone. I want to stay here. I need to stay here."

"And you also need a doctor to look at you."

"You're a doctor."

He shook his head. "Lainey, I'm trying to do the responsible thing. Will you help me?"

She turned away. Several lines of brown blood

had run down her neck, disappearing under her dress. When she turned back to him, she was frowning, serious. She lifted her big, roughened hands. "The problem is, you and I are working with two different definitions of responsibility."

"Still, I am asking you to," he said again. "For me."

"And I won't," she said gently.

He stood. "Well, then. I'd better dress it, hadn't I? What do you have?" He crossed to the medicine chest. "Any gauze?"

"Yeah. I think so." She started to get up, but he signaled her to sit.

"I can find it." He opened the medicine chest. On the shelves inside was a precariously jammed jumble of makeup—tubes, compacts, brushes, and wands. He found some gauze and brought it back, with tape and a pair of scissors. "Are you dizzy at all?" he asked her. She had sat again, was hunched forward with her head hanging.

"Oh." She paused. "A little. I don't know. It scared me. You know." Her voice was tremulous.

"I'll have to stick the tape down partly on your hair, if you don't want a bald patch, okay? You'll have to be careful taking it off. It'll pull."

"Okay," she said.

"Your dress is a mess too. Bloody."

She began to cry.

"Lainey." He stepped quickly to the door and shut it. He sat on the edge of the tub and reached over her, his hands on her back. Her size, her shape, were as familiar under his fingers as if he'd never been away.

"Oh, God," she whispered.

"Lainey," he said.

"I don't think I can do it anymore," she said.

He bent his head over her. Soundlessly her body

shook under his hands. They sat that way for some minutes, until she stilled under him.

"Ugh," she said.

He sat up, and she turned and reached for the toilet paper. He glimpsed her face, swollen, glistening. Then it disappeared behind the clump of paper, and she blew her nose.

She looked up at him, ruefully. "Sorry," she said.

"What on earth for, Lainey?" he said softly.

"Well, for crying," she answered. "It's so predictable. At it again." He didn't answer. "And for dragging you over here."

He shook his head.

She gestured up, vaguely. "For this too," she said.

"That? That's hardly your fault." She shrugged. After a moment he said, "Besides, you can always look on it as simply a new kind of stigmata."

There was a silent pulse of time in the room, like a missed beat; and then she whooped with laughter. He laughed too, in pleasure at her laughter; and for a few seconds they sat facing each other, watching each other's brief happiness.

Then she stopped and wiped her eyes. Her glance fell to her dress. She yanked it around to look at the bloodied neckline, her chin doubling as she pulled it in. "What a mess," she said. She threw the paper in the trash and stood up. In one quick motion she reached down and pulled the dress over her head. Under it, she was wearing a white cotton bra, large, matronly, and a half-slip. She wadded the dress, crossed the room, and violently threw it into the old hamper.

David had turned quickly away the moment she lifted her skirt. He didn't feel he could bear to look at her so nearly naked, whether because it would draw him or repel him he wasn't sure. He had stood and gone to the sink. He busied himself rinsing the washcloth, soaping it again. When she sat back down, he came and pushed her head forward. His fingers parted her hair. Gently he stroked the cut with the soapy cloth, then spread several of the gauze pads over the slice. He cut two lengths of tape and pressed them down, trying to connect as much as he could with the grayish, dead-looking flesh of her scalp.

"All set," he said finally. He turned back quickly to the sink and began to rinse the cloth.

"Is it going to be all right?" she asked. She got up. She was standing by the hamper. He looked at her, then back to what he was doing. She was touching the dressing gingerly with both hands, exploring. The plucked-looking shadowed flesh of her underarms was exposed to him. The heavy curves of her arms and shoulders were nearly as white as the bra. There was some deeply female dignity to this whiteness, this heaviness, he felt, in spite of her absurd costume.

"We'll see. I think so."

Her arms dropped. "I guess I'll go stretch out, then," she said in a small voice. "I feel a little . . . not dizzy, exactly. Just shaken, I guess."

"Okay. Just a second, I'll help you."

She waited by the door as he squeezed the last faint pink rinse out of the washcloth and hung it up. He dried his hands and then stepped to her. He took her elbow. Her arms were crossed over her breasts now.

"I'm sorry," she said. "You're embarrassed, aren't you?"

Without answering, he opened the door and guided her down the hall, her silent escort.

"I'm sorry. It never occurred to me . . ."

"Clearly," he said, dryly.

She extracted her arm from his hand. "I'm not really dizzy," she said.

"I just want to keep an eye on you." They were in their room now. Her bedroom. She turned on the bureau lamp, and he was instantly shocked at how unchanged the room was. As though his absence should have made a difference, especially here. But everything was just as she'd arranged it years before. He looked at the family portraits on the wall. Even the members of his own family in these pictures seemed part of her world, not his, claimed by her arrangement, by her very wish to include them. When he'd lived here, he'd completely stopped looking at any of them. They were as familiar and unseen as the pale paisley wallpaper—which he noticed now was peeling away over a brown spot close to the ceiling. There were stacks of books on the bedside table and floor. Several empty glasses cluttered the bureau.

She had turned back to him. "Well, I'm going to get ready for bed." She gestured helplessly in mock modesty.

"Okay. I'll come back in a few minutes. Can I get you anything from downstairs?"

"Yes, as a matter of fact. I'll have a drink, I think. Bourbon. Rocks."

"Okay." He started out.

"And get yourself one too, if you want one," she called out.

When he came back with their drinks she was propped up among the pillows, wearing a nightgown, a white one like Nina's. She'd brushed her hair, he noticed—and felt a moment's worry about the gauze bandage. He sat down at the foot of the bed.

"Thanks," she said, taking the glass. She drank two quick long swallows. "Lord!" she said, and leaned her head back.

He lifted his glass and drank too.

"Are the girls okay?" she asked after a moment's silence.

"They're fine. They're watching TV. Some late-night thing."

"Oh. 'Creature Feature.' "

"Yes, I suppose so."

"They aren't too upset?"

"Seemingly not." He slid back against the foot-board. "I'll go down and sit with them in a while."

"Oh, you don't need to do that. You should be getting home, probably. We probably interrupted your evening."

"Not at all. I was reading." He sat for a minute, remembering the stillness of his apartment, the shat-tering call of the telephone. It was the time on a Satur-day evening when a single person without plans might suddenly feel the impossibility of getting through the night alone; a time of night when David had occasionally found himself trying to imagine whom he might telephone. He had thought he knew who it was the moment he picked up the receiver—a younger woman he'd been seeing up until a few months earlier, a woman who'd often called him late at night, drunk or stoned. Sarah's slow, small voice itself had startled him, and he'd been ready to be frightened, alerted by his quickened pulse for what followed. "God, it's a good thing I was there."

"I know." She took another swallow and set her glass on the bedside table next to the pile of books. From the side, her bandage looked absurd, like a bea-nie set low on the back of her head. She looked at him and frowned. "It's worrisome, isn't it? And it isn't good for the girls. Seeing all this. I mean, at least when Mack was still here . . . Then there was someone nor-mal—I mean, a boy."

"Well," he said. "Of course, there's Bob."

"Oh well, Bob." She shrugged.

"He seems perfectly nice to me," David offered.

"He's nice enough. It's just that he's kind of . . . well . . . eunuchy."

"Eunuchy, Lainey?" He laughed. "Eunuchy? It sounds like a flavor of fudge."

She smiled. Then said soberly, "But you know what I mean."

"Maybe I do," he said.

"It's just that I hate to think that their sense of what's masculine, of what's male, is shaped by seeing Randall. And he's more sexual now too. They've had to learn to cope with that."

"Well, they're tough cookies," David said.

"Poor things." She grimaced and then relaxed back among the pillows. Her hair pushed forward in a dark, soft frame around her face, making her young momentarily.

"I'll spend the night, I think," David said.

She flushed quickly. She looked almost frightened.

"I'll sleep downstairs. Or Mack's room."

"You *don't* need to do that," she said firmly.

"I want to. I'm concerned about you. And Randall may wake. I didn't ever take him to the bathroom, because I wanted to get him to bed fast."

"Oh." She reached for her glass and drank from it again. "So you think this bump might be some kind of a problem?"

He lifted his shoulders. "It bears watching for twenty-four hours. It was a hard whack, and anytime you lose consciousness, it's a troubling thing."

Her eyes were unreadable dark in the low, yellow light. Finally she said, "Mack's bed is made up, I think."

"It doesn't matter. Don't worry about it. I'll find a way to get comfortable." They sat in silence, each lost in thought, for several minutes. David wondered if she had the sense he did of the deep confusion of everything that stayed unarticulated between them.

But when he spoke again, it wasn't about any of that. He asked her where Mary was.

"Oh, she's on a sleepover," Lainey said. "She's suddenly very popular in school. It's hard on Nina, actually."

"Nina's not?" he asked.

"Nowhere near as much, no."

Suddenly Sarah appeared in the doorway.

"Hi, Poops," Lainey said. Then, with a touch of concern in her voice, "What's up, lovey?"

Sarah looked shyly at David as she came in and stood by the bed. "Can I sleep with you, Mom?"

David felt an unexpected pang of jealousy. For what? For their intimacy, for the way Sarah turned so quickly from him to Lainey?

"Was it too scary on 'Creature Feature'?" Lainey asked.

Sarah's eyes shifted quickly to David again, and then she nodded.

"Okay," Lainey said, and patted the bed next to her. Sarah climbed in, flashing her long legs momentarily, her too-big feet. He saw that her toenails were painted a bright pinky-red. "But you know the story. I'll take you to your room in the night, right?"

Sarah slid down. Only her face was visible.

"I'll do that when the time comes," David said. He had stood up now and moved over by the bureau. He was uncomfortable and almost unable to look at the two of them. Sarah was lying close to Lainey's body, and her face on the pillow looked younger than her age, blissful and shy.

Now they could hear Nina coming up the stairs and down the hall to Lainey's room. His eyes met hers as she stood in the doorway—hers were cool, assess-

SUE MILLER

ing—and then she turned to her mother and sister. "Did she say I teased her?" Nina asked Lainey.

"I did *not!*" Sarah said, propping herself up.

"I didn't," Nina said. "She's just not old enough to watch that stuff."

"But you *did* go 'Whoooooo,' " Sarah said.

Nina had come in and sat at the foot of the bed on Sarah's side. Now she made her hands into claws and did it again.

Sarah shrieked and flipped the covers over her face.

David turned away and watched them in the bureau mirror. Nina was bent over Sarah, tickling the wiggling form under the covers. Lainey, laughing, held her glass out away from the commotion.

"Don't!" Sarah shrieked, "Don't! You're killing me!"

When she thrashed too hard against Lainey, Lainey tickled her also with her free hand.

He had a feeling they were doing this for him, all of them. But he couldn't understand—and maybe they wouldn't have known either—whether they were trying to pull him in or push him away. It made him nervous and sorrowful, simultaneously. He felt the chilliness of his own personality as if it were weather. When he had lived here, been part of them, they had needed him, and he had been aware of what he gave them—some coolness or perspective in the hot glare of Lainey's emotionality.

Now he wasn't sure. He knew he hadn't been a good father to them in these years away, concentrating too much of his attention on Mack. On Mack, because he resisted so. On Mack, because he was the boy. On Mack. Because the little girls seemed all right, happy, and Mack didn't.

And now here they were, giggling and wrestling, showing him what he'd missed.

"Careful, girls," he said. "Remember Mom's head."

They sat still, panting. Sarah emerged from the covers, her hair mussed and wild. They all looked at his reflection in the mirror.

He turned to face them. "I'm getting another drink," he said. He held up his glass. It was only half empty, he noted with surprise. "You, Lainey?"

"No. Bedtime. Bedtime for me and Sarey-Berry." She set her glass down and slid farther under the covers, throwing several pillows onto the floor. "But if you'd get the light, please?"

"I will."

He picked up the dirty glasses from the bureau and went to the door. Nina had stood up too. "I'm watching the second half," she said as she pushed past him. A pulse of perfumed heat from her exertions enveloped him. He was startled to realize how tall she was. As tall as Lainey, almost. Her eyes stared into his, nearly level with his own, and then she ran down the hall, down the stairs, her hair like a broad dark ribbon waving across her back.

He flicked the light switch off and stood in the doorway for a moment, looking back. "I'll come get you in a while, Sarah," he said.

"Okay." Her voice was dreamy already.

"Good night, David," Lainey called, as he started down the hall.

He hadn't been alone in the kitchen for three years, he realized. The yellowed paper shade on the lamp allowed light only over the table. He looked up at the wall around it. The picture of Freud with his family in the garden was still there, spotted and browned with age. There was a clipping of JFK laughing, a photograph Nina must have taken of Randall and Mack together. There were three art postcards, two of annunciations, David saw, moving close to them, and one of Paul as a Harlequin, by Picasso. Underneath all of this someone had taped a three-by-five card with a recipe for Rice Krispies Treat.

David looked again at the Picasso and realized that it was there because someone must have thought it could have been a portrait of Randall at an earlier age. He stared at it—the pretty, otherworldly face, the dark empty eyes. Randall. David thought of how he'd looked this evening, huddled in fear and misery in the corner of the front hall. Had he recognized somehow that he'd hurt Lainey? David suddenly imagined that moment, the frantic push, and Lainey stumbling back, the sharp sickening noise as her head struck. He saw her lying crumpled, as she must have lain, the blood beginning to pulse out under her head in a dark pool.

What if she had died?

What if?

David tried to imagine himself returning to this house, supervising the children, helping them with homework, insisting on chores. Abruptly he recalled a time, years earlier, when he was telling Liddie what to do in what he thought of as a calm, businesslike way—a way he congratulated himself on for being so different from Lainey's way. Liddie had turned to him in fury and said, "Why do you always have to *preside* over us? Why can't you just *live* with us, like Mother does?"

David added more bourbon to his glass. He stood for a while at the kitchen sink. The plates and glasses from supper were recklessly heaped in it. The potted plants on the windowsill—geraniums—were leggy and brown from underwatering. Dried leaves were sprinkled all along the ledge around them. He was thinking of a patient he'd terminated with recently. She was an older woman who reminded him vaguely of Lainey's mother. She'd been in therapy for two years for depression. In one of their last sessions together she'd said, "I know you have great theories about why I'm better, but you're wrong. It's not because of any of your theories. The reason I'm better is on account of you. On account of the way you are."

He had been moved by this, touched. But he had said quickly, "Well, that would fit the theories rather nicely too, you know." She had laughed and said she should have known it would.

But he kept coming back to it later, as he did now. It had made him confront, finally, the growing sense he'd had for, he supposed, years that in the end, all his training, all his ideas about psychiatry, probably mattered less than the fact that somehow he had a gift, a way of hearing, of responding, that helped his patients. Nothing he could congratulate himself on then. Just luck. He had worked with it, to be sure. He had honed it. But it was, at its root, luck. He felt a sudden sense of emptiness, recalling this, and he turned back to the lighted table, to the cluttered images on the wall above it.

When David came into the living room, carrying his freshened drink, Nina, who had been lying stretched out on the couch, tucked her legs under her nightie and shifted to the side to make room for him. "I'm warning you, Dad, you're not going to like this stuff," she said. Her eyes were glassy and unwavering on the set—"two burned holes in a blanket," Lainey would have said.

He sat down and looked at the screen. A man with a boar's snout and tusks clutched a struggling woman, his human hand over her mouth. Her arched eyebrows rose in anguish, and when his hand slipped, she uttered a series of piercing shrieks from immaculately painted dark lips.

"Wrong," he said. "There's nothing I like better

than when the hairy beast carries off another nubile maid." He chuckled theatrically.

"Oh, Dad," she said, and shifted again, away from him slightly, so that he was looking at the rise of her butt in her white nightgown. They watched together in what David hoped was a companionable silence as the sad tale unfolded—the misunderstood monster, the finally sympathetic beauty, the terrible death. Each time a commercial came on, David went upstairs to listen outside Randall's room for sounds of his waking, at Lainey's to be sure she was all right. There was only a steady silence behind Randall's door and, in Lainey's room, the twinned slow rhythms of her breathing and Sarah's.

When the movie was over and Nina had stood up to turn off the television, David asked her abruptly, "Was it scary, Neen?"

She turned around to face him. "Dad! I'm fourteen years old."

"I don't mean the movie. I mean when your mother passed out."

"Well, I didn't *know* it right away." Her voice was bored.

"Did you find her?"

"No. Sarah did. We were upstairs, and she came down to see what was on." Silence. These were not events she wanted to talk about with David.

He cleared his throat. "Well, I just wanted to tell you how well you handled everything. You did just the right things—and in a very grownup way."

She was swinging nervously, just slightly, from side to side. Her nightie billowed gently with her motion. "Thanks," she said, in a small, embarrassed voice.

"It must have made you angry with Randall, though, in some sense."

Her voice tightened. "There's no point getting angry at Randall," she said quickly.

"Occasionally, though, people have been known to get angry when there is no point to it."

She didn't answer. She had lifted the dark rope of her hair from her back and now was twisting it, pushing the coil against her head as her mother had pressed the bloody towel to her head earlier. She was beautiful suddenly, dark and grave, like a younger Lainey.

"Of course, these occasions are rare indeed. Only a few documented cases in the entire history of Western man. Statistically insignificant . . ."

She sighed dramatically, impatiently. "I *know* what you're trying to get me to say, Dad."

He smiled at her. "Well, then say it, dammit!"

She laughed suddenly, dropping her heavy hair, and David felt she'd offered him a gift of great value. "No way, LBJ," she said, grinning. "Anyhow, I'm sleepy. It's like, one in the morning or something." She started out of the living room.

David pushed himself off the couch. "I'm headed up too. I have to check on everyone." He switched off the living room lights and followed her up the creaking stairs. At the top, Nina opened the door to the third-floor stairwell. The light from above fell across her straight flat hair, her face was in its looping shadow. David reached out, saw her tighten, but touched her anyway, her silky hair, her narrow shoulders.

"Night, Neenee," he whispered.

She relaxed a little. "Night, Dads," she said, and stepped up and pulled the door shut behind her.

Sarah woke at his touch, but her eyes stayed blank, without recognition; and then she moaned and turned away. He held her arm, shook it gently. She whined and jerked her shoulder forward. Lainey stirred on her side of the bed.

David decided to carry Sarah. She fussed a little when he slid his arms under her, but her weight was dead as he swung it up, she was utterly limp against his shoulder. His hands touched the bare flesh of her thigh and bottom under her nightgown, where her skin was damp and warm. She smelled of sweat and soap. He shifted her and felt the dry wadding of a bandage, a cotton pad between her legs. Sarah. His heart lurched abruptly for her, for all he didn't know about her, about any of them.

When he laid her down in her own bed, she curled immediately away from him, whimpered once, and was quiet. He yanked the covers out from under her, then pulled them up again to her chin, patted them close around her huddled form.

He was heading downstairs when he heard Lainey's faint call. His name. He went back down the dark hall to her room. "Hi," he whispered.

"Hi," she said. "Everyone's asleep?"

"On the way, anyhow," he said. "How are you?"

"Fine, I think."

"No headache? No nausea?" He'd crossed to the bed, stood by it. He couldn't really see her, just the darkness of her hair against the pillows.

"No," she said. There was a silence. Then she asked, "Randall hasn't waked?"

He sat down. "No."

"I don't know how to thank you for coming over." Her voice was almost her normal speaking voice, but rustier, softer with sleep.

"You don't have to, Lainey." He reached out, touched the dark mass of her hair, thicker than Nina's. The white circle of her face turned toward him on the pillow.

"Are you sleepy?" she asked, and he felt the sudden weight of the evening, a yearning just to lie down next to her.

"I am," he said. "You know, I was actually on my way to bed myself when Sarah called."

"*Sarah* called?"

"Yes."

"For some reason, I just assumed it was Nina. She usually takes charge." She had turned on her side toward him.

David's foot was touching a pillow. He bent down and picked it up. He propped it against the footboard and then stretched out, his feet toward Lainey's head. "She did take charge," he said. "But she was guarding you. She told Sarah to call."

"Guarding me? Oh, good Lord, what a horrible thought." She flopped onto her back. "Oh," she moaned. "Ick, ick. I can't stand it, David."

He didn't answer.

After a while, she asked, "Do you have a cigarette?"

He patted his jacket. "Yes."

She wiggled up to a sitting position in bed. Their hands reached for each other. He took hers, put a cigarette in her palm, then lifted another to his own mouth and found his matches.

They sat back, the bright glow of their cigarettes marking their locations, head of bed, foot of bed. A matched pair, he thought. She moved suddenly sideways, then back, and he felt a little weight by his outstretched leg.

"Ashtray in the middle," she said.

He reached forward and found it with his fingers, dropped the match into it. They sat for a while, smoking in silence. David was intensely aware of her, of the flare of orange when she inhaled, of her movements on the bed. Abruptly they both started to speak at once, then stopped.

Lainey laughed, a scratchy intake. "You go," she said.

"No, you."

"No, really," she said. "I'll remember, and go after you."

He drew on the cigarette and leaned back. "I miss the girls. Or I've missed the girls. I've not thought about them enough." He wanted to explain about the pad between Sarah's legs, about how beautiful Nina had grown, but a kind of shame that any of this should have been a revelation to him prevented him. "Seeing them tonight makes me sad. That's all." He tapped his cigarette on the ashtray. "What's yours?"

She didn't answer for a moment. She stirred, and the bed moved under him. "Oh, mine is foolish," she said.

"Come on. You promised."

"I feel bad, especially after yours." She reached forward toward the ashtray. "I was going to tease you about being home alone, in bed early, on a Saturday night."

"Ah."

"It seems mean now, and I didn't intend it that way."

"Well. I have slowed down."

Her voice was suddenly sarcastic. "I've ground to a halt, myself."

"Lainey." He didn't want her to veer off into bitterness. He wanted to sit here, peacefully, out of time, for a little longer.

When she spoke again, her voice was gentle, musing. "But it is true, when I think of it, that the girls give me something that's nearly the same." Her cigarette glowed brightly, then died. "I don't mean it's the same, really. Or anything like sex. But I do. I touch them a lot. They touch me, and it is. It's very physical. It's pleasure." They sat in silence. Somewhere in the dark, the house shifted, creaked. "It's hard when they won't, then," she said. "When they outgrow it. Like Nina." The tiny circle brightened again. And then he felt the motion of her arm, reaching for the ashtray. "I'm not sure what I'll do when they're gone." Her voice was soft, hollowed.

"Maybe you'll have sex," he said. "To get what the girls used to give you."

"I'll be—what?—around ninety-two by then?"

"You're as old as you feel."

"Maybe ninety-three."

He laughed and sat up, felt for the ashtray to put his cigarette out.

She had sat up too. She leaned toward him. She was waiting for him to be finished with the ashtray. Her hair fell forward; he could smell it, he could feel it moving the air close to his face.

While she was putting her cigarette carefully out, he lifted his hand to her head, he slid his fingers under her thick hair to the bare skin of her neck, her jaw. There was a little clicking noise in her throat.

Her head came forward and rested on his shoulder. Her hands gripped his forearms. He bent toward her, kissed her neck, moved his hand down over her heavy breasts, the familiar paths of her flesh. He felt an old, deep desire.

"No," she whispered.

For a moment he ignored her, but then he felt that her body had frozen, and he dropped his hands.

"Lainey?" he asked.

"I can't, David."

"Is it a bad time?" he asked. Their old password.

She laughed. The spell was broken, and she leaned back among the pillows. "A bad time. No. Just that I can't." After a moment she was, he thought, weeping.

"I've managed . . ." she began; and was unable

to go on. He sat tensed at his end of the bed. He felt disqualified to comfort her. Then her voice came again, thicker, but willed to calm. Harder too. He was glad he couldn't see her face. "You can't know what it was like for me after you left. I was terror-stricken. I felt that . . ." He could hear her gulp. After another moment she said, "I've gotten to a safe place now. And it's where I want to stay. I don't want to want you. Or to miss you. And I'm not interested in being someone you want momentarily. Or even occasionally. If you were ready to come back it would be different." Her voice was flat, with no question or hope in it. She wasn't asking him for anything. Then, much more gently: "Maybe you're just confused about the girls too. All that nice touching."

"I don't know," he said. "I don't know about any of it." He had swung his feet down. He was sitting now on the edge of the bed, staring at the dark.

"What do you mean?"

"I don't even know that, Lainey. What I mean. What I feel. I'm sorry. I was . . . I was relieved to go, to be away. I had felt for years that it was a kind of death, our life together. That I was dead. That I'd watched you die. And that all my relations, with you, with the children, were false. A kind of . . . nattering designed to keep me away from my own misery."

"And were you more alive out there?" Her voice was tender, full of pity. "With other women?"

"More *out there*." He turned to where she was. "Yes. I was. I have been. For a while I was. But I wouldn't have gone unless you had wanted me to go."

Her voice was suddenly colder, louder: "That was hardly a whim, if you recall." He reached out to where it was coming from; he was saying "Shh, shh" while she spoke. His fingers grazed her cheek, her lips. She paused, then spoke in a softer tone again.

"It more or less had the quality of a forced hand, wouldn't you say?"

After a long wait, he said softly, "We could go back and back, Lainey. 'You made me do this.' 'You made me do that.' 'If you hadn't done this, I wouldn't have done that,' ad infinitum. It's like trying to find a prime mover."

She didn't answer, and after a moment he said, "If Randall had been all right." There was silence. He went on. "If the pill had been invented ten years earlier. If I hadn't slept with anyone else." She stirred. "A thousand ifs," he whispered. "A thousand mean, desperate things we each did. And I am . . . sorry. For my share." He could hear that her breathing was uneven. "I hope you can believe that." He waited a minute, then spoke again. "But tonight I wanted you. Maybe *because* of all that, all we've done to each other. Because, in some way, it's all been done. And we've forgiven each other so much. Because we've passed through it."

She leaned forward and reached for his arm. Her hand struck him gently, then opened and held him.

He turned to her and touched her legs under the covers. "Because I know you so well, and you know me. Because I miss the girls."

After a long moment she whispered, "I can't, David."

"I understand," he said. "I know. I'm sorry if I hurt you by asking."

She sat back again. He could see her head moving slowly back and forth on the pillows. Then she stopped. Finally she said, "It probably is a bad time anyway. I mean, I barely remember from one month to the next. But it would be our luck. Can you imagine?"

"All too well."

She laughed. She said, "I'm so tired."

"Me too," he said.

"*Don't* sleep on the couch," she said. He thought for a moment, then, that she'd open the covers to him as she had to Sarah. "Mack's bed is so much more comfortable."

He was surprised at the sorrowful pinch of rejection he felt. But he made his voice jaunty as he stood up. "Mack's bed it is, then."

But in Mack's doorway he stood, unready for sleep. Across the third-floor landing, he could hear Nina move and sigh. He stepped into the room and shut the door, waiting until then to turn the light on, so it wouldn't disturb her slumber.

This room was the mirror image of Nina's, with its sloping walls, its window seats. But Lainey had papered it differently. Boy's paper, tiny antique automobiles, although Mack had never had even a passing interest in cars. That hadn't been the point, though. The point, David thought, had been that Lainey had done it herself, showing him once more how competent she was. Demonstrating to him how well she could manage everything. Trying to refute his marriage-long argument that for all their sakes, Randall should be sent away. He remembered the smell of wheat paste in the house, he remembered her leading him up the stairs to show him her latest accomplishment. He hadn't responded the way she wanted him to, he recalled; there was a fight. She'd cried, the children had retreated to their rooms. The house was suddenly a study in closed doors.

Now he thought of how many of their positions they'd taken in response to the other's. For him to say that Randall's care was burdensome meant she papered Mack's room, put new linoleum down in the bathroom, picked the scraggly clumps of grapes from the slanting arbor in the backyard and made jam. And then, hot, tired, drunk, she would slap the children, weep, accuse him of retreating into his work, never helping, not caring.

The year they found out about Randall, she'd been so full of household achievements, so lost as to seem crazy in her desire for these useless accomplishments. Always worn, frantically moving on to another project at the children's expense. The psychiatrist had used the word *autistogenic* to David, and it was all too easy to believe it.

And then they'd had Nina.

He had been terrified after Nina's birth. She was a quiet, placid baby, and her docility, her gentle, passive nature, had frightened him. He half believed she would develop as Randall had. He could feel the fear stiffen his arms as he held her. He was afraid of hurting her, of damaging her. He tried to have as little to do with her as he could; but he watched her more anxiously than he had any of the others. And before that was even resolved, before Nina had sat or said a word, Lainey was, unbelievably, pregnant again. This time he had known better than to talk about abortion, than even to bring it up with her. But his very silence made her worse. It became the goad, the driving force, the impulsion—to chair the PTA, to write letters to the editors, to knit matching shapeless sweaters for all the children, to paper the walls of their rooms.

He remembered now. When they had stood here, in this room, he had said, "Well, if wallpaper could cure this family, we'd certainly all be in great shape." This was the edge he always played close to in his humor; he had thought she might laugh.

But she had spent too much time on this, she had hoped for too much from it, to let it become part of one of his jokes. Her face whitened, her mouth turned bitter. She had begun the familiar litany of

complaint against him—for his coldness, for his remove from her, from the family. It had escalated
quickly. She had shut herself into their room, crying.
He had left the house. Then returned and apologized.
Perhaps they were still at the stage then when they
might have made love. He couldn't remember.

It made him tired, and sorry for them both, to recall it. He sat down in Mack's desk chair. On the wall
in front of him was a poster for a movie called *Reefer
Madness*, with a photograph of a demented-looking
young man showing the effects of marijuana. Next to
it was a series of sketches by Mack—cartoons really—
of musicians playing, or singing. Negroes, they
seemed to be. There was a portrait that David recognized as Al, done in one long slow black line, a separate squiggle above the forehead for his looping
pompadour. David looked at the objects on Mack's
desk, neatly arranged and dusted by Retta in his absence. Sports awards. A mug full of pens. There were
several jars of ink, a stamp pad, and in a little saucer
were spilled some pennies and several keys. David
thought he recognized one as the key to his own
apartment that he'd given to Mack, hoping they could
somehow be closer. It hadn't worked, though Mack
had always been civil—too civil—to him. But he held
all his anger and resentment in, and it came out eventually in cutting asides. He remembered Mack's saying
to him after he'd been accepted at Harvard, "Well,
now I'm out. Free and clear, just like you."

David had been so shocked that he hadn't been
able to answer.

Mack had smiled then and said, "I wonder how
they'll manage. Women and idiots."

David forgot what he'd said in response. Probably something wise, remote—"headshrinky," as Mack
called it—about Mack's anger. But it didn't matter in
any case. Mack had intended to wound him, he saw

that he'd succeeded, and he'd moved on, he was talking about whether he'd try out for a sport, about which one he was likely to make the team in.

Now David got up, restless, and pushed away from Mack's desk. He went to the front window, which looked out over the square. From this steep angle, it looked small and unreal, stagelike. The streetlight on Harper was burned out, and all the contrasts were muted, the shadows longer and muzzier than they should be. Abruptly David saw, superimposed on all this, his own bright image reflected in the window. All those subtle shifts in the real world disappeared to black behind it. He stood, solitary, filled with a sudden burning self-hatred for the tall, trim man in the glass. He crossed quickly to the light switch, then lay down on the mattress pad and felt, nearly instantly, the deep dizzying pull of his fatigue.

He slept, he wasn't sure for how long. He was dimly aware of one, then another, train roaring past.

And then suddenly he was awake, listening hard to a quieter noise in the house.

He got up quickly, staggering slightly in the dark. He hurried down the stairs, down the hall to Randall's door. His head bent to touch it, he listened. There was only silence. He waited for what felt like several minutes, but the noise didn't repeat itself. Slowly he could feel his body relaxing. Now he went to Lainey's doorway and listened to her even breathing. Then to Sarah's room, silent also behind her closed door.

Standing there, he imagined Lainey doing this night after night, making this round among the closed and opened doors, listening for the children's rhythmic breathing, their dreaming, while he slept alone in his apartment, the bedroom door flung wide to the silence beyond.

But this was dishonest. It was just as likely that he hadn't been alone, that he'd been with one of the women he'd slept with over the past several years. He stood still in the dark hallway and they emerged up at him, faces, bodies, aspects of sex. There were several whose names he'd forgotten, he realized. Six or seven, in three years. That wasn't so many, perhaps. And as he'd told Lainey, it had pretty much stopped.

But it wasn't their numbers anyway, or the fact that some of them had been young—nearly as young as Liddie in one case—that disturbed him. What had pained him, shamed him, was the adolescent hunger he had felt through it all for its melodrama, its mindless excitement.

Liddie's doorway yawned blackly open at the end of the hall. He made his way slowly to it, touching the wall. He went in and sat on the bed. He was thinking about the woman who'd been her age, the last woman he'd been involved with. Charlotte. He hadn't even liked her much, but he'd felt nearly out of control with an almost self-willed passion for her, for her life. She was a graduate student, a self-proclaimed radical, a "liberated woman," which seemed to mean that she slept with a lot of people. He had smoked dope with her, he had eaten peyote. He had danced wildly and without self-consciousness. He had fucked her in ways he'd never even wanted to fuck anyone. And while he was living through all of it, he felt utterly free, in a mean, desperate way. He felt it was the only reality—or at least the only life he could learn anything from.

And then he'd have the children over, or take them out somewhere, and realize that everything else he was going through was negated by their irrefutable claims, by the immediacy of their daily concerns: Mary's humiliation over her braces. Mack's near expulsion from school for insulting a teacher. Nina's struggle with Lainey about a curfew.

Finally those claims had caused a series of arguments with Charlotte, and the last one had just about ended it. He'd had to cancel an evening with her because of one of the kids; she'd said she was tired of the way his children took up their time, took his energy. He yelled back. She called him a fucking asshole.

There was a long silence. Then he'd said, "If you could see your face when you say things like that, how hard, how ugly it looks." He knew he was trying to hurt her, but it was true too. Her face, in its eager meanness, was ten years older.

"You like it well enough when we're fucking," she said. Then her face changed and she cried out frantically, "Fuck me. Fuck me. Fuck my cunt." They were exactly the excited tones she used when he was in her; her face was suddenly stamped with that same ecstasy.

He was shocked at the skillful imitation. He said quickly, "I've even grown a little tired of it then." This was true too. The pounding emphasis on the forbidden words sometimes did seem merely silly to him.

But now she was smiling, hungry to hurt him too. "Well, let me say then that I've grown a little tired of what passes for a hard-on with you." They'd both drunk a lot.

For a long time he couldn't think of a response. Then he said, "Perhaps it's just a generational thing." He was trying to make light of it, trying to bring them back to a place where something might be retrievable between them.

But she wanted this; her face was unusually animated. She said carefully, "No, I don't think that's it."

"What is it then?"

"It's that I'm out here, in the real world, the world that's changing. And you're just fucking around with it, fucking with ideas about change. Do you give one shit, really, about Laing or Norman O. Brown or any of those guys? They're just ideas to play with for you. To me, to us, they're real.'' She had stood up. She crossed the room and planted herself in front of him. "I've changed my life, David. I've made me who I am. And you're still so fucking hung up. You're still married, for God's sake. You don't even know how to make yourself free.'' She tilted her head and smiled at him. "Fuck you," she said lightly. "Watch my ugly face now.'' She leaned forward and thrust her face at him. "Fuck you. Fuck your family.''

He had left that night, but that hadn't ended it. She'd called him about a week later, her voice slurring on the telephone. She was weeping. She said she'd been at a party, she'd smoked too much, drunk too much. That she'd gone into a back bedroom and had sex with several people—"Maybe three or four, I don't know"—and now she needed him.

It was raining. He couldn't catch his breath as he started to drive. He wanted to fuck her, to hit her; he felt a deep excitement in this trashy drama. He was driving fast down Fifty-fifth Street, and he ran a red light. He saw the pedestrian just in time and swerved, his brakes squealing. He came to a halt sideways in the intersection.

The man stood and pounded David's car in his rage. He was wearing a poncho; his face was lost in the black hole of the hood. He was like a nightmare, a death figure from a Bergman movie. His angry breath frosted in the dripping air. David sat inert and watched him as he came around to the door by the driver's seat and kicked it several times before he disappeared into the dark downpour.

Cars were honking. David started the engine and pulled over to the side of the street. For a long time he sat there gripping the wheel, his heart pounding, and wondered how he could have allowed this to happen to him. Finally he turned the car around and headed back to his apartment. His door still bore the dents the man had kicked in it.

Now he heard a distant thump: Randall. He moved quickly and silently down the hall. He shut Lainey's door, wincing at the hard click of the catching lock, and opened Randall's, fumbled on the wall for the light switch.

Randall was on his hands and knees, rocking, groaning. His mattress had skidded drunkenly out into the room. He looked like a mad shipwrecked survivor on his raft.

David began to speak, softly, almost crooning. He crouched and touched the boy's back, and smelled the pungent odor of urine. He felt the bunched and corded sheets under Randall. Wet. Cold. He slid his arm around his son, under his armpit, and lifted him to a standing position. The boy shuddered, whinnying, but he didn't resist. Maybe, David thought, because he'd gotten used to a man taking care of him, with Bob. David led him down the hall to the bathroom, speaking softly, slowly, the whole while.

In the bathroom's bright light, he pulled Randall's damp pajama bottoms down, unbuttoned the top, trying not to look at the heavy swing of the boy's penis, the dark patch of hair around it.

Blinking, his face wrenched closed against the light, Randall lurched to the toilet and sat down. He pushed his penis between his legs and then bent over to watch it. David heard the hesitant spurt, then the driving flow. He turned away. He hadn't seen Mack naked in years, but how different he would feel, he realized. How proud, even aroused a little, he might be by the vision of Mack's maleness. With Randall, there was only something sad, repugnant. He thought of what Lainey had said about the girls, about their sense of what being male meant. He looked back at

Randall. There was a light beard griming his jawbone, and David wondered, irrelevantly, who shaved him.

The flow of urine into the toilet slowed, stopped. Randall was still hunched over, though. Now his belly tightened, and he grunted.

David knew he should stay, that the boy would need wiping; but some instinct for privacy—probably his own, if he were honest, more than his son's—made him leave. He went back to Randall's room and stripped the bed. A corner of the red blanket was damp too, but he decided not to risk the noise of a tantrum by taking that away. He left the sheet, the rubber pad, the pillowcase in a wadded heap by the stairs, where he'd dropped Randall's pajamas. He got clean bedding from the linen closet and tossed it onto the mattress. He found dry pajamas in Randall's drawer.

He went back down the hall. Randall was still on the toilet, his arm was still wedged down between his legs, but he had relaxed, he sat quietly. the rich stink of his bowels rose around him. David shut the door and stepped forward into it.

"Okay, let's try this," he said. He unwound some toilet paper, wadded it, and held it out to Randall. The boy seemed to wake. He took it, arched his back, and reached around behind himself to wipe, slowly and carefully. "Good boy," David whispered. "Good job." Three times David wadded the toilet paper. Three times Randall wiped at himself as laboriously as a little child just learning how. All the while, David whispered his praises.

Then he helped Randall on with his dry pajamas and they returned down the narrow dark hallway to Randall's room. David quickly sailed the rubber pad, then the sheets, onto the mattress and pushed it back against the wall. "Here you go, come on," he said, squatting, patting the mattress. Randall stood and stared just beyond David as though he hadn't heard him.

"Here we go," David whispered in a singsong voice, feeling some desperation. He stroked the bed. Randall didn't move. David stood and picked up the red blanket. "Here we go," he said. "Lie down." He waved the blanket, like a deranged matador, as Randall knelt, then awkwardly flipped over onto his back.

David's hands were trembling as he tucked the blanket in. He knew for the sake of ritual that more was expected—a song, or for him to lie down too. But he felt incapable of any more patience or tenderness. And it wasn't that he was angry at Randall or blamed him. In so many ways he was the same sweet animal-child he'd always been. His clubbed penis, his beard, his pubic hair, all were like terrible accidents that had happened to him.

And to David were the denial of the hope he didn't know until that moment he'd still entertained: the hope that his son could change. An autistic boy, a beautiful autistic boy, is one thing. An autistic man, another. And this had happened in his absence, this final crushing aspect of the bad luck, the accident that was Randall. With shaking hands he carefully locked Randall's door again.

He scooped up the urine-soaked bedding and went downstairs through the silent house. Again he felt the sense he'd had earlier of doing this in Lainey's place, perhaps even on her behalf. There was something calming about this. He descended the second set of steps now, to the basement laundry, made over after Sarah's birth, at Retta's insistence. The light was fluorescently bright when he turned it on, and the appliances gleamed meanly. The bright boxes of soap and bleach stood in a neat row on a shelf on the wall.

It was as he carelessly, Lainey-like, began to

shove the damp sheets into the washer that he felt how blameless he held her, and stopped, astonished.

And then was not astonished. Then he felt that he'd known this for a long time, without realizing it: he had known that this was luck too. Just luck. That Randall's illness was only bad luck, fate. He'd known that Lainey hadn't caused it, he'd known that he was wrong, had been wrong, to think so. The years seemed to roll by in his mind as he looked for the moment when he must have seen it first; and couldn't find it.

The light above him ticked and flickered, brought him back to life, to time. When he began again to push the sheet into the washer, he wasn't sure how long he'd stood there, frozen, but he was conscious now of a deep exhaustion. His hands, his arms, felt heavy and clumsy. And when he turned to go back up the stairs, his whole body seemed to be moving heavily, as though he'd taken on some burden.

When he came up to the kitchen, she was there, summoned, he thought irrationally, by the power of his emotion. He heard her as though from a distance offering to make coffee or to fix him another drink. She said she'd waked up when he was tending Randall, but didn't get up because she thought it might make him somehow worse. When she turned to the sink, he saw that on the bandage she wore there was blood. She was talking steadily, but he could barely hear her. He was startled when she set a glass in front of him, when she sat down opposite him at the table.

He sipped at the drink. The cold shocked him, and he set his glass down too quickly. A little liquid slopped on the table.

"Thank you for doing all that," Lainey said. His face must have looked puzzled, because she added, "With Randall, I mean. I know it's not pleasant."

From somewhere he heard his own voice. It

sounded creaky, old. "There's no need for thanks. It's as much my job as yours." He cleared his throat. "I've done too little of it."

"Well, I'm grateful anyway."

"I should look at your wound. Your cut."

Her arm went up and she patted the gauze cap. "Why? It feels all right." Her cheeks were flushed from sleep, her hair messy.

"There's blood on the bandage. It must have opened again."

"Oh." She felt around. "Not much, though. It's not wet or anything."

"Still, I'll check it."

"Well, first things first. Let's finish these, why don't we?"

Silently they sat and drank. After a few minutes, David felt the sense of disorientation diminish; he felt returned, somehow, to himself. He looked up at the wall next to him, at the pictures again.

Lainey followed his eyes. She said, "I know it's crazy."

"What's crazy?"

"Two annunciations."

He was about to say, "That's the least of it," hoping she'd laugh, when she continued.

"It's just that they're both so beautiful, but in such different ways. See? The Fra Angelico is classic and peaceful. The angel comes, and Mary's so . . . unruffled, so accepting." She moved her face closer to the little images, squinting. "But Botticelli. He's got all this motion, right from the angel to her. The angel rushes in, and his air moves her too, all in one line. It seems sexual, as though she really is being made pregnant. And she's turning away too, see? It's as though some part of her is wanting to run. Not to have to do it."

" 'If this cup may not pass from me.' To quote Adlai."

She looked over, and now she did laugh. "Well, yes. Lord, I bet he wishes he'd never said that." Her face sobered. "But I love both interpretations. Or I'm intrigued by them."

"I vote for Botticelli," David said, after a moment.

"Do you? Interesting. But you were always more sympathetic to ambivalence than to certitude. Or belief anyway."

He was startled. "Was I?"

"Oh, yes! Didn't you know that?"

"Apparently not."

She had turned and was frowning at the postcards again. Then she sat back and looked at all the pictures, as though trying to make sense of them together.

"Lainey," he said. And was surprised at the tenderness in his tone. He couldn't remember when he'd spoken to her this way.

She turned to him, and her face widened eagerly to hear whatever he would say to her.

His voice was as loving and gentle as though he were proposing marriage. "Lainey, we need to talk about sending Randall away."

Her face didn't change, but tears brimmed, glittering, on her lower lids. "Yes," she whispered, and closed her eyes.

Spring—Summer 1966

12 THE spring David came back to the family seemed to last forever. Long before anything blossomed or turned green, the air was ready for it. The university students ambled down the streets, arm in arm, slowed as much by the weather as by love. At breakfast the kitchen door was always thrown open, and the gentle wind sighed around everyone, reaching into all the cold corners of the house, seizing their paper napkins, ruffling the magazine pictures tacked on the wall. Everywhere, people talked about it—how warm, how sunny, how unlikely—as they never did about the more remarkable terrible weather Chicago usually had. They seemed nearly dismayed by their collective good fortune. At school, the kids in Nina's classes sat lost, staring out the open windows at the greening world, often not knowing what to answer when one of them was called on.

If she'd been thinking about it, Nina might have seen the long spell of tender weather as a blessing, a benediction on them all, on their new life as a family. But to her the weather, her father, these were backdrop only. Nina was almost fifteen, and she was going through one of those stages that come in adolescence when you think you can change everything about yourself, you can will your life to be different from that time on. She could barely see the events in the world of weather or in her parents' lives, she was so blinded by those taking place inside her. Later she would try to remember the day her father came back, as she could remember—would remember forever, she was sure—the night he left. And she couldn't.

They did talk about it. Their mother sat them down in the living room—picked up for the occasion, Nina noted—and stammered like a young girl as she broke the news. Their father took them out to dinner at Morton's to answer any questions they might have. There was ample psychological preparation. But the day of his return was foggy in her memory. He began coming over to dinner more, staying on into the long, warm evenings. But it seemed to her that she simply didn't notice—perhaps didn't want to notice, or have to think about—when he spent the night again. When the door to her mother's bedroom was shut to them all once more. The main differences in their lives, anyway, were that they had to be neater and that their mother seemed happier, but nervous, as though something might go wrong at any moment.

And Randall was sent away. Whether this happened before or after her father moved in, Nina couldn't say later, but she remembered the general coincidence in timing—though both parents insisted this had been decided separately, that one had nothing to do with the other. But Randall's departure was the event outside her own life that Nina remembered most clearly from those months.

He was sent to a school in Connecticut, a school Lainey had known about and been in contact with for several years through her autism correspondence. There were only minimal preparations necessary. His few possessions were packed into a dark brown duffel bag like the ones Mary and Sarah always took with them to camp, and he got a haircut—a terrible haircut. He was at the mercy of the barber anyway, since he had no ideas to announce—or any way of announcing them—about how he wanted to look. And he moved constantly in his fear of the scissors, so that he always wound up with various gaping stripes of white flesh showing through his dark hair. But this haircut seemed to Nina uniquely brutal, unkind. He was, after all, still beautiful sometimes, in a nearly spiritual way. And this one robbed him of that utterly. It made him only physical, and therefore ugly. She thought he looked faintly like a thug.

Nina cried when he left with her parents for the airport—because he was smiling and placid that day, because in his haircut and new clothes, the pants worn just slightly higher at the waist than a normal person would have worn them, he looked like a child. She cried because she hadn't paid him any attention in weeks, years, except to get angry at him for messing something up or for eating sloppily. She cried because he seemed like a trusting, cheerful pet who's being taken to the pound and understands nothing of that.

He was holding Lainey's hand as they stepped out into the soft spring air, and he barked joyfully at the sound of a train rattling past.

"Yes, train," Lainey said, and they walked together down the long path to the curb. He was taller than she was, but he still walked like a four-year-old, and when he saw the car he let go of her hand and ran toward it, excited to be going for a ride.

Nina was in charge of the house while her parents were away, but she didn't do any of the things her mother had asked her to do. Twice they were all late to school because she hadn't set the alarm. They sat up watching television until one or two every night. And she never cooked. Not once. Instead she used the emergency money Lainey had left, and they ate out—once at the Tropical Hut, once at the Medici, a coffeehouse around the corner. And she bought packaged baked goods—Twinkies, cupcakes, stale little pies wrapped in cellophane—which they all snacked on at odd times. Nina had worked up a story to tell Lainey to explain all this, a lie that might even make her mother feel guilty, about burning her hand. But Lainey never asked.

She seemed stunned. For several days after their return, her eyes would fill up and spill over at odd moments. She would wipe the tears away and go on with her chores as though this were merely a physical phenomenon, like a hiccup or a sneeze, that had nothing to do with what she was feeling. Nina hated this. She wasn't sure whether she wanted her mother to make her grief more ceremonial or more private; but in any case, this kind of bizarre, unexplained incontinence was unbearable to her. Once she was in the kitchen, setting the table, while her mother walked back and forth between the sink and the stove, making the usual racket with dishes and pots and pans, her eyes and nose streaming freely.

Finally Nina couldn't stand it anymore. "Mother!" she said.

Lainey started, as though she'd forgotten Nina was there. She looked over at her daughter guiltily, waiting like a child to be told what she was doing wrong. She was barefoot, wearing an old shirt and shorts that had grown too big for her in the last few weeks.

"Stop it. Stop it!" Nina couldn't think what it was she needed to say to her mother. If Lainey had been a smaller woman she might have taken her by the shoulders and shaken her. "Just stop it," she said.

Lainey set everything down. "I can't," she said, and gulped. And then she left the room.

But of course she did. She stopped, though for a long time she still got up in the night regularly, as though Randall were waking her. Nina imagined her wakefulness as being like the pain that amputees report in a phantom limb. In the morning, though, when they all trooped downstairs, she'd be gone, back in bed, and whatever the traces might have been of her agony were picked up. David would fix breakfast. After their silent mornings in his absence, with Lainey shuffling sleepily back and forth from the counter to the table, smoking, drinking coffee, it was hard for Nina to get used to her father's energy, to his questions, his jokes. Often he'd sing, one of his absurd songs: "The *pope,* he leads a jolly life—jolly life."

But for the most part, all this was merely the stage on which Nina's life was acted out. Actually she barely saw them, rarely thought about them. And this in itself was new for her, an exciting change: she felt free of them at last, in some sense. In her earlier memories they were always the ones on center stage, the ones she could recall most clearly. The Nina that watched them barely existed for herself. She was just a way of seeing them, a way of looking. She couldn't remember what she had looked like, looking. But years later, when she thought back on this period of her life, they were the ones she could barely remember. It was Nina, Nina whom she saw. Their lives, their doings, were blurry and unclear.

And so what seemed of greatest importance to her during these three or four months when so much was happening to them was that she inherited Randall's room.

Prior to this she had always shared a room with Mary. It seemed to her that Mary's asthmatic breathing had been part of her dreams from her earliest memory, that speaking to Mary in the dark was a way of thinking, and Mary's replies were like part of her own consciousness. But Nina was tired of Mary now, of Mary and Sarah both. She'd grown four or five inches in the last year, and that great surge in height seemed symptomatic to her of the distance she felt she'd traveled from them. When Lainey offered her Randall's room, she leapt at the opportunity. For days she sorted through her possessions in preparation for the move, throwing away or giving to Mary or Sarah all those embarrassing remnants of her own immaturity—dolls, Cray-Pas, dress-up clothes. Keeping only those things that spoke of the new life she planned for herself.

Together Lainey and Nina had chosen a feminine, very delicate paper to cover Randall's scarred walls— a cream-colored background, with birds flying among blue and yellow flowers. Lainey hired a painter-paperer to do the room, an old man named Mr. Money. He called Nina "Princess."

All this seemed magical to Nina: Mr. Money's name, his apparent adoration of her, the emergence of the room from its nightmare form to conventional and, to Nina, completely satisfactory prettiness. From somewhere Lainey had found for her a kidney-shaped dressing table with a threefold mirror. It was unlike any of the other pieces of furniture in the house. Everything else was from Lainey's family, or else only functional, simply utilitarian. This had a flower-printed skirt and a little upholstered stool to match it. It seemed a remarkable concession on Lainey's part to something Nina was confident was visibly emerging in herself. After she moved downstairs she would sit in the indented waist of the table for hours, looking at herself from every angle, with every conceivable hairdo. *Me,* her life sang, and she believed it. *Me, me.* So it wasn't until Mack came home from college that she thought very hard or seriously about the changes that had taken place in their lives together.

Lainey had written to Mack, had been trying to call him for days to find out his exam schedule, to find out how he was getting home; but he hadn't responded, hadn't called back. Then one evening as Nina and Lainey and Mary were in the kitchen, cleaning up after dinner, there was a noise over the clatter of dishes and the running water. They all turned, and Lainey was suddenly in motion. It was Mack, grinning in the doorway. He was rumpled, with several days' growth of dark beard shadowing his face. His hair seemed shockingly long to Nina. It was still that time when you took someone for a girl if he didn't have his hair trimmed with clippers on the sides, and Mack's came down nearly to his collar.

In Mack's absence her memory of him was always shaped by the way Randall looked, by that angelic vacancy, the queer childlike haircuts. It was as though in her mind she always saw Mack under a superimposed image of Randall. So she was very startled now to see this large, dark man, full of energy and personality. Startled, too, to see the power of the embrace he gave Lainey—when his arms went around her, her heels lifted off the floor.

For several seconds after the embrace ended, Lainey stood exclaiming with her back to Mary and Nina. Until she turned to them, Nina couldn't see that she was again weeping openly in that curiously unselfconscious way. *"Look,* look who's here!" she cried, as though they couldn't see him, as though he didn't exist, until she pointed him out. She crossed the kitchen to the back door. "David!" she started to call. "Mack's here! Macklin's home." Her hands didn't even lift to clear her flooded face.

When he held her, Mack's beard scratched Nina's cheek, he smelled of sweat and funk, and she was aware of her breasts being squashed against his wide flat chest. Her heart seemed to be banging loosely in her rib cage. When she stepped back from him she couldn't look at him. She felt a heat like shame rise to her face.

But then her parents came back in, and Sarah, and she could disappear into the folds of family, into that familiar hubbub of people bumping into each other, speaking, moving with a kind of comfortable unconsciousness of each other.

While Mack showered and shaved, while Lainey fixed him something to eat, Nina went to her room to get her camera. She set it on the dressing table for a minute and sat down. She leaned forward. The shimmery silver of the old mirror was flecked and streaked behind the glass, and she looked hard into this softened version of her face for what it might reveal about herself, her secret thoughts, to someone else. Then, suddenly, she sat back. She picked up her camera and lifted it to her face, looking through the viewfinder into the glass at the hidden girl looking back at her from behind her camera.

She was just emerging from her new bedroom when Mack stepped out of the bathroom, holding a towel wrapped around his waist. He stopped when he saw her, then walked down the hall toward her.

"Your room now?" he asked, smiling.

"Yes," she said, and stood aside.

He rested in the doorway, surveying it. She felt somehow a growing sense of awkwardness. She wasn't sure if it had to do with the prettified room or with Mack's body, large and wet and nearly naked, standing so close to her. He gave off a soapy-smelling damp heat that seemed to surround her. She looked down at his feet, noted that hair curled on his big toes, on the tops of his high white arches.

"Some transformation," he said.

"I know," she answered.

Mack had always been Nina's favorite. There was a kind of inevitability to this. Mary and Sarah were younger, too much like her; Liddie was too old, she left home too early; Randall was autistic. Mack was the only one left, in a sense. But also, he was male, he was powerful. He reminded Nina of her father. Those were the logical reasons, but finally even they didn't explain the importance to Nina of his attention and approval, the wrenching pain she felt each time circumstances reminded her of how inconsequential her life, her existence, was to him. There was some yearning affinity she was always aware of whenever he drew near to her world. Even as a little girl, through all the summer nights they had played their endless round of games in the square or on the street—Spud, Sardines, Hide-and-Seek, Red Rover, Statues—when the big boys descended, it was always exciting. They frightened the littlest ones, they paid the girls to take down their pants, they whipped everyone with the naked wiry branches from the tree of heaven. They forced the girls to eat things they told them were poisonous. And yet the children would have followed them anywhere; they loved them for the excitement, the sense of evil, of danger, they carried with them. For Nina, Mack carried all that, and then more.

And the summer after her father returned, Mack began once more to do things with Nina occasionally. To include her. They were odd adventures, meant in some sense again just to fill time until one of his friends arrived—he seemed incapable of solitude, of reading or even just being alone in his room.

He never actually asked her to do these things, though. For the most part, everything seemed just to evolve, to happen. Once, they sneaked into the freight elevator of an expensive apartment building on Dorchester and spent a half hour or so sitting on the roof, their backs propped against a chimney, looking at the black stripe of the lake against the lighter evening sky. Mack was talking, a disordered monologue Nina had to make a concerted effort to understand, about "purity," how hard it was to have it in this world, how you had to struggle for it in yourself. When she looked over at him in the glowing air, she was startled and moved to see that his eyes were swollen with gleaming tears.

Another evening they went to a playground together. Later Nina was sure that he was stoned that night too, but again she didn't realize it then. She was aware, though, of something self-conscious in her own pleasure, something slightly false; but also something exhilarating that made her push that recognition away, that made her tilt her head back and laugh with almost pure delight as he pushed her on the iron whirligig and then jumped up to join her.

But probably this would have been the extent of his interest in her that summer—he would have swooped down occasionally into her life out of boredom, out of idle affection or curiosity about her, and then pulled back into his own world—if David hadn't found his attention to Nina objectionable.

They were all still sitting at the table in the dining room, though everyone was through eating. Lainey had had Mr. Money repaper this room recently too, perhaps in celebration of David's return, and Nina thought maybe it was on account of this that they had all been behaving with a kind of stunned propriety. But maybe it was just the newness of having David back, or Mack home from college, that caused the politeness; and the magazine elegance of the room had nothing to do with it. In any case, it seemed a little false to Nina, after their years of odd meals served anywhere in the house; it seemed like playacting. But it was also pleasurable, just as the pretense of childish innocence in the playground with Mack had been pleasurable.

Mack was talking. The windows were open—had been open since mid-June in deference to Chicago's steady summer heat—and a little layer of grit sat on all the sills in testament to that. A commuter train rocketed past outside, and they all froze momentarily, sat like a tableau of American family life, mid-sixties. And for those few seconds, Nina felt that quick sense of heightened awareness and self-awareness that stops your heart periodically through adolescence, that promises you you'll understand life if you remember this moment, freeze it under clear glass, look at it unblinkingly over and over. "Yes!" her heart said with a sudden *whump,* and she consciously made herself record the details: At each end of the table her parents sit, Laine;'s face open and eager in love as she waits for Mack to continue; David's composed, minimal smile revealing nothing of what he thinks. The evening sun slopes sideways outside the tall windows—yellows the air, touches the trees—and the room is full of a reflected greenish light. Mary's and Sarah's faces across the table are lifted to Nina and Mack, together on their side; Nina feels connected to him, she feels a sense of tender pity for them. Of love. Of love for them all, as they are at this moment. Of love even for the old familiar dishes on the table, the way her own hands lie curled next to them, the way the trellised arbor on the new wallpaper encircles them all in a false, pretty world.

Then the train was gone and Mack started talking again. Nina couldn't even hear what he was talking about, so concentrated was her need to record the context, the feeling. But in a few minutes he got up, and the spell was broken. They all began to push their chairs back and reach for plates, glasses, silverware.

Mack, bending over the table, turned to Nina. His long hair fell forward across one cheek. "We're going to the Clark tonight, Neen. W. C. Fields. Want to come along?"

She was already saying yes, unwrapping this gift in her mind, imagining the events of the evening to come, when David, unmoving yet in his position at the head of the table, said, "I don't think Nina needs to trail along for that one, Mack."

Mack seemed to uncoil slowly up into a standing position. "I didn't say *trail along*. She won't *trail along*. I asked her to come with me."

"Mack," Lainey said, and then she smiled uselessly, pathetically, at him.

"Well, come on, Mom. What does that mean, *trail along*? He's always doing that, that weird sarcasm. It's like . . . a fucking *trick* or something."

Nina's father was smiling now. "I'm right here, Mack," he said. "You can address yourself to me."

Mack stood, not looking at anyone for a moment. Nina's eyes met her sisters' across the table. Theirs were scared and excited. She realized that they'd all been waiting, they'd all known this moment was going to come. Even the happiness of the few seconds before this, she saw suddenly, was made potent and worth noticing by the inevitability of this moment's arrival.

"Why can't I go?" she asked abruptly. And then she felt it: she'd chosen sides! She gripped the back of her chair.

"I didn't say you couldn't," her father said. "I'm only asking Mack to think about the situation."

"Look," Mack said. "I don't see what the big deal is. Why you're making such a big deal out of it. God."

"I'm not," David said. "But it's my responsibility to look out for the best interests of everyone in this family, and this isn't in Nina's best interest. In my opinion."

"Why the hell not?"

"Oh, come on, Mack. There's no need for all this righteous indignation. You're nineteen. I'm just not so sure that a fourteen-year-old is the appropriate partner for you in your adventures."

Simultaneously Nina protested, "I'm fifteen," and Mack said, "We're going to a W. C. *Fields* movie, for Christ's sake."

"Please don't say that, Mack," Lainey said.

He turned quickly to her. "For Christ's sake?"

"Yes. I'd just rather you didn't." This was a tic of Lainey's, born of religious feeling. It had nothing to do with foul language. It was an era when they'd all begun to swear violently. The world had. *Fuck, shit, asshole:* they used these words freely, often in front of their parents too. And David and Lainey no longer objected, except sometimes for a pinched look on their faces, as though they'd smelled or tasted something not right. But the idle use of *God* or *Christ* still wounded Lainey.

Mack shook his head. "We must live in the only house in the nation where it's more acceptable to say *shit* than to take the name of the Lord in vain."

Lainey smiled. " 'If the foo shits,' " she said.

Mack laughed, and for a few seconds Nina thought that her mother had brought them all through it, that the moment was over.

But her father was standing up now, and he said, "Listen, Mack. All I'm asking you to do is just think about this little romance you're conducting. It's like *Catcher in the Rye.* Pretty great for Holden, but maybe not so fair to Phoebe."

Nina hadn't read *Catcher in the Rye.* She didn't understand her father's reference. But the word *romance* caught her breath and made her blush, made her happy and embarrassed.

"All I'm asking you to do is examine your motivation," he continued. "Think about it."

"I don't need to examine my motivation," Mack said. "There's no reason Nina shouldn't go." And then he said in a mean voice, "I don't know what your trouble is, but it's your trouble. It's got nothing to do with reality, man, nothing at all."

"Mack," Lainey said. Her tone was pleading. It asked, *Don't wreck this, don't spoil this, for me. For us.* There was a long silence in the room, maybe as long as the silence when the train passed.

"Look," Mack announced coolly. "I'm taking Nina with me. If she wants to go."

"Oh, I do!" Nina said. She looked to her mother for support, but Lainey wouldn't meet her eye.

"Of course she does," David said. "That's my point."

"But I can, can't I?"

No one would look at Nina.

"Naturally it's your choice, Nina," David said coolly. "As long as you're home by eleven."

Willing herself unaware of the tension in the room, Nina carted several loads of dishes to the kitchen and then went up to her room to get ready. She was struck by the smell of fresh paint as she entered it, a smell that had made her joyous and hopeful for weeks, that called up for her the pleasure she saw on Mr. Money's face whenever he called her "Princess." And that night, as she got ready to go out with her brother, she was thinking that she'd crossed some threshold, that she'd stepped away from her sisters into some new world that Mack was the owner of. That from now on it would all be different.

They did go to the Clark that night, Al and Soletski and Mack and Nina, and she disappointed them all by not understanding what was funny about W. C. Fields. And after this, Mack began to ask her along more frequently. She went out with them five or six times before it all blew up, but her memory later gave it back to her expanded, repeated over and over.

Her father never again spoke about her "trailing

along" with them, though it was clear he was annoyed by it. But this was his way. It was the way of many of the parents on their block, in their world. They explained their positions clearly and left the choices up to their children. Aside from curfews established for their safety, there were few rules in the children's lives. They were allowed enormous freedom, once it was clear to their parents that they understood the risks and problems in their options.

Nina took a kind of dark pleasure in being the focus of the tension between her father and her brother. She felt vied over by the most important people in her life. She wasn't clever enough then to see that if Mack hadn't chosen her he would easily have found any number of other issues to struggle over with David. It was only later, remembering, that she realized that Mack had announced his position about the new shape of their family in any number of ways since his return.

He seemed unable, for instance, to tolerate the gentle solicitude that marked their parents' new relations with each other.

"Did you sleep well?" Lainey would ask David.

"Very well, thanks," he'd say. "And you?"

"Pretty good," she'd say.

"Not me," Mack would intrude, his voice just slightly too loud. "I made one mistake after another."

He called the family "the expurgated version"; he called David "the wandering gentile," "the prodigal dad." It seemed to Nina that he was using her father's own weapons—humor, sarcasm—and turning them against him. And it worked. David couldn't respond. It would have been impossible to call Mack's bluff or to choose to take offense, because all of this was so perfect an imitation of David's own style, of what he'd been doing to all of them for years.

But Mack didn't bring Nina along only because

it annoyed David. It was just at the beginning of that
period in the sixties when a reverence for childhood,
for childlike innocence, began to flower. Suddenly
you weren't supposed to be cool anymore; you were
supposed to be goofy, charmingly wacky, unselfconsciously eccentric. And through sheer naïveté Nina still
had some of those qualities, those qualities Mack admired and wanted for himself.

And it was partly for this reason that he wanted
to turn her on, to teach her how to smoke dope. Because it was also that time when people who'd discovered marijuana had a kind of proselytizing passion
about it. They believed in it. They thought if everyone
used it, it would bring peace and joy to the world.
That the war would end. And he seemed to think that
if Nina used it, she'd never have to grow out of her
childhood, in some sense. That the quality he saw in
Nina and saw himself as having lost would have been
saved in her if she discovered another way of thinking
about life early enough.

He'd offered it to her even that first night when
they went to the Clark, but because she would have
had to smoke it—and she didn't know how to
smoke—Nina turned it down. Sometimes, though, as
they drove around on various adventures after that,
the boys would pass a joint back and forth in the car,
and Nina could feel herself getting a little dizzy from
the smoke, slipping into a kind of strange associative
way of thinking. They'd grin at each other then and
try to keep her talking. It wasn't until nearly midsum-
mer, though, that they actually succeeded in getting
her high.

It was a night when Nina's parents were going
out for the evening to a dinner party, leaving her
alone in the house—Mary and Sarah were away at
camp, and Mack had said he'd be in charge of his own
supper. To Nina, they looked youthful and happy as

they went down the front steps into the pale summer evening. Lainey had lost a lot of weight just before and after her father moved back in, and they were built remarkably like each other again, both tall and slim and dark. They could have been brother and sister.

Nina called good night to them from the front porch. After they'd turned down the block, out of sight, she went back in and shut the door. The front hall smelled of her mother's perfume, a wonderful complicated aroma, sweet and dark. Nina went up to their room and found the bottle sitting out on Lainey's bureau. Tabac Blonde. Nina knew this stuff had the quality of holy water for her mother. You couldn't get it in the United States. Lainey had a college friend who lived in Paris send her a bottle once a year. Nonetheless, Nina unstoppered it, touched the glass stem to her neck once on each side. Instantly she felt transformed, sexual. She opened her mother's drawer and rummaged through her makeup. Lainey never threw any of it away, so there was a huge assortment of greasy eye shadows, rouges, stubby bright lipsticks. Nina spread everything out in front of her on the bureau and began to try one, then another. Berry Blue eye shadow. Then Misty Gray over that. Candy Plum lipstick. She penciled moles here and there. She spit into the little tray of mascara and brushed the gummy stuff on her lashes.

Below her, she heard the front door open. There were voices—male—and the door slammed shut. It was Mack and company. Their feet bumped heavily in the hall and the living room. Suddenly her image in the mirror changed. What had seemed glamorous to her only seconds before looked cartoonish and idiotic. She headed quickly down the hall to the bathroom to wash her face.

"Is that you, Nina?" Mack called up. As she passed she could see him standing at the bottom of the stairs, his big hand nearly covering the top of the newel post.

"Yeah. I'll be down in a minute." Nina locked the bathroom door and washed her face carefully, leaving a faint trace of lipstick but cleaning off the moles, the goop from her eyes. She brushed her teeth. Music started from downstairs, the powerful voice of a black woman begging over and over to be rescued.

Nina came down into the pulsing beat. They had the volume turned so loud that you could hear a nasal vibration in the air, as if all the glass, all the metal, the house owned were singing along. They were back in the kitchen, shouting at each other. Nina went to the doorway and stood watching them for a moment. Mack was stirring something in a big pot on the stove. Al stood dazed, smiling, in the back doorway. Rob McKinnock sat at the table with his eyes shut, his mouth moving inaudibly with the music. She could smell her mother's perfume on herself under the soap. "Take me, baby, Hold me, baby," the black voices sang urgently. The back door was open, and the light in the room changed suddenly as the wind shifted the leaves on the mulberry tree. The air touched her face, it moved her hair slightly. *Let my life stay like this forever*, she thought. And she stepped into the room.

They were stoned, more stoned than she'd ever seen them before. It took Al a few moments to make sense of why she was there. Mack was making spaghetti for supper, and they'd brought her brownies, brownies cooked with grass, to turn her on. There was a sense of ceremonial generosity as they peeled the tinfoil back off the pan and showed her the bruised-looking cakes.

Nina sat down at the kitchen table and ate two or three of them while the boys smiled idiotically, benevolently, and cooked their dinner. Then the music had changed, the hornlike voice of Otis Redding was rocking the house. They ate spaghetti, sprinkled, too, with a little grass. Nina was beginning to feel strange. When they all cleared the table, she noticed that it took the plates a long time to slide into the sink, and that two of them broke neatly into perfect halves. This seemed utterly remarkable to her, though when she tried to speak of it to Rob, she said something else.

In the dining room and living room they danced, the three of them and Nina, with the music all around them. Time seemed to stand still, then to rush forward. When Nina closed her eyes, she felt the music was part of her, that she didn't have to think about moving—it was inevitable, the music told her how to, she'd been there, doing it, an infinitely long time. After a while the windows were dark, and then it occurred to someone to turn on the lights. They danced some more: the Stones, the Supremes, Junior Walker.

Sometime after that, they were suddenly up in Nina's room, all of them, peeling the wallpaper in memory of Randall. Mack was the one who said it, again and again: "Do this in remembrance of me," and they all pulled the long strips down. It seemed so clear; later Nina could remember the sense of beautiful logic as the paper came off in patches and strips and the horrible wrecked walls were visible again. She felt Randall then, among them; she was stunned by the odd beauty of the walls with the multiple layers of pattern and paint. It was solemn and right. It seemed the only meaningful ceremony of goodbye she'd been allowed to have for her brother. She cried, and Mack held her, his face changed to grief, too, by her tears.

And then they were in the basement, giggling, getting the bicycles out, all the different sizes. When they came up out of the bulkhead, the air was dark and cool, and it silenced them. They each got on a bike and started pedaling. Nina looked back at the house as they left—the windows all burning brightly, the door flung open. She thought how beautiful it was. *Home,* she said, her lips carefully shaping the word. She was startled by her voice in the silent night.

They pedaled for a long time in the black air. They were in a row, at the edge of traffic, and the headlights moved across the boys' pumping legs ahead of her. She watched them all going up and down, up and down, and there was some confusion about whose legs they were, though it helped her to touch her own, to feel that they were the bare ones. Someone was laughing, and the impulse washed over her too: their foolish legs, the joke of all of them doing this in a row.

But when they went through the black tunnel under the Outer Drive, the air changed, it was suddenly cold and damp. Nina's lungs hurt, and she was afraid the air was too cold in them. She was trying to hold her breath.

At the Point, the only noise was the swish and suck of water against the rocks. The lake heaved slowly, massively, gleaming in the moonlight with the silvery schools of dead alewives that had washed to shore in huge numbers that year. Nina sat with her back firmly against the granite pilings, convinced that this way the water couldn't get her, couldn't pull her in. The boys stripped down quickly. They were silver in the moonlight too. They dove in and disappeared under the magic iridescent mass of alewives. They waited to come up until they were out beyond the fish, too far for Nina to see them. And even though she could hear their voices out there, their laughter, she was also sure they were in the fish, that they were dead too. She held her cool knees close for safety, so she wouldn't slip away into the silvery water, and she began to cry again.

When they came back they pulled her up into their midst. They huddled close to her, wet, naked, to comfort her. They were all talking at once, too fast for Nina to understand them. Their bodies were cold, pressing against her. "I thought you were dead," she said. She was touching their bumped, glistening flesh as they jittered around her. Then they were holding her, rocking her, the way you do a child you've trapped in a circle game. Nina let them, she let herself stagger against them, she let their bodies rub together. Al danced away, holding his penis out, calling to her that he wasn't dead and lifting it, waving it as proof. Nina laughed at him, at his flat wet hair, his jiggly penis, and then he pressed into the close ring again, and they were all laughing and moving against her. She could feel their cold, strong bodies, she could feel the kisses of their soft, floppy penises on her legs. She could hardly breathe, she was so excited, so happy. She wanted this dance never to end.

She was too tired to pedal back, so they left her bike and she sat on the crossbar in front of Mack. She was dizzy and sleepy, swaying gently from side to side with the rhythm of his pedaling. But when they got home and she stepped off, she felt as alien as you do after a long boat ride—heavy and earthbound—and she knew that it was nearly over, that she was coming back.

She went into the house and up the stairs. When she turned on the light in her room, her father grunted once, raised his hands to cover his face, and then sat up on her bed, swinging his feet down to the floor. The room was a shambles. Nina's fingers lifted to her mouth, involuntarily. She and her father looked at each other a long moment. Then Nina looked down. Between them, on the floor, were strips of the flowery wallpaper—here a rose, there a bird's opened wing.

Her father's voice said, "Is there an explanation for this? Nina?"

Nina looked at him again. His pale eyes seemed to cut through her, his mouth was a tight line. The overhead light made his high domed forehead gleam.

Nina wanted to take the blame but to share it too, to escape. She was appalled and terrified. "We all did it," she said, and realized that this was her own, her true voice, that it seemed to be saying exactly what she intended.

"You and . . . ?"

It took her a moment to remember. "Mack and Rob and Al."

"I don't suppose you can tell me why."

She shook her head. Nothing could explain this. Then it came back to her. "We did it on account of Randall."

"I see," he said. His composed face tightened even more, but at the same time his shoulders shifted forward. He looked defeated. Nina saw then how much power they had over him. She felt a sudden pity for him.

After a few seconds, or a minute, he asked, "Where is he now?"

"Randall?" she asked. And then she knew that was wrong. "Mack?"

"Yes."

"Outside."

He nodded. His expression hadn't changed. "And whose idea was this?" He gestured at the room. "Who, exactly, was the dim bulb?"

"I think Mack. But I'm not sure."

Her father stood slowly. He was still dressed, though he'd taken off his shoes, his jacket and tie. He stepped noiselessly toward her in his socks, and she stood facing him, tensed for anything: To be hit, though her father had never hit her. To be screamed at. To be wiped from the earth's surface.

"Let's go," he said. He took her arm, and she felt alive again. She turned, and he held her by the elbow as they walked down the hall, down the unbearably loud, groaning stairs. The windows were all glowing with a soft gray light, a light that seemed holy and judgmental to Nina.

Nina and her father stood together in the open doorway. Muted colors had begun to live in what they saw. The sky was almost pink, an oyster color. Rob lay on his back next to his fallen bicycle on the gray-green grass of the square, and his soft giggling noise floated across to them, along with the repeated metal squeal of one of the other bikes. Mack and Al circled around him like circus performers, pedaling slowly. Mack's face was tilted up in a kind of blind ecstasy, opened and closed at the same time. Nina could feel her father's cool grip tighten on her skin as they watched him going around and around and around.

"You are responsible for this too, Nina," her father said to her suddenly. And though later she realized that he'd meant just the events of the evening, the state of the house, when she spoke then she was looking only at her brother, at the chemical innocence on his face, feeling a sense of kinship and protection deeper than blood. "I know," she said. "I am."

And then her father let go of her and stepped forward to call the boys in.

PART

TWO

13

WHEN you read about families like ours, where one member is very ill—*special,* they're sometimes called now—you discover that often when the problem is removed—because the ill person is sent away, or dies, or gets cured—someone else in the family takes on that role. And maybe that's all it was: that after Randall left, there was suddenly room for Mack and me to go crazy, to be as mad, as bad, as we wanted.

On the other hand, maybe we were really only angry at my father for leaving us, *acting out,* as he would say. Or it could have been just that it was the sixties and there was a perfect congruence between the time—which heaped its praise on acting out—and our lives. Or maybe it was a result of living in Hyde Park, where being troubled or in trouble was equated with being sensitive and bright, where the high premium put on eccentricity drove half the people my age then and later into a kind of wasteful extravagance of personality. But perhaps it was all more elemental than that—hormones only, singing in our blood, driving us to wildness.

But whatever the immediate circumstance, the need, there was also—for me anyway, but I suspect for Mack too—the exciting sense of inevitability, of stepping toward a waiting fate that was part of who we were. We *did* go crazy, we *were* bad; and suddenly the balance in our family shifted, the dividing line moved. Where before there had been "the extras" and then the others—*the giants*—with Randall in their center, now the line was drawn between those who were seemingly normal, happy, proceeding well, and then Mack and me, who suddenly were something else. And of course, somehow inevitably connected to us in our wildness, our craziness, was my mother.

This might have been when I was nine or ten years old: Mary and Sarah and I came out late to play. It was almost dark, and we could see that most of the other kids had already gone home. As I went down the front steps, the few who were left out there, running and whirling on the black grass in the square, looked sprightly and otherworldly. They made me think of an illustration in a picture book of mine—a dancing circle of elves and fairies in the moonlight—and I was stopped still for a moment on the steps by the power of the similarity.

Then I heard voices behind me and, turning, saw my mother and Mrs. Gordon on the swing, nearly invisible in the deep twilight of the porch. Their cigarettes were bright soft beacons that swayed with the swing's slow motion. Mary and Sarah were already crossing the grass to the game, being transformed into the magical anonymity of the other children by distance and darkness. I let them disappear. I sat down at the bottom of the porch stairs. I took one of my shoes off and pretended to hunt for a pebble in it, while I listened to the women behind me. The slow squeak of the swing provided rhythm, the cries of the children a kind of music. I stuck my hand inside my sneaker and sat there.

For a few minutes I couldn't understand what they were talking about—some news of Mrs. Gordon's that my mother thought was wonderful and Mrs. Gordon wasn't so sure about. Then Mrs. Gordon said, "I'll tell you what it is with me." Her voice was gravelly, loud. "With me, it's simply that I'm not sure I can bear to do it again."

"Oh, I know," said my mother. "It is so much work those first few years. But, Jane, lovey, then it's done, isn't it? Out of dipes, off to school . . ."

"That's not what I mean," Mrs. Gordon said emphatically. "I don't mind anything once they're here. It's just the goddamned labor." Her cigarette flared orange as Halloween when she inhaled. "I dread it. I dread the thought of it. And all those *hands* up you."

My mother laughed sharply. "Well, yes, there's certainly that," she said. Then there was a thick silence. It seemed female to me—the slow-drifting cigarette smoke, the sense of heavy, physical companionship. When my father talked to his friends, there weren't these long, rich silences full of meaning, full of another kind of communication.

Mrs. Gordon spoke again. "I mean, I can't imagine how you did it six times. What could you have been thinking of, Lainey? Six of them. God!" She laughed.

For me, the air was suddenly thrumming over the beckoning cries of the game. This was it, then. The mothers were talking about *us!* About their children.

"You must have been out of your mind," Mrs. Gordon said.

After a moment my mother said, "Well, in a way I suppose I was." Her voice sounded hollow. I squinted over at the darkened porch, but I couldn't see her face. It was lost in the shadows, in the funny angle up. "Quite mad, actually."

"Oh, God! I didn't mean it that way," Mrs. Gordon said.

"Oh, I know, I know," my mother said in a tired voice. Somebody moved a glass, and ice chimed. "But I was. That's all."

I drew my hand out of my sweaty shoe and cupped it over my face. I breathed deeply the rubbery, familiar, comforting odor. My shoes, my feet, my hand.

"Is that you, Neen?" my mother asked in a different voice.

I bent to put my shoe on. "Yes."

"You'd better play before it gets too dark, sweetie. I'm calling you girls in at nine o'clock."

"It'll be dark before nine o'clock," I said, tying my shoe. I hated for my mother to use that tone of affection with me, especially when others were around. It seemed to me that she was trying to force me to join in pretending to Mrs. Gordon that the two of us were loving and close; and I felt swallowed whole by that notion. "It's actually dark now."

"It's not so smart to point *that* out," said Mrs. Gordon, and she laughed again.

I walked away without answering. I didn't like Mrs. Gordon. I could hear my mother's lowered voice say something, something about me; but then I was crossing the grass, onto the children's terrain. The game, the shouts, swept me up. The bodies bumped around me. The puzzling world of the grownups fell away, and I forgot it nearly instantly.

When I thought about it in the days afterward, though, what haunted me was nothing it might have revealed to a wiser listener about not having been planned—as with the nicknames, there seemed to be a pushing under until much later of any consciousness of that idea. Instead I seized on the notion that my mother was crazy when she had us. "In a way I suppose I was," she had said; and when I recalled this, it seemed to me her tone had been flat and undeniably truthful, different from the voice that made extravagant claims in anger ("You are driving me out of my mind!") or her occasional playful pretense to nuttiness. It seemed a statement of bald fact: She had been crazy. She had been mad. And we were her symptom, the shape of her madness.

When I suggested this to her on that visit home a few years ago, explained to her the way I'd thought about it during those adolescent years, her face twisted up with anguish. We were sitting together on her porch in the almost-dark, and it was this coincidence, actually, that had brought it back to me—the memory of the other porch, the other twilight.

"Oh, don't say that to me, Nina," she cried. "It breaks my heart to think you felt that way. If anything, you girls were my absolute cure."

I laughed then, and after a second she did too, I think purely in response to me. I doubt that she understood that what amused me was her automatic continuation of the metaphor: we were "the cure." *Madness, illness, cure.* Sickness and health. This was natural language for us, the terms in which we understood life in my family—because of Randall, I suppose, and because of my father's work.

And yet—and I have come to see this only slowly—for my mother these metaphors were more complicated and had more layers than they did for the rest of us. Because illness—and madness too—were also affliction, suffering. And as such they had a spiritual element for her. Certainly she did think in terms of cure. She was no saint; she would have chosen health for Randall, for herself, and for all of us if she had had the choice. But she also thought in terms of acceptance and endurance. And that made her see much in life as a given, as something one *would* or *would not* learn from. I remember hearing her once, in one of the terrible arguments that grew more bitter in the months before my father left us, saying to him, "You think there's some other Randall in there, locked inside this Randall, waiting to come out, to be born. But you're wrong. He is who he is. *He* is our

Randall. He's the only one we even have a chance to love."

One of the reasons I was in the Midwest—one of the reasons it was such a bad time between me and my first husband—was that I'd had a miscarriage. I'd been in the fourth month of a pregnancy that was unplanned and, as Will put it, "inconvenient." I found this word, which he repeated whenever we talked about the baby with friends—or even just casual acquaintances—repellent. It wasn't that I had wanted a child. In fact, until I got pregnant, I hadn't. But then almost immediately I'd felt, in addition to the sense of a door closing in my life, a kind of eager leap of my heart, a readiness to welcome this change, this new person, whoever it might be.

But in any case, I lost the baby. Something began to go wrong early one hot evening in August. We were taking a nap, waiting for it to cool off enough to make dinner, when the pains started. I lay in the darkening room, watching Will breathe heavily in heat-stunned sleep, watching the light change on the brick surface of the apartment opposite, and when I knew the pains weren't going to stop, I woke him. We took a cab to the hospital and they put me in a private labor room. Will had gone out for a few minutes to find a nurse and a bedpan, which I thought I needed, when the baby was born.

Afterward the doctor told me that there were various anomalies. That was the word he used. He said he knew that it was difficult, and he was especially sorry I'd seen the baby—they tried to avoid that. But that often an early miscarriage like mine was Nature's way of dealing with defective children. "You'll be back to work, back to your old life, in a few days. And then there's no reason why you and your husband can't just go ahead and have a healthy, wonderful child." I'd decided almost right away, though, to go to Chicago, sweet home Chicago, instead.

While I was there, staying in my room at my mother's apartment, I had trouble sleeping. Not falling asleep. Usually that came easily. But at three-thirty or four in the morning I'd wake abruptly and absolutely. Sometimes I simply never got back to sleep. Other times, it would take several hours, but slowly the gray light would seep into the room, touching first the white of the sheets, a nightgown draped over a chair; then making the whole room smaller and safer; and I would feel that welcome dizzying pull into irrational thought, timelessness, and know that I was dropping off again, escaping my life for a few more hours.

Troubled by such sleeplessness at home, in my own apartment, I would have risen, put on music, worked. Will could sleep through anything. But in my mother's guest room, I was always aware of her, worried that I might wake her if I got up. The one time I did—to heat some milk in the kitchen—she joined me after a few minutes. We sat together awhile, as I imagined she'd once sat with Randall in the night. We started talking about my father, and after a long silence I asked abruptly, "Tell me something. Did Dad have an affair with Tony? Years ago, I mean."

She looked sharply at me. "Why do you ask?"

"Because I think I remember that. But I'm not sure."

She took a sip of the warm milk. I'd fixed her a glass too. "Dad had a number of affairs at a certain period in our life together. Tony was one." Her voice was flat. She was silent for a few moments. "But he'd always been attracted to her, I think. And it was his way of dealing with everything that had gone wrong. His way . . . of mending himself."

"What was yours?"

"My . . . ?"

"Your way of mending yourself."

She laughed, once, a single bitter cry, and then her mouth twisted. "Mine was not so efficacious. Or fun. I drank too much and had hysterics, which you may recall. I don't know . . ." She frowned at me. "You children, maybe. Religion."

"Do you mind that he's marrying Tony? I mean, that it's Tony?"

She shrugged, and swirled what was in her glass.

"I mean, you must have been jealous then," I pushed. "Doesn't this make it all come back?"

"I was jealous. Of course. That's really why we separated that first time. I couldn't stand it. Tolerating it. The others. But I was always jealous of your father. That was part of the problem. I think I always loved him so much more *intensely* than he loved me."

"Even at the start?"

"Mmm. I think so. No. I know so." She went to the sink and ran water into her empty glass. Then she turned around and leaned back, folded her arms. "I remember before we were married," she said. Her voice was recollective, almost dreamy. "I was still teaching, fifth grade, and David and I had started to sleep together. And I was so overwhelmed, I so wanted to have him, that I used to pray for it. 'Let him want me. Let him love me.' That kind of thing. I'd imagine it, our lovemaking. In church, I mean. And I found that so . . . shocking, so disturbing—that all I could think of when I was praying was David, was sex—that I went to the minister." She smiled. "That kind man. You don't remember him, but I couldn't have survived without him. Especially Randall. It was a loss to me, a tremendous loss, when he died. And then that callow buffoon who succeeded him." She shook her head, looking stern for a moment. "But Dr.

Norman was marvelous. I mean, here I was, this cow-eyed, moonstruck, whimpering thing, worrying so about the fastidiousness of my prayers. And yet he took me into his study and listened. So patiently, with such attention.''

She stopped and looked at me, but I could tell she wasn't seeing me at all.

"What did he say?" I asked.

"Hmm?"

"The minister. What did he say?"

"Oh! Wonderful advice!" she said. "Basically he said that God understands. That he's hardly surprised by the nature of earthly love. Human love. Even physical desire. That man's love, woman's love, is always earthbound anyway, even his love of God." She came and sat across from me again. "He quoted Scripture. That beautiful passage from Paul: 'For now I know in part, but then shall I know, even as also I am known.' And he said that all earthly love *is* necessarily partial. Is like passion. And that God expects our love to be partial, partial in every sense. And to be flawed and selfish. But that if we come to him through it, even through that kind of love, we've still come to him. And even if we come to him by praying just for what we want, what counts in the end is that we've come. To Him.''

"And you believe that?" I asked.

"I believed it absolutely then. I believe it enough now.'' She got up from the table, and I rose too, took my glass to the sink. She stopped at the door. "But now I also believe in a more Job-like God.''

I looked over at her. "A punitive God?"

"Oh, no, not necessarily. But a God who is just absolutely unknowable to us. Inexplicable and remote.''

"Doesn't sound very comforting." Trailing after her, I started out of the room, down the hall.

"It's not. But that's not so much what I'm looking for now anyway."

I watched her walk to her room. She was wearing a T-shirt and sweat pants. Evidently she'd been sleeping in them. I'd noticed that since she was single again, she tended to fall into bed wearing whatever she'd had on all day, just as she'd often done in the earlier years my father lived away from us. She turned at her door and called good night to me, softly, as though there were children in the apartment she was afraid of waking.

After that I stayed in my room when I was wakeful, so I wouldn't get her up too. Occasionally I turned the light on and moved around the little space, rifling through the trunks. I read old letters, sorted through the images that had dotted the kitchen walls for years, unrolled old paintings of ours, the colors dried to a brilliant dust that clung to my hands.

But often I just lay in the dark, waiting, longing for sleep. And then, unsolicited, all the memories would come rushing back—harm I'd caused, damage I'd done, pain I'd inflicted on other people. There's a kind of egocentrism in this sort of nighttime self-blaming that borders on madness, I know, and it seems to be fed by the dark, the quiet, the lack of the corrective *otherness* of life, at that hour. I would see Randall's wincing face as I hit him, Mary's as I told her to go away, to get out, the baby's face, tiny, gummed, and grayish on the bloodstained hospital sheet. And once, just as I was dropping off, I remembered a moment when I told Will I'd never loved him, and I imagined his pinched face as frozen and grainy—a mean photograph taken in a moment of revenge. When I woke I felt a kind of despair at what seemed compromised and ugly in every corner of my life.

Once or twice I pulled the telephone into my room from the hall and called Will at that terrible hour.

He was kind usually, patient. It was in his interest to be so, because he wanted me back. But it was in his nature too, and I knew that. The last time I called, he asked me when I might come "home." For a moment I couldn't think of an answer. I was lying in bed. The trunks and boxes were pushed untidily around, ranged in an unwelcoming disorder. I thought of all the emblems of my childhood lying jumbled in them, and the word *home* made me feel suddenly bereft.

"I don't know," I said at last. "I honestly don't."

"Well, then, do you have a clue as to how you'll make this decision?"

I could see Will—he's very beautiful, a much more beautiful man than I ever thought I'd be involved with, much less marry. Even now that we're no longer together, I sometimes remember how he looked with a kind of surprise at my own accomplishment. Before him I'd "specialized," as my father called it, in eccentrics—artists, musicians, dropouts, returnees from communes and mental institutions— difficult men who dressed weirdly, who wore beads or cowboy boots or elaborately patched blue jeans, who did drugs and didn't want to be "tied down." I hadn't wanted it either. I was well suited to my weirdos. But when the time came I'd married Will, who had disarmed me with what I took for his steadiness. And his beauty. I imagined him then in his pajamas, sitting up in our bed in the dark in the middle of the night, attentive and attractive, even at that hour. A part of me yearned just to give in, to go back. To be lying next to him, looking at him, smelling him. After all, what was I accomplishing here, what was I doing, hanging around on the fringes of my parents' changing lives? But I said again, "I don't know." And then suddenly, seizing at straws, "I want to stay for my father's wedding."

"So after that you'll come home?"

"I just don't know," I whispered.

"What?" His voice was sharp with irritation. "I can't hear you. You what?"

"I don't know if I'll come home," I said.

Now he was silent. Finally he said, "Well, Nina, I wonder what the portents will be that will let you know. A full harvest? Snow before December?"

"Will," I pleaded.

"Or are you waiting till you see the man dance with his wife?"

"Be fair, Will," I said.

After a moment he said, "Just tell me this, then. Are we separated? Because I'm having trouble explaining this to myself. Is this the beginning of the end of our marriage, or is this just a long visit home? Should I be dating?" He laughed harshly. "Should I be *dating?* Tell me what I ought to do about this."

"Can you wait?" I asked.

"I can wait awhile," he said. "If you tell me what I'm waiting for. If you tell me how long I have to wait, for a start."

"I'll try," I said. "I feel awful too, you know. But I'll try to figure it out. Next time I call you, I'll try to have an answer."

There was a pause. I could hear a rustling noise at his end, and for a moment I wondered if there might be someone with him, lying next to him in our bed. From Lainey's apartment came a deep, black silence.

"I'll look forward to that, Nina," he said, and hung up.

The next day I telephoned and made an appointment to see Dr. Dusek. Really just a social visit, I said to the answering service.

*　　*　　*

I left plenty of time before my appointment and walked over slowly. It was October already, but the day was warm and breezy. The wind rattled the dry brown oak leaves still clinging to the trees in Jackson Park and skittered those that lay on the sidewalks and grass. When I finally turned onto Kimbark, I felt the same sinking reluctance I'd felt every time I turned this corner in adolescence; but at the same time my pulse and breathing quickened with that ancient excitement too.

I wound my way slowly up the three flights of specially built, narrow stairs that went nowhere but to her office. The waiting room was the same, track lights and blond wood. There was a big framed Frankenthaler print on the wall, news and educational magazines arranged tidily on an end table. New chairs, though, I noticed, upholstered in bright colors. Then the door opened, and she leaned out. When she saw me, she stepped quickly forward, smiling. She held her hand out and gripped mine, her other hand patting my arm as she shook it, in a kind of reduced embrace. "Oh, Nina!" she said. "What a great pleasure! To see you." She seemed smaller than she had in the past, a tiny, delicate woman with untidily pinned up gray hair. Deep wrinkles scored her face now, where before she'd had just lines, but otherwise she was unchanged. She was dressed as beautifully as ever, in a pale draped suit, and as she turned to lead me back into her office, I saw she teetered on the same kind of preposterously high, tarty heels she'd always worn. At the start of my therapy, this had fired a private contempt for her that I was determined to hold on to. The vanity! The idiocy! As though anyone would think she was anything but a middle-aged midget! Now I found it charming.

I was babbling mindlessly as I followed her in. I sat down in the chair in front of the desk, the same chair I'd occupied twice weekly for all those years in high school and college. I looked around as she made her way—a little awkwardly, I noticed—to her own chair, behind the desk, facing me. The room, tiny anyway, was more crowded now than it had been, and when I turned around I saw the reason. There was another chair behind me, and an analytic couch. Everything else had been pushed toward the window to accommodate them.

"Tell me what you are doing in Chicago," she said after she sat down. She still pronounced it Chew-caw-go.

I laughed. "Well, as usual, that's exactly the right question."

"How do you mean?"

"Oh, nothing," I said. "There are some good reasons too." And I explained about my father's wedding, my state of limbo because of the grant.

She had heard about my parents' divorce but hadn't known my father was going to marry again. She asked me to convey her wishes for his great happiness. Then she said she'd seen my photographs from time to time in the *Christian Science Monitor*. She liked them.

I talked about my career, about what I hoped to do with the foundation money if I got it. I told her a little about my parents, about how strange it felt to be moving back and forth between their homes. Too quickly we fell into the familiar pattern: she was more silent than not, and I talked about myself. From time to time I would jolt to an awareness of this, and then I would make myself ask her a question, to restore the sense of dialogue I was trying to insist on: after all, this was a friendly visit, not a medical one.

Her family, she said in answer to my query, was well. The children were all on their own now, or in

college. "No more sounds of playing or disaster drifting up from downstairs. Do you remember?"

I did. When I'd been seeing her, the children
were small, and occasionally from somewhere deep
in the house you could hear the thud of an accident,
or shouts of pleasure or pain muffled by wood and
plaster. When this happened I would watch her face
carefully for signs of betrayal I could have pounced
on, signs that they claimed her attention away from
me. And never saw one, not a flicker.

"And I think they are doing well. Though one
never truly knows, as a parent, of course. But certainly
it is . . . well . . . an easier time in the world than when
you were that age." She shook her head. "I strongly
feel that you, your parents—everyone who survived
that era—should be awarded a medal. Or at least a
diploma, a certificate of graduation. Many would dis-
agree with me, of course. In times of order, we yearn
again for disorder. And no doubt we will discover,
too, the price we are paying for our present peaceful-
ness. But there is always a price. Life is an expensive
business, finally."

I asked about her practice. It was full-time now,
as it hadn't been then, with the children, and "part
sitting up, part lying down," she said. "You understand these complicated distinctions." When she
smiled, her eyes virtually disappeared into the deep
wrinkles around them.

"Yes," I said.

"Mostly women. And what we used to call girls.
Now known as women too, of course. Though really,
for women, so extraordinarily young. Only one man.
Still the men are not so interested in a female shrink.
When that changes, the world will truly be a different
place, I believe."

"Yes, that would be some sort of ultimate barom-
eter," I said.

She let a silence fall, and I looked past her out the window at the trees, the houses beyond. Occasionally in my desperation for a topic early in my reluctant therapy, I'd report on something in the rooftop view. "The leaves are all gone," I'd say. "Now you can watch your neighbors all you want." Even this, though, she'd been able to turn to use: "Why would I want to?" she'd ask; and then pursue me into my assumptions about her.

In fact, the leaves were mostly gone now, and the light shone in so brightly behind her that it was hard for me to see exactly what was going on in her face. She seemed to be studying me. Finally she spoke. "Well, Nina," she said. "And what are the bad reasons?"

"The bad reasons?"

"Yes. You said there were good reasons 'too' to being in Chicago—and you told me those. But didn't you want to tell me the bad reasons?"

"The good news and the bad news," I said.

"Yes." She smiled.

"Okay, the *real* reason I'm in this room . . ." I grinned. "No, I did want to see you also," I said. "But beyond that, I thought . . ." And I knew suddenly the absurdity of my impulse. I wanted to laugh. "I thought maybe, too, you could tell me whether or not I should stay married." I shrugged.

Slowly a smile changed her face. Then left it. After a moment, looking directly at me, she said, "I don't think so, my dear."

"I know."

"I'm sorry there are problems," she said.

"But there aren't," I protested.

"I'm sorry for that, then," she said, and her eyes disappeared into the folds again.

"It's just me," I said. "It is."

She tilted her chair back and shook her head

wearily. "I tell you, this could be the title of a book on doing therapy with female patients. *It's Just Me.* In spite of all the political work of feminists trying to teach us to say, 'It's just them.' Neither will really work, you know."

We talked a little longer. I told her about the miscarriage, about Will. "I think in some measure I married him for what I saw as his stability, you know? Because I'd been in relationships for so long where everyone was free to do what he wanted. She wanted. And we all went crazy and hurt each other and cried. Will was—is—so different. And I suppose I always thought the trade-off would be that he'd be a great family man. A good father. I think in some ways I'm disappointed because he didn't want the baby." I leaned forward, put my hand on her desk. "No, I *know* I am."

I was thinking of the morning I'd come home after staying overnight in the hospital. Will had called the office to say he'd be late for work. He'd hovered over me. Before he left, he told me he'd pick up Chinese food on his way home, and I could hear a kind of pleased caress of the notion in his voice: our life, returning to normal.

"What do you mean, *trade-off?*" She was frowning.

"It's a term, you know, from the business world, I think—"

"No, no, no, no, no." Her hand swept the air impatiently. "I'm not still fresh off the boat. What I'm suggesting is that surely you meant to say something else. *Trade-off* is the wrong word. I think you meant that you would get something as a *concomitant* of his stability. Along with it. Not as a trade-off for it. Not as the negative aspect of it."

I was silent a moment. "Well," I said. "The classic *lapsus linguae,* I guess."

"Perhaps this is worth pursuing?" she asked. I didn't answer right away. "Is there something, can you think, that you were—or are—giving up to get Will's . . . stability?"

"The usual, I suppose." I shrugged. "Drama. Excitement. Abuse."

"Ah, yes. Abuse. So necessary in a relationship."

I smiled. "Well, I always liked the struggle in all those tempestuous relationships, I must admit. But I felt crummy about them too. Because I knew that they were a way for me to avoid being close."

"Intimacy."

"Yes."

"And now you have intimacy."

I looked out at the blank sky. "I have something like intimacy anyhow. Peace." She moved somehow—a protest, I think—and my gaze shifted back to her. "We do get along. We genuinely like each other. We do."

She looked at me across the desk. Then she pointed at me. "You know," she said, "I was not only joking"—I heard *choking*—"when I said earlier that I was sorry there were no problems in your marriage. Because, my dear, you come from such a life, such a background, that problems and conflict have been of central importance for you, and for your family. Always there was drama. But such meaningful drama. In a way, I think your job in life will be to adjust to the aftermath of that."

I said nothing.

"Perhaps this is what you're struggling with in part, with your Will. Hmm?"

We talked awhile more. When she looked once at her watch, I knew she'd allotted me the standard amount of time and that it must be nearly over.

"Well," I said, starting to stand. "Our time is up, I believe." I was imitating her accent.

She laughed and stood too. "Famous last words," she said.

At the door, her hand in mine was warm again. "You look wonderful, Nina. I'm so glad to see it. To say it. It is a great pleasure for me to see you again."

I could feel a deep blush rise to my face.

"And if you should want to talk again while you are here, you will call me. I will always take time."

As I went down the stairs, I had to move out of the way of another patient, climbing up. Our eyes met briefly, and then we both looked quickly away, wherever else we could.

On the long walk back to my mother's, I was remembering my therapy with Dr. Dusek. For the first few years—my senior year of high school, my freshman year of college—I hadn't wanted to be there. I was forced to go. My father had insisted on it, was paying for it, after I'd had what my parents called "some hard times." How she must have dreaded my arrival twice a week! A sullen, angry adolescent, full of hostility, of inanities. I always wore a ghostly pale lipstick—in photos I remind myself of Al Jolson—and I circled my eyes with black liner, dark shadow. I smoked then—she did too—and the two of us would sit in her office, often through long silences, filling the air with stale clouds of tobacco. Sometimes when I saw my boyfriend right afterward, he'd pull his head back from my stinky hair and say, "Pew: therapy!"

Usually I tried to concoct a subject for discussion on my way over to my session—something trivial, something that would keep her away from the realities of my life, which consisted then of cutting most of my classes and working on art and political projects like staged happenings. A group of us would stand up in Harkness Common and first read and then slowly eat passages from the *New York Times* about the Vietnam War. We thought we were very avant-garde.

It was in this mood—evade, distract—that I began one morning to tell her about a game we had invented in my dorm the night before, a game we called The Good News and the Bad News.

We had been sitting around, six or seven of us. Cheryl started it. "Well, the good news is my father finally divorced his cruddy second wife," she said abruptly.

There was a cheer, halfhearted at first, then gathering force as we realized the absurdity of cheering this news. "But the bad news . . ." Cheryl paused to suck on the joint, and the bad news was delivered in the constricted, high-pitched tone of someone desperately not breathing out: "His new girlfriend is already pregnant, so he married her right away. A real slut."

As the moans of sympathy went round the room, she exhaled a thin stream of smoke.

"What fuck-ups they are," someone said. "What cosmic fuck-ups. I wonder if we'll fuck up as badly as all that."

"Well actually, I don't know if she's really a slut or not," Cheryl apologized. "I've never even met her, actually."

After that there was a disorganized kind of turn-taking, and at some point I found myself offering the details of my family's life. (The good news: after two years they made love, finally. The bad news: she got pregnant *again!* The good news: she had me. The bad news: she had me.) My turn took longer than anyone else's: there was so much in our history I could use. As a group we had grown more and more hysterical—stoned, uncontrollable laughter that fed on itself. And I felt high, too, with the success of my long, mean narrative, the triumphant distance I felt from it all as I cast it this way.

I was glibly retelling all this to Dr. Dusek, hoping

she would think I was a very clever girl—even if I didn't want her to know much about me, I cared very much that she think I was clever—when, to my surprise, I began to cry.

Dr. Dusek was very still for a few minutes. Then she leaned forward and pushed the box of tissues on her desk toward me. "You did not weep then, when you were playing this game?" she asked.

"No, just now," I blubbered.

"So you feel something now, something you were not aware of then," she said gently. And after a long moment, in which the sound of my strained, irregular breathing was the only noise in the room, she asked, "Why is it so sad now?"

"I think," I said, "because I see that, in fact, it's true."

"It's true," she repeated.

"Yes," I said, and couldn't go on for a few minutes. But finally I said, "That the good stuff in our family—all of it—*was* the bad stuff. And all the bad stuff . . ." She sat with the light glowing from behind her, her face lost in shadow, only listening. "And all the bad things, even Randall, were . . . were *good* also."

I wept for a long time in her office. I wept because I felt so confused by life—I was eighteen—and its strange mixture of beauty and ugliness. Because I was frightened at the idea of giving up what I felt was all I had inside me—my rage at my family, my pain. Because I saw that therapy, the terrible cure my father had forced on me, had brought me to this moment, the moment I thought I was evading even as I began to tell the story that contained it. I wept because it had released me and helped me in a way I never would have chosen, hadn't in fact consented to.

*   *   *

When I met Will, I was involved with what Dr. Dusek had earlier called one of my dangerous men. He was an artist, a kind of sculptor, whose work consisted at that time of tracing the effect of certain conditions on a number of busts he'd had fabricated of Richard Nixon—freezing, being left on an interstate, being submerged for months in the top tank of a toilet. He made his money, though, dealing drugs: grass and speed, some hallucinogens, and various prescriptions—tranquilizers, painkillers, Quaaludes. Will came with a woman my lover knew to a party in his loft. At about four in the morning, the only people left were named either John or Susan. This was more than okay. It was almost necessary, everyone was so stoned. They all said each other's names and laughed a lot. Only I wasn't named Susan or John or stoned. I'd had a fair amount to drink, but I was somehow still very aware, very clear about everything that was happening. I saw, for instance, that my lover, also a John, had his hand down the back of some Susan's jeans, though she was leaning forward and talking animatedly, as though that were someone else's ass back there.

I'd been through this many times before. The routine from this point on was pretty standard. In a while someone, usually John, would replace the Stones or Marvin Gaye with Pachelbel's Canon, and everyone would get suddenly serious and start putting the moves on everyone else. In the morning on my way to coffee I'd have to pick my way through the undressed, the partially dressed, the partially coupled, couples. This time I'd know their names. Often I didn't.

So when one of the Johns headed into the bedroom for his coat, I followed him.

"Are you going?" I asked.

"Yes," he said. I couldn't believe how straight-looking he was, how preppy. He had a very British thatch of straw-yellow hair, combed floppily to one side. I wanted to leave with someone because I needed to balance the score with my John. For a moment I hesitated, though, not sure that this guy would even carry weight in the scale. But he was just so purely beautiful when he asked if I wanted to share a cab that I decided what the hell.

"Why did you leave?" I asked in the cab.

"My name isn't John," he said. "And you?"

"My name isn't Susan."

We both laughed, and this seemed reason enough that night, in that crazy world, to invite him up to have a drink, to go to bed with him.

The next morning when I woke he was still there, already awake, alert. He reached over and smoothed my hair back off my forehead with the cool flat of his hand in a gesture that reminded me of one my father used when I had a fever. "What would you like to do today?" he said gently. Three months later, I asked him to move in.

Will was a lawyer, and he *was* very straight. At first I couldn't see what it was that attracted him to me. The women he knew wore stockings, silk blouses, pearls. They made money. At that stage I was still working on and off as a waitress to support myself, and shooting a lot of weddings and bar mitzvahs. I had a whole variety of costumes I'd assembled to go into the world in, but very little of what he might have thought of as clothing.

It was only slowly that I realized my cachet in his world—that it was my very funkiness, my poverty, my art. People from his office would say to me, "I hear you're working on . . ." and describe some half-baked idea I'd been toying with out loud. Or, "I understand you're going to have a show at . . ." and name a gallery whose owner had once been polite about my photographs.

It was hard to know what to accuse Will of, since clearly he was proud of me, of the life I'd made for myself. It wasn't until much later, after we were married, that I began to notice that his friends seemed to know also about the kind of personal life I'd been leading—names of former lovers, for example, a few of whom were beginning to have a minor celebrity in New York. Or even some of the circumstances of my growing up: the autistic brother, the psychiatrist father, the troubled adolescence.

There was a period of a year or so when, in response to all this, I tried to behave so badly it would shut Will up. Even at the time, I realized that that's what I was doing; but I also felt purely out of control, crazy. And I took a kind of pleasurable meanness in everything that happened. Once Will wept so hard after I'd been gone for a few days that he burst a small vessel in his nose, and blood pumped lavishly over his face, over my hands and body, as we held each other. And what I felt, even as I cried too, was a perverse kind of enjoyment of the drama of this.

But that need passed, and I turned back, finally, to my work, to our peaceful life together. And it *was* comfortable, truly comfortable, just as I told Dr. Dusek. And certainly much easier for me than it had been earlier, when I was alone and struggling financially, or sleeping with someone who was also doing the deed with several others. So much easier that I did at least know what Will meant when he called the pregnancy inconvenient. It was only very occasionally that I felt that nagging sense of Will's desire for ownership of my eccentricity, or the impulse to make him pay for it.

*　　　*　　　*

Aside from my parents, the only members of my family left in Chicago were Mary and Mack. I didn't see much of her. Partly it was the fact that she was very pregnant. To my surprise, this disturbed me. But also, she continued to work until nearly the end—she was a pediatrician in an HMO—and between that and her marriage, she didn't have a lot of free time. We did a few things together the last week before she delivered, but I relied much more on Mack for company.

He was a bartender—actually the co-owner of the bar—on the Near North Side. He'd created a tiny, self-sufficient world for himself, and he seemed to live safely and happily in it. I worked for him a dozen or more times when he needed an extra waitress. I liked the work. I'd done it often enough in New York before I got married. It was absorbing and comforting, and as close as I wanted to come at that time to being sexual—the constant bumping into other bodies, turning, reaching around the other "girl." I liked, too, the music, the dim, smoky intimacy, the slightly risqué banter from the customers.

And I especially liked the hour or so after closing, when Mack and I, sometimes with another bartender or Melanie, the regular waitress, would sit around with most of the lights off and talk. No one was anywhere near ready for bed, even though it was two or three in the morning. We were all keyed up from the hectic pace of the work. And stirred too, I think, by the intimacy of the rhythms we'd set up with each other all night.

When the others were there, the talk was often political, locally political. Mack had been active in his alderman's losing campaign for office the year before, and he was already thinking about the next election. They talked of Mayor Washington, of the Council Wars, of the abiding power of racial feeling in the city. Though I understood very little of the specifics, it had the fascination for me that Chicago politics always had.

And Mack, so absorbed in it, seemed at peace to me finally, healed almost. I could forget, looking at his face, the occasional uncomfortable moments when I saw the other side of him, the crazy side, the side that seemed to want to throw everything good in his life away. Only every now and then there might be a sudden visible flash of those impulses that had brought two marriages to an end, that had made his second wife say to me after she'd moved out, "I love Mack a lot, but you just can't live with him."

One time it was a drunk who wouldn't leave. It was late. The place had completely emptied except for him. He was loud and seemed ready for a fight. He knocked over a couple of the tables. I was frightened and went to stand behind the bar. Mack talked to him gently for a long time, trying to persuade him to go home. He actually got him standing up, got him near the door. But every time he'd mention the need for departure, the drunk's voice would move higher, shift into a dangerous gear. He'd accuse Mack of trying to get rid of him.

"If you don't like me," he said finally, "at least do me the fucking courtesy—the *fucking* courtesy— to say so." His feet were widely planted. He held his arms rigid at his sides, his hands balled into fists.

"Oh, no," I heard Mack say, mildly. "I like you. A lot. You're one of my favorite people." And then I could see his face lift with a kind of pleasure: he'd thought of a new approach. "Let's shake," he said. "We like each other. Let's shake on that."

The drunk was wary, but he extended his hand. As soon as Mack gripped it, his own left hand lifted and punched hard twice, once quickly to the man's chest, once again under his chin. The man made several strange noises, and his knees buckled. Mack grabbed his crumpling form and half walked, half carried him to the door. Neither Melanie, across the room, nor I seemed to be able to move, and the cold air blew in the open doorway for the entire minute or so Mack was outside. I could see him lower the man carefully into a sitting position on the curb and then bend over him, arranging him as if to make him perfectly comfortable.

Melanie had started to cry. When Mack came in and heard her, saw her, his face changed instantly into a composed kindness that made me think of my father. He went to her and held her, stroked her back. Melanie buried her face in his striped shirt and let him comfort her. She'd been behind Mack when he punched the guy. She'd heard the quick dull whumps, the grunting push of breath out of the drunk's lungs with the first blow—but she hadn't seen, as I had, the transforming cruel excitement in Mack's face the instant before his fist moved.

When Mack and I were alone, we talked about the family. Sometimes he would be doing some final chore—washing glasses, wiping down the stainless-steel sinks behind the bar, checking and restocking the bottles in the vast display along the mirrored wall. There was a pleasant music to this—the steady burble of running water, the clinking of glasses or bottles—and it moved us easily back in time.

I was surprised, always, by his insistence on early, happy memories. Memories of the years before I'd been born, before they knew what was wrong with Randall. Surprised by the power of those memories to change his face, to smooth it into youth again. Once he told me a long story about how he and Liddie had found a bunch of coins under the ice in the square. As he spoke I could imagine the two of them, shapeless in their woolen snowsuits, hunched over the discovery. Then stomping the clear ice to get at the bright coins: quarters, dimes, half-dollars. He said that every time they freed one, they'd carry it carefully across the ice to Lainey, who was sitting on the front steps in the winter sun in her old blue coat. "I remember how huge the square seemed then, how far away Mother looked, watching us coming across all that snow, carrying our treasure." His expression was as awestruck, as deeply pleased, as it must have been when he lived the moment.

He, in turn, was startled by the pain, the fighting, the discord, in my memories. He had forgotten the time he cut his foot. He hadn't been there when Randall pushed Lainey into the newel post. "The amount of blood alone is appalling," he said.

I'd been to see Dr. Dusek only a few days before this. I'd been thinking ever since of what she'd said about the importance of struggle, of pain, in our family's life. I said, "Well, maybe that's what you get when you go into therapy. You remember all the gory things you'd really rather forget."

"One good reason I'll never try it."

I watched him for a moment. He was moving steadily behind the counter, washing the glasses in a quick, practiced sequence. His longish dark hair fell forward across his forehead, masking his eyes.

"Well, you know the argument," I said at last. "All that pushed-under stuff gonna get your mama one day."

He laughed. "I'm sure that's true. I'm sure you're right. But I sort of feel, at this point—you know—it's what I'm made of." He lifted his face, and his motion stopped for a few seconds. "Pushed-under stuff." He was still smiling, looking over at me. "I'm like some stretch of the city built on polluted fill, fill packed with PCBs and toxic waste. But I *am* all built up, see? And you've got your choice. You want to get rid of the bad stuff, you've got nothing left. Nothing."

He was sober, suddenly. "But you're right. It is true. It does come back. It all comes back anyway. In dreams sometimes. Same with certain memories of Vietnam. It's all distorted, of course. Sometimes, you know, I rescue myself from things that really happened, things I couldn't escape from then. I'm doing things the way I wished I'd done them at the time." His voice became abruptly deep and ministerial. "Or *I'm leaving undone those things I should not have done.*"

I brought over a tray of dirty glasses and stood for a moment leaning on the bar to be close to him, hoping that brought him comfort. I was afraid to ask him anything about Vietnam. Once I'd said to him that it must have been awful in battle, and he'd looked at me as though I were a stranger. "Battle," he'd said contemptuously. "I was never in battle. I just tried to kill people who were trying to kill me."

When he went on now, his voice was his own. "Sometimes, though, it's worse than it was," he said. "Sometimes it's as though I'm seeing some concentrated version of whatever was evil in me at a given moment. Sometimes it's stuff I don't even want to think about in the morning. Very interesting ways, for example, of causing people pain. Or sexual things." His face had gone dead. Then he looked at me. "Do you have that?"

"Sure," I said. "Horrible stuff. But I always try to remember it. To figure it out. But that's from therapy again."

"Yeah. Therapy."

"It brings you good things too," I said. And then backed up, raising my hands. "I'm not trying to convert you. Honest."

"Don't," he said. "Besides, I get the good stuff

too." He slid my tray closer to him and his arms shifted their movement, started to pick up the glasses. "I dreamed about Randall not so long ago."

"Did you?"

"Yeah. Somehow . . ." He looked up, and the faintest line of concentration moved in his forehead. "This was it: *He* was Mary's baby—she'd been pregnant with him, that's why he was here. But he was adult too. You know, magical stuff. And he was walking past the house, our old house. He walked right past me. I was on the porch or something. And I called to him, but he didn't stop. So I ran and caught up with him and grabbed him, turned him around. I was tremendously excited, touching him. Not surprised at all, you know, just happy. And he was looking at me with his same face, but it was, like, intelligent. Normal. And I said, 'Don't you know me, Randall? I'm your brother. It's me. I'm your brother, Mack.'

"And his eyes got . . . just very tender and concerned. And he reached over and touched my face and he said, 'But what *happened* to you? What's wrong? You look so worn out.'

"And I realized that he didn't know me because I was older, older than I'd been. I'd aged. And he thought it was . . . a disease or something. Anyway, that seemed funny to me; I actually laughed, in the dream. And then I said to him, 'I've been alive. I've just been alive, that's all.' And he looked so sorry for me, like he was the one who pitied me.

"When I woke up I didn't remember it. But I was just so fucking *glad;* I knew something good had happened, that I'd been dreaming something I wanted to get back to. And then I did, I remembered why, that I'd seen him again. That he'd talked to me. That he was all right. Cured."

"God, what a wonderful dream," I said.

"Yeah. Done entirely on my own. No therapy."

He smiled for a moment. "You know, the only other person I've told that to was Mother. That I'd dreamed of Randall, talking."

"Was she excited?" I asked.

He laughed and stopped moving again. "You might say so. She said—and this is a quote—'Oh, what did he *say?*' "

He had imitated perfectly her eager inflection.

Afterward, driving home in my mother's car, I thought about her response to Mack's dream. The night sky was black over the lake, away from the glare of streetlights on the Outer Drive, and the moon rode along with me, speeding south too, leaving a trail like a blur of sequins on the water. I was thinking of how different my father's reaction to the dream would have been if he had been the one Mack told it to. Of how he would have seen it as a clue to Mack's way of thinking about himself, about himself and Randall. But to my mother, it could still have a nearly biblical quality. She was like some pre-Freudian who believes that dreams, even the dreams of others, carry messages for her. That word can come this way—if not from God, then from a beloved son. I imagined her listening to Mack as though he were bringing this kind of report from another world, a world where Randall was safe and forever young and could speak, in a shy, unused voice. "Oh, what did he *say?*" she had asked. I could see her face as she waited for Mack's answer—open, ready to believe, grateful for the word Mack brought her, her first meaningful words from Randall's lips.

14

AT the moment when Mack's plane lifted from the runway at O'Hare and all the buildings and streets began to fall backward—to become toylike miniatures—Mack was elsewhere. He was pushing one steel blade after another across the gleaming gunmetal of the ice, sending up the slightest splash with each stroke.

He had the rink nearly to himself: there was a group of squealing teenage girls, four or five of them, at the far end; and a small child, lumpy in a green snowsuit, staggering on her ankles, making her way slowly around the loop, her mother holding on to one hand. After each tortured circuit the two of them disappeared for a break into the heated changing room.

But Mack never stopped. On the long straight runs he leaned forward, arms swinging, to build up speed. On the curves, he watched the same skate cut in front of the other over and over in a precise hissing repetition of angle and force. Already his legs ached from the unaccustomed exercise—he'd done no more physically, this fall, than occasionally throwing a Frisbee with his roommate at Harvard. But he pushed himself harder, enjoying the strain, enjoying his own speed, elaborately enjoying this moment, so that he wouldn't have to think of all the other things that were happening somewhere else—the plane rising above the cloud cover to blue sky and blinding sun; his mother at home, trying to invent reasons for his not showing up; his room at school, darkened, stale-smelling, empty, waiting.

And he didn't; he didn't think of any of it. There was gay music, something by Strauss, perhaps, pumping in over the loudspeakers, echoing in the cavernous empty space under the stands. And he was sweating, adrenalized, thrilled by his own speed, by the emptiness of his mind.

He wasn't dressed for this—his hands were bare, his long, uncovered hair flew back in the wind he made with his steady forward motion. He'd chosen this abruptly, gratefully, when he'd spotted the little flag trembling on its pole above the unused football field, the flag which had signaled throughout his youth that the long, sheltered rink under the stands was open. If he hadn't come to the rink, he might have gone home and let his mother drive him to the airport—it could have happened that easily. Chance. Luck. He believed this as he went around and around. The thought made him laugh out loud, and the teenage girls, who had been watching him intermittently, laughed too, at him, with him.

Mack was the last to leave—the music had been turned off for some time, and twice the student manager's voice had come over the loudspeaker, asking that the ice be cleared. Finally he cut half the lights, and Mack did one last loop, standing straight, gliding with his feet together, listening to the slowing sibilance of their doubled slice. When he sat down to unlace the skates in the changing room, his legs jumped and trembled against the bench, and his first steps in his own heavy shoes were awkward and uncertain, brought him staggering against a rectangular silver radiator on his way out.

But once in the dark, cold air again, he took long strides, heading down the empty streets away from home. He realized abruptly that he was hungry, hungrier than he'd been straight through this Thanksgiving holiday, in which he'd felt like an outsider at each family meal amid his noisy, dramatic sisters. They were full of exclamations, excitement, pronouncements—someone was *weird beyond words, a complete dink.* Or *unbelievably groovy, super.* He'd shoveled in what he had to and fled each evening to be with Al or Rob or Soletski. To get drunk or stoned.

He found himself now thinking of hamburgers, of thick, stinking slices of onion, of half-sours, potato chips. He turned east down Fifty-fifth Street toward Blackstone and then walked up to a little bar and restaurant called The Eagle. It was brightly lighted and quiet—a Sunday-night crowd. There were two men at the ornate bar, and only four of the tables were full. Mack could see that if he sat at the bar he'd have to talk to the men—they were speaking loudly down its length to each other—so he chose a small table near the window.

The waitress was young, not attractive, but she called Mack *sir* in a small, sweet voice. He ordered a beer, then the hamburger special. When it came he ordered another beer, and then another; and then he ordered a second hamburger, plain this time, with another beer. The waitress served him silently, politely, and he smiled a tender smile of real gratitude at her.

He was sitting, full finally, sipping this last beer and watching the sparse walking traffic on the street outside, when a middle-aged couple, making their way to the door from the back of the deep room, stopped at his table. The man touched his shoulder and had his hand extended as Mack struggled to his feet, trying to place the face and then succeeding: Mr. Stahl, the father of Annie, his high school girlfriend. Mrs. Stahl stood smiling just behind her husband's right shoulder. They all chatted. Mack felt proud of the smile lifting his face: how pleasant he was being! He inquired about Annie. She was at Northwestern, in her senior year, like him. She was happy there. They got to see a lot of her. They asked how he was, what his plans were after graduation.

He hoped his face was falling into thoughtful lines when he said, "Still formulating." He wanted to laugh.

Mr. Stahl nodded. "I know how it is. You need a strategy now. This Vietnam thing. You can't just do what you might have done. There's too high a price, with this goddamned war." He patted Mack on the shoulder. His hair was longer now than it had been when Mack was dating Annie. His sideburns curled wildly down his cheeks and made him look younger—much younger than his wife—in spite of the gray in them.

"Well, take care of yourself, Macklin," Mrs. Stahl said, frowning and serious, as though she wasn't sure she should trust Mack with the job.

"You too," Mack said, his head bobbing.

When they shut the door behind them, Mack sat down, relieved. He leaned back in his chair and stretched his legs, feeling the ache, the pull in his muscles. On the street, the Stahls seemed to confer for a moment, then turned north, toward Fifty-third Street.

Mack ordered another beer. He was thinking of Annie, of how energetic, how unselfconscious she was. Sometimes he would cue her lines in one of the student productions she acted in. His reading was always embarrassed and mechanical. But Annie would respond with stage-level commitment: passionate, amused, weepy, thoughtful—whatever was required to be the exact person in the exact moment she was pretending to live. It had astonished Mack, turned him on.

Mrs. Stahl looked a little like her daughter. And her frowning face had reminded him of his mother's, of the frown that made a curved vertical crease, like the print of a sharp thumbnail, between her dark eyebrows whenever she looked at him. Yesterday she had asked him what time he was leaving, and when he'd been vague, when he'd said there might be some guys driving back, that very frown had appeared.

"So you didn't get a round-trip ticket?" she asked. They'd sent him a check to cover the airfare for the holiday.

"No, I didn't," he said.

"Well, why not, darling? That's what it was for."

He smiled at her. "Because, Mom, I didn't know if I'd be flying back," he said. The frown had already vanished; she had capitulated before he'd even begun to speak.

It was almost ten when he got to Jimmy's, a dark bar formed of two adjoining rooms behind a double storefront on Fifty-fifth. It was as close to a student hangout as the University of Chicago had, except it was graduate students, some well into their thirties, and hangers-on who came here—people who should have left Hyde Park long before but hadn't, people still working every now and then on their theses, people who had part-time jobs in bookstores or bars, who were disillusioned teachers, or worked for Legal Aid or poverty programs, or made music or art that didn't sell. The mismatched tables were randomly placed, perpetually pushed around by customers forming parties. The floor was bare wood, worn. The bartender for the most part drew big glasses and pitchers of beer, with the occasional shot of whiskey. Mack went up and stood at the bar. He ordered another beer. The bartender asked to see his ID.

While he was looking at it, the big man next to Mack leaned toward him. "Be grateful, kid," he said. "When they stop carding you, it's all over. Easy pussy, for instance. It's *all* over. Sleeping through the night without getting up two or three times to piss. Eating without gaining weight."

"All that good stuff," the bartender said to the man as he pushed Mack's ID back across the bar and turned to draw the beer.

"Damn straight," the man said. He set his glass down, hard. "You a student?" he asked Mack.

Mack said yes, and the man was off. He'd gone downstate, he said. Not U of C. Basketball scholarship.

Mack barely responded, a polite noise.

The guy explained his high school career, said that he'd been an all-state player eighteen years before. He described his specialty, a fadeaway jump shot. "It was like I was floating backward, you know what I mean? Like I was flying, but in reverse."

Mack nodded. The man must have been very good-looking once, but everything in his face now was too thick, puffy and coarse.

"And do you know, that year, on that all-state team, there were a total, a *total*, of three black guys? Three black guys from the city of Chicago. Isn't that amazing?"

Mack turned away slightly—he could tell, suddenly, where this was heading—but the big man leaned forward. He took up the little distance Mack had created between them. "That'll never happen again. It's a black man's game now. Within ten years, I promise you, there won't be a white guy in the NBA. Playing in the NBA. And you want to know why?" He burped, and his hand rose delicately in a halfhearted gesture that suggested that if he'd been sober, he would have covered his mouth prettily. "They're better than we are. That's the truth. They're better. Genetically."

The bartender had moved again at this last. He caught Mack's eye from halfway down the bar and shook his head.

"Stan, my man, give it a rest," he called.

The big man turned, perplexed. "It's the truth," he said, once his gaze found the bartender. His voice was petulant.

The bartender shrugged. "Give it a rest anyway. It's boring."

There was a short pause, and Stan laughed, with a forced good nature. Then he leaned forward across the bar. "That's because you don't care. You don't care about basketball. You're short anyway. A short guy. But I care, and my friend here"—he reached out and rested his hand on Mack's shoulder—"he cares too."

The bartender came down and stood in front of them. "Let me put it this way," he said quietly. "I'll give you a free beer if you shut up about the black race. This isn't a good place for this kind of public discussion, see?"

"I get you," Stan said. "I understand exactly what you mean." And he waited with a child's attentive eagerness as the bartender drew him another beer. "A done deal," he said, and scooped the beer toward him.

But almost as soon as the bartender moved away, he started up again, comparing the game as it had been played in his day with the game now. Mack looked around the room, hoping for a familiar face, a way to excuse himself.

The man was relentless. Black people moved differently, jumped differently, used their bodies differently. It was undeniable. It had changed the sport completely. Yet, he revealed to Mack, no one would talk about this. Except him. Not the newspapers, not TV. "Lookit even this guy." He gestured toward the bartender. "A little guy like that, what does he know? But you still can't talk about it. Can't bring it up. Can't mention it. But I do. I do." He was nearly whispering. "Because you know and I know: the *truth*. I mean,

I'm not saying anything *bad* about the colored. I'm saying they're good. I'm actually saying they're better. Better than we are. Why should that bother anybody?"

"You're saying they're different," Mack said.

The man's face eased into a big, grateful smile. "Right. That's what I'm saying. They are *different.* They are different."

"Kind of, like, less human."

Now he frowned. He was very thoughtful. "Now, there *might*, there might be a element of truth to that. Because, for instance, did you see that *Hustler*, that *Hustler* magazine with the African guy? With his dick, you know . . . ?" His face was serious, intense, and his big hands made a complicated circling motion in the air.

"Afraid not," Mack said.

"It was tied in a knot. His dick. It was so fucking huge he had to tie it in a knot. I saw it!" His voice had risen with enthusiasm.

"In a reputable magazine."

"Right. Now, you won't see a *white* guy with his dick tied in a knot. I guarantee you that much."

From farther down the bar Mack saw the bartender's head lift from a chore, his eyebrows pull together. He began to move in their direction.

"But you might see a white guy with his head up his ass," Mack said pleasantly, smiling.

He watched as awareness slowly dawned through the smog of alcohol in the man's heavy face. He felt a thrill of fear, of adrenaline, as it turned ugly and angry.

The big man straightened. "You want to say that again?"

Mack turned so he was directly facing him. He said slowly and carefully, a little louder this time, "You might see a white guy with his head up his ass, though."

The bartender was right there quickly, his upper body lurched across the bar in one move, grabbing Stan's arm before his slowed reflexes allowed him the punch.

Mack had stepped back, grinning, happy. He was nearly dancing in his excitement as the two of them struggled. "Hey, okay," he said. He laughed. "It's okay now." He lifted his beer glass above his head.

"Hey," he said. "Look here!" And carefully and slowly he poured the beer out onto himself, a sheet falling onto his hair, down his shirt.

After a long moment's pause, the big man's arms relaxed, dropped to the bar. "I'll be goddamned," he said. He began to laugh. "I'll be goddamned." And then the bartender laughed, too, and slid back onto his side of the bar; and those nearest the bar in the room turned and saw Mack dripping, grinning, in a spreading puddle, and they all began to laugh.

When he got home, everyone was in bed. Drunk, stinking of beer, he washed his face in the first-floor lavatory and took a long, gratifying piss. He left his shoes and socks there, carefully lined up under the sink. He turned the lights off behind him before he tiptoed up the stairs. He congratulated himself on his precision, his thoroughness.

For a moment in his room, he stood still. He imagined himself getting undressed before he went to bed, but it seemed like a lengthy and a complicated task; so he slid, fully clothed, under the covers. His legs in their damp trousers were tired and sore. His bare feet felt chilled at first from the cold of the stairs on the way up, from the icy sheets; but he concentrated on skating, on the memory of it, of that rhythmic alternation, and they slowly warmed up. It was all he thought of—that motion, over and over—as he dropped quickly into a heavy, drunken sleep.

*   *   *

He would go back, he told his mother the next day.
He would, in a couple of days. He just needed some
time to sort things out. Things hadn't been so good
at school. He'd been having some real problems with
work; he wasn't happy. But he would go back. No one
would notice his absence for a few days.

In the daytime he stayed up in his room, sleeping, or listening to music, or reading. Late in the afternoon, before his father got home, he went out:
sometimes to a movie, or to Rob McKinnock's apartment—he was a senior at the U of C—or to a bar or
restaurant. He tried to stay out until midnight or so,
when they'd all be in bed. When he did see his father,
David was silent, but Mack had the sense of being
watched. He knew that his mother had spoken up on
his behalf, that she'd told his father just to wait a bit,
to allow Mack some time. The question was only how
long he had.

The truth was, Mack had barely gone to school
this fall. He'd met with his adviser, he'd registered,
signed up for the requisite courses. He'd even gone
to the first few weeks of classes. But then he'd
stopped.

He'd slept a good deal. Three or four times he'd
seen a shrink, but the man seemed stupid to Mack,
not as bright as he was, and what was the point of
that? He sat or walked along the river a fair amount
until the weather got too cold. He'd gotten drunk or
stoned nearly every night. He'd been thrown out of
the Bick, out of Hazens and the Casablanca. He'd written long letters he didn't mail to a girl he'd been in
love with earlier.

His roommate was gone nearly every weekend,
campaigning for Humphrey in Maine and New Hampshire or western Massachusetts, and those were the
worst times for Mack: the empty, silent room, the liq-

uor bottles lined up on the mantel. He played Ray Charles endlessly. He read, almost never anything connected with school. He read *The Sound and the Fury*. He read Camus. He read David Cooper and R. D. Laing and Philip Slater. He read Sylvia Plath and the New Testament. When he got so drunk that the lines blurred, he would shower and go out for coffee or a movie. Occasionally he found someone to go with him.

This long slide had begun in the summer. He'd decided not to go to Chicago. To stay in Boston instead and do community work in North Cambridge. He signed up to live in a group house in Somerville with seven other students involved in the community or political action. Margaret was one of them. When he met her she was standing in a bandanna-print bikini and a faded blue work shirt in the messy kitchen, making French toast amid a lot of vanilla-scented smoke. She turned to face him, squinting through the perfumed clouds, and he saw she had freckles everywhere—all over her face, her chest, her flat, tanned belly, her slightly sunburned kneecaps. She was laughing, and her long red hair was pulled back in a sloppy ponytail. There was nothing about her that Mack didn't like.

They were lovers for almost a week. Mack moved his things into her room and the two of them stayed there, with the door locked, for hours in the late afternoon and evening. They'd get up in the middle of the night and go for a walk down the deserted, black, treeless streets, bumping into each other in their fatigue. They'd point out absurdities to each other: an ornate iron gate attached to a chain-link fence, a madonna in a blue-painted shell in someone's littered front yard. "A bandshell, with a one-woman orchestra," Margaret offered.

"Or a censored version of *The Birth of Venus*," he said.

They'd shop in the all-night store in Union Square, buying ice cream, fudge sauce, cherries, lime soda; and come home and make a sugary meal, trying to suppress their giggles so they wouldn't wake the others.

Mack had never been so happy. It was like being stoned all the time. Margaret was skinny and strong, with tiny breasts, all upturned nipple. Her favorite position was squatting on him, her feet planted next to his rib cage, her bony freckled knees rising so he could grip them and rock her with his motion. He called her his jockey; he told her he loved her.

She was an artist. She drew him over and over in those few days, naked, sleeping. She drew his cock limp, and erect. Her room was a mess, as his sisters' rooms had been at home—strewn with underwear and projects, things her Head Start kids had made for her or she for them, sketches and paintings. It smelled of oil paint, of her, of sweat and funk. She was the most uninhibited lover he'd ever had. She walked around her room naked, she bent over unselfconsciously in front of him. She loved him to look at her; in fact, it excited her. He drew her once, in charcoal, the first drawing he'd done since high school. She was sprawled on the bed, one knee up, her thighs spread wide. She got so aroused by the intensity of his gaze, she made him stop and enter her.

It was the day after this, actually, that Jay Staley moved into the house, and when Mack came home, late, from work, he knew it was over. The group was still eating at the table in the kitchen—he could hear them when he came in the front door—and over the rumble of their voices Margaret's laughter rose shrill and almost hysterical. He could tell she was excited, she was turned on by someone else. They made love a few more times after that, but she was passive, absent. The last time, he pulled his cock out of her when he'd finished and said, "That was very polite, Margaret."

Her body rolled away. "I'm sorry," she said in a small voice.

"It's Jay, isn't it?" he said, and she began to cry.

He wouldn't let her help him move his stuff back out.

Jay was a photographer. He'd come up from Yale to do an inner-city arts project. Jay Staley the Yalie, Mack called him. He spoke of *making contact* with street kids.

"How is that different from, say, hanging around with them?" Mack asked. They were all at dinner again, a few days after Mack had moved his belongings out of Margaret's room. This was the first time Mack had spoken during the meal.

"Mack!" Margaret said, and blushed.

"What?" he asked.

She made a face at the others around the table, a request for their support.

"What? It's a reasonable question," he said.

"It's *hostile*," she said softly. "It's aggressive."

Jay touched her arm. "I can answer it," he said. He smiled at Mack and began to explain his philosophy—that you couldn't impose yourself on the kids. You just had to be there, waiting for the right moment. He called the Polaroid camera a *godsend* to his work, said it drew them in in a way nothing else could have. The whole time he spoke, Margaret watched his face as though he were a holy man, a guru.

Mack was doing a sports program in the parks. He was working with high school kids, coaching basketball, volleyball, organizing tournaments. He drove around from park to park in a battered project station

wagon filled with balls and nets. He worked with Portuguese kids, Irish kids, black kids. Many of them were dropouts, a few of them recent high school graduates. Already three or four kids he'd come to know pretty well had been drafted. Sometimes, stringing up a net, demonstrating a serve, or blowing his whistle, he felt like an asshole—as though this could do anything to change their lives, their possibilities. It was just a way to make privileged guys like him feel better about themselves.

Jay seemed to have no such doubts, no hesitation. He seemed really to believe that he could have an impact. And maybe, for all Mack knew, that was true. Maybe his work did offer the kids something that Mack and his work couldn't.

Jay tended to be out in the evenings a lot—a good time to make contact, apparently—but sometimes in the late afternoons, when Mack was just getting home from work, he could hear them making love in her bedroom: the loud pumping squeak of the bedsprings, sometimes the repeated thump of the frame as it smacked the plaster. Once Mack sat down in the hall to wait it out, his back against the trembling wall. Finally the bed was still. Then, faintly, he could hear them talking for a long time, murmurs and laughter. After half an hour or so, the door swung open and Margaret came out in a bathrobe. She nearly tripped over Mack and then stood there, looking down at him. He could smell her, smell the sex. He could have reached out and touched her freckled bare leg.

"Jesus Christ!" she said, and then she spun around and went back into her room.

Margaret had pointed out to Mack when she split up with him that they barely knew each other, really, that she was sure he wasn't in love with her truly, deeply. In his clearheaded moments Mack suspected that this might be true. But at the same time he wanted to feel it wasn't. And he enjoyed his misery, in some perverse sense. It made him feel alive, intense, and that gave him the only comfort he could find in the situation.

In August, three people from the house went to Chicago for the Democratic convention. Jay was one of them. Margaret couldn't go because the Head Start program she worked for couldn't spare her. On the third night Jay was gone, Mack stood in the hallway outside Margaret's door and invited her to come on a drive with him. She'd been napping. She was wearing shortie pajamas, and her red hair was wild and snarly, the way Liddie's used to be in the mornings. She looked at him guardedly.

"Truce," he said. "Just friends."

"I don't want any scenes," she said.

"The scene will be a drive. Wherever you like. The Charles. Or Walden Pond."

She chewed her lower lip. "It's not going to change anything."

"I'm seeing someone else anyway," he said. He had, actually, slept once with the older woman who ran the parks program office. "This is just to prove we can talk to each other like human beings."

She turned and stood looking back into her own room. Behind her he could see the mess, the clutter. Scattered around her feet on the floor were clothes she'd shed over the last days, or weeks.

"I always liked to talk to you," he said gently.

"All right," she said. "Why don't you wait on the porch? I'll be down in a few minutes."

They drove to Walden Pond and walked past the beach, still crowded now at eight o'clock, to a cleared spot by the path that circled the shore. Neither had brought a swimsuit, but Margaret was wearing shorts

and a T-shirt. She took her shoes off on the soft dirt bank and walked slowly in.

Mack stripped down to his jeans. The water was just slightly cooler than a child's bath, and they laughed and splashed each other in their pleasure in it. It was as though Jay had never happened, Mack thought.

Margaret's hair darkened to a deep brown and straightened with the pull of the water's weight. When she stepped slowly toward the shore, Mack could see through her wet shirt that she was wearing no bra.

They sat side by side at the shoreline for a while, talking about their jobs, about the house members, warming and drying out in the summer air. Then slowly they ambled back to the car. On the way, Margaret began to speak of Jay, to talk about his work, his sense of political commitment. Mack tried to change the subject several times, but she kept coming back to it, to Jay. He could feel how she loved to say his name, to conjure him by talking. He was expected to agree, to praise Jay, to think him a wholly admirable person.

When they got back to the car and were about to get in, Mack smiled across its roof at her. "You used to think those things about me," he said. Then he bent his body into the hot, airless space inside. When she appeared opposite him in the passenger seat, Margaret's face had changed. Soberly she looked over at him. Already her nose and upper cheeks were glistening with perspiration. She leaned forward and touched his damp jeans on the thigh. "I still think them about you too," she said. "I still love you, Mack. I'm just not *in love* with you."

He turned on the engine. "Ah, one of those delicate distinctions."

She was silent a moment. Then she said, "I don't like it when you start getting sarcastic."

"Well, I have problems when you start getting so subtle."

"I'm sure you understand the difference," she said coolly.

He drove out of the lot, away from the pond. "Why don't you explain it, though," he said at last. The houses around them were pretty Victorian cottages, set far apart. Planted, groomed.

Margaret began to talk. "Well, when you just *love* someone, you feel . . . calm and good about them. And that's the way I feel about you. I admire you. I want you to be in my life in a friendly way. I care for you."

"Thanks," Mack said.

"No, really, Mack," she said.

They drove on in silence. The wind from the car's motion whipped her hair around her head. It was curly again.

"Give me the *in love* part," Mack said.

She shrugged sullenly and looked out the window.

"No. I want to hear it." He smiled at her. "Please."

"There's just tension," she said.

"Tension," he repeated.

"Yes." Her voice was irritable. "If you must know, when I'm with Jay, or just even when I think of him, I feel a tremendous tension—eagerness, anxiety, whatever. I'm very . . . distracted."

"So even now, even when you're with me, and you think of our mutual friend, you get this . . . *tension?*" They were coming up the main street of a town. Concord. It was lined with pretty, old-fashioned shops.

"Oh, Mack, why do you do this? You said you wouldn't make a scene."

"I guess I didn't figure you'd try to tell me how wonderful Jay is."

After a silence she said, "Mack, I like you so much. You just mean a lot to me." Her voice was kind and concerned. Mack wanted her to shut up. But she went on. "I think of you so often, and I'm just sorry there has to be this . . . mess between us. I just keep hoping, I guess, that we can rise above it. That we can have what was nice between us be that way again."

Mack pulled over abruptly to the curb. The guy behind him braked sharply, honked, then yelled something over at Mack as he drove past.

When Mack spoke, his voice was too loud for the tiny space they sat in. "What was nice between us, Margaret, was sex. Was when we fucked."

"Mack," she said. Under her freckles, the flesh around her mouth was suddenly white.

Together they watched a very elderly couple teeter past, staring in at them from under matching sunshades. Then Mack said in a reasonable voice that she'd better get out. He wasn't sure where he was going, but he wasn't going back to the house that night.

"But I can't get out here. This is miles from home."

"Well, I'm only going farther."

"But how am I supposed to get back?"

"I don't know. It's a town. There'll be a train, or a bus."

"You're not serious."

"Yeah, I am." He looked over at her.

"I can't believe this. That you'd do this."

"Just get out, Margaret."

She waited a few moments for him to relent. When he didn't say anything, she burst out, "This is just so fucking . . . immature. This is just absurd."

"This is immature? *This* is absurd? You broke my

heart, Margaret. You fucking wrecked my life. And you . . . you're cavalierly screwing your way through the house. I can't feel too bad for you that you have to take a *train* home."

"They're not the same."

"You bet they're not the same. That's my point. Now get out."

When she didn't move, he reached across her and yanked the station wagon's handle. The door groaned and swung out. Her face was inches from his. Mack could smell her breath, that familiar sweetish Margaret odor. She hesitated.

He leaned back and gripped the wheel. "I'm not driving you back there." His voice was rising, getting harder. "Just fucking get out. Get out of the fucking car." He could hear the threat, he felt it; his heart was pounding.

She looked at him silently for a long moment, then stepped out onto the street. She slammed the door so hard that the handle rattled. He pulled away, tires squealing.

He drove on the winding country roads for several hours as night fell. Finally, when it was truly dark, he turned back and wove his way home. It was around eleven when he got in. The air in the house seemed hot and smelled of sweat, food. No one was around. He went into the living room and turned on the television. He watched the end of a detective show.

Then the news came on, and there on the screen were the crowds of students and radicals in Chicago, swarming back and forth in front of the Hilton Hotel—bloodied, excited. When the lights and cameras played over their faces, they cheered and chanted, "The whole world is watching! The whole world is watching!"

Perfect, thought Mack. Sitting alone in the flickering blue light, he laughed once. "Fucking, fucking perfect," he said out loud.

The following week, by a vote of five to two, with Margaret abstaining, he was thrown out of the group house. His behavior was called provocative and antisocial. Mack had known how the vote would go, had known who would vote for and against him. He'd prepared a short speech, actually, to make to the house members after the verdict was reached, a speech in which he defended his immaturity, his pettiness, as being more authentic, more *felt*, than their rules, which ignored human feeling. But in the end, surveying the closed sorrowful faces in the shabby room, he decided not to waste his time.

It didn't matter that much, in any case. He spent a couple of very drunk nights with the project secretary. And then several of the Harvard houses began to open for early arrivals—the football team, the upperclassmen in charge of freshmen orientation—and it was easy enough to sneak in and out of unoccupied suites until they opened his hallway and he could move back in.

Sometimes, though, waking early in some bare room in order to get out before the maintenance crew arrived and found him, Mack would look frantically around the strange shabby elegance of the paneled walls, the empty fireplace and bookshelves, and he'd wonder, not so much *where am I*, but *who am I*.

Mack was watching the five o'clock news with his mother—he had gotten up only a few hours before—when he heard the front door open. Though it could have been any one of his younger sisters, he knew immediately that it wasn't. He knew it was his father. And when David appeared in the open archway to the living room, Mack had pivoted to face him; their eyes met and locked for a long moment. Then there was the explosion of rifle fire on the television, and they both turned their heads that way. The young man on the screen flung his arms wide and tilted back into the tall grass. "My God," whispered his mother. No one had greeted his father.

"Is this what we mean by *bringing the war home?*" his father asked.

Lainey set her drink down. "David, you're early!" She got up and crossed to the set, turned it off just as the narrative started up again, the deep, melodramatic voice of the combat reporter.

"I know. I wanted to see Mack before he made his nightly escape."

Lainey seemed embarrassed, flustered. Her big hands wandered aimlessly in the air. "Would you like a drink?" she asked.

"No." He sat down and stretched his feet out on the pale rug. "Yes. Yes, all right."

This room had changed more slowly than the others after Randall left—but now the couch was re-covered in yellow, and there was a rug, there were curtains at the windows and some paintings his mother had done in art class on the walls. The whole house looked more or less normal now. And they—they could be a normal family too, about to have a normal discussion. Mack's mother went back into the kitchen. He could hear her in there after a moment, getting ice cubes out.

The long silence enveloped him and his father. His father broke it. "Well, Macklin," he said at last. "Is this a *convenient* time for you to talk?"

And instantly Mack felt the ancient rage this sarcasm always triggered—and the wish to defend retroactively the small boy in himself who'd always been confused and rendered speechless by this tone of his father's. Even when it was addressed—as it usually had been when he was small—to his mother. "I'm at your disposal," he said.

"Wonderful," his father said. He shifted on the couch. His posture seemed relaxed and comfortable. "Let me say, then, for starters, that I'm concerned about you."

Mack was sitting up very straight, as he'd been since he heard the door open some minutes before. "You don't need to be," he said.

"Well, nonetheless, I am," his father said. He smiled fleetingly, the slightest lift of his lips. "And my concern is, quite simply, that I get the feeling you don't know what you're doing at the moment. With your life, that is."

"I guess that's fair."

David waited.

Finally Mack said, "But of course, it is my life."

"Well, but not in every sense."

"What do you mean?"

Lainey had come in. She set a glass down for David. She stood awkwardly, resting her thigh against the arm of the couch, looking from one of them to the other. Mack wondered if she had known this was coming, if she and his father had talked about it ahead of time. Her face was anxious. If she had ears, Mack thought, they'd be lying back. Then he smiled, because of course she did have ears. And they weren't.

His father seemed offended by the smile. He sat forward, suddenly, as though to insist they were all business here. "What do I mean? I mean that you're living at home, seemingly. It's been a week and a half. That we're paying your room and board."

There was a shocked silence in the room. Then Mack said, "I didn't realize that money was a problem."

"Oh, it isn't!" his mother cried. But his father had started to talk too, and he continued on after her cry:

". . . this pretense of independence. An independent person does not . . ." Now he sat back and took a sip from his glass. His voice was quiet when he began again: "does not bring the war home." He set his glass down with a little *clink* on the coaster Lainey had brought. "And we're paying for it doubly. We're paying for a meal contract there, an empty room there, while you sit here and get stoned and sleep till noon every day, like some inert . . . *lump* in our midst."

"David," Lainey said. Her hand was resting on her bosom as if she felt pain there.

He looked up at her.

"Surely this isn't the point," she said.

"No," he said then. "No, you're right." He sounded tired, suddenly. He looked at Mack. "You explain the point, then, Lainey."

She stepped away from the couch and sat down between them, on the decorated wooden chair—Aunt Lalie's chair—pushed against the wall. It was uncomfortable, rarely used except as extra seating at parties. Lainey had to perch forward on it. She was frowning. She looked like an earnest schoolgirl. "The point is just . . . that we *are* concerned, Mack. You seem so . . . lost, at the moment. And there are just so many—so many real consequences to being lost at your age. Especially as things are now. Not just school—whatever's happening there—but . . ." She gestured at the TV. "The war. Getting drafted."

David moved restlessly on the couch, and she looked quickly over at him, then back at Mack. "We'd just like to feel that . . . it *is* your life. In this sense: in the sense that you do what you decide to do, but because you know the consequences."

"But you can't always know the consequences."

"Of course you can't, but certain things are predictable."

"Such as?"

His father's voice was hard. "Such as, if you don't go back to school, you'll flunk out."

Mack looked at him and slowly smiled. "Yeah, but chances are, if I do go back I'll flunk out too."

"What do you mean, *chances are?* What sort of a hell of a way to talk is that?"

"Just that my chances of passing anything this semester are not good."

"Because you haven't worked."

"That's right."

"And why haven't you, may I ask?"

"Because I don't belong there. Nothing I might have worked on seemed . . . interesting or important to me."

"But what does, darling?" Lainey asked. "What *is* important?"

Macklin shrugged. "To see how this all comes out."

David sat forward suddenly. "You are in *charge* of how it comes out. Don't speak as though you had nothing to do with the course of your life."

"Well, I feel differently about that than you do, Dad."

"You feel you don't have control over your life."

"That's right."

Lainey leaned toward her husband, as if she wanted to interpose herself between them. "Well, of course he feels that way, David. I mean, look at this world we live in. Just ceaseless violence. Assassination. This unholy war."

David lifted his hand. "Mack has a choice about how to deal with that."

"You believe I have a choice, Dad."

"I know you have a choice, son. That is something I know. And even more immediately, you have many small choices. And it's time for you to make a few. It's time, for example, for you to get back to school. To get back to work."

No one said anything for a moment. Then Mack spoke. "Well, I choose not to do that."

"I see." His father sat very still for a moment. When he spoke, there was sarcasm in his tone again. "I assume that's final."

Mack felt a furious leap of anger. "Yes, it is," he said.

"Well, then, I'd like you to withdraw. To take some responsibility for that decision. To withdraw officially. Maybe I can get back some of the hundreds of dollars I shelled out in tuition."

"David," Lainey said.

"All right," Mack said. "I'll do that."

"And I think you'd better get a job. Life is an expensive proposition when you're in charge of your own."

Mack stretched. "All right," he said. "I can do that too, I think."

Lainey said, "I don't think we should be so hasty here."

Mack turned to her. "It's all right, Mom. This is what I want. This is just putting me in motion."

"But, darling, it's not so simple. They'll have to let the draft board know, and then where will we be?"

"We'll see, won't we? It's coming up anyhow, one way or another."

"But it doesn't have to." She was frowning with intensity, pondering what she imagined was the future shape of his life. "You don't have to lose the 2-S. You might want to go on to graduate school, for instance." Mack smiled, but she didn't notice. "And in June, if you waited until June, there'll be so many others. I mean, this is just sticking your neck out, all alone. Surely they'll take you. David, don't you think . . . ?"

"Lainey, there are lots of options to play out before that happens. I wouldn't worry about it."

"But unless he does something, he's going to get drafted. Mack, surely you can't imagine fighting in this horrible, immoral war."

"There are a lot of other people doing it, Mom," he said; but at the same time David was saying, more loudly, "There are a lot of options to play out, Lainey." And apparently reassured, she nodded. She didn't seem to have heard what Mack had said.

Two days later, Mack got a job at Kroch's & Brentano's. It was just for the holidays, wrapping and preparing gift books to be mailed. The pay was minimum wage, but Mack didn't care. He didn't have to be at work until four—the store was open until nine each weeknight up to Christmas—and he could wear whatever he wanted because he wasn't on the floor. And he liked the big store, the smell of the books, its quiet.

After work he often stayed downtown for a while, wandering among the expensive shops, looking over the lavish display windows, the twinkling amber lights. Everywhere, Christmas carols were piped in, and sometimes you could catch people humming or singing them under their breath as they hurried around. Mack felt a pleasant sense of isolation from it all: this was life as other people lived it. He, he was on another tack.

At some point he'd head back to Hyde Park on the IC. Occasionally he'd take his mother's car late at night and go out again—to Jimmy's or to Rob's apartment or to hear Soletski's band, which played every now and then in some seedy joint for a cut of the door money. Sometimes he'd stay on with the band after they closed a place, or move with them to a party in someone's apartment. There was a lot of drinking, a lot of drugs. The female singer, Irene, and one or two of the musicians were occasionally shooting heroin, and everyone else smoked dope and drank constantly. There were times when Mack fell into a stuporous sleep in some strange bed and woke still slightly drugged in the early morning hours. He often had to drive around for five or ten minutes in his mother's car before he figured out where he was, which direction to head in to get home.

Sometimes he felt a kind of revulsion at his life, and then he did something with Nina. Once he took her to see *King of Hearts,* and she seemed wildly excited by its vision of life—the loonies in charge. And when the people he'd gone to high school with, his classmates, began drifting home for Christmas vacation and Mack suddenly had his choice of parties to go to almost every night, he took Nina to a few of those too.

One was at Jennifer Furman's house. Late in the party, he noticed a guy he'd hardly known back then talking to Nina. Her head was lifted to listen, her long dark hair fell like a luxuriant shawl over her back and shoulders. She was wearing a lot of makeup these days, and it made her look older. He had thought when she came down the front stairs that night that she looked old enough to be someone he was dating. Across the room now she laughed suddenly, and her face, which in repose seemed full of sorrow, leapt to girlish life.

On the way home, she thanked him for bringing her along. "It's wonderful to get away from all the people who think that you're just . . . a certain kind of person," she said.

They drove in silence for a while. Nina was smoking. She never did at home, and Mack wasn't sure whether his parents knew about it. She tapped her cigarette on the ashtray. Finally she said, "What's going to happen, Mack?"

He looked over at her. "What do you mean?"

"With you. Are you going to Canada?"

"I dunno." He smiled. "Is that what you'd do?"

Her look over was careful, thoughtful. "I'm not sure. 'Cause you couldn't come back, after all."

"That's the argument, all right. For me not to go, I mean."

She inhaled, and watched the cloud of smoke she blew back out. Then she turned to him and said, "But why don't you just go back to school? It can't be so bad." She made a face. "It can't be as bad as it is every single day for me."

"Is it?"

"Yes," she said. She shrugged. "Or maybe not. I *am* Miss Mysterioso. A veddy veddy unusual *personne.*" She pulled a veil of her hair across her nose, hiding the lower part of her face. Then she threw it back. "Wondered about by thousands," she said.

"Loved by none," he said.

She laughed. "So true." She leaned forward and stubbed her cigarette out. "I can tell you exactly what it's going to say under my picture next year. Want to know?"

"Sure."

"Still Waters Run Deep."

He laughed, and then there was a moment's silence.

Then she said, "I don't understand it, really. Just because I'm sort of . . . shy, I guess. But it's like I've got this infectious disease or something." Suddenly she arched her fingers so they looked like claws and leaned toward him. "I touch you, and you die."

"Oh, please, please, Miss Mysterioso. Don't don't touch me." He swerved the wheel hard, and the car rocked sideways.

She shrieked and laughed. They settled back.

"Well," he said. "It's not that much longer."

"Except it's forever. It seems forever."

"I know."

She leaned back and sighed dramatically. Behind her, the plain of the Midway stretched flat and black. "But why don't you?" she asked. "Go back, I mean."

"Because I'm tired of that. Of just consenting to my life. I hated school. I wasn't learning anything. I felt completely false, and after a while I just stopped anyway." He shrugged. "Besides, I withdrew officially. Dad made me."

"He made you?" Her voice was incredulous.

"He made me *choose*. Supposedly so he could get his money back. Actually"—Mack grinned—"because he was so fucking pissed he couldn't see straight."

"I didn't know that. God, what was he thinking of? I can't believe he did that! Doesn't he *know* what'll happen?"

"Well, as I said, it'll happen anyway."

"But when it happens, then what?" He didn't answer, and after a moment she said decisively, "I think you should be a CO."

"Do you?"

"Yes. I knew a guy. Well, I didn't actually know him. I read this article about him. And he was a CO, and now he's doing some work in a hospital somewhere. A mental hospital."

"Well, it's a possibility. Too bad I haven't been to church in years. That do help with CO."

She was watching him. "What are the other possibilities?"

"Well, I could render unto Caesar."

"You mean *go?*"

"Yeah."

"But your life isn't Caesar's! Or the army's. Or whatever."

"It is as much as anyone's is. Is anyone's?"

"Well, some people want to go."

"Huh. I wonder if that could be true." He down-shifted and turned the steering wheel. The car nosed onto Harper Avenue. "But of course, Dad will offer to fix it too. There's that way out. Go to a shrink and be pronounced crazy. Be cured of the army by being found nuts."

"Dad does have that way."

He looked sharply at her. He remembered abruptly all he had wanted to do for Nina once, all he had wanted to show her. He'd been so caught up in the events of his own life that he hadn't thought of her in what felt like years. He hadn't considered who she was, or was becoming. Until this moment. He noticed now that the fingers that had held the cigarette were ripped, chewed around the nails. He knew she seemed lonely, she almost never went out. And he saw now that her way of being pretty—dark, sober, *handsome* really—was not something that would be useful to her in high school. He felt a sweep of concerned tenderness for her suddenly. He wanted to help her, to touch her—to reach beyond himself— and this unsummoned sensation was so welcome, such a relief, like shedding an imprisoning garment, that he wasn't able to speak for a moment.

But just as he had gotten control of himself, just as he was about to say something to her, Nina reached over and rested her scabbed fingers on his arm. "I want you to know, Mack," she said softly, "that I'd do anything I could to help you."

He parked the car and turned off the engine. He looked at her tender, pretty face in the dark for a moment, and then he laughed out loud.

Mack had to work on Christmas Eve. Customers kept arriving up until the moment the doors closed. Many of them bought eight or ten books, all to be wrapped separately. The tables had been out on the floor for four days, and Mack worked frantically, yanking the expensive paper, the multicolored ribbons, off their large spools. But there wasn't the feeling of impatience, of being rushed, that had hummed through the store for the last several days; the customers had a pleasant air of resignation about them. Mack commented on it to one of the last people waiting in line, a black man in an elegant camel-hair coat. "We all know we've been bad," the man said. "We're not out to prove anything."

The cleaning crews were already descending by the time Mack had finished picking up the mess around his table. And when he stepped outside, the streets were nearly empty, in sharp contrast to the sense of urgent bustle when he'd come in to work at four.

The night was cold and clear, and Mack's ears burned as he walked to the IC. Even the train was nearly empty—a few late workers, like himself heading home, and, in his car, two weary-looking women with shopping bags packed tightly around them as though propping their bodies up. He got off at Fifty-seventh and walked the length of the wooden platform, looking down at the lighted town houses below him on one side, at the dark park on the other. His footsteps on the boards were the only sound. In the viaduct under the tracks, too, his solitary scuff echoed in the empty space.

No one was home, but he'd expected this. He had warned his mother that he'd probably be late, and she'd said they would go on to the Christmas Eve service. He could join them there if he got back in time. He saw that the keys to his father's car were on the hook in the front hall as an invitation.

His coat still on, the collar turned up, he went

into the living room and sat down on the couch. The lights on the tree were plugged in, but otherwise the room was dark. The bubblers made the walls shimmer with underwater motion. Under the tree, the presents were heaped—a smaller pile in recent years, so many ancient relatives had died. Liddie had been due to arrive home this afternoon after Mack left for work, and he could tell she must have added hers—dotting the top of the slope, there were numerous packages wrapped in the equivalent of tie-dyed tissue. And scattered here and there among them all, glamorously wrapped, were Mack's presents too, books, bought with his employee discount.

He got up and went over to the tree. He knelt by the presents. He looked through them, squinting at the tags, opening the little folded cards taped on the various odd wrappings. Every possible family permutation was there. It was like one of those sociograms he'd failed to study this fall: Sarah to Liddie, Liddie to Nina, Nina to him (a square flat package, a record), and so on. He was touched, abruptly, with a sense of the crisscrossing, weblike love that held the rest of his family together. And ashamed of how careless he'd been in his own selections.

He went back to the kitchen. It was just ten. He must have barely missed them. Standing in the silent room, he could hear the minute hand click, move. He decided abruptly that he'd go, he'd join them. Hurrying now, he went back to the front hall and lifted the keys from the hook. He pulled the door hard after him to lock it.

The seat in his father's car was icy under his ass and legs, and Mack shuddered and hunched over the steering wheel as he drove through the lifeless streets. Everywhere, there was this silence. Everywhere, lighted trees in the windows, and no people. A wild desolation seized him. He turned on the radio, fiddled with the knob until he got a talk show, relaxed into the sound of the impassioned, argumentative voices.

He had to park about a block away from the church. As he approached it, walking, he could hear the singing from within. Appropriate: "O Come, All Ye Faithful." He smiled and felt eager in spite of himself. And when he opened the door, the music, the hundreds of voices, embraced him as viscerally as heat.

He stood behind the last row of pews, trying to spot his family; but the congregation was standing too, a wall with their backs to him, and he realized there was no possibility of finding anyone. Singing himself as he walked forward, he moved up the side aisle, looking for any empty space. He finally found one about two thirds of the way up. When he stepped into the pew, the woman standing next to him turned and handed him the hymnal she'd been singing from, then moved closer to the man on her other side to share his. Mack finished out the carol with the rest, then bowed his head as the minister intoned a welcoming prayer.

When everyone had sat down, Mack saw that his family was only about four pews ahead of him. Mary was leaning to whisper something to Sarah, and they made faces at each other. His father's head turned in profile, surveyed the church, and turned back again. Was that a search for Mack? Impossible to know.

Mack thought of all the Sundays he'd sat in this church with his family, almost always without his father. His absence was reasonable enough—he was the one who stayed home with Randall. But it fed Mack's sense of perplexity about just what, if any, his father's religious convictions were. About a year ago, Mack had read *The Future of an Illusion* for a course, and he was sure it held the answer, that this must be it. But when he'd tried to talk to his father about it, David was dismissive. He'd said something brusquely about his not necessarily believing every idea of Freud's just because he was a psychiatrist.

His mother's feelings, on the other hand, were transparent, always had been. She'd appeared in the parish hall every Sunday of his youth, waiting for them as they trooped down from Sunday school. They would follow her into church, like imprinted goslings, Mack thought. He remembered her hopeful face before church, her rapt attention during the service, taking in the message, which would seem to lift her, change her, until the next crisis—someone's temper tantrum, an act of destruction by Randall—brought her around again to hysterics, to slaps, then remorse for her own weakness. Sometimes in church, though, he would hear that odd dull click in her throat and, without turning his head, know that she was weeping in quiet joy. Her head even now was unswervingly fixed in the direction of the chancel. Mack followed the track her gaze must be taking. The chancel was gaudy with color—white and red poinsettia, the lush green of their leaves.

The minister was reading about God having set Jesus above the angels, his voice imitating God's, pronouncing richly, "Thou art my son, this day have I begotten thee." Mack stared up at him. He was a young man with long sideburns and wire-rimmed glasses. He was new since Mack had gone to college. Lainey had pointedly mentioned his work with draft resisters several times to Mack.

When the minister was finished, he turned and walked back to his thronelike chair. There was coughing, stirring. The organ began with the last two lines of "Hark! the Herald Angels Sing," and the congregation rose, began lustily. They did all the verses, and Mack's throat was dry and aching slightly when he sat down. He was grateful for the long prayer the minister launched himself into, but he didn't listen hard. He was thinking about his family with a tender feeling, like regret. Then the children's choir performed several pieces. After they'd sat down, the minister came forward again and began to read: "In the beginning was the Word," he intoned majestically. "And the Word was with God, and the Word was God." Mack knew this passage by heart—he'd had to learn it for Sunday school, and it had always intrigued and puzzled him. He was startled, then, when it changed suddenly, when, in the middle, there were several lines he'd forgotten utterly, not about Jesus but about John: "There was sent a man from God, whose name was John. The same came for a witness, to bear witness of the Light. He was not that Light, but was sent to bear witness of that Light." That was it; then it moved right back to the lines Mack remembered: that Jesus was the Light, that he made us sons of God if we believed. The minister wound it up: "And the Word was made flesh, and dwelt among us, and we beheld his glory, the glory of the only begotten of the Father, full of grace and truth."

During the next hymn and the short homily, Mack kept thinking about those strange lines—old John the human being, stuck right into the middle of the Bible's strangest passage about Christ. It pleased Mack, and touched him.

As the minister pronounced the benediction, Mack felt suddenly that he needed to cling to this feeling, that he didn't want to talk to anyone, not yet. He tried to thread his way quickly toward the side doors, but the cheerful throng, shaking hands, greeting one another, slowed him. He knew if he looked hard at the wrong face, it would open in recognition and welcome, so he kept his eyes cast down as he slid around people, murmuring apologies. Just as he was about to step outside, he turned to see if his family had noticed him. Through the crowd his eyes met Nina's; recognition animated her face, but he raised his finger to his lips and turned into the dark night.

He felt he was holding on to something, something he thought of as solitary and pure in himself. He drove out to the lake and headed south. He drove around for a long time, through the ghetto, into South Shore. There were bars and restaurants open, he saw, but he didn't want that either. He didn't know what he wanted; he didn't know where to go to find it.

At a stoplight under the el, a black man knocked on his window. It frightened Mack. He tried not to look at the man. But the man called to Mack: "Mister. Mister." He was drunk, slurring the word. "Merry Christmas," he shouted on the other side of the glass. "Mer-ry Christmas, mister." Mack got his wallet out. He didn't have much. A five and some ones. He rolled his window down and gave the man the money. The cold air, and the rich, horrible stink of the man's breath washed into the car. "God bless you," the man said earnestly. He was gripping the edge of the window. "You're a good man." Mack noticed that his fingers poked through the worn tips of his gloves. "You're a good man, mister."

Mack drove home. When he brought the car to a stop in front of the square, it was after twelve by the greenish light on the dashboard. He cut the motor and sat for a moment in the stillness. Then he got out, locked his door, and walked to the house.

The tree was still on, for him to pull the plug, he guessed. But just as he crouched to reach the outlet under the window, his father's voice stopped him: "I've been waiting for you."

Mack lurched, nearly fell. His hand spread flat on the carpet, and he pushed himself up.

"Sorry to scare you," his father said. He held up a white china cup. "Want some eggnog? Spiked?"

"It's not my drug of choice," Mack said.

His father smiled and sat down in the deep chair. Mack sat too, on the couch. He was surprised, for a moment, at how relaxed he suddenly felt; and then he realized that he was eager, in a way, to have this over with, this last hurdle he'd known he'd have to leap before he let his destiny take him. He looked over at David. His father's head was bent, as if he were still in church, praying. His hairline had receded slightly over the years, and when he lifted his face to Mack, his high forehead added to his aura of severity, of dignity. He was frowning. He cleared his throat. "Well, as you said, this thing is in motion now." Upstairs, someone's slippers slid down the hall to one of the back bedrooms: Sarah, or Nina. A door closed.

"Somewhere out there, yes, I guess it is."

"I've no idea how long, but I suppose not very, and you lose your 2-S."

Mack didn't answer, and David took a sip of eggnog and set the cup down on the fat upholstered arm of the chair. He was still wearing a tie and a tweed jacket. His eyes on Mack seemed big and black in the shimmery orange light. "What's your plan?"

Mack laughed, but David's face stayed immobile, and he stopped quickly. David leaned forward and rested his elbows on his knees. "We'll support you, whatever you choose to do, Mack. I want you to know that."

"But what if I choose to do"—Mack made his voice dramatic and raised his eyebrows—"nothing!"

David watched him, and Mack felt suddenly foolish. He shoved his hands into his jeans pockets and slouched back.

"That would be asinine indeed," David said quietly.

After a minute, Mack said agreeably, "Well, gee. Thanks, Dad."

David's eyes were steady on Mack. The pale skin on his brow had furrowed. "You cannot be serious."

"It *is* my life, man."

"Not to throw away, it isn't."

"Why would it be throwing it away?" And before David could answer, he said, "Remember what our fearless leader said so long ago? 'Ask not what your country can do for you. Ask what you—' "

"Stop it, Mack."

Mack shifted, sat up straighter. "There was a time we all thought those were words to live by."

"Times have changed," David said harshly.

Mack shrugged. They both watched the tree a moment. The tinsel stirred slightly in a draft.

Then David said, "Okay, let's just start again here. Let's lay this out. In terms of our options."

"What you mean, *our,* white man?"

David ignored Mack's smile. "I mean what's possible here." He took another swig of eggnog and set his cup down again. He licked his upper lip. "CO is possible," he said. "It probably means a legal fight, but it's possible."

"CO is not possible."

"Why not?"

"Oh, come on, Dad. I know guys who are doing CO. Their lives . . . have a certain recognizable pattern, you know? They've been fighting against the war all the way. They're the ones throwing blood on *my* file, for Christ's sake. They converse, like on a regular basis, with their consciences. They go to fucking church. Or Quaker meeting." He shook his head. "There's no way I'd make CO."

"All right. Supposing that's true. Let's suppose it is. Then there's Canada."

Mack said nothing. He was watching. It had suddenly become clear to him that there was no need to respond until his father came to his point.

"But I think, to be honest—she'd never say this, but I will—it'd about destroy your mother. If you want it, we'll support you, as I said. But keep that in mind."

Mack sat.

"Then there's the option I think you should take."

After a long moment, Mack bit. "Which is?" he asked.

"Well. I think I could get you disqualified psychiatrically."

Mack smiled. "I knew this was coming." He shook his head. "I knew this was coming. God."

"It's no disgrace, Mack. There are even some elements in your life that would make it seem very easy."

"What? Like using drugs?"

"Yes." His father's gaze was direct. "And dropping out as you did. When you had the deferment. There's a very . . . self-destructive image that could be established."

"And you're just the guy to do it."

"Well, of course I wouldn't be the one to do it. For all the obvious logical and ethical reasons. But there are colleagues of mine who do feel strongly about the war, who are willing to help."

Mack didn't answer.

"This is nothing to be ashamed of, Mack. There are lots of boys doing this." When Mack didn't answer again, David began to explain. He'd arrange an appointment. There were several men to choose from. He'd pick someone Mack could feel comfortable with.

As his father talked, Mack watched him warming, becoming animated in that oddly distant way—gentle, concerned, but professional. He remembered how safe that had once made him feel; he remembered turning to his father when his mother seemed out of control. At what point, he wondered, had his father's calm begun to seem a liability? At what point had his mother's craziness come to seem honorable and appropriate? He couldn't remember.

"It's a matter simply of an interview," his father was saying. "Maybe two. Possibly three. And you've only got to marshal the evidence. You don't need to lie. Just some selective remembering. Things you've done, events—hell, even I can think of two or three— that show you . . . well, under stress, let's say."

"Hell," Mack said. "I can think of four or five."

"Of course!" David said. His smile was almost boyish. Then he saw something in Mack's face, and it dimmed.

Mack's voice was quiet and flat. "But I don't want to do it, Dad. I'm not going to."

David nodded slowly, two or three times. "Well," he said finally, "I don't see that you've got an option, son."

"I'm going to do what I told you I'd do."

"Which is?"

"Which is *nothing*. Exactly that. Nothing. And maybe, all on their own, they'll think I'm nuts enough for 4-F."

"Don't be provocative, Mack."

"Well, then, take me seriously for about two seconds, will you? I've thought about this."

"Mack, boys like you do not get drafted. You're better than that, and you know it. I won't let this—"

"Fuck that!" Mack's body jerked forward on the couch. "Fuck it! I'm better than *nobody*." He stopped for a few seconds, and his voice was soft again when he spoke. "I'm no different from anyone else, Dad. Just one of the guys. Just one of the fucking guys, like all the others." He stood up. "And I don't want you in my life anymore, arranging anything. Dispensing favors. Presiding. Like some . . . fucking god."

There was a long silence. "Well, I accept that, Mack," David said finally. "I think that is fair. I'd argue you are different from everyone else, but I understand that I can't be the one . . . that my judgment isn't the definitive one." He was looking down, at his clenched hands. "But let me offer you . . . let me suggest, though, one possible interpretation for your behavior."

"Oh, Christ, Dad." Mack stood up and stepped quickly to the doorway.

"No, wait a minute. I've heard you out. Now I'd like you to listen. Will you listen, just for another minute?"

Mack stood, looking over at his father, looking down. He remembered a time years earlier—a fight?—when he'd stood over his father in just this way, feeling this same distance, this power.

When it was clear that Mack would stay, David began. "I'd like to say, Mack, that I know I've been a . . . a difficult father for you. Partly the separation, literally disappearing that way. But I know, too, that I've been . . . withdrawn, and I regret that. I regret how cut off from all you children I've been. How much I've missed. And I don't excuse myself. I know some of the reasons I turned away from the family, but I don't excuse myself." Mack had come into the room a step while his father talked, and now he sat down on Aunt Lalie's chair. David smiled gratefully. "And because of that, I know"—he shrugged—"there are a lot of unresolved issues. For you, and for the girls. And I wouldn't blame you if you felt like punishing me. Or testing me."

Mack was stirring.

"No. Wait a minute. Here's what I want to say, Mack. Hear me out." David was leaning forward, one hand out. It was as though he wanted to touch Mack. But he didn't. "It's *don't.* Don't test me on this. This one hurts you, not me. Or you as much as me. If this is a test, find another. Find another one, son, that just hurts me, not you."

Mack was shaking his head. He grinned momentarily. Then he said, "Well, that all sounds noble as hell, doesn't it? But I have to say—I mean, I don't like to say it, but I have to say, Dad, that that's one of the most egocentric things I've ever heard. This has nothing to do with you. This is me. This is *me* looking for some honesty, some authenticity, somewhere in my fucking life. Which is—no, listen, man!—which is a fraudulent, bad-faith piece of shit at the moment."

"Oh, God, Mack! All this existential crap."

Mack stood up quickly. He pointed to his father. "And your psychiatric crap! Your crap, Dad. I don't believe it. I don't believe it. You've fucking got me coming and going, but I don't care. I don't care if this is Oedipal, or acting out, or some other shit. Those are just words, Dad, just your words for it. And I'm not interested, I'm just not interested anymore." He stepped toward the doorway again, on his way to his room, but he stopped just inside it. "You don't believe in *my* words: well, I don't believe in your words. I just don't happen to believe in them. They don't describe it for me, Dad. They don't have anything to do with the way I feel it." He turned away.

David rose quickly. "Mack!" he said.

Mack's hand rested on the newel post. He looked back. David came and stood in the archway, and they stared at each other for a moment. David said, "I guess my question for you, Mack, is what *do* you believe in?"

Mack took a deep breath, then exhaled slowly.

"In not faking it," he said. "Not pretending to be what I'm not: noble, or worthy of exemption. Or better, I guess, than anyone else."

David's gaze was intense on Mack. When Mack

was finished, he frowned, and then he said, "But you notice, don't you, that those are all negative?"

Mack didn't answer.

"You're being very scrupulous, but to what end? There's no reason here. No center. No positive belief."

"It's what I've got, man." Mack lifted his empty hands. "It's all I've got."

Mack went up the stairs slowly to the second floor, feeling his father's eyes on him as he rose. After he'd shut the door to the attic stairs, though, he sprinted up the last flight, and a cry, a muted caw, escaped from him. He went into his room and shut the door, whirled around in the familiar dark.

He wanted to shout, to bang the walls in victory. He went to the side window and looked out over the train tracks. Beyond the black ridge of the embankment, the bare treetops of Jackson Park made a feathered horizon line against the lighter sky. He remembered abruptly dreams he'd had as a child—still had, occasionally—of being able to fly. Dreams so vivid that on waking he sometimes felt for a few moments that they were true—that the slow ascent through just such pale, light air, above just such naked trees, was memory, not wish.

He crossed the room to his desk, flicked on the harsh glare of his desk lamp, watched his hands moving under it, rolling a celebratory joint. He lighted it, then turned off the lamp and carried the joint with an ashtray back to the window seat. All there was left now was to wait. Easy. He could do that.

He fell asleep at the window. His head snapping forward woke him. He got up, stripped, and staggered to his bed. His body felt hard and clean in the cool sheets, his cock stiffened in pleasure, and he reached to stroke himself. But before he'd even really begun, he fell asleep again.

Sometime in the middle of the night he heard the noises of his father's sleeplessness in the kitchen—the muted, slight scrape of the kettle on the iron grill as he started a pot of coffee. But Mack was so lost in his stoned dreams that he understood it as the sound of childhood: he believed it was his mother, awake with his brother—that Randall was among them again—and he smiled in his sleep to know that everything was back the way it was supposed to be.

15

WHEN Nina came back to high school after her long week's absence, everything had changed. It wasn't that she'd been popular before and now wasn't—and it wasn't the opposite either. It was just that whatever kind of success she might have aspired to earlier was now impossible, and her only hope lay in the aura of mystery and danger, tragedy even, that surrounded her.

She felt as she lived through it that she would always remember that first day back, walking down the wide halls lined with lockers, nodding at the few classmates who spoke to her. Hearing the whispers starting up behind her as soon as she passed. "She . . . She . . . ," a long hiss trailing her like a cloud wherever she went. Certain movie images helped her then, oddly pictures of men, mostly. Marlon Brando, staggering bloody and beaten through the crowd at the end of *On the Waterfront;* a Spanish bullfighter walking with strained indifference away from the bull and his tossing horns.

Nina had run away, something so scandalous in her world that she knew it was all that would matter about her for the rest of her senior year. She had run away, and she wouldn't tell anyone why or where she'd gone or what she'd done. Everyone had a version, even people who'd never been remotely interested in her before. Mary repeated them all to Nina. She was the only one Nina talked to about any of it, though she wouldn't tell even Mary why she'd gone.

The sessions with the psychiatrist had already started, forced on her because of her stubborn silence. If she wouldn't talk to her parents, her father said the night she returned, she would have to talk to someone else, someone responsible. His face was composed when he said this, his voice was calm, but Nina could tell by the tightness around his mouth that he was deeply angry.

She had arrived back at home midevening and let herself in quietly with her key. She had stood in the front hall, staring at herself in the mirror and listening to the noises in the house—tinny radio music and the sound of running water from the kitchen, upstairs the on-and-off voice of someone on the telephone.

And then a laugh.

A laugh! Nina couldn't help being shocked. They had gone on, then. Life had gone on.

But she should have known this. Hadn't she gone on with all of them when their father left? When Randall was sent away? Hadn't she laughed?

Lying across the bench in the front hall were Mary's ugly tweed coat, Sarah's green one. On a newspaper on the floor under the mirror there was a row of boots drying. Here and there on the ancient wood, the ghostly white Rorschachs of melted salted snow recorded everyone's comings and goings over the time she'd been away. Nina looked at herself in the mirror. She had been gone six days. She felt she had changed so deeply and profoundly that she would never be the same, but she saw no signs of that in the mirror.

Her sister—Mary, it was Mary—was saying something about an aptitude test: "There's no point in getting nervous. It just makes it worse." Nina tilted her head back until suddenly the overhead light ignited the tears that distorted her vision. She watched her blurred reflection with contempt. "Cry," she whispered. "Go ahead." And then she grinned sorrowfully at herself—at her flat, unwashed hair, her greasy skin, her bus-smelling, rumpled clothes.

She spun around as her mother strode quickly out of the kitchen, drying her hands with an old towel, her head already tilted back to yell up the stairs to someone. Lainey stopped, frozen, when she saw Nina. And then it began, it began just the way Nina had known it would. "Neenee," her mother whispered, and she rushed forward in only a few long steps and threw her arms around Nina. Nina felt the long shudders shake her mother's body. She smelled her perfume. After a moment Lainey drew back. She gripped Nina's shoulders, shook them, hard, and cried out in a shrill, anguished voice, "Where were you? Where were you? I was so worried!"

Nina had gone to Columbus, Ohio. She'd looked it up in the encyclopedia at school. Columbus was close enough but far enough. It was big enough but small enough. After she'd paid the bus fare she'd have $272 to get by on for a while. And it was where her lover, a graduate student, had gone to college.

She had seen Philip Olson for the first time from the stage in Mandel Hall. He was sitting behind the director in the nearly empty auditorium, his feet draped over the back of the seat in front of him. When Nina and the other high school girls trying out stepped onstage in a group, he swung his feet down and leaned quickly forward to say something to the director. They laughed together loudly, and Nina knew instantly by the sound of their laughter that he'd said something sexual about them.

The girls were all trying out for the bit parts in *The Crucible,* a university production. The other actors, college and graduate students and a few quasi-professionals, had been in rehearsal for a while. The girls would have only a few lines each—mostly they had to scream—so they were being added later, only a few weeks before the production. There were seven

of them trying out. One by one they had to step forward, say a few lines, and then act frightened and
scream very loudly. When Nina took her turn, her
heart was beating so hard she could feel it shake her
chest, and she was afraid she would open her mouth
and be unable to make any noise. When she
screamed, her voice did break, but even she could
hear that it made her sound more convincing, more
frightened.

Nina hadn't wanted to do this particularly, but
she had a friend this year, one of the popular girls,
Stephanie Lombauer, and Stephanie had talked her
into it. Nina hadn't had a best friend before. She
would have done almost anything Stephanie asked
her to do. Each of them had sworn that if the other
didn't get a part she wouldn't take one. But when the
calls came that evening, both of them had been chosen. They talked on the phone for more than an hour
about it.

Philip was the producer of the play. Nina wasn't
sure what this meant, except that whenever there was
a problem, Tony, their director, would call him from
backstage or out in the empty theater and Philip
would appear next to the director, clipboard in hand.
He would frown and make notes while Tony talked—
about the lights, about the props, about the sound
system, about the costumes—and the next day the
problem would be solved.

Nina couldn't take her eyes off Philip when he
was around. He was tall, big-boned, with softly curling
brown hair. He smiled a lot, a teasing, sly smile, and
he was very attentive to all the women in the cast.
Stephanie thought he looked like Warren Beatty in
Splendor in the Grass.

Tony was a short, slight, ugly man, with a British
accent that occasionally lapsed. You could hear then
that he was from someplace hard and gritty and with-

out grace. He called Philip "my bonny prince." He called the high school girls "the nymphets," which made the other actors smirk or laugh. When he wanted them to scream, he'd cry out from the darkened auditorium, "Nymphets, *s'il vous plaît!*"

Nina was playing Betty. She had five lines. As opening night approached and the rehearsals were more continuous, the full cast was asked to be present every night, and Nina and the other high school girls would bring their books along and sit studying backstage until they were needed. Five nights before the opening, she was slouched cross-legged on the floor in the hallway outside the dressing room, her back against the wall and a book on her lap. Philip came out and stood over her. She looked up, and her breath shortened. Then she looked down again, trying to concentrate on the swimming lines in front of her.

His foot snaked under the book, tilted it against her chest. Nina looked at him. His head was bent sideways to read.

"Ah, Latin! Working on . . . ?"

"Declension of *x* nouns," she whispered. "*Pax, lux,* those guys."

He had let the book fall flat, an apron across her opened lap. Nina reached up and unhooked the hair from behind her ears. Then, to disguise this gesture, she idly pulled a handful of it forward over her shoulder, began to separate it into strands, to braid it.

Philip was watching the stage again, the actors moving and talking in the opened box of radiant light. "Okay," he said suddenly, without looking down. "Decline . . . Ex-Lax." His voice was low, hoarse, so he wouldn't be heard onstage.

Recklessly Nina plunged. "I'd rather not have any Ex-Lax, please," she whispered.

He looked down quickly and grinned. "Very well done. And so polite."

She shrugged. "I can be rude if I want."

"Okay," he said. "Let's hear that."

"Get away from me with your fucking Ex-Lax," she said.

He laughed out loud and walked back into the dressing room. Nina's hands holding her tangled braid were trembling.

After that he called her "Mademoiselle X," or "the X-girl," and Nina was even more preoccupied with him. She and Stephanie talked for hours about him, analyzing every nuance of his behavior. When he had rested his hand on Nina's back, was he trying to feel if she was wearing a bra? When he stood with his arm around the woman playing Abigail, did that mean he was her boyfriend?

Stephanie said he was too old for Nina, that it would never work. In Stephanie's pretty bedroom, Nina agreed. But when she was alone, she marshaled the evidence against Stephanie. The year before, one of the senior girls at U-High had married Mr. Avery, the English teacher, and dropped out of school. This year you saw her sometimes, pushing her baby carriage, looking suddenly a lot older than anyone who'd stayed in school. Also, Nina knew that her father had had younger women for girlfriends when he lived apart from them. And only a few weeks earlier, when Nina had gone down the street to the Gordon's party to give her mother a message from Liddie in New York, Mr. Gordon had put his arm around Nina's shoulders and pushed his face so close to hers that she could smell the booze, the aftershave. "Why don't you stay awhile, Nina?" he said. "We need young blood at these tired old parties." Nina had blushed and was beginning to try to think of a way to extract herself, but then Mrs. Gordon had yelled at him from across the room, "Hands to yourself, Hank," and he'd laughed and moved away.

It seemed to Nina that it might have been the kids who invented the boundaries between children and adults, not the other way around. Besides, Philip was probably not much older than Liddie; and wasn't she still a kind of kid, after all?

On opening night the attendance was sparse. Snow had been falling steadily all day, and the air rang with the scraping of metal plows. The applause after the final curtain seemed scattered, only polite. An air of depressed hush hung over the group Nina and Stephanie drove with to the cast party. But Nina was on the lap of the man who'd played her father, Reverend Parris. His arm circled her waist, and she was aware of his hard, muscular thighs under her bottom. It made her feel sexy and adult. The party was to be at Philip's apartment, and she was excited about that too.

When they all got out of the car, it took Nina a disoriented moment to realize where she was—on Blackstone, only a half mile or so from her own house. She'd baby-sat down the block from here.

Philip was already home. The door to his apartment was open, and operatic music poured out and down the narrow, steep stairway as they all slowly thudded up. His apartment was small, two rooms open to each other and a tiny kitchen tucked in back. Philip was coming out from it as they entered. He embraced the two women in the cast, then gave Nina a light kiss on her cheek. When he stepped away from her to take someone's coat, she saw Stephanie smiling at her.

Nina moved over to her friend quickly. Together they walked into the front room. "My God, he kissed you!" Stephanie whispered. They stood close to each other in Philip's bedroom—his bed took up half the space—and looked out the huge multipaned window, which faced onto Blackstone, as they talked and giggled. They were up higher than the streetlights, and from here the snow outside seemed to be floating rather than falling, making its way hesitantly into that world of light, sidewalks, people. Behind them the older actors and the stage crew were slowly filling the rooms, moving back into the kitchen for food and drinks, talking loudly. Nina and Stephanie sat down together on the windowsill to watch them and whisper to each other.

Tony came up to them. He held two cans of beer. "Interested, my darlings?" he asked. He handed them over ceremoniously, like someone awarding diplomas. Nina was parched, thirsty from the screaming. She drank half the beer down almost at once. Someone had changed the music since they'd come in, and now it was ragtime, what her mother called "jiggledy-pop music." They watched the apartment grow crowded, the grownups move among each other, and finished their beers. Stephanie dared Nina to get another. She stood up and made her way through the rooms. Only every fourth or fifth person was someone who'd actually been in the play. The music had changed again. Jefferson Airplane. A few people had started to dance in the middle room, bobbing up and down among the little groups of two and three standing around screaming at each other over the music. The smell of dope floated in the air.

In the kitchen, Philip touched her shoulder. "Little Miss X," he shouted into her ear. She could feel his breath on her neck, warm and damp, and her skin tightened under it. After she'd pulled the beers out of the refrigerator, she stood in the doorway to the middle room awhile before she started back for Stephanie, drinking her beer and hoping Philip would touch her again. But then she saw that he was dancing with the woman who'd played Abigail, wildly jumping up and down.

Behind her, someone shouted, "Artie—what a jerk! He specializes in black girls. Likes it when they call him honkie."

"Sick."

Nina turned and saw the woman who'd played Sarah Good, Rikki something. She noticed Nina looking at her and held up the joint she was smoking. "Toke?" she yelled. Nina shook her head no. She moved into the middle room, into the heart of the music, and stood against the wall, next to a man she didn't know.

"I don't even know what they were," he was saying. "Some were red and some were little blue ones. But they sure made me happy. Nirvana."

Then Nina saw that Stephanie was dancing too, dancing with Tony. He had an absurd, ducklike motion. Suddenly she felt conspicuous. All alone. Slowly she threaded her way back through the moving mass of bodies to the bedroom. Someone had pushed all the coats to the back of Philip's bed, and several couples were sprawled along its edge, talking. Nina sat on the windowsill again. The window was open now, and the cold air pumped over her butt and back, making her feel feverish. The woman sitting next to her said to someone Nina couldn't see on her other side, "He told me I couldn't use Eliot. Said Eliot was passé. Said I'd have to restructure the whole thesis. I said *fuck this.*"

Nina finished her own beer and started on the one she'd gotten for Stephanie. When a man came out of the bathroom off the bedroom, Nina got up and went in. She was light-headed. She locked the door. It was an old-fashioned room, heavily tiled in white, with a black tile stripe around the upper edges. The walls above were painted a shiny orange-red. Nina peed for a long time. Over the roar of the flushing toilet and the steady *whump* of music from beyond the door, she looked at herself. She'd deliberately left on her stage makeup to look older—Stephanie had too—and her extravagant dark eyes startled her. Someone banged on the door. "Emergency!" a voice shouted, and there was laughter. Nina used the comb on the sink to rat her hair, and then she went back out, went and stood again in the doorway to the middle room.

The music was Sam and Dave, "Hold On, I'm Coming." Everyone in the room moved in concert, a waving mass, and many of them were singing along—shouting really. It made Nina want to laugh. She had almost finished Stephanie's beer. She went to the tiny kitchen for another. Philip was there.

"Aha!" he said. "I've got you." He led her back to the dancing room. The floor was jammed, and they had to move close to each other. They bobbed up and down too, sometimes touching as they made the gentle fucking motion everyone else rocked to. Nina and Stephanie had practiced this together, all the moves, and Nina knew she was better than Stephanie, better than most people. She held the beer in one hand, sipping from it every now and then, and tried to think of what she would say—something bright, something sophisticated to keep him with her—when the music stopped.

But when the sudden silence came and their bodies straightened, she only laughed. He put his arm casually around her shoulders and said, "You're a mighty delicious girl, Nina."

Her mind went blank. She tipped the beer can up. Nothing. She swallowed anyway. She said, "I know."

I know. *Stupid.* She wanted to die. He danced two more numbers with her, and then he thanked her and moved away, just as Nina had known he would. Stupid, stupid.

She floated at the edge of the rooms, had another

beer—perhaps two beers? Stephanie found her, and they sat together again, but then Tony asked Nina to dance, and then someone else she didn't know. She was happy for a while, moving without self-consciousness in the swaying mass of bodies, but she kept hoping Philip would ask her again. She tried several times to catch his eye, but he just grinned at her. When later she saw him lift the hair from Rikki's neck and then bend forward and bite the pale flesh there, she felt foolish, even more stupid.

At midnight, Stephanie found her, and they picked their coats out of the tangled mass on Philip's bed and went downstairs. Stephanie's mother was waiting in a car outside. She said nothing to them about the way they smelled, the way they walked.

Nina was silent during the ride home. She felt that her heart was breaking. Almost as soon as she stepped out of the car and slammed the door, she began to cry. But she remembered to wave to the idling car when she reached her porch. She watched its glowing taillights move away, toward the corner of Fifty-seventh Street. Instead of going in then, though, she pushed the slatted strips of snow off the swing and sat down. Alone in the pale darkness of the snowy night, she cried and cried. And then she went to the porch railing and threw up over the side.

The snow had stopped the next day. By noon the streets were plowed and salted down to the glistening asphalt, and the theater was crowded that night and for the next three shows. The adults in the cast freely made arrangements to go to Jimmy's, to The Eagle, to The Courthouse, after each performance; but there was always some parent with a car waiting for the nymphets. Riding home each night with the other high school girls, all of them happy, giggling, Nina felt trapped and desperate, as hemmed in as she had felt years before by Mary and Sarah and the little world she made with them.

On the last night of the show, after the curtain calls, after she'd changed into her own clothes, Nina went to look for Philip. She hadn't told anyone she was going to do this, not even Stephanie. She was terrified. She found him giving instructions to the stagehands about breaking down the set. She knew he'd noticed her—he'd nodded once in her direction to signal he'd speak to her in a minute, she should wait. Nina stood obediently until they all said good night. Then Philip came over to her. He was standing in front of her. Nina took a deep breath and said, "I think I'm going to die if I don't see you again." Her voice was trembling.

He looked at her for a long moment. She tried desperately to read his expression—repulsion? attraction? pity? She couldn't tell. Like her father, like Mack, he had a still, almost blank face in repose.

Finally he smiled gently and said, "Well, we can't have that, can we?"

He called, as he promised he would, a few days after the show closed. They met at the corner of Fifty-seventh and Harper and walked out to the Point. On the way, he told her about himself, that he'd grown up on a farm in Ohio, that he'd gone to Ohio State, the first person in his family to go to college. That he wanted to write plays, that he worked part-time at the Goodman Theater. Every detail was rich and fascinating to Nina. She imagined in pictures the context and the characters.

Haltingly, she told him a little about herself too, what little there was that she thought might interest him. They came back by the Fifty-seventh Street beach. Philip began to skip stones over the leaden lake. Nina tried a few. She was better than he was. She felt relaxed with him, suddenly.

"Okay," he was saying. "That was just warming up. This one—this is really the contest that counts."

She beat him again, and they both laughed. She jumped up and down, with her hands clenched over her head. "The winnah!" she yelled. "The winnah!" He ran after her, grabbed her, and suddenly she was still. His arms were around her; he rested his chin on her head. And then he stepped back from her. His face was kind. "Nina," he said. "You think you'll die without me, but you won't. There'll be lots of men for you. Lots of men in love with you. I promise you that."

Nina felt slapped. She turned away and walked a little distance ahead of him.

He came up just behind her. "What's wrong?" he asked. He reached for her, put his hand on her shoulder, and she stopped. "Nina, I didn't mean to hurt your feelings." He came and stood in front of her. The cold had whipped tears into both their eyes. He touched her cheeks, then leaned forward and kissed her. Nina willed her love up to her lips, willed him to feel it, to feel how much she cared for him. His mouth was so warm; his tongue ran over her lips and teeth. She thought she might swoon, and when he dropped his hands and stepped back from her, she actually did sway a little with the sudden motion of the cold wind.

After a moment they both turned and began to walk along the beach again. She started talking to him, slowly and carefully. She'd thought all this through while she waited for today, waited for her chance to win him. "I know you're much older than I am," she said. "And you think you know all about love. Much more than I do. And maybe you do know about some parts. But you don't know anything about me, about what I am, about what it could be with me. You're all . . ." Nina couldn't think of the word, and she stopped walking. Then she found it. "Sullied," she said. He looked over at her, and she thought she saw the slightest smile play across his face. "It could be different with me," she said angrily, fiercely. She hit his arm. "You're just afraid to try."

Just then the air changed, shifted somehow. They both felt it and relaxed. They smiled at each other, and Philip started walking up the beach to the pedestrian bridge over the Outer Drive. When they got to the middle they stopped and leaned on the railing. The cars sucked and whizzed under them. Philip said, "It wouldn't be fair, Nina. I'm just too old for you. I am. It isn't that I wouldn't like to try, that I'm not attracted to you. But it would be wrong." Then suddenly he quoted a line from the play, a line spoken about Nina's character, Betty. " 'The Devil is out and preying on her like a beast upon the flesh of the pure lamb.' " He grinned, but she didn't respond. "I don't want to feel that way," he said gently. "I don't want to prey on you. You see that, don't you, Nina?"

"No," Nina said stubbornly. "I don't know what you're talking about."

"Yes, you do," he said. "Yes you do." He took her hand and they walked. At the Museum of Science and Industry, Nina said she was cold, so they went in. They walked back to Main Street, the reconstructed nineteenth-century village. The photographer in his handlebar mustache and derby hat was there, standing outside his studio, trying to drum up business. He called to them, and Philip offered to pay for a picture. In the antique car, they fooled around. She took the driver's seat, but he pushed her out. Finally they settled on a pose—very formal, very Victorian and upright, his hand resting on her shoulder.

As they waited for the print, they walked slowly up and down the timeless fake street. Nina felt completely happy. She would have gladly stayed here, in this world, forever. But the photographer stepped out and waved to them. It was ready.

When Nina held the picture and looked at it, she was appalled at the image of herself. That stringy hair? That skinny long neck? She lost her nerve. She was silent as they headed out the doors, down Fifty-seventh Street again. Silently, too, they walked under the IC, past the entwined hearts, the graphic drawings, the amazing suggestions. When they got to the corner of Harper, they stopped. Philip touched her shoulder. "I'll see you, Nina," he said gently. "I'll see you around."

She lifted her face to him, hoping the tears from the cold were making her eyes beautiful, hoping he'd kiss her once more. But he just smiled at her and then turned and crossed the street.

For more than a week, Nina couldn't sleep, couldn't do her homework. She snapped at Mary, she fought with her father over her right to use the car. At canteen after school, she got into an argument with Stephanie, who said that Philip was a tease, that he hadn't cared in any particular way for Nina, that he had just wanted the whole cast to fall in love with him. "If you don't eat more than that," her mother said, "you'll shrivel to nothing before our eyes. Your hair will fall out."

One afternoon she followed a couple down Fifty-fifth Street. They'd attracted her by the way they walked, brushing against each other with every step; and the way they looked at each other, with a kind of intensity Nina felt she would never have in her life. When they stopped to look in a store window, their bodies kept up a kind of conversation too, by touching constantly. Though it was cold, the woman wore no hat on her head, and her hair, which was long and blond, blew wildly around. Once, when she turned to say something to the man as they waited to cross a street, a long strand of it whipped forward across her face in the wind, and he reached over tenderly and lifted it back, as though he were lifting a veil. Nina recorded every touch, every gesture, and used it to feed her misery.

The next day she was walking past Gordon's when she saw Philip in the back, drinking coffee in a booth with a woman. She went inside and stood by the doorway, watching, until the waitress came over and said, "We don't seat you. You can just plop down wherever you like." Nina turned and went home.

On Saturday morning, she woke up knowing she had to try again. He was wrong, he would see. And there was nothing for her to lose anyway. She got dressed and applied her makeup carefully. She walked quickly through the icy streets to his apartment building on Blackstone and climbed the narrow stairs. It all looked different in the day. She could hear the life behind the other doors she passed.

No one answered her knock, so she sat on the top step of his landing to wait. When she heard the door open far below her and someone start up, her breathing tightened, as though she were the one mounting the steps. But then she saw the figure two stories down, weighted with a grocery bag, moving slowly. It was a woman. As she turned to mount the last flight, she stopped and looked up. Nina was getting up to move out of her way.

"You waiting for someone?" the woman asked. She was bundled up, a wool hat pulled low on her forehead, a scarf covering her chin. You couldn't tell what she looked like, whether she was pretty or not.

"Yes. Philip. He must have been delayed, I guess."

"Yeah." The woman passed Nina and went to the other door on the landing. She bit off one mitten, juggled the bulky grocery bag while she fished, bare-fingered, in her shoulder bag for the keys. Just before she unlocked the door, she pulled the mitten from her mouth and asked, "You from the Goodman?"

"No; U of C," Nina said.

"Oh. *The Crucible* stuff."

"Yeah; I was in it," Nina said.

"Well, I hope he shows up soon." The girl went in and shut the door.

Nina sat down. After a few minutes, the girl's door opened. Her coat was off, and she was in socks. Her hair was matted and full of static electricity. Her cheeks and nose were still red from the cold. She was heavy, stocky.

"Look, I've got a key to his place. You know, in case of an emergency or whatnot. It's silly for you to sit out here. I'll let you in. If he gets mad, send him over and he can yell at me."

"Thanks," Nina said, unbending again. She rubbed the bones in her butt. "He should be here any minute."

The girl worked the key and swung the door open. As Nina stepped into his apartment, Philip's neighbor shook her head. "God," she said. "Every time I look in here, it makes me think I ought to sand my floors too."

Nina looked down. The floors were nearly white, brightly reflective. She hadn't noticed before. "Yeah," she said. "Well, thanks."

"S'okay," the girl said as she shut the door behind herself.

Nina stood and looked around. Everything was neat, bare, orderly. She was shocked at how small it was. With people in it, it had seemed bigger. She crossed to the tiny kitchen. The window in the back door looked out over a wide porch, which circled around behind all the other apartments on this floor of the building. She vaguely remembered, the night of the party, that this door had been opened finally, to cool everyone off. That she had stepped out onto the porch at one point with damp sweaty hair that had stiffened instantly in the cold.

She opened the refrigerator. The bottom two shelves were still packed with beer, and there were several partly drunk jugs of wine on the top shelf. Nina got a glass from the dish drainer and poured it full of white wine. She paced the two other rooms of the apartment, sipping, picking things up, reading, looking at the photos tacked to the walls. They were mostly from theatrical productions, but there were three or four of Philip with friends, women sometimes; and there were two of him with what clearly was his family—another young man, who looked very much like him, and his smiling parents. It was spring somewhere. There was a lilac bush in bloom behind them.

The evidence of this full life scared Nina. She could feel the nervous energy that had gotten her here slipping away. She poured another glass of wine and drank it off quickly, like medicine, standing at the kitchen sink. Then she washed the glass and set it where it had been in the drainer. She went into the bathroom and rubbed toothpaste over her teeth with a finger, scratched it onto her tongue. She reapplied her eye makeup and went back into Philip's bedroom.

An open, broken straw basket on the floor held his dirty clothes. Nina looked at them. Jeans, socks, Jockey underwear. Jockeys. She was glad. She and Stephanie had talked at length about men's underwear, about how peculiar boxer shorts were. She sat down at Philip's desk. The radiator banged once, and she jumped. Then it banged again, continuously, a machine gun sound, and she relaxed. She looked at the papers around her. She read Philip's notes to himself. *Friday: Desitin. Order lights and tape recorder. Appointment with Dean.* On a torn scrap of paper was the name *Lizzie* and a phone number. Nina wadded this and put it in her pocket.

When she heard someone coming up the stairs, she went into the central room. She placed herself in the middle of the bright white floor, in a square of sunlight. The key slid into the lock, the door opened. He was alone. He looked startled and beautiful, and Nina was so happy she stepped toward him and began to laugh.

They made love in the bed, in the kitchen with Nina sitting on the counter. They made love standing up, Nina backed against the wall. They made love in the tub with the water slapping over the edges the way it had in childhood when she and Mary slid together. They made love with Nina bent forward over the desk, her weight resting on all the papers and notes, and she read Philip's words as he slid in and out of her.

Nina came over mostly in the afternoons, afternoons she was supposed to be working on the yearbook, afternoons she had formerly spent sprawled on the bed in Stephanie's room or gossiping with the girls at canteen. She didn't miss any of that, her old life. And there was suddenly nothing to say to anyone in that world anyway. All she thought of, all that mattered, was being with Philip, making love with him; and there was nothing she could safely have told anyone about that. Sometimes she caught Stephanie staring at her, or someone else, and she realized she was seeing them as *the enemy*. She would be scared momentarily: could they tell? could they somehow see that she wasn't a virgin anymore? that she was being fucked for hours, several times a week? But her parents and her sister seemed completely oblivious, and she always decided, in the end, that she must be hiding it well.

There were no curtains or shades in Philip's apartment. When she first arrived, the afternoon light flooded the little rooms and made Nina self-conscious—their flesh was so exposed, their skin so white, so white and then so purplish. Their nakedness so intense. She joked about it once by tenting his cock with her long, dark hair, hiding it while she touched it. But as the shadows grew deeper in the little rooms, Nina relaxed. And when it was almost dark, then she liked to look at him, to hold his penis near her face and ask him how this felt, how that felt. And to have him look at her. She was most eager, most careless of herself, as the afternoon drew to its dark close, and that excited Philip too. Often she had to ask him to stop, to remind him that she needed to be home for supper.

They made love perhaps only a dozen times in all, but each time it was for hours, over and over. Each time they promised each other this was it, the only time, then the last time, just this once more. They made love until the sheet was soaking wet, until Nina was swollen nearly shut, until her legs shook when she stood up and her mouth was puffy and raw inside.

Nina was eager for instructions, desperate to please him more than anyone ever had. "What haven't you done?" she would ask. "What would you like?" She never came, but that wasn't the point. The point was to make him yearn for her, to do whatever he wanted so he'd love her. She had chosen him, and it was inconceivable to her that he didn't love her, wasn't going to love her—that she couldn't make this happen.

He wanted to please her too. He spent what seemed like hours lying between her legs, licking, playing with her gently. It was a revelation to Nina to be looked at, to be desired there too. To see that doing these things—pushing his fingers into her, into her ass, moving his face slowly on her—were things he liked, were things that made him hard again; but still she didn't come. She was always thinking too much about making him want her, about getting the power over him she had let him have over her.

Once, he washed her before she left, so she wouldn't smell "like a come factory," he said. And as she bent this way and that, opening herself to the warm cloth, to his stroking, she could see that he was getting hard again; and she knelt down and sucked him for the little juice left. When she was done, he lifted the washcloth—it was cool now—and gently stroked her mouth too.

She came home with damp hair, her face chapped and dreamy, and sat at the dinner table, benevolent and remote, conjuring sexual images as Mary and Sarah chattered, as the plates were passed up and down the table, as her parents frowned at her and exchanged long looks with each other.

And then she was late. She didn't know how late at first, because she'd never kept track of these things. But finally she remembered: she had been having her period the night Stephanie had a sleepover—she'd had to go to the bathroom two or three times to change the pad, and someone had commented sarcastically on her bladder size. She checked the calendar and saw that it had been almost seven weeks since then.

She couldn't tell Philip. A few days before, he'd vowed once again that they had to stop seeing each other. He was too old for her, he was ruining her life. And she'd promised not to call or come over for two weeks anyway, although she had been sure when she agreed that he would call her before then. But besides that, the first time they made love he'd stopped just before he'd entered her and said, "You're protected, aren't you?" and she had said yes because she couldn't have endured it if he'd stopped. Because she couldn't get pregnant if they did it just this once, which was all they were going to do.

For the first few days she was terrified. Sitting in class, she sometimes felt dizzy, sometimes broke out into a cold sweat at the thought of all she was about to lose. But then, slowly, it became a story to Nina, she saw clearly how it could happen, she had the pictures in her mind: she would go away, she would live in an apartment a little like Philip's, but with higher ceilings and curtains of a light white fabric. A bowl of bright oranges would sit on the table. There would be pictures and photographs on the walls. She would have the baby alone. This would be easy. She had recently read an article in one of her mother's *Ladies' Home Journal*s called "Childbirth Without the Agony," in which a woman described her natural labor as being hard work but painless. Philip would miss her desperately, and when she returned to finish high school, beautiful again—a mother with his child—he would marry her, just as Mr. Avery had married Leslie Rogoff.

And so began the plan, the suitcase stored in a locker at the Greyhound terminal, the allowance and baby-sitting money drawn out of the bank, the note to her parents taped on the inside of her closet door.

She left on a Friday, so she could say she was spending the night at Stephanie's house. That way it would be late afternoon on Saturday anyway before they would miss her, before they would find out it was a lie. As she walked toward Fifty-ninth Street, she kept thinking that this was the last time she'd walk past the Bakers', past the Masurs', past the long triangular empty lot at the end of the block. The IC was packed with commuters heading downtown for work, but Nina pushed through them, close to the windows on the Harper Avenue side of the train. She saw her house flash by for the last time too. Her throat felt swollen.

The bus was only half full. Even so, a young man in a pea coat and sailor's hat asked Nina if the seat next to her was taken. She smiled at him but told him that she wanted to sleep, that she'd like to keep it for herself for now.

The bus moved slowly out of Chicago, through the blocks of blasted, burned-out ghetto, past the hellish smokestacks of Gary, onto the blank snowy interstate beyond that. The road was edged with darkened plowed ridges of old snow that looked as though they'd been there forever. Nina felt a powerful, frightened sense of exile she tried to push under. She closed her eyes and pretended to sleep. But every time she opened them again it was the same: the wide empty fields a luminous gray under the gray sky, sometimes a few black trees or a weathering farmhouse sitting in desolate solitude, or a truck or a car in the distance along some parallel two-lane highway. She thought of herself as moving out of life, as entering this timeless landscape, and she was scared.

In Indiana the bus pulled off the highway, the turn indicator clicking loudly. The driver parked and stood up to announce a thirty-minute rest stop.

Inside the cafeteria, the sailor carried his tray to her table and sat down opposite her. The lies came easily, Nina was surprised. She was visiting Ohio State to see if she wanted to go there. Her brother went there and liked it. The sailor wasn't listening very hard anyway. He was just waiting for his turn to talk. He was going home from Great Lakes for a last visit before he was shipped out. His sister was meeting him— maybe they could give Nina a ride; did she have a ride?

Yes, she said, she did.

They were sitting at a wooden table, maple, with a thick plastic finish. The coffee was weak, yet somehow acidic too. Nina didn't usually drink coffee, and she had put two, then three packets of Coffee-mate into it, until what was in her cup was a gummy pale grayish-brown. The sailor was young—younger than Philip. Younger than Mack too. Maybe only a year or two older than Nina was. They talked about the food, about their fellow passengers, scattered as far apart from each other as possible in the large, ugly room. His neck and lower jaw were thickly covered in painful-looking pustules, some of them scabbed or honey-crusted. He grinned at her and asked again about the ride. No, she said. She was sure her brother was meeting her. Even if he was a little late, he'd show up.

Someone walked quickly by the window, collar up, hurrying against the cold. The snow was blowing lightly sideways. It was hard to tell whether it was actually falling or just lifted by the wind from the surface of the whited landscape around them. When they went back out into it, following the bus driver, trailing like schoolchildren on an educational expedition, Nina imagined herself as looking like that huddled person—anonymous, sexless, helpless. Stuck in it.

The sailor sat next to her. He had a lot to say. Nina was struck by this. After they graduated from high school, perhaps, it happened: they realized that their stories were the ones that counted, and all those columns in *Seventeen,* in *Mademoiselle,* about getting them to talk became obsolete and pointless. Nina smiled and nodded, *how interesting,* and thought of all the secrets he didn't know: that she was pregnant, that she was running away, that there was no brother, no place to stay, no future at Ohio State. He had taken the little information she'd given and constructed his own perfectly sufficient version of her life. Just as Philip had; because really, he never knew the most important things: her father's leaving and coming back, Randall, the sharp divisions in the family. To him, she had been a lucky girl, a girl with educated, gifted parents who'd given her every opportunity.

But hadn't everyone, always, done this to her? Who had cared to know her really, to ask what she felt, how she suffered? What did it mean, after all, when her father called them "the little pitchers of health"? when her mother called them her babes, her perfect babes? Nina felt a quick vindictive pleasure in the secret mess she was making of her life. It made her smile sweetly at the sailor, and he leaned forward, closer to her.

What he was really concerned about, he said, was the very good chance that he was going to be sent to Vietnam. She was lucky she was a girl, he said, not to have to think of these things. And Nina said yes, yes, she was certainly lucky, she knew that was true. After a while she pretended to sleep again.

Later Columbus began, and was reassuringly like Chicago in its outer stretches—the black neighborhoods, the sturdy, squat houses and apartment buildings. But then she was shocked by the downtown area, which was shuttered and deserted. Blocks of storefront windows were blank, or backed with ripped paper, or soaped. Here and there was a spot of neon, a bar. But there were no restaurants, no hotels, none of the life Nina thought she could step into.

The sailor's sister didn't want to leave her at the station, wanted to wait with her. Nina assured her her brother would come. He'd told her he had an afternoon class, but he'd be there, that she was just to wait. The sister was a fat woman, friendly and loud. She insisted on giving Nina her telephone number, just in case.

After they'd gone, Nina asked the man behind the ticket counter if there was a Y or a cheap hotel nearby. He barely looked at her as he recited in a monotone, "Gorham Hotel two blocks south on Summit." His pointer finger lifted in a minimal gesture. "YWCA six blocks west on Broad."

Before she left the station, Nina took all her change and fed the snack machines. She bought two dry-looking sandwiches wrapped tightly in cellophane, a package of potato chips, and several candy bars. She put them in the top of her suitcase and went out into the deserted streets.

Nina walked slowly to the Gorham Hotel, stopping to change hands on the suitcase several times in each block. The hotel's lobby was large, full of empty orange plastic chairs arranged in rigid rows, as though someone were going to show home movies. It smelled strongly of Lysol. No one was at the desk, but there was a doorway behind the counter, and from somewhere in the space it opened into, Nina heard a TV, and voices. When she rang, a woman's voice called out, "Give me a minute." Nina set her bag down and waited.

The woman who finally appeared behind the reception desk was middle-aged, but she wore her hair in a strangely old-fashioned, tight hairdo that looked like something out of the 1940s. She had on a kind of housecoat with bright flowers and birds printed on it. She was smoking a cigarette, and she looked startled to see Nina. "What do you want?" she asked.

"I need a room for just one night," Nina said.

The woman looked around the lobby, then at the streaked glass doors Nina had entered through. "You alone?" she asked.

"Yes," Nina said. "I'm moving to Columbus, but it's too late today to find an apartment."

The woman squinted at Nina through her smoke.

"Yeah," she said after a while. "Okay." She pushed the register across the counter. "Sign in," she said. "It's four bucks."

Nina signed the register *Liddie DeLacey*, in a careful handwriting not like her own, and fumbled in her purse for the money.

The woman's eyes were steady on her the whole time. When Nina laid the money on the register, she scooped it up and tucked it into her pocket in one movement without lowering her gaze. Then she gave Nina the key and told her where the room was. She was putting her on the second floor, she said, because the elevator was temporarily out of commission.

As Nina started up the stairs, the woman called out, "Honey?"

Nina turned. The woman was standing in the open doorway that led back to wherever she'd been when Nina arrived. Her eyes were slits looking up at Nina. "Put that chain lock on your door before you go to sleep tonight, okay?"

Nina nodded, and the woman disappeared.

The next day, Nina found the bus that went down High Street toward the campus of Ohio State. Slowly, as the number of stores increased, as they became more and more the kind of stores that might support student life—record shops, pizza parlors, an army-navy store—she began to feel reassured. At the end of a long block that had two houses with Rooms for Rent signs in their first-floor windows, she pulled the cord and struggled off with her suitcase.

An elderly man answered the door in the first of these houses. He seemed completely incurious about any of the story Nina had worked up—a new lie, about being a part-time student at the university, the first in her family to go to college. He just wanted it clear, he said, standing in the hall, that she couldn't have men in her room, that she couldn't cook up there. That she couldn't play a radio. The rent was fourteen dollars a week, payable in advance.

Nina was so grateful for the ease of this that she didn't ask to see the room, and so she was stunned when he led her upstairs and into what must once have been the master bedroom of the house—a huge room with high ceilings. It had a bay with three windows that nosed out over the yard into a tall bare tree. She was thrilled, too, to see that she had her own marble washstand in a corner of the room, though the toilet and the tub, he told her, were down the hall. It wasn't until after he left her that she noticed that the bed, an old iron camp bed, sagged luxuriantly toward the middle. That the carpet was filthy and stained. That dust balls roamed freely across the floor and the sink dripped steadily. When she went to the window and moved the curtain back, her hand came away feeling faintly greasy, and the dust motes danced wildly in the still air for a moment.

She yanked open the sticky bureau drawers and began to unpack her bag, neatly arranging the underwear, the socks and tights, the sweaters. Then she folded the covers back on the bed. She looked hard at the pillow and the sheets. This was what she'd been afraid of, she realized: that the sheets would be somehow vile. But although they were worn—actually darned in a few spots—they were clean. And when she lay down, the air that stirred around her head smelled reassuringly of strong bleach.

Nina lay in bed for a long time. Sometimes she slept. She thought about Philip, about his worshipful attention to her, the way he smelled after they'd made love—she'd only slowly realized that the smell was partly hers. She woke up and washed her face, then lay down again. At one point, staring at the grayed, cracked ceiling, the light ebbing outside, she thought,

Now: now her mother was beginning to worry, now she was calling Stephanie's house. In the gathering dark in her room, she stared up, openmouthed, and tears of pity and self-pity began to form.

She was hungry, she realized. She took a twenty-dollar bill from her wallet, then looked around for a place to hide the rest of her money. She tucked it, finally, under one edge of the rug, first pushing aside the sandy dust that lay evenly distributed on the worn dark wood.

She walked four blocks down High Street, until she saw a five-and-ten. She went in. There was a lunch counter, she was relieved to see, just as there was in the one on Fifty-third Street. She ordered French fries, two hot dogs, and a Coke. She ate slowly. The counter woman stood watching her from the end of her work space, and Nina felt that the sound of her own chewing and swallowing were explosively loud. Before she left the store she bought an alarm clock, soap, a plastic soap container, shampoo, a glass, and, at the last minute, *Mademoiselle.* Her change was $7.27.

She walked slowly back, looking at the stores, thinking of employment, of how it would be to work here—in a record store where a young man maybe Philip's age was sorting through the bins. Or here, in a pizza place, where the sign on the door gave the hours—noon to midnight daily—and the old man kneading dough in the storefront window watched her gloomily as she passed, his dirty apron whitened with flour over his belly.

The sun had set, and Columbus was dark. She stopped in a drugstore on the corner near her house and bought a Butterfinger and a Baby Ruth. As she was paying, it suddenly seemed very important to her to know the time. She asked the counterman.

"Nearly five," he said.

"Four forty-five?" she asked.

He looked quizzically at her, then squinted at his watch. "Four fifty-two. And a half," he added sarcastically.

As she walked quickly back the remaining half block, she was calculating the minutes it was taking. Her hands were shaking as she turned the key in the lock, as she virtually ran up the wide, worn staircase. In her room, she dumped everything onto the bed and tore open the packaging around the clock. Hurriedly she set it, plugged it in. For a few minutes she sat on her bed watching it, watching the slender hand spin off the seconds, count out these empty moments in her life. She was near tears, but she made herself breathe slowly and evenly, and after a few minutes she felt calmer. She went to the closet and carefully hung up her coat. She began to unpack and arrange her new possessions.

Later she heard the tenants coming in, the doors shutting, the stairs creaking, the toilets flushing. There were footsteps above her. She read *Mademoiselle*. She read an article on the pill and how it had changed our society. She read another one, on how to get a man to propose. She slept for an hour or so, with her mouth open and dry.

Someone was running a tub. Nina needed to pee. She used her water glass, squatting over it, and then emptied it into the sink. Carefully she washed it out, rinsed it.

Later in the evening she ate the candy bars and went to sleep again, without brushing her teeth.

Nina passed four days this way. She tried to think of herself as exploring, as *getting ready*—to find a job, a life. The third afternoon she actually walked miles down High Street, to where the campus started, but then she was confused by its size, by the ugly modern buildings, the vast parking lots, the sense of no center. She asked questions in a foreign accent, maybe French, which made everyone expansive and patient. She found an administration building, but the employment office in it was for students. For outside employment, the woman at the desk told her, she'd have to go to the personnel office, in another building. The secretary gave her a map of the campus and pointed it out, Nina got lost on the way. It was getting dark too, so she found someone to direct her back to High Street, and she went home.

That night when all the noises in the house had stopped and everyone seemed to have gone to bed, she took a bath in the rust-stained tub, scouring it thoroughly both before herself and after.

Nina woke in the night and turned over. Sticky, wet, her thigh made a faint ripping sound as it came off the sheet. She reached quickly between her legs. She brought her hand up to within inches of her face, trying to see in the dark. Then she licked her fingers: Blood! She pressed her hand to her face, smearing the stickiness over herself, making a muted, eager noise.

In the low wattage of the bedside lamp, the blood was blackish on the sheets—it looked as though a violent deed had happened here. Nina's nightgown was smeared and clotted, and she took it off, wadded it up and jammed it between her legs. She shuffled naked across the room to the sink. She wet the washcloth and rubbed its steamy warmth slowly up and down her inner legs and thighs, and then bent backward and moved it over her streaked buttocks. Then her face where she'd smeared it. She went to her bureau, opened the drawer, and slipped on a loose sweater and a skirt.

She stripped the sheets and the mattress pad off the bed. Blood had soaked through into the mattress, joining the other, fainter stains there. Nina brought the bedding over to the sink. She ran a basin of cold water and began to dunk the bloody spots into it. She rubbed the bar of soap across them and scrubbed and scrubbed. Her hands reddened in the cold, they ached sharply. The water turned pink. A good girl, she worked for a long time, holding the sheet up repeatedly to the inadequate light, turning it, sliding another patch of it under her gaze to check for stains. She talked to herself as she worked, planning her next steps, and twice she laughed out loud.

When she was finished, she pushed the old, stiff curtains back and draped the sheets on the bared rods. Then she lay down on the lumpy stained mattress, with the nightgown still between her legs, to wait for the sheets to dry, to wait for day. It seemed to her she could feel the blood ebbing, seeping slowly out of her. Clearly she pictured the long hallways at school, her Latin class, her room at home. She tried not to think of Philip, but when she did, it was as though his power were in the waste blood flowing so slowly out of her body. The very images that had made her nearly cry out in longing for him in that other life—his darkened cock stiffened as flat against his belly as a sword strapped to him, his face shiny from licking her—these seemed suddenly distasteful, even foolish. And she felt a sad and emptied sense of freedom, a reluctant joy at being returned to her solitary self.

When she woke, it was early morning. The sunlight was glowing through the hanging sheets. They were lifting, shifting in the breeze that flowed in through the drafty old windows, as the heavier, real curtains, stiffened with ancient dirt, hadn't been able to. They were, for a moment, the curtains she'd pictured when she still loved Philip, the curtains that would have blown lightly into the rooms she could have made in that beautiful, trapped life. As she reached to pull them down, to remake the bed, they fell on her face as cool as snow—soap-smelling, still slightly damp. Beyond them through the dirty glass Nina saw the lustrous wash of the early-morning sun strike the buildings across the way, and the world seemed to beckon her, to glow through the film with an infinitely bright, steady promise.

16

NINA was the first to arrive, and so she had the summer house to herself for several hours before anyone else got there. It had been closed up all year. She went around the rooms, banging open the sticky windows and wiping down the high trailing cobwebs before she started to make the beds. The linen closet still bore little signs on each shelf in her grandmother's printing—the ink bleached to a pale, dreamy blue now—telling you the size of the sheets stacked in each pile. Nina had no memory of her grandmother, but she thought of her always in connection with what was welcoming, what was orderly and gracious, in this old shingle house. And she herself felt unexpectedly a sweep of generosity as she unfurled the first sheet, as she let the air lift it above the bed—there was something so graceful, so expansive, in its sailing motion.

When she was finished in the bedrooms—the beds all neatly made and towels set out for everyone—she went downstairs. There seemed to be no real coffee, but she found a bottle of instant in the pantry and put some water on to boil. She had to chip away at the hardened dark crystals in the bottom of the jar. When she'd loosened enough and mixed the brew, she took her steaming mug and went outside, onto the porch, to drink it. The air was clear and dry, but the smell of the sea was still heavy in it, and the gulls cried anxiously to each other as they circled. There was a couple walking on the beach far below, and a few sunbathers sprinkled here and there on the sand, but no one was in the dark water. It was too chilly for swimming today. Nina pulled her sweater around her, hunkered down in the chair. She had driven up from New York that afternoon in a borrowed car. Everyone else would arrive sometime later today, except Liddie, who was coming just for the service tomorrow.

It was her father who'd called to tell her that Randall had died—he'd been hit by a car when he broke away from a group walk and ran out into the street. It was no one's fault, her father had said. Just a terrible, terrible accident. The service would be performed by her mother's brother Paul in the tiny church in this shore town in Connecticut where her grandfather had always summered. Her parents had chosen to have it here because it was near Randall's residence and because so many of the children lived in the East now—they wouldn't have far to come.

Nina had been alone in her apartment, working, when the telephone rang. She almost hadn't answered it; she often didn't when she was working. Her father's voice had startled her, shocked her really—he never called. He was direct and quick with the news, and Nina felt she'd stepped within seconds into a kind of emotional limbo. She was unclear what she ought to feel, whether she could feel anything.

She hadn't seen Randall in almost a year. Even then she'd gone to visit mostly out of a sense of obligation. There was no sign that he had recognized her, though he'd been comfortable enough going out for a walk with her on the residence's grounds. Perhaps he'd thought she was one of those supportive, cheerful-but-firm staff people—and in fact, Nina had tried to keep her voice, her whole bearing, in that mode during the visit.

Randall had thickened and coarsened as a man. Probably he didn't exercise quite enough, even though part of the program at the home was work: he and Nina had walked among orderly planting beds of vegetables that the residents labored over daily, tiny unidentifiable tender fronds of green the only growth at that point. His face, which had always seemed startled and dreamy when he was younger, now looked simply dull, tuned out. He had a thick, square beard too, because it was easier for the staff to trim that once every few weeks than to shave him daily. Many of the male residents had beards; Nina felt as though she were wandering around the grounds of some strange religious order. She stayed only an hour or so, and when she left, her throat ached from talking nonstop the whole time.

She'd responded to her father automatically on the telephone, without thinking, but she could hear the sympathy and compassion in her tone, and part of her thought, *Good, good.* After she'd hung up, she stood for a moment looking around the apartment. Will had moved in about six months earlier, and the sight of his handsome possessions—a tweed sofa, the pretty rug, the antique backgammon game—seemed unwelcome, out of place momentarily among her hand-me-downs. She felt disconnected from her life with him. But then she went back to what she'd been doing before the call and finished up. And she was so absorbed in her work that she'd actually forgotten about Randall's death for several long periods that afternoon.

But when Will came home that night and she started to tell him, she suddenly thought of that face again. Not the dull face of the silent, heavy man she'd visited, but Randall's face in youth—Randall's, Mack's, her brothers', lost and sweet as they'd both been then in their different ways. She felt a quickening pity for them, for all of them—herself too—and she wept for the first time for the distance they'd all come from their past, and for the price they'd paid for that accomplishment.

*　　*　　*

Now she got up and headed for the kitchen. She was thinking about Will. He'd arranged for the car she was driving, an Audi, of all things. And he'd given her a couple of hundred dollars before she left. When she protested, he told her she could pay him back later but that it would be stupid, wrong, for her to have to worry about money for the next few days.

Will wanted to marry her. She knew that some of his concern, his kindness, at this moment had to do with that campaign. But some of it, too, was just who he was. As she got in the car and drove down the shaded winding streets to the Higgledy Piggledy in town, she thought of how it would be to be Will's wife—to be taken care of, to drive in a car that smelled of leather, to have enough money, not to worry about how much groceries for the family would cost. To be able to weep openly to someone who you knew would want to comfort you. She had felt, when he held her, a kind of relief at having managed, with his help, what seemed like a normal response to her brother's death. She'd even had a sort of picture in her mind's eye of how they must have looked in their embrace. She was feeling real sorrow, she knew; but almost instantly a part of her was observing that sorrow also, seeing it as Will might. But that was her fault, she thought—that second step. That had nothing to do with him.

When she got back with her bags of groceries, there was another car parked in the driveway. She pulled in behind it over the crunching gravel, and Mary and her parents appeared as shadowy figures on the porch, then came out from behind the screen to greet her. As they stepped into the late-afternoon sun, their hands lifted in a peculiar pathetic synchrony to shield their eyes, and Nina started to reach next to her for her camera, forgetting for a moment that she didn't have it with her. Then she stepped out onto the driveway with them, and they were taking turns holding her.

There was an odd collection of booze in the pantry—Kahlúa, Cherry Heering, half- and quarter-filled bottles of hard stuff, a silvery slice of vodka at the bottom of one. Nina had bought some beer and wine too, on her trip to town. But no one, she noticed, was really very interested in any of it, except for her. Mary had never indulged much, and her parents, now that she thought of it, had sipped slowly at wine on her last few visits home. Health concerns? Age? Would it make them judge her harshly?

Nina didn't care. She'd bought ingredients for chili, and put herself in charge of dinner. She made sure her glass was full as she worked. Upstairs she could hear her mother running the vacuum. Her father had taken the telephone into the sun porch off the living room and was calling Chicago about patients and their medications. Mary was in the dining room. When Nina stepped forward she could see her there, hunched over her books on the table, her heels hooked on a rung of their grandfather's chair, studying something—Nina thought she'd said the circulatory system. The house was calm and peaceful. Nina remembered suddenly a time in her childhood when she'd yearned for this kind of peace, imagined herself as she was here, at its heart, cooking for everyone, making it possible. It all seemed so sadly different now, herself most of all. She reached for her drink. The fat hissed as she flattened the meat in the pan.

No one was clear on whether they should wait for Mack and Sarah, who were driving down—Mack all the way from Vermont, with a stop in Boston to pick Sarah up. But finally Lainey insisted that they couldn't any longer. It was dark, perhaps nine o'clock, and they'd shut all the windows a while before against the damp chill of the night air.

Nina was grateful for the decision. If she didn't concentrate on focusing, a second image of whomever she was looking at—a twin! she thought—floated gently sideways and sat there too, chatting. She had poured herself a big glass of water, and she hoped that between the food and the liquid she'd sober up a little.

"Sorry to be such a mess," she said loudly for perhaps the second or third time. They were at the table. They'd talked briefly about Randall, bumping up against his death and then veering away from it with a discussion of the residence: how good it was, how *it wasn't their fault.*

Then somehow her father was remembering with Mary his decision to specialize in psychiatry. "It infuriated everyone I'd worked with," he said. "They saw it as a real betrayal. Primarily, I think, because psychiatry was seen as passive and soft then. A way out of the hard work of true medicine. I felt very brave, very much the radical young man, defying them all."

"Oh, you were!" Lainey cried.

"Gee, I feel just the opposite about it," Mary said. "I mean, I'm no good at it, but when we were doing psychiatry, what I found so interesting and what scared me—what I really didn't have the courage for, to be honest—was that lack of absoluteness. And to me, it takes much more courage to be functioning as a physician in that gray area, that sort of edge of what's known, than . . ." She frowned and stopped a moment. "I mean, look, it's perfectly easy when you have these three symptoms to say, 'Aha, it's this disease,' and then you look up the medication and the course of treatment, and that's that. But in psychiatry, those rules aren't there. It's just the physician and his intelligence, sometimes working even *against* the patient. I mean, defenses and so forth." She shrugged. "It does seem brave."

Nina had risen, and now she went to the kitchen to get another glass of water. She'd had the sense, suddenly, of being an outsider, the sense of how much they saw each other, these three, how comfortable they were together. A family. She stood alone at the sink with her finger in the bubbling rope of running water, waiting for it to get cold, and she thought of Will again, of how comfortable and easy her life with him seemed. Like that, she thought. Like a family. That was what it ought to be, wasn't it? Supportive. Grownup. Peaceful. The voices in the dining room rose and fell, together and apart, gently. Someone laughed. Her father. She could have that.

When she came back to the table, Lainey was passing around photographs she'd culled from the albums at home. About half of them were shots Nina had taken, and she couldn't help looking at them with a professional eye. She was pleased with the sense of composition, with the feel for what was complex, evocative, in a situation, which she'd had even then. Here was a shot of all of them by the Christmas tree in their ratty bathrobes, Randall behind the circle, his eyes seeing something else. And here a picture of the dining room, the table a mound of paper and books, Mary hunched over the piano—her elbows, her rounded back; and Randall standing as though transfixed by her music in a patch of light in front of the window. Here another of him at breakfast having a tantrum, his body blurred slightly in frantic motion. Sarah and Mary were at the table too, eating and smiling nervously.

"I didn't realize," she said, "how many pictures I took of Randall."

"Didn't you?" Lainey said. "Well, of course, I picked out a lot with him in them to bring along. But you *were* fascinated with him in that way. I used to think that you were trying to get some handle on him by taking his picture over and over. That you were trying to solve some mystery. Oh! Look at this!" Lainey held one out. "You girls, all three of you." She was silent for a moment while Nina looked at it. "It's amazing to me how *like* you girls used to look." Nina reached for her water, gulped it. "Now Nina looks the spitting image of Audrey Hepburn in *Roman Holiday*—you do! that wonderful haircut!—and Mary looks like a younger, darker Virginia Woolf."

Mary wadded her paper napkin and threw it over at Nina. "You win again," she said.

Her father cleared with Nina. Lainey had gone upstairs for something else.

"I don't know why I do this," Nina said.

"Do what?"

"Drink till I'm stuporous and then have to work my way back."

"Well, I suppose it keeps you busy."

She looked over at him. His charming, small smile moved quickly over his face and was gone. She felt all her old affection for him in a drunken rush. "Out of harm's way," she answered.

"And it gives you something to do with your hands."

"And my liver."

He was rinsing the dishes in the sink. He turned the water off and looked at her. "If it really worries you, Nina, maybe you shouldn't." His face was serious and concerned, and Nina was suddenly offended.

She stood up straight. "It's so easy, is it? To change yourself? To break a nasty habit?"

His pale eyes were unmoving on her. He had rolled up his sleeves to carry the dishes in, and his bare arms were shapely and corded. How handsome he was, she thought.

"Don't you think there comes a time when all the elements support you?" he asked. "When you simply have enough separate reasons to stop doing whatever it is you're doing?"

"And then you just clean up your act? Get your shit straight?"

"That's been my experience."

"You should know, I guess." She tried to keep her voice light, teasing, but she could hear that she hadn't quite succeeded.

His face looked tired, suddenly. He shook his head. "You know, Nina, I wouldn't mind talking about any of this with you when you're sober. Anytime."

She turned away and scraped a platter into the trash barrel. "I'll try to remember that," she said. *I'm sorry, I'm sorry, I'm sorry,* she wanted to say.

In the dining room, Lainey had a piece of paper lying in front of her on the table. She was explaining the order of the service to Mary. She looked up. "Nina, listen too," she said. "I want to be sure you approve."

Nina had started to stack their dinner plates up her arm, as she did when she was a waitress. "I approve," she said.

"But it was absolutely our decision—well, ours and Paul's—and I'd like to be sure all the rest of you are happy with it."

Happy? "I'm happy with it," Nina said. She lifted the last plate into place. It was magical, the way they sat there, all four of them.

After dessert and coffee, Mary came out to help wash, and Nina turned on the radio. An oldies station. Mary said, "It's hard to feel anything about this, isn't it? I mean, I was like twelve or something when he left."

"How are the parents?" Nina asked.

"Same as ever. Mother weeps a lot. Dad doesn't. But he's very . . . silent about it, I guess. Anyhow, they both seem really at a loss too."

"I wonder how recently they'd seen him," Nina said.

"Well, I know Mom still flew out every month or so."

"And Dad?"

"Less. But he did. I don't think *I'd* seen him for maybe three years."

On the radio, a man named Big Anthony from Bradford called up and wanted "Deep Purple" by Nino Tempo and April Stevens. The DJ honked a horn, and then the music started. Nina and Mary sang along. Then "Help!" came on, and Nina showed Mary the monkey. "Didn't you do it?" she panted, punching the air. "Were you too young?"

They put the dry dishes on the kitchen table: a stack of creamy plates, the jingling silverware.

"Remember how Randall liked music?" Mary asked.

"Some music," Nina said. "Some music he hated."

"Did he?" Mary said. "See? I don't remember that."

"I don't either," Nina said. She was looking out the dark window to where she knew the ocean moved. "I don't remember exactly. But some he did. Some he really hated."

What she was seeing was Randall, howling suddenly when the arm dropped on a record he didn't like—the first few notes identifiable to him, before there was melody or word. Long before Nina would have known what the music was. And once she had stepped into the living room and there he was, rocking from foot to foot, seemingly happy. He was holding one of his arms across his face with the other, so he could chew slowly on his sleeve. She had felt such a wave of disgust, of rage at him, that she would have hit him if she had had the nerve. Instead she stepped very close to him and began to sing "Au Clair de la Lune," a song he hated. His mouth had ovaled in pain, his eyes had shut tight, and he began to whimper along with her, trying to ride over her noise.

There was a serving spoon missing when Nina put the silverware back in its box.

"Maybe it was missing before," Mary said. "I wouldn't worry."

"No, I know I set it out."

"Well, it'll turn up. It's no big deal."

Mary said she would stay up—she needed to study, and she wanted to wait for Mack and Sarah. Their parents had gone to bed already—it was almost eleven—and Nina was feeling more and more tired as she sobered up. She left Mary alone in the living room, lying on the couch in the light of an old lamp with a parchment shade.

When she lay down, Nina was so exhausted that she was sure she'd cross over easily into dreamless sleep. But in the unfamiliar dark her thoughts began to swirl faster and faster, dancing over endless ugly scenes—a moment she'd pushed him too hard on the swing, hoping he'd fall; a time they'd locked him in a closet in a game and forgotten him. Her head swung back and forth on the pillow. Then, suddenly, she saw the serving spoon in her mind's eye, sliding slowly off a plate with some leftover chili into the green trash bag under the sink.

She got up quickly and pulled on a nightgown. Downstairs, Mary had fallen asleep on the couch, with the heavy book open across her chest. It lifted up and down, up and down, with her slow breathing. Nina looked under the sink, but the green bag in the wastebasket was new, nearly empty. She turned on the outside light and stepped into the cool, thick air. The bag sat in an open, dented galvanized can next to the back-porch stairs. Nina pulled it out, sat down on the steps, and untied the knot that held it closed. It was in here, somewhere. She knew it. She looked down into tinfoil, the plastic trays the meat had come in, an empty vodka bottle, bits of chili, coffee grounds. Her heart failed her for a moment. But then in memory she saw the spoon again. It was here, buried treasure, she knew it was.

And when Mack and Sarah turned up the drive a little after midnight, this was the first thing they saw: Nina on the stoop under the diffused bright light as though on a tiny stage. Nina with her sleepy hair haloing her head, garbage strewn around her, tears running down her face; Nina with her arm plunged deep into the green bag, feeling around for what she'd lost.

Mack had arrived in Boston about noon, even though Sarah had said she wouldn't get off work until much later. But he'd been restless in Vermont, cut off from grief by his distance from the family. He'd thought the sooner he was in motion, the sooner he might be able to feel something. And he thought, too, that it might be useful to visit Cambridge, to retrace his steps, to try to think his way back to the moment that had sliced his life in two all those years ago—a moment that he knew was connected in some way with his complicated feelings now about Randall and his death.

He'd forgotten it would be Reunion. He had to drive blocks from the Square to find a parking space, and as he walked back, he found himself increasingly among middle-aged men wearing matching hats and name badges, some drunk already. He saw that a few of them were wearing '69 badges—his year!—and realized abruptly that this would have been his tenth reunion, that some of these men were people he'd been in college with. He began to look at the faces. They seemed fleshy and prosperous, complete strangers.

Mack felt uncomfortable. He went to Elsie's and bought himself a roast beef sandwich and a raspberry lime rickey. He carried them down to the river. Behind him, in the courtyard of Eliot House, there was a tent. Alumni in pastel shirts—older, white-haired—were gathered under it. Their voices carried across Memorial Drive over the noise of the traffic, a low, steady rumble. Mack went close to the water's edge where the sloping bank blocked his view back, where the algal smell of the Charles and its slow rhythmic lap seemed to enclose him. There were sunbathers down here, and two young men playing Frisbee. Mack ate slowly and then lay back in the sun. He felt peaceful. He swung his head on the grass and looked in the other direction. Not ten feet from him lay a nearly naked young woman, her body gleaming with oil, her belly flat, her breasts flattened too on top, but pouched where they drooped gently down against her sides. As he watched, she turned restlessly and flopped onto her stomach. In a moment her elbows rose like wings above her back and she unhooked her top. Then slowly she lowered her arms again along her sides. Her eyes had never opened.

Mack turned away, propped himself on one elbow to look again at the Frisbee players. He hadn't slept with a woman in four or five months, not since the poet after her reading at the local state college. She'd come into the bar he worked in, come in with some of the faculty. Mack knew them. He knew nearly everyone in town. They introduced her, and she stayed on after they left and then until he closed up. Before that there had been another gap between women of three or four months; and Mack knew this was the way it would go as long as he stayed in Shelbyville. Unless he wanted to start sleeping with married women, the wives of his customers.

He had moved to Vermont seven months after he got out of the service. He'd been living at home with his parents, trying to figure out where to go next and watching a lot of television. It was all wearing thin quickly, all the love and concern that had poured over the ocean to him when they thought he was in danger. He had felt, all that time in Vietnam, so scared that home had become a kind of icon, a religion. The idea of *getting home* had been what kept him going, and he saved their letters, folded in his pocket, until the ink wore off, the damp paper literally disintegrated. It was less the words he cared about than the notion of their having touched the paper too, of its having lain in all the familiar places—the kitchen table, the little desk in the living room. It made it seem possible that he could cross that distance too, that it was possible he could get back there.

He had managed to save a few of them, and he remembered others—not always the exact words but the sense of them. It had astonished and moved him to feel how they loved him, how they reached out to him and wanted him to know it. Sometimes he wondered if the reason he'd ended up moving to Vermont, living so far away from his family, was that it made it easier to remember them that way—full of the urgent expression of love. His father especially. His letters had been so tender and regretful, so apologetic for the distance between them.

And yet within a week of his return, it all seemed to dissipate. His father had asked him over dinner one night what he planned to do. When Mack answered, "I thought I'd let my hair grow," he could see David's jaw shift under his smooth flesh; and he'd thought of the letters abruptly, with a sense of deep loss.

Two days later, he'd gotten the job at Kroch's, selling this time. And he liked it—touching the books, talking to people. He had a picture of himself reading through the store, using his employee discount to begin his real education. He felt something like the same excitement he'd felt at the beginning of each semester for the first couple of years of college.

But he found he couldn't read. He'd bring things home and start them, but within just a page or two he'd have a sense of disorientation; the print would seem jumbled and senseless, and he'd be flooded by memories, by the thought of where he'd been, of how he almost hadn't come back. He'd feel again, with a sense of sharp disjuncture and puzzlement, how frightened he'd been, how reduced, altered. It didn't seem possible also to be this Macklin, beginning *The Tempest*, trying *Lord Jim*. Sometimes his heart would start pounding, his breath would shorten with the physical memory of his own fear. And he'd go downstairs and watch TV, whatever was on.

A few months after he'd started work, he got a week off and made a trip east. He'd visited Randall in Connecticut, Nina and Liddie in New York. He'd gone to Cambridge, too, and talked to a dean at Harvard, who explained how easy it would be to reenroll. But then he'd come home and fallen again into his former pattern, work and then that welcome sleepy lethargy.

He'd met Celeste at a party at the U of C. She was short, very fair, a little plump, with lips as full as the wax ones Mack's sisters used to buy at the candy store. She had smallish, wonderfully blue eyes. A sexy baby face. She was getting a master's degree in teaching, and she was the first person he'd met who didn't look shocked when he said he'd been in Vietnam. He told her that, and she explained that she was from a tiny town in Vermont. That about a third of the guys she'd gone to high school with had ended up over there.

He dated her through the spring, and when she went back to Shelbyville in July, he went too. They were married a year later. His parents came out for the wedding, and all his sisters drifted in from wherever they were. Celeste looked shorter, blonder than ever, standing among his slender, dark family. For a wedding present, his father offered to pay his tuition whenever he wanted to finish school, but Mack and Celeste asked instead for the money as a down payment on an old farmhouse near town they'd been dreaming of. Mack planned to spend the next few years working on it, while Celeste taught.

He'd started off with an ambitious schedule, and for three or four months he kept to it. By the time the first maple leaves were turning pinkish red and Celeste reported to work at Shelbyville District High School, he had the plaster off and several rooms insulated on the first floor. They'd have their morning coffee in the partly done kitchen, the Indian-head pattern on the silver foil of the insulation like a strange nightmare kind of wallpaper around them.

Sometime in the late fall, though, as the weather began to turn really cold, Mack stopped. Part of it was the car. He'd begun driving Celeste in to work and then coming back to town in the late afternoon to pick her up, "in case" he needed to have the car during the day. But then he started to hang around town for a while after he'd left her at school. He went to the hardware store or the record store. He stopped in Jack's Variety for coffee and talk. He collected anecdotes to tell her from the shifting group of men who whiled away bits of time there. Sometimes he'd have lunch. He'd get home and stoke the stove, read the paper, and often get dinner started, before he had to get back in the car and drive to town to pick Celeste up.

But in spite of his dwindling energy for the house project, he had more energy for lovemaking. And oddly, Celeste seemed to become more and more passive in the face of it. After they made love, she would often doze off, and he'd let her sleep awhile before he began moving over her again, trying something else. He felt in love with her body in a way he'd never been with anyone's before. He felt safe and whole while they were making love. Sometimes he lay still for a long time with his cock inside her, not moving, not even thinking about coming.

That second summer, when she was home all day, he'd worked hard again: he'd gotten Sheetrock up over the insulation, he'd sanded and painted the walls. But winter hit him that year with the same force, the same result as the year before; and this became their pattern, was their pattern for the four years they were married.

One afternoon in the late fall of that last year together, they were lying still on their mattress, covered with a thick, ragged quilt Mack had found at an auction. Pumping over her minutes earlier, he had sensed her impatience, her remove. She'd turned away from him after he came, so that now he was lying against her back, with his chin resting on her shoulder. He moved his free hand around to the front of her sturdy body and gently covered one of her small, round breasts. She stirred enough to make it clear she didn't want him to touch her. Then she said in a mean voice, "You know, Mack, sometimes I think your problem is your mother didn't breast-feed you long enough."

He didn't speak for a moment. He had a sense of whirling dizziness, of a dangerous world opening wide in front of him. He tried to make his voice light. "I didn't know you thought I had a problem," he said.

She flung herself over onto her back. "I think you need to get a job," she said, not looking at him, just at the ceiling, dotted with wide sanded circles and stripes of joint compound. "I'd like you sometimes to be out of this house. I'd like to be able to be alone every now and then. Not to have to hide in the bathroom to get some time to myself."

"Jesus," he said. "Where is this coming from?"

She threw the covers back and lurched up, scooping her clothes off the floor as she rose. He watched her body as she nearly ran from the room, the dimpling jiggle of her wide buttocks. The bathroom door slammed with a force that stirred the air over him seconds later.

Celeste moved out—"for a while," they agreed—to a tiny apartment over Aubuchon's Hardware in town. Mack got the bartending job, he insulated an upstairs bedroom, he started sheetrocking the walls. Celeste came back for a couple of weeks, but then she said he was hovering. Couldn't he just stay away from her, give her some space?

She moved out again, to a little house near town she shared with another teacher. Mack got a second part-time job, as a reporter for the Shelbyville *Post*. His days were almost full. He covered town meetings, basketball tournaments, local fires. He slept with a few women. Celeste heard about it and came back again. They both cried, they both comforted each other. She took two sick days from school, and they were happy, making love a lot. They brought the mattress in by the wood stove, so they could lie naked in comfort.

Then she told him she'd had several affairs too, one with another teacher, one with the divorced father of one of her students. They were sitting at opposite ends of the kitchen table, sitting naked with blankets like shawls over their shoulders. She'd been drinking when she started talking about it, and she offered a few details, almost giggling. Mack had been drinking too, and he got up his chair and hit her. It was pure impulse—he just wanted to stop her words, her mouth—but his hand had tightened into a fist just before impact, and he could hear that he'd hit her much too hard. She lurched sideways and nearly fell off her chair. When she righted herself, he saw the redness, the swelling already starting on her cheek, next to her pretty eye.

For a while after that, Mack lived in a commune halfway between Shelbyville and White River Junction. He liked the company; he liked driving up to the house at almost any time of the night and seeing one or two windows lighted, smelling coffee when he opened the door. There were two children in the commune, little boys four and seven, and Mack took them with him when he could to the games he covered. But it turned out that there were deep-running divisions in the house, ancient feuds he hadn't known about when he joined them. About eight months after he moved in, they were down to three members. They had a meeting and decided they couldn't afford to renew the lease.

Mack moved back to Shelbyville, back to the farmhouse. He cleaned up the damage the mice had done, moved the bed into the other bedroom, asked for and got a raise at the *Post*. His divorce papers came through.

A couple of nights later, Celeste drove up to the house. They made love, almost wordlessly, for a long time. She left before morning, and he hadn't slept with anyone again until the poet.

She had been older, Jewish, urban. She had made him remember all the smart girls he'd gone to high school with. She lived here, in Boston, and for a moment, lying on the grass by the river, Mack thought maybe he'd call her. But then he knew he shouldn't. He knew he'd end up talking about Randall, about his death, trying to puzzle through his own feelings; and he didn't want to hear anyone else's observations about them. He looked over at the sunbather again.

Abruptly he remembered the urge he'd have toward sex after someone he knew had died in Vietnam, so that late in his hitch he was regularly buying women when he could—he, who'd been sure when he first arrived that he'd never touch the pretty, pathetic little girls with their thick makeup and their crazy, mimetically learned obscenities. In the end he'd gotten good at bargaining them down, making them throw in variations for free. All to celebrate being alive. Fucking dirty on behalf of the dead. Maybe what he was feeling now was just that same randiness. Then, suddenly, at the thought of that word, the pun, he laughed out loud. The almost-naked woman's eyes snapped open, found him. She frowned and watched him for a moment—was he a rapist? a killer?—but as soon as he began to gather up his trash, to stand, she drifted back into sunbaked sleepiness.

Walking past her with the greasy papers in his hand, Mack had the impulse to bend down, to whisper something foul—or maybe just the word *randy*—to her. But he kept moving, up to the wire-mesh trash barrel.

There were still a few people sitting around at tables under the striped tent top at the Tenth Reunion luncheon, while the students cleaned up around them. Mack tried walking in, but a young woman at the gate stopped him.

"Do you have your badge?" she asked.

"I lost it," Mack said.

"I'm sorry," she said. "You can get another one at the Freshman Union, but I'm not allowed to let you in without it."

"But I'm in the class of 'sixty-nine. Honest."

"I'm sorry," she said.

Mack looked over at the men. Most of them seemed heavier, older than himself, he thought. Infinitely more respectable anyway. Mack was wearing a worn T-shirt over jeans and sandals. These men had on sports jackets, the goofy hats, pressed shirts. Only here and there was there a pair of jeans, and those were neat, new. No one looked familiar. He turned back to the girl. "You don't believe me, do you?"

She was pretty and young, in a loose smocked sundress. She looked frightened. She turned to see who was nearby to help her.

"Look, it's all right," he said. "I won't make trouble."

She had backed up a few steps, and now she looked at him dubiously.

"You're right; I didn't pay my dues or whatever. I admit it. I was a dropout anyway." He held his hands out, empty. "Before it was fashionable. You can tell by my uniform." He gestured down at his worn jeans. "I just wanted to peer at them for a moment. My ex-classmates." Two men walked toward them, and Mack and the girl stepped apart simultaneously, as though they were all doing a kind of country reel and the reunion men were supposed to dance out between them. When they stepped back toward each other, they were both smiling, as though they'd shared that thought.

"What class are you?" he asked her after a moment.

" 'Eighty. Next year is the big one for me," she said. She had long straight hair. She wore no makeup, and her eyelashes and brows were almost white. She looked like a remnant of the sixties, a flower child.

"And what comes then?" he asked. He slouched against the pillar on his side of the gate, comfortable.

"Oh . . ." She changed her voice, to put quote marks around it: *"Life."*

"In one of its many forms."

She grinned. "Exactly." She had a wonderful, wide smile.

"Well, don't be in any rush," he said. "Before you know it, you'll look like these guys."

She looked back at the few people left in the courtyard and then at him, critically. "You don't," she said.

"I take that as a compliment."

She blushed and did a little mock curtsy. "You may." Then: "What are you doing, in 'life'?"

"Well." He paused and leaned forward to read her name tag. "Well, Sophia. I'm at a crossroads. And I'm not exactly sure what comes next."

"Kinda like me."

"Kinda like you. Only very different."

"Why should it be any different? I mean, isn't everything that's open to me just as open to you?"

"Is everything open to you?"

"I think so, yes." Her face was very sober, suddenly. A child's, full of expectation and solemn hope. He felt sorry for her.

"Magic," he said. "Then it is."

"And it isn't for you?"

"No. I've chosen a few things. And that . . . well . . . that shut some doors in my life."

"You mean like dropping out."

He laughed. "That was one anyway. That certainly got the old ball rolling."

A whole cluster of alumni passed between them. Someone was saying, "It was a veritable circus. I was embarrassed to be part of it." Mack looked at the man. He was smoking a pipe. Who *were* these people? How had this happened to them—this weight they'd taken on—and not to Mack?

"So," Sophia said. "What are your options? What is . . . the crossroads?" He looked at her. She blushed a little. She was flirting.

"Actually it might be more like a rotary."

Her laugh was a little too loud, a little shrill. When it stopped, they stood silent for a moment. Then Mack said, "Christ, I don't know. I just can't go on quite the way I have been. And . . ." He plunged: "My brother died. That might be the most important thing."

Her face sobered instantly. Death. She was impressed. Mack had known this would happen. All of it.

"You mean *recently?*" she asked.

He nodded. "Just now. I'm on my way to his funeral."

"But that's terrible!" And when he didn't respond: "What did he die of?"

"An accident. *Life*, I guess. Bad timing. Bad luck."

"Oh, God, I'm *really* sorry." She looked away for a moment, and then back at him, intensely. "Were you close?" she asked.

Mack didn't know what he was going to say; it just came out. "We were twins."

"God!"

"Yeah. At one time, I thought I would have given my life for him." Four or five more alumni, the last stragglers, passed between them. Her face remained there, waiting, looking only at him as the men filed out. So much sympathy. Mack was ashamed suddenly—of his lie, of his use of the truth. His tone was harsh when he spoke again. "Imagine my surprise when I found out that I'd rather live, that I didn't want to die. For him, or for anyone. Imagine my . . . *self-loathing.*" He put the same quotes around it with his voice that she'd put around *life.*

Sophia's face twisted in perplexity. She didn't get his tone. She felt, perhaps, wounded by it. "I'm sorry," she said finally. Her voice was cooler. Her expression had closed somehow. "I don't understand. I don't understand you."

"Don't be sorry for that," he said. He looked at her pretty, sad face. *"I'm* sorry. I'm sorry." He'd been like a dark cloud drifting across her blue, blue sky. "But you've been . . . nice. To talk to me." He held his hand out.

"Well, it *was* nice to meet you." Her voice was full of regret, and her hand in his was cool and strong.

He'd gotten partway down the block when it occurred to him how he could use her. He swung around and walked quickly back. Her face lifted hopefully to him; but fell almost immediately when he said, "Look. Sophia, I need to get into my old room. Can you just get me into Adams House?"

She waited nervously outside, on the stairway, in case anyone came. The paneled living room was the same, dark and airless. Two student trunks were shoved into the middle of the room, labeled and ready for summer storage. He pushed the door to his bedroom open. The furniture in here was arranged differently from the way it had been—the bureau was where Mack had had his desk. But the narrow bed still stretched out under the window, and when Mack lay down on it, the rooftops, the trees, the church spire were all still there against the sky, all just as they had been years before. He'd lain here that whole fall, essentially, looking up at this view, trying to figure out what he should do. It was hard now for him to remember the bottomless grief he felt, the sense of falseness in everything he did. Even going to meals was painful, sitting next to someone in the vast, elegant dining hall, smiling, acting pleasant. He'd seen a movie that fall, a Bergman movie, *Persona*. In it, Liv Ullmann played a woman incapacitated to the point of speechlessness by her sense of horror at the falsity of her everyday exchanges. Mack had wished he could be that crazy, that lost.

The only place he'd really felt comfortable was at Randall's institution. He'd visited his brother three or four times in October and November, but the last time he went he'd told a staff person to fuck off when she said he needed to leave, that it was time for Randall's gym class. The institute had written to his parents, told them he "romanticized" his brother, that his visits were disturbing to Randall and the other residents, and that for the time being, he wasn't welcome.

The weeks had worn on, he'd stopped going to classes, seen fewer and fewer friends. Late one night a couple of days before the Thanksgiving break, Mack had walked into Somerville. He made his way through the ugly treeless streets to one of the parks he'd worked in the summer before. Alone, under the glaring night spotlight in the cold, he sat on one of the sagging swings and thought of the kids he'd known— Al Inguagiatto, Ray Diglio, Mike Carney. They had all talked about their fate—about the draft, Vietnam— with a kind of careless bravado. If it happened, it happened. If you bought it, you bought it. At least you weren't working for Earl's Auto Repair the rest of your life, for Somerville Lumber.

Probably not all of them had gone—they joked that Ray might get 4-F on account of his acne—but Mack remembered the casual excitement in their voices as they talked about their chances. "At least something will be happening," Mike had said.

Now Mack thought maybe that was the moment

he'd made his choice—to be like them, to stand in for them, for others like them. For Randall.

And it had been wrong, the wrong choice. It had done no one any good, had rescued no one, changed nothing. Some of them were surely dead. Or damaged. Randall was gone now. And his own life felt alien and strange to him, like a long, pointless dream he was forced to live slowly through.

He lay on the bed and watched the fat, cottony clouds move with infinitesimal slowness behind the high spire of the Catholic church. His chest felt as though someone were pressing heavily on it. "Oh, God, Randall," he whispered into the still, close air. "What do I do now?"

The service was oddly intimate, David thought. Four or five staff people came from Randall's residence, but aside from that and one other of Lainey's brothers—Pete—the immediate family were the only people in the tiny church.

Paul didn't wear a robe; Lainey had asked him not to. He stood in front of them dressed just as they were and offered them all the ancient comforts. Near the end of the service he read the passage from Luke: "Whosoever shall not receive the kingdom of God as a little child shall in no wise enter therein." Lainey's breath caught. David could hear that she was beginning to weep, and he put his arm around her.

Paul looked up and was silent for a moment, as though waiting for inspiration. Then he began to speak of Randall. He said that Randall had lived always in a state of childhood, a state of grace, as it were. That he'd escaped time, lived untouched by the struggles that dominated our lives—the struggles of choice, of will, of love and hate. "He was free, in some sense," Paul said, "of human experience, which the rest of us must suffer, endure, and try to learn from. And part

of what those of you gathered here have had to learn
from is the experience of Randall himself." He looked
directly at Lainey. "It's hard to say you wouldn't have
wished him different; in all honesty, you probably
would have. But because he was the way he was, you
are all different; your lives have taken turns they otherwise wouldn't have taken. And you've grown and
changed. It has sometimes hurt you, and been costly,
but it has made you what you are." Now he looked
across the pews at all of them. "Randall is in you, forever and ever. In who you have become. He is, he will
always be, your child. Even those of you who were
children with him have passed into adulthood, while
he stayed, in every fundamental way, the same. He is
your child too." He stopped for a moment and
opened the heavy Bible to the bookmark. "Let us remember the words of Our Lord from the gospel of
Mark: ' "Suffer the little children to come unto me,
and forbid them not: for of such is the kingdom of
God." And he took them up in his arms, put his hands
upon them, and blessed them.' "

Paul bowed his head. The organ began slowly to
play. Farther down the pew, Mack's body shook helplessly, his hands rose to his face. David pulled out his
handkerchief and passed it down. He knew he
wouldn't be able to cry. Not here. Not in front of all
the others.

Now Lainey and her brothers had gone for a walk on
the beach. Mack was somewhere upstairs, behind a
closed door. David was lying down in the living room.
He'd thought he might take a quick nap, but he found
himself instead listening to his daughters through the
open window above the couch. They were outside,
on the porch. They'd started to compare stories about
where they'd been, what they'd been doing, when
he'd called with the news; and David realized,

abruptly, that they would remember that moment a long time, that Randall would join Kennedy or Martin Luther King in that phenomenon: you'd never forget where you were, what you were doing, when you heard about his death.

Mary and Sarah had both been in the shower, and Sarah in particular found this coincidence astonishing. "Isn't it, like, so weird? Just so totally bizarre?"

"Please," Liddie said. "Next you'll be comparing what stage in your menstrual cycle you're in."

Someone must have gestured somehow—Sarah gave Liddie the finger?—because there was a beat of silence, and then they all laughed.

"Well, where were you, Lid?" Sarah asked.

"Not in the shower."

"But where?"

"Actually I was just coming back from a rehearsal, a session with one of the soloists in this chorus I'm supposed to be directing—ought to be directing even as we speak." Her voice warmed to her story. "And I was coming up onto the porch of this boarding-house where I'm staying through the festival—such a very glamorous life!—and I could hear the phone start, and I knew. Actually I did know. That it was for me. And that it was bad news. And when I came into the hall, sure enough, here was the lady, the board-inghouse lady, you know, in one of those flowery bo-somy dresses you can't believe they even make anymore. And she was holding the earpiece and just turning to me. And she said, 'Oh, Miss Eberhardt, it's your father.' And I thought, *Oh, God, it's Mother.* And I took the phone, and she went discreetly into the living room. And listened to every single word I said, I'm quite sure."

After a little silence, Nina said, "I was working in the darkroom. And the appalling thing is, I went right back to work."

"Well, I can understand that, Neenee," Sarah said. "I mean, he'd been gone so long. I hadn't even seen him in years. In a way, he was already dead for me." After a moment's silence, she said anxiously, "Don't you think we all feel that way?"

"Certainly I do," Mary said. "I mean, I was saying to Nina, I was about twelve or thirteen maybe when he left."

"See, I don't think he left," Nina said.

"What *are* we speaking of?" Liddie asked.

There was a pause, and David imagined them in their chairs, all the pretty women. All clearly from the same family, except perhaps Liddie. She'd cropped her hair short and lightened it, he thought. She was very blond, very glamorous now, in a brittle way. It had shocked him, seeing her this time.

His body had tensed on the couch, and he realized he was waiting for Nina's answer.

Finally it came. "I don't know. Just, if anyone had asked me about our family—where we all were and so forth—I might have said there was one still at home. *By which I mean,*" she said pointedly, as though someone had made a face indicating protest, or incomprehension, "that psychologically he was still there. Among them. That he was always the one who needed them, needed their protection. The one who had to be arranged for, even a thousand miles away." In the silence that fell, David could hear the gulls beyond them, and the steady noise of the surf. "Don't you think Mother and Daddy must have been worried sick about who'd be in charge of him when they died?" she asked. Then she said, "He never left."

"And now he has," Mary said dramatically, after a moment.

"It's so weird, when you think of it," Sarah said. "Because there's actually a room for every other person in the family to come home to but him, but he's the only one who . . . well . . . like Nina says, stayed. Psychologically anyway.''

"And now we get to watch chapter two," Liddie said. "After the longest chapter one in history."

"What do you mean?" Mary asked.

"What comes next. What they do next."

"You think it'll change things?"

"God," Nina said. "I feel it'll change things even for me. That something's finally, finally ended in my past."

"Too late for me," Liddie said. "For better or for worse, I hurled myself out of the nest long ago. And look at me now."

"What? You like what you're doing."

"I adore it, actually. But it's a far cry, that's all I'm saying, from what I once thought I'd be doing."

"So? I'm a salesgirl, for Christ's sake," Sarah said.

"You're twenty-something. And you're a fiddling salesgirl."

"Yeah, but the band will never make me any money."

"Well, you're wise, my precious, if you know that now."

Someone stood up—David heard the chair scrape, then the other chairs. Sarah said, "Cripes, I should find Mack. We need to get going."

David stood up quickly, too, and went into the kitchen. He could hear them talking, laughing, dispersing through the house, their footsteps moving across the living room, up the stairs, spreading them in their various directions.

They'd leave soon, all except Mary, who was returning to Chicago with him and Lainey tomorrow. Liddie would go back to prepare for the festival. Sarah and Nina would return to their marginal lives, Mack to his in Vermont. And he and Lainey would be alone with it finally, just as Nina had said. And alone with each other.

At almost every step of the way so far, he'd felt distant from her, and guilty on account of that distance. He'd known first—he'd been the one the residence could reach. Lainey was downtown for the afternoon, at classes at the Art Institute and then shopping.

And so he'd canceled his appointments, he'd gone home to the empty house. For a moment now, remembering it, he thought of what Sarah had said, about how Randall didn't have a room there anymore. Because the first thing David had done when he got home was to go upstairs, to go and stand in the doorway of Nina's room, the room that had been Randall's, hoping to be able to find something to feel for his son. The room was strange, the walls half papered, half painted with a forest scene Lainey had invented after Nina and Mack wrecked it. But it called up nothing of Randall, only the anguish David had felt over each of them during their adolescence.

He'd gone to his study then and started to make the calls. Liddie had an answering machine on, directing him to a number in western Massachusetts, and he reached her there just as she came in. Her voice was frightened, but it eased when he told her the news. She moved directly into practical considerations. It would be a little tough, she said, but she'd get there, wherever they decided the service would be.

Mack was speechless. David had done all the talking, assuring him he'd get back to him with details of the service. In the background he could hear the wail of country music playing.

It was Nina's voice that had made him feel something, the instant swell of sympathy in her tone. He had been afraid he'd weep on the line, and he presented all the information quickly, dryly; but he wanted to stay on with her, to hear that warm, sorrowful voice.

He'd had to wait for five or ten minutes to compose himself before he called Mary. The two youngest girls were sweet, concerned; but by then what David had to say was nearly routine for him.

When he was through on the telephone, he'd sat for a few moments in his study. Then he got up and walked methodically through all his children's rooms. Though he felt a kind of repulsion as he did it, he forced himself to think of the loss of each of them, trying to increase his sorrow for Randall. In Liddie's room he sat and remembered the night he and Lainey had decided to send Randall away, the night he'd known he was going to come back if she consented to it. He lay down on Liddie's bed, staring at the ceiling, and thought not so much of Randall himself as of everything Randall had cost him and brought to him, all the years between that first frightened vision of him as ill in the Fourth of July parade and the empty, excruciating visits with him in Connecticut.

Had he loved him, ever? There were moments, he recalled, moments of love so stabbing and selfless, when Randall would lift his face in pleasure at something simple David had done for him, would smile ecstatically. At those times, David felt that the love he bore for his other children was tainted—by their will, their demands, by his expectations of them to change and grow, to reward his love in some way. That it was only Randall, pure soul, pure need, who called up what in some sense might be defined as pure love.

But he remembered, too, his own rage—when Randall soiled himself, when he woke the household in the night, when he dispassionately destroyed something: curtains, furniture, dishes. Once he'd stood in the pantry squealing and wincing with pleasure as he dropped glass after glass from the shelf to the floor. He'd nearly finished by the time David got to him.

He heard the door opening and sat up quickly. Lainey's voice was pitched to reach him in his study, and he called back that he'd be down in a minute. He heard a rustle and thump as she dropped packages and her purse on the bench. Then she went to the kitchen. He'd gone into the bathroom and splashed water on his face, toweled it, looked carefully at himself in the mirror. There was no sign, none, of whatever he felt of grief, and he was aware of a familiar tug of dislike for all that was self-contained, *dry,* as he thought of it, in himself.

He came slowly down the stairs. She'd turned the radio on—he could hear it from the second landing—and she was pulling pots out. They struck each other with metal song. He felt almost dizzy, moving back toward the kitchen. He didn't know what he would say. He wished he didn't have to be the one. He stepped into the room and stood for a moment watching her before she looked up. Her face froze; she stilled completely. "What?" she said. "What?"

And somehow he said it, just his name, then that he was dead. Her arms fell and she dropped the pot, it clattered across the floor. A helpless low cry escaped her. He went to her, he held her, felt the way her sorrow shook her body even before she began to weep. He felt weak. He pulled a chair out with one hand and guided her onto his lap as he sat down. He held her close for a long time before she began to ask him questions, before he had to tell her about the car, about the train that had wailed in the distance and the cry of pleasure Randall had made before he let go of his partner's hand and began to run across the street. And it wasn't until then, until that moment of recounting this detail for the first time, that he let himself remember Randall in the yard, crowing happily, his head swinging toward the clatter of the IC or the heavy rumble of the freight cars. It wasn't until then that he cried too.

By late afternoon everyone had gone. He and Lainey and Mary sat down to an odd meal of leftovers and talked peacefully among themselves.

Lainey said, "Maybe the next time we all get together, it'll be something to celebrate. A wedding. Or a baby."

"We had a wedding already," he pointed out. "And it wasn't much to celebrate."

"Maybe Nina will marry this guy," Mary said.

"What makes you say so?" Lainey asked.

Mary shrugged. "She just seems to feel safe with him. He's not like her famous rat series. He sounds nice. She really does seem tempted."

"Did she say all that?"

"More or less. But I could tell too. I can always tell about Nina."

They spoke idly, with long pauses between remarks. It was easy, like dozens of meals they'd shared with Mary in Chicago when she came over or they met her at a restaurant. Surely their sunniest child, she seemed uncomplicated and serene in the way she moved through life, in the genuine affection she bore for all of them. David remembered his nickname for her and the other little girls: "the unexpected blessings." How true that seemed now.

While Lainey went upstairs with her coffee to collect bedding and clean, David and Mary did the dishes. He had a sudden sense of how like Lainey she was physically. The other girls were all thinner, more like him. Mary was big, broad as well as tall. Not heavy, just strong, the way Lainey had been as a young woman. Moving back and forth beside his daughter, he remembered those comfortable evenings with

Lainey early in their marriage, before they knew about Randall, when the ease between them as they did their chores had seemed deep and complete and erotic.

Even Mary's frown was the same, the little curved line between the dark eyebrows. "How do you think Mother's doing?" she asked abruptly.

Mack had asked him this too, and Liddie. It was as though Lainey were the only one they expected to suffer because of Randall's death, as though David were somehow an impartial observer. *I loved him,* he wanted to say. *I loved him too.*

"About as well as you could expect. It'll take her a while, I think."

Mary nodded.

Just before they left the kitchen, Mary picked up the square white box that sat on the shelf over the table.

"What's this?" she asked, and gave it a slight shake.

"It's Randall's ashes."

"Oh! God. *Sorry,*" she said. Her face was frightened. "It's just . . ."

"No; it doesn't look likely," David agreed. He had thought, when the cheerful funeral director handed it over, that the white cube looked like the endless stream of corsage boxes that had sat in their refrigerator on Harper during the girls' high school years, holding wilting baby roses, flattened gardenias, the odd shriveled orchid for weeks after the event; until Retta, usually, insisted whatever girl it belonged to face facts: it was gone.

"Where will you put them? Or will you . . . ?"

"Scatter them. Yes. I think so. Probably on the lake. We haven't talked about it much. Here. I should take it up and pack it." He took the box from Mary and turned the lights out after them. Following her up the stairs, he was thinking of Mack. He'd lifted the box too, earlier in the day, before the service, and asked the same question. When David had told him what it was, he'd been silent a moment. Then he'd smiled that strange distant smile he had, and said, "Boy, he ain't heavy." And sung, "He's my bro-the-er."

David had felt his head shake, involuntarily.

Mack's hands lifted. "Okay. Okay. Bad joke."

"Just if your mother had heard you, Mack . . ."

Mack had grinned, almost wickedly. "For Mother I would have said, 'His burthen *is* light, by God.' "

In spite of himself, David had laughed.

And now David, carrying the box slowly upstairs, was suddenly struck by it too—all that power that Randall had held, reduced to this, a few pounds, most of that probably the plastic jar the ashes sat in. Surely some of what he felt himself was the weight falling away, the yoke lifting.

In the middle of the night, he heard Lainey get up. They hadn't bothered to pull the curtains because they needed to rise so early to catch the plane, and he watched her silhouette cross in front of the glowing white windows. The floorboards of the old house protested every step. Once she'd gotten downstairs, he sat up partway. He expected to hear her in the kitchen, but the house was deeply silent, no noises rose above the heavy push and pull of the ocean that washed in from the open window.

He dozed very briefly, and when he woke, he immediately got out of bed himself. He'd been dreaming her sitting in the dark living room, or at the dining room table, weeping silently in order not to wake him or Mary. He felt around on the chair for his bathrobe. He was standing in front of the window, about to put it on, when a movement in the moonlight on the wide lawn that stretched down from the house to the sea caught his eye. He turned and stared. It was Lainey in her nightgown moving up the lawn, her white feet winking on the black grass as she ran. He saw her stop and turn back to face the ocean. He could feel himself stiffen, and only after she turned again and continued on her way back to the house did he realize he'd been holding his breath.

He went quickly down the dark stairs, stumbled across the living room, and opened the front door. She was perhaps ten feet from the foot of the porch stairs, standing on the lawn. Her arms were wrapped around herself, and she spun to him when she heard the door, her nightgown swirled, and she lifted her face. It was open, alive; her dense hair was blown back from her forehead.

He stepped forward to where the moonlight fell on him too. "I was worried about you," he said. His voice sounded thin and puny in the expansive air.

"You needn't be."

"I didn't want you feeling sad by yourself."

"Sad! Oh . . . ! David." She stepped toward him, and her face was anguished and jubilant at once. "That's not it, not at all. It's terrible. It's terrible, I know. But what I feel . . ." She stopped and looked at the ocean again. Then after a moment she turned slowly once more to face him. "Don't you see?" she whispered. "I'm *free.*" Silver tears glittered in her eyes. "I'm free as a bird!"

17

IT was my mother, it was Lainey, who wrote chapter two for them—Lainey who ended it, finally, though it was my father who moved out again. And it's clear she was set in motion by Randall's death. Certainly not so quickly as I was: I married Will about a month later; or Mack—by Christmas of that year he'd sold his Vermont farm and used the proceeds to buy into the bar in Chicago. No, for Lainey and my father it took longer, it was all more tentative and gradual. But the first impulse toward change was immediate. It came when they returned from the funeral. Lainey called a realtor to ask what they could get for the house. She wanted out, she said. She knew it as soon as she walked through the front door and set her bag down by the newel post.

It was my father who resisted, who said he wasn't ready to give it up. She was surprised, she told me, at what seemed sentimental to her in this, sentimental and out of character. Still, she canceled the appointment, even though she felt almost physically uncomfortable at home now: all those useless rooms, all that wasted space. But then she started in the set-painting program at the Goodman, and for a while they were both very busy. They seemed to settle in again. Her letters and phone calls were accounts of all they were accomplishing in their separate worlds.

But the dramas had run out, and slowly the engine of their marriage stopped. She was the one who felt it, keenly. For two years in a row she spent most of each summer away from my father, at her family's house on the shore. I went up from New York a couple of times each of those years to visit her, to get out of the city. And it was late that third fall after Randall's death—the fall of 1981—that my father moved out. Harold Baker had had a heart attack and died quite suddenly, and Lainey said it made her feel a need to be decisive, to make the changes she'd been thinking of. That was the explanation she offered all of us at the time anyway. And it was the way she spoke of it to me too, on those dreamy nights on her front porch while I was visiting her. But it's occurred to me more recently that it might have been more complicated than that. That perhaps she realized in some way when Harold died that there would always be women for my father—women like Tony. That she wouldn't in any sense be abandoning him if they separated.

At any rate, they separated. He moved out, and after a while he did begin to see Tony. At first it was because she was an old friend and they were comfortable together, they understood each other. And then, increasingly, it was out of a sense of potential, of joy.

A week or so before their wedding, my father and Tony asked me out to dinner with them on the spur of the moment. They would pick me up, they said. There was a restaurant they wanted to try on the North Side. Maybe we'd stop by Mack's for a drink afterward.

I wasn't ready when they arrived. I pressed the buzzer and then stepped barefoot out into the chilly hallway. I could see it was just my father down there— he stood alone in the little lighted space at the bottom of the stairwell, his dark coat widening out under his shoulders and head. I called down to him to come up, and he lifted his face blindly to my voice.

"Let me signal Tony," he said. He disappeared for a moment, and then I could hear him begin his ascent.

"Good Lord, Nina," my mother said softly when

I went back into the living room. "You might have warned me." She was still in work clothes, stretched out on the couch with the newspaper spread around her. She was barefoot too, and I could see that the soles of her feet were a dusty gray.

The room was a mess. What's more, she had recently taken the canvas off a flat from her latest set and tacked it up on the wall. It showed part of the front of a stone house, a mansion. The big granite blocks it was made of were deeply chiseled at the edges; the front door was wooden, the grain done with careful exaggeration. There was a grotesque brass face for a knocker.

It was astonishing really—you stepped into her quite ordinary apartment and there seemed to be this other fantastic building there, making everything in the real world around you small and colorless by comparison. When my father came in, he was silent for a moment, looking around. His head swung back and forth, taking in all the different elements.

"Hello, David," my mother said. She was still on the couch, though she'd sat up. She'd hastily folded the messy newspaper, too, and taken her glasses off.

"Well, Lainey." He stepped into the room. His face looked suddenly oddly animated and eager. "Still making scenes, I see." He gestured at the wall.

She looked up, and then she laughed, her old loud, whooping laugh. "I'd *never* thought of that," she said. "No wonder I like to do it." She was still beaming across at him as he sat down on the chair closest to the hallway.

"The place looks nice, though," he said with some generosity. "All the old stuff looks good in here."

"This is hardly *all* of it," she said. "There's tons more in my storeroom downstairs. And just boxes and boxes of junk shoved in the guest room and the study. I had no idea what to do with anything.''

I'd started down the hall to find a pair of panty hose with no runs, which was what had held me up in the first place. ''There's even all our old stuff,'' I called back.

''Really,'' he said.

In the guest room, I pushed my hand into one pair after another of ragged hose. I finally found one on which the run was for the moment confined to the foot area. I touched nail polish to the point where the ladder ended and waved the hose through the air, blew on it to speed its drying. When I pulled it over my foot, I twisted it so the run would be almost entirely hidden by my shoe. The whole time I was doing this I could hear my father's quiet voice and then Lainey's—more animated, more alive, than it ever was when she talked to me or to one of her friends. *She still loves him,* I thought. But of course, she'd never said she didn't.

I stood still for a moment even after I was ready, listening intently—as I had listened so often to them when I was a child, trying to understand the mystery that had brought them together, that kept them locked in their endless struggle with each other. Somehow I felt a kind of anger at what seemed their ease with each other now, their comfort. Then I noticed, under a pile of other books on my nightstand, the worn journal my father had given me those weeks ago. I extracted it and carried it back down the hall to where they sat smiling across the room at each other.

''This is yours,'' I said, holding the book out to my father. He squinted at it as he reached up.

''Oh, good Lord!'' Lainey cried. ''It's that horrible diary about how crazy I was.''

"No, no, no, no, this is about Randall," my father said, turning it over in his hands.

And then he looked up, his face suddenly pained. There was a moment of stunned silence in the room as we all took it in: the long, hard history laid bare in their quick exchange, the claims implicit in their different versions of the meaning of my father's written record. And I was aware of a sudden guilty sense of myself as provocateur. I realized that I had wanted all this somehow when I picked up the book. That I had deliberately created this moment—this moment in which Tony sat alone outside in the car and the three of us in here stumbled once again over the events in our past that bound us together, in some sense forever. With an almost clinical distance I noted that I was a little breathless, that my heartbeat was bumpy and fast.

But my father had recovered himself. He was saying, in his gentlest voice, "Actually I think it's neither. Or both. It's really just a young man's very philosophical discussion about which came first, the chicken or the egg." He smiled tentatively at Lainey, as though asking her for something he wasn't sure she'd want to give him. After a moment, my mother smiled back. Then both of them stood, nearly simultaneously, as though this had broken a spell that held us all in place.

As my father and I were going down the stairs, my mother called out, "Give my love to Tony." Her voice sounded strained, and I looked up quickly, but all I saw was her back disappearing into her fun house of a living room and then the blank door shutting.

My father was quiet in the car on the way north. But he'd taken the back seat, and Tony was chatting about the restaurant—a friend of hers had invested in it, it turned out—so I don't think she noticed anything. Every now and then I looked over at him, at the passage of streetlight after streetlight across his smooth, almost skull-like face. It revealed nothing.

When we got to the restaurant, Tony excused herself, and my father and I were seated together. The room we were in was dark and plush and old-fashioned, with leather banquettes against the walls and portraits everywhere, in heavy gilt frames, of horses and dogs. It felt simultaneously genuinely rich and deeply phony.

As soon as we sat down, the waiter came over for our drink order, but my father said, "We'll wait for my wife." I was caught by surprise; for a moment I didn't know what he meant. Perhaps I made a noise of confusion, because he dipped his head toward me as though in apology and explained, "Tony."

When the waiter had gone, we sat for a moment in awkward silence. Then my father leaned forward and rested his folded hands on the white tablecloth. "You know, Nina," he said, "I wouldn't have ended it. It wasn't what I wanted at all."

"I think I know pretty much how all that happened, Dads."

He smiled coolly. "I doubt you do. I doubt Lainey explained to you how hard I fought for it." I was looking at his hands, at how slim, how pretty, they were. Like a woman's really. He said, "I thought we could be happy, perhaps." His voice sounded suddenly bitter, and I looked quickly up at him, but his face, as usual, was unreadable. "Lainey said an odd thing to me, you know," he went on. "After Randall died. She said she felt free. And I was foolish enough to think I could join her in that, that we could be free together somehow." He shook his head. "That was not what she meant." Then his quick smile passed over his face, and I felt my own face lift too, in automatic response. He said softly, "You should know, though, that I'm very happy now. Tony and I are, I think, better suited to each other in some ways than Lainey and I were."

I murmured something.

At the table next to us, a couple sat in awed silence while the waiter ceremoniously lifted rolls from a basket with a pair of silver tongs. My father sighed abruptly and said, "Lainey had—still has, I think—such a need for drama, for everything to be high-pitched." He shook his head. "I was no good at living on that scale. Everything, even sex, had to have a nearly sacramental quality."

Far across the room I could see Tony being directed to us, nodding, her chin lifting.

"And after Randall died, my incapacity for that was all too evident. There just wasn't enough there for Lainey. In me. In our life. I didn't have the power to draw her back to it." Then he looked intently at me and smiled again. "Perhaps what it is is just that Lainey has no gift for what Freud calls 'normal misery.'"

I laughed, too loudly, to signal him to stop talking. Tony was nearing the table, her pretty dress swirling behind her, her face open in greeting.

But he went on: "Life, in other words, as we mere mortals have to live it."

And then she was there, smiling down at us, smelling freshly of perfume—a lilacy, light odor—and he rose to pull her chair out for her and signaled the waiter that we were ready to start.

After the meal, my father said he was tired, too tired to go to Mack's. I was relieved, actually. I had drunk too much, and I was exhausted too. Both of us had been preoccupied through the dinner, and as though she could sense that something was wrong, Tony had been talkative and charming, directing our conversation easily to the world outside of us—politics, the theater, the food we were slowly eating. Even in the car on the way home, she kept things light and sociable.

When I opened the door to my mother's apartment, Lainey stirred on the couch and slowly sat up. She was wrapped in a blanket. An opened bottle of wine and a sticky-looking glass sat on the coffee table. "Nina," she said.

I felt I'd known all evening that she would be waiting up for me. Without taking my coat off, I sat down in the chair my father had occupied earlier.

"I fell asleep," she said. She licked her lips. "I was so upset when you left. I . . ." She looked confused, and then her eye fell on the bottle. "Would you like some wine?" she asked.

"I've had plenty."

"Me too," she said, but she leaned forward and filled her glass again. "I don't know when I've had so much to drink." She took a swallow and then looked up, smiling. "A bald-faced lie. I do know very well when I've had so much to drink. But it has been a long, long while."

She sat back, with the glass in her hand. Her short hair was oddly ruffled and then flattened around her head. In another situation it would have been comical, I would have joked about it with her. Now I felt a powerful surge of remorse for her suffering. I said, "I'm sorry about the notebook thing, Mom."

"How could you know, darling?" she answered quickly.

I watched her for a moment. I felt dismissed rather than forgiven—and I suddenly wanted her to understand that I'd intended to stir things up. "I knew," I said, too loudly.

"Oh." Something crumpled in her face. She set her glass down. "Then what on *earth* did you think you were doing?" Her voice was flat and cold.

I shrugged. "Maybe I was being like the prover-

bial child of divorce you read about in the literature.
Trying to bring her parents back together."

"Well, you ought to know it's much too late for
that."

"Or else I'm just the wrong child."

"What is that supposed to mean?" She was scowl-
ing. Her face looked old and sexless.

I got up, went across to the black windows.

"Nina, no one could bring your father and me
back together."

I turned around, quickly. "I'd like to know why
not, when you finally had a chance for a peaceful life
together." I had the sense, oddly, of speaking in my
father's behalf, of pleading his case.

She shook her head. "No, we didn't. Not really."

"Why not? Just why not?" My voice sounded
childish and shrill, even to my own ears. She stared
at me a moment before she answered.

"Because after Randall died . . . it was like there
was an empty place, a hole, in the center of my life
where he used to be." Her hand had lifted to her
chest and rested there. "I measured everything
against what it had felt like before, and everything
seemed . . . diminished. Unimportant. I couldn't help
that. That feeling."

"Oh, come on, Mother. You didn't even want to
try. At least Dad wanted to try."

"It wasn't that, Nina. Or it was. But . . . but he
wanted to—I don't know—just close over the past. He
wanted something from me. If he could have let go
of me, just let me go on, it might have been all right.
But it would have been starting all over. With all new
rules. And I just didn't have the strength. I'm glad for
your father—and for Tony—that they have that energy. But I wouldn't have wanted to begin again." She
looked up at me, and her face shifted, became sly.

"He suggested *therapy* to me." It was like a joke she was trying to share.

I felt a quick pulse of anger at this, at what seemed a request for my allegiance, for my betrayal of my father. "So?" I said, the fifth-grade taunt.

"As though I could be *cured* of turning away from him."

"There *are* cures for some things. Didn't you agree to that when you sent me off for mine?"

"Nina!" She had started to reach for her glass again, but now she froze. "We hardly *sent you off*. What an expression!"

"Forced me to go, then."

"And are you sorry?"

"Of course not. It did cure me. Or it helped. But that's what I'm saying." I sat down in my chair again. "You know, sometimes I think you and Dad got locked in so early to the terms of your argument that you've never even tried to negotiate, or compromise. You're absolutely stuck."

Her face was white suddenly, shocked. "You may not speak that way to me, Nina. About your father and me. We worked hard to be loving to each other. Harder than you know."

"Yes, for Randall's sake. And then when he died, that was it."

"That's not true."

"Well, it sure wasn't for my sake, was it? Or Mary's or Sarah's. Clearly none of us ever even counted in this mess." My voice was shrill again. I could feel my heavy heartbeat.

"Nina, how can you say that? If you knew the love I felt for all of you . . ."

"But I do know that love. I know that love so very well, and it's completely conditional. It's be quiet, be good, be happy, be well. Be well. And I'll love you. I'll love you, *my perfect baby.*" I had started to cry.

"Nina." Her voice was pleading. I could see the pain I was causing her.

But I didn't care. I was suddenly lost in my own pain, a pain I would have sworn I'd left behind long since. But now the ancient child in me had come to life. Lost in my drunken sorrow, I wailed, I could hear my own noise as though someone else were making it. What I wanted, I think, was for someone to hold me; but not this mother, not mine. It was an impulse, a desire more abstract and primitive than that.

And my mother seemed to understand that. She didn't rise, she didn't rush to embrace me. She sat with her pouched, sad face and watched me and waited for me to stop.

And when I did, finally, and was blowing my nose, she said quietly, "Nina, no one gets love without *some* conditions. It's not in human nature to love that way, even your own children. You want certain things from them. You want things *for* them. I wish I could have loved you, all of you, that much. But that's not in me. It's not in anyone."

"You loved Randall that way. Randall got love like that."

She looked anguished. "Oh, Nina, don't you think I wish I *could* have loved Randall with all those conditions? What a gift that would have been! That's the only kind of love I ever really wanted to feel. The other kind . . . who would want to feel that unless they had to?" She waited, but I didn't answer. "Nina, I know I wasn't a good mother. I railed at you, and . . . I hit you. There's no excuse. But I loved you all so much. Couldn't you feel it? At all? It had so much more of *me* in it. It had all of me, in all my terrible weakness. The other kind. It asked too much. It was too hard. Maybe it used up too much of me. But I gave you whatever I had."

She leaned forward on the couch, toward me.

"Nina, when you have children . . ." I turned my body sharply in the chair. "You will, lovey. I know it. And when you do, you'll want to love them . . . imperfectly. That freedom, Nina, to be who you are, in loving. Not better than you are." She sat back. When she spoke again, her voice was softer, almost hoarse. "Randall got that. You're right, of course. But I wish you could understand. It made me feel . . . yes, a kind of excitement in some way. I rose to it. I admit that. And part of me loved that—rising to it. I wouldn't change that in my life. It's just . . . part of who I am now. But it was my love for you other children that I loved. It was that love that held me to the earth."

After a long silence I asked, "And what about your love for Daddy?"

"I don't know. I don't know. When we came back together . . . something had happened. And then of course we had to get through everyone's adolescence." She laughed. "Minefields. And we knew why, that it had to do with everything we'd done to you, everything that had happened. It brought it all back, it made us—I don't know—so . . . so careful with each other. Considerate. Even making love." She reached for her glass now, held it a moment, then sipped.

"I think maybe I can't forgive him, that's all. For reacting so differently. For wanting to make the best of it. For wanting to put that part of our lives—the part that had cost me so dearly—behind us. To move on. To move on? Nina, I couldn't. How could I?"

I sat there, thickheaded, and tried to think whether I needed to answer her. And then I felt, suddenly, as though I couldn't anyway. The accumulated emotion of the evening seemed to press in on me with a rush, and I felt as though I might fall asleep in the chair if I continued to sit there. "I . . . I have to go to bed," I said.

"Yes."

I got up and started down the hall, almost staggering in my fatigue. But halfway to the guest room, I stopped. I turned around and went back. She was sitting just as she had been. "I'm sorry, Lainey," I said.

"Oh, darling, me too."

And then I went back to the guest room and shut the door, and fell nearly instantly into a heavy, befuddled sleep. But at the usual witching hour, I woke again, quite suddenly. The light was still on in the hall, the crack at the bottom of the door a luminous wand. Everything in the room glowed dimly in its light—my clothes heaped on the back of the chair, the hulking trunk and boxes. My mind was working frantically, running over the events of the evening, and I realized, staring at the shadowed medallion in the center of the ceiling, that I'd never heard Lainey speak of *forgiving* or *not forgiving* my father before this night. That through all he'd done to her with his passionate belief in one particular version of Randall's illness, she'd never let on that she saw herself as injured or damaged by him. And even tonight, of course, she hadn't spoken of that ancient, deep wound that had sat at the center of their marriage for so many years. But I felt that it was there, it was the source of the anger she clung to. For wasn't the thing she found unforgivable his wish to move away from it? From Randall, and what she'd become in response to him, of course; but also from what my father had done to her. Maybe, I thought, when life has bent you, has changed you in the cruel ways it bent and changed Lainey, it's too much to ask that you ever move beyond it. Even in the name of health. Even in the name of happiness.

It seemed to me then that although my father was right in his wish for my mother to move on with him, she was right, too, to want to cling to the memory of that earlier time when she'd lived a life whose dimensions were so cramped by duty and love but also so spiritually expansive. Lying in the dim light, I could see what they both wanted, and why. And I realized that I held them blameless for that. I had the peaceful sense of forgiving each of them on behalf of the other, as I drifted back to sleep.

About halfway through the wedding reception, our parents, *the grownups,* as I couldn't help thinking of them, had for the most part retreated into the kitchen and dining room of Tony's house, surrendering the hot, crowded living room to us, *the kids,* men and women in their thirties and a few in their early forties. There was some drifting back and forth by a few brave souls, but then Al Baker and Mack began playing records in the living room, and even that pretty much stopped.

I had stepped out onto Tony's deck and pulled the sliding door shut behind me. It was so unseasonably cold out—it had been for a few days—that the students she had hired to help with the party had stacked the cases of champagne out here. I'd noticed, the last time I'd come out for a couple of bottles, both that there was a light snow falling (what will be the portents, Nina?) and that the deck was already gaily dotted everywhere with popped corks.

Now I stood outside for a few moments. The bare ground was still warm, and most of the snow had melted at the rising touch of its dark heat; still, the white laced the grass delicately, it lay in a thin, transparent sheet on the deck, it lightly veined the branches of the trees. It stroked my face like cold tears.

The deck was in the bend of the L made by the square living room and the narrow dining room. From out here the wide glass doors opened onto the theater in each. The house looked hectic and hot, full of motion, of life. The conversation was muted through the glass, dulled to a gentle roar that reminded me of the constant sound of an ocean. The lights inside were warm and yellow. Candles flickered on the mantel in the living room and on all the windowsills, as though it were already Advent. In their wavering tender light, the men with their suits moved dark as grackles behind the exotic plumage of the women. I saw Tony weaving back to the kitchen through the crowd, her coral dress a brave flag of color.

The music pulsed under the hubbub. In the living room, Al was dancing with Mary, both of them frowning, intense, comical, looking down at their own working bodies, their busy feet. Her husband, Peter, was standing in a corner of the room, talking earnestly to someone I didn't know. On his belly was the little striped sling the baby was sleeping in, and he kept stroking the bulge of bright fabric while he talked, with the proprietary air of pregnancy.

It had been the simplest of weddings, all of us, family and friends, standing behind Tony and my father in the crowded living room while the businesslike justice of the peace went quickly through the service. He was Irish, and he praised them in a thick brogue for a job well done after every successful repetition of his words: "*Ver*ry fine; *ver*ry good." When each of them pronounced "Till death us do part," I had a sense, watching the backs of their heads—the one fleecy white, the other thinning and gray—of the gravity of this promise. I remembered, suddenly, the feeling I'd had when I made the same vow with Will, the feeling, I'm sure, that rang in my defiant voice: it will *take* death to part us. But Tony's accepting murmur, and my father's too, acknowledged death as the sorrow that would inevitably end their marriage, as the irrevocable final stage of their life together.

Now that I've said this vow for a second time, I recognize that there's at least one other way to mean it. *Till death us do part,* my husband and I pledged: but we intended it as a wish, a prayer. We were acknowledging that we knew all too well how many other reasons for parting there might be in our lives, acknowledging the power of luck, of chance, to change or govern the course of our marriage. We were hoping for the good fortune, the descent of a kind of grace, *a gift,* to last us through till then, to hold us fast to our best intentions.

That night, though, watching my father officially begin his life with Tony, I knew only about Will and me, about our foolish doomed assurance. And when my father at last kissed her and the spontaneous applause and cheering erupted in the crowded room, I'd had to turn my face away to hide the tears.

Suddenly Mack was standing close to the living room glass, his hands cupped on either side of his face, peering solemnly out at me. He slid the door open, and the noise burst forth with him.

"Aha!" he cried, too loud. "What are you doing out here in the cold?"

I bent over one of the cardboard boxes. "Getting more booze," I said. "Help me open a couple, will you?"

He shut the door again and stood with me on the deck. Together we unwrapped the thick foil, untwisted the fragile wires, and shot the corks off into the still gray night. Mack's face had the sober delight of a boy's at each explosion. He had been drinking too much, which was unusual for him—in recent years he'd grown more careful about booze. He'd been dancing a lot too. He'd taken his jacket off at some point and rolled up his shirt sleeves, and I could see big circles of dampness under each arm and down the middle of his back.

When we were finished, he helped me carry the opened bottles in. He filled a glass for himself and went off, holding a bottle out in offering, stopping to fill each glass held up to him, talking to each person he served. Periodically after that as I moved around, as I helped Tony serve the trays of catered food, I could hear his voice through the noise, too loud, sometimes nearly frantic.

A little later Tony took over the records for a while, and the music shifted to big-band stuff, fox-trots, swing. Some of the older group came out again from the dining room, and we danced too, *the kids,* to the brassy, smooth sounds. I stood by the fireplace through one number and watched Tony and my father moving in that stylized way, as though their bodies had been made for each other. Lainey and my father hadn't been so well matched, even though they had looked so much alike. They were too much the same size, and she had too much energy. When they danced, she often seemed to be out of his control, as though she were trying to lead. They weren't graceful together.

Tony and my father looked as though one brain, one set of directions, governed both of them. They didn't speak, didn't look at each other while they danced, but the intense intimacy of their doubled movement was almost embarrassing to watch. When the song ended, he slid his arms around her and bent his head for a moment into the soft cloud of her hair.

Al asked me to dance. I did the jitterbug with him to a couple of Glenn Miller songs. He was an athletic dancer. He twirled me around under his arm; he caught my hand exactly on the beat, just as I was about to spin off to some far corner of the room. It felt dangerous and exciting, dancing with him, and I was sorry when he said that he had to take a break. He was panting. He went into the dining room to get something to cool off.

I did a fox-trot with Peter. The baby in his pouch

pushed into my belly and made me silent and awkward with him. And then Mack put on a few more old forty-fives, and the grownups drifted away again. By now he was dancing wildly, blindly, sometimes without a partner. And he was drinking directly from a champagne bottle. He swung it freely as he moved, and people left plenty of room around him.

When a slow song came on, I asked him to dance. I tried to hold on to him, to contain his motion a little. He stumbled against me, he stepped all over my feet. We ended in an embrace, Mack drooped on my shoulder.

"Nina," he whispered. And then suddenly he was weeping, a violent, raw sound in my ear. The next song began, something by Aretha Franklin, and I moved with him quickly into the empty front hall. I stood there holding him, hoping no one else could hear. "This is so hard on me," he blurted between his gasps for air. "Christ. This is so hard."

It was startling to me to hold Mack, to feel the grief shake his body. I wanted desperately to say something, I wanted to be sympathetic. After all, hadn't just these confused feelings—just this amount of booze—triggered my tears, my grief, with Lainey? But I felt so distant from him that it was like holding a child weeping over an imagined slight or loss—I had that sense of understanding his pain but also of having moved beyond it. I murmured vague comforting phrases and patted his strong back.

Then Al was there, standing behind Mack. He touched my brother's shoulder, and Mack turned easily to him. Al was bigger than Mack, built the way his own father had been, and Mack looked slender and vulnerable in his embrace. Our eyes met over Mack's head, and Al began talking steadily to him. He was guiding him toward the stairs. "Come on, my old friend," he was saying. "I want you to take a time-out."

"Time-out, Al," Mack said. "I need a time-out, Al." They started up. "Al," Mack said. "My pal Al."

I watched them stagger and lurch over the carpeted steps. "Al, my pal," Mack was saying. "Al, you're my brother." Suddenly he pushed Al away and stood facing him, swaying on the landing, his face a parody of drunken astonishment. "Al, you're my brother!" he said. "Did you realize that? You—are—my brother."

"You're damn right," Al said. His arm encircled Mack again, turned him once more to face the rising stairs.

"Isn't that great?" Mack said in tender amazement. He was watching Al's face, touching his chest. "You're my brother, Al." They heaved up. Just before they got to the second floor, Mack stopped and yelled, "My brother is dead! Long live my brother!" I turned and looked to see if anyone had heard it. Then he yelled it again, but only a few heads swung in my direction. Most people were talking too loudly over the music or were busy dancing; and Aretha was doing her part, wailing "Dr. Feelgood" on the stereo.

From across the dining room, though, I saw my father—motionless, tall, and erect. His head was lifted, his smooth face was frozen and attentive, as though he thought he'd heard someone calling for him from across some great distance.

But then one of the guests must have spoken to him, because he turned quickly and his face opened, he was smiling slightly, sociable and polite.

Much later I went upstairs to the bathroom and saw, as I passed Al's old room, that Mack was curled up asleep on top of the bed. Someone had taken his shoes off, spread a red blanket carefully over him. I stood for a moment looking in at him. His hand was loosely fisted near his mouth, and to me his face looked childlike—almost pretty. Before I went back down, I shut the door carefully and quietly so the noise from the celebration below wouldn't disturb him.

It was late when I left, but there were still perhaps ten or fifteen people there, scattered through the rooms, talking quietly. My father was in the kitchen with Tony's daughter, Susan, and another, older couple. I kissed him good night, and he held me hard against his chest for a moment. When I stepped back, I saw that his eyes had reddened behind the thick glasses.

Tony saw me to the door. She thanked me for all my help, and then she hugged me too. I was struck by how small, how fragile she felt in my arms.

"Mack's upstairs, you know," I told her. "Big Mack, that is." He'd assigned himself this nickname to hide his pleasure when he heard what Mary and Peter had named the baby.

"Yes. David said he'd tucked him in."

"I wondered who had," I said. I thought of my father bending over Mack—bending over each of us when we were small, stroking back our hair with his smooth, gentle hands.

"So much for your honeymoon," I said.

She laughed. "That's certainly the last thing David and I need," she said. And then, unexpectedly, color rose to her face, and she was silent. I had never seen Tony at a loss before, at the mercy of her emotions. I felt touched, and embarrassed too. We were both awkward as we said good night, and I was so caught in my confused emotions that I walked past five or six houses before I began to take anything in.

But then I realized that the street was asleep anyway, most of the old familiar houses completely dark. As I passed the Masurs', though, I saw that there was a dim light on somewhere deep on the first floor. They'd been at the wedding, along with Mr. Rosenberg and the Gordons, the Lees. Except for the ones who had died, Lainey was the only member of the old group who hadn't come. When I got to the square, I stopped and looked at the whited lawn. It seemed so small compared to the way it loomed in my memory.

On an impulse, I turned in and went down the path to our old house. I knew that a family with young children had bought it; Lainey had told me that. I had certainly peered in this direction each time I'd gone to Tony's house to see my father. But I hadn't wanted to walk in before, to get that close to it. Now, abruptly, our reign there seemed over, seemed like ancient history. And I felt like marking that sense of a time gone by. I was ready to look at what had become of it.

There was a light on upstairs, in the largest bedroom, the bedroom that had always been my parents'. The shades were drawn, and the bare branches of the silver maple crisscrossed like stylized ink drawings in front of them. There was one other light, a spotlight in back. It shone brightly over a new deck, like Tony's, which jutted prowlike off the kitchen. Everything else was dark.

I walked along the side of the house into the yard. I stood for a while as far from the spotlight as I could get, my back against the fence that ran along the bottom of the embankment for the IC. I was shivering in the cold; my feet were wet. The snow hissed gently around me as it landed.

When the light went off upstairs, I felt bolder. I went slowly across the yard, climbed the steps to the deck, and tried to peer in the glass doors to the kitchen. Our kitchen. I could see a table and chairs in the middle of the room. And as my eyes adjusted, I could see that the cabinets were new, a pale color, that the room was completely transformed. From where the pantry had been, I saw light. For a moment

I thought it was a mirror, reflecting the door and the light over me. But then I realized that those were windows—that the pantry simply wasn't there anymore, that the room was open on that side, too, to the snowy night. The dark cave that had been our kitchen, the seat of all our family drama, was gone. In the daytime this would be a bright, airy room. Pretty, I imagined.

A train screamed past behind me. I stepped back, and suddenly the dim world inside the glass vanished and what I was looking at now on its surface was myself, myself revealed under this bright light. The wet snow had flattened my hair around my head. I looked bedraggled and even colder than I felt. It made me think of a story I'd read over and over as a child, Andersen's "Little Match Girl." I'd used it then to feed my own sense of being an outsider, an onlooker among my family: the little girl, shivering, dying in the cold, while inside there was warmth, life, drama. Now I saw abruptly that the theater was equally out here. That the figure who hovered on the other side of the glass, looking in, yearning, had her story, her drama, also—her beginning and middle and end. And that standing outside, looking on, offered no escape from the roll of events, from the steady pull of time.

I looked hard at myself for what seemed like the first time in a long time. I'd borrowed a dress coat of Lainey's because I had brought nothing with me I could wear over my clothes to the wedding. It was black and sleek, and in it I didn't look like a girl, which was how I still thought of myself most of the time. My face was pretty, I think, but not with that open, eager expression a girl has. There was something sad in it. I saw that I'd changed, in spite of the way I had thought of myself, in spite of everything I'd done to stay safe from time—even when, as with my marriage to Will, I imagined I was plunging into its pressing

stream. Looking at myself under the spotlight, I realized that that choice, too, had been a kind of retreat,
just as Dr. Dusek had suggested. That it had always
been the touch of the random that had changed me—
the accident, the unwilled event, out of my control:
therapy, or Randall's death, or the loss of the baby.
These were the things that had claimed me in spite
of my best efforts, that had given my life a shape, a
sense of forward motion. That had brought me here,
this strangely forlorn woman looking back at herself
under the falling snow, in someone else's expensive
clothes, outside someone else's house.

I went back to New York two days after the wedding.
I felt as though whatever I'd come for had been somehow achieved. Or else that it didn't matter anymore.
I brought back with me several of the odd family pictures that had hung for years on the kitchen wall at
home: the brittle, spotted magazine photograph of
Freud and his wife; the two postcards of the annunciation; a photograph I'd taken once in youth of my
brothers together, smiling, looking like twins. I hadn't
asked if I could have these things specifically. I'd just
taken them. After all, Lainey had said to take whatever
I liked. Naturally I'd chosen pictures, images. And I
brought back several rolls of film I'd shot during my
stay, including some pictures I'd taken of Mary while
she was still pregnant.

She had stopped work finally, the last week before she gave birth, and I spent a day with her helping
her pass the time. After lunch she decided on impulse
to take a bath. It was the only place she felt comfortable, she said. We talked of everything inconsequential as she lay back in the tub, her feet propped against
the wall above the nickel faucet, her belly rising solid
as an island out of the lapping water, white and immense and taut. I was sitting on the toilet seat. I had

trouble not staring at her. I actually thought I saw, once or twice, the moving pressure of a tiny heel or fist pushing her flesh from within. My body hadn't changed much with my pregnancy to anyone's eye but my own; but in Mary's packed roundness I could see what might have become of me finally, how my instruction in giving myself over to someone else might have begun.

It was as she heaved herself to a standing position in the tub and reached for a towel that I asked her if I could photograph her undressed. I was a little surprised when she consented.

I hadn't ever enjoyed the life photography courses I'd taken—those posed naked bodies seemed sterile to me, robbed of context, of the vitality I looked for in even the most ordinary human situations; but I liked taking Mary's pictures. She vamped for me at first, making seductive calendar poses as though she were mocking herself for what wasn't sexually beautiful about her body anymore. It was clear that she felt awkward and uncomfortable. She kept saying, "This is completely crazy"; or, "I've never done anything like this before." But then, finally, as it sometimes happens with people in front of the camera, she just relaxed. She was able simply to turn in the light as I asked her to, to lie back, to squat, to dance to the music on the radio. She had one gesture that I caught in several of the pictures—that of holding her belly as though the baby in there had made her own body precious to her in a way we aren't usually allowed to feel about ourselves.

When we were through and she was getting dressed, I said, "Do you remember when we were little, Mary, and we'd play those dirty games up in our room? Or the basement sometimes? Or Bumping Bottoms—remember that?"

She had been carefully pinning the sprung waist

of her maternity pants. Now she looked up at me and shook her head, smiling. She said, "You know, Nina, I think maybe we need to sit down together while I explain to you the function of repression in human life."

I clicked the lens at her several times, even though there was no film left. "The hell with repression," I said. "I want to remember it all. That's why I love taking pictures. My little victory over all those Freudian processes."

Suddenly she frowned. "Actually, Freud says something like that somewhere."

"Does he?"

"Yes. You should ask Dad. It's not as literal as what you're saying. But it *is* something about art. About art being a way to . . . maybe not escape neurosis but to make use of it, or transform it somehow. I've forgotten."

"Interesting." I watched her. Her hands were still on the big safety pin, and she was staring at me, trying to remember Freud. Her face was softened and made younger by the pregnancy, and she looked for all the world like the earnest little girl she'd been, the Mary who'd trailed after me for years and years, sweet and grave and utterly convinced I knew all the answers. I was sorry there was no film left in the camera.

That film sat on a shelf in my darkroom for a month after I came back to New York. But one night late, unable to sleep, I got up and went in there, looking for something, anything, to do, and I remembered it. Frantic with loneliness, I began to develop the pictures, to fool around with light in the ones I liked.

Will had moved out a week or so earlier. Splitting up with him had been both easier and harder than I had thought it would be. Easier because as it turned out, he felt we were at an impasse too, because he wanted to end it as much as I did. Typically, though, he thought the problem, the drama, was mine, was internal. In his version I was frightened. I was withdrawing from him because there had been something wrong with the baby, because I was fleeing the possibility of producing a damaged child, a child like Randall.

"I know how much you wanted that timeless scene," he said. "The happy family, the beautiful baby."

We were sitting across from each other in the living room, as we had for the last four or five evenings. It seemed to me that we clung to these conversations, these companionable postmortems, because we weren't quite ready yet to say goodbye. We even had several quickly developed rituals: now we were both sipping expensive Calvados from tiny crystal glasses we'd received as a wedding present and barely used since. He spun his glass slowly on the arm of his elegant couch.

I didn't want to end this comfortable sense of aftermath by fighting with him, by saying that I thought it was he who had wanted a changeless, pretty life. Instead I skittered around the topic. I reached for abstraction. Safe. "But time is everything in that scene," I told him.

"Fine," he said. He set his mouth. "Let's not argue."

And we didn't. We went over all the old stuff, even my infidelities, with what seemed almost like Lainey's distance as she talked about my father on the porch. There was never the sense of something deep and abiding between us, though; never the sense of something to forgive, on either side, that had run under even my parents' most peaceful moments. And that made it seem easy when the time finally came, when the Gentle Giant movers pulled up in front with their battered truck.

The hard part, of course, was how much I missed him, all that was steady and reliable and comforting about him. For a while after he moved out, I called him with some regularity, and I only felt at home when I was listening to his voice. But then, once, a woman answered. When he came to the phone, I said just that I was sorry and hung up. And after that I tried to do something else with the energy that wanted to reach out to him.

My repertory, though, was pretty banal. I drank too much, I listened to maudlin music—sometimes even descending for sorrow to country and western stuff. I often stayed up until two or three in the morning, watching anything I could find on TV.

This night I had music on, loud. The *Orchestral Songs,* by Strauss. I was trying not to think about having a drink. I spread four or five of the finished prints of Mary out on a big worktable. And then I noticed, still stacked on the table's corner, the pile of pictures I'd brought back from Chicago. I spread them out too.

For a while I pushed everything idly around on the table—the photographs, the postcards. I began thinking of them as elements in a kind of Rock-Scissors-Paper game, which contained the mystery of my childhood. Which had the most power? Freud? That analytic version of my parents' life, which insisted that Randall—and their misery—had its source in my mother's wackiness and should be struggled against, fought, cured? Or the annunciations, which said, in effect, that Randall was holy, that the failure was my father's in not accepting what was a given, what was fate—as both of the annunciation Marys did in their separate ways, as Mack did in his twinship with Randall. And what was my sister Mary, with her striped, heavy belly, in this game? Perhaps the reality of gestation and birth, which should have taken over the argument anyway with its simple, pressing insistence on life.

In the end I did get a drink. In between sips, I tacked all the pictures up on the wall. And finally I went to bed with the music blasting and the bedroom light still on, curled up on myself in a half circle of misery, hugging my own bare knees.

For weeks, for months, the pictures stayed there. Eventually I simply stopped seeing them, except occasionally when I would suddenly think of something that had happened while I was in Chicago; or something from childhood. Then I'd go and stand in front of them again, staring stupidly at one and then another image, as though if I looked hard enough, long enough, their meaning would become clear.

I hadn't gotten the grant, it turned out; and separating from Will meant that I was broke again. I'd started to do weddings and bar mitzvahs, birthday parties. In the late spring, I accepted a job in Darien for a sixty-fifth wedding anniversary. Will and I had filed for divorce only a few weeks earlier, and I had a sense of facing an appropriate kind of punishment as I assembled what I would need for the day, as I walked down the street through the pale sunlight to the rental car place. But then a rumpled old lady with her bags set down around her looked up from feeding the pigeons and said, "You're up early this beautiful morning, my darling." And I saw that there were blossoms on many of the trees; New York suddenly looked pretty and new. I realized I was glad to be walking through it, that I was taking pleasure in life again, in spite of myself.

The woman who had called me had said the party would be huge—all the generations, "thousands of grandchildren and great-grandchildren." Thinking about it had made me conscious not just of my own

failure with Will but of the strange inability of anyone
in my family but Mary to take up what most people
would call a normal kind of life. Liddie wasn't interested at all, that was clear. Mack didn't seem to be able
to stay married long enough. And Sarah—it was hard
to tell with Sarah, she was so cheerfully promiscuous.
I knew she had slept with at least four members out
of the other five in her band. Somehow she and her
friends reminded me of those line drawings of bun-
nies, hundreds of them, that turned up everywhere
in domestic life in the mid-seventies—on coffee mugs,
on aprons and dish towels. Their innocent randiness
was so blank-eyed that it had taken me a long time
to realize that I was looking at—could there be such
a thing?—bunny orgies.

I found the place easily. It was a mansion on the
coast that the town owned and rented to residents for
special occasions. The family wasn't there yet, but the
woman who'd phoned me, a granddaughter—plump,
red-haired, about forty—was waiting, bustling around
in the elegant, wide entrance hall, ordering a couple
of young women in maids' uniforms to carry food and
big bags of ice here and there. She gave me a name
tag—*Nina Eberhardt, Photographer,* it said—and told
me just to snap whatever was "fun." "Try to get as
many different people as you can," she instructed.
"Everyone's going to want a memento of this. We'll
do the big family portrait after the meal." I could tell
she was nervous. Her eyes in her plump face darted
everywhere, never coming to rest on anything for
more than a fraction of a second. She was carrying
around an extra-large paper cup of Dunkin' Donuts
coffee, and there was another one, empty, resting on
the table where all the other name tags sat.

I pinned the label on myself and meandered
through the grounds. Everything was in bloom here—
rhododendron, mountain laurel, dogwood. It made

the street scene in New York seem retroactively inadequate and skimpy. The dew wet my sneakers.

I watched the family slowly gather, trying to get a sense of its shape, of the logical groupings within it. A brass quintet wearing tuxedos arrived too. They were young, probably college students. They blew and spat into their mouthpieces for a while, and then they began tootling Gabrieli on the wide back lawn.

When the car with the celebrating couple started up the drive, the granddaughter who was running things came onto the veranda out back and shouted the news. The quintet played an impromptu cavalry charge and then ran for the front of the house. We all followed. The musicians stationed themselves quickly on either side of the stairs. As the car doors swung open, they blew a complicated, glorious fanfare, and the hundred or more children, grandchildren, and great-grandchildren cheered and yelled.

The couple was white-haired but not as ancient-looking as I had expected. They were both little and round, and each sported a huge corsage. I noted, too, that she was wearing makeup, though the eyebrows—high, irregular arches—were drawn on with a wavering pencil. Clearly they were ready to enjoy the day. They turned this way and that, like royalty on display, waving and smiling to the group around them. Then a younger, larger relative appeared at the elbow of each, and they began the laborious process of ascending the wide stairs.

A receiving line formed in the entrance hall, and I stood opposite the old couple at its head. Over and over I caught the warm embraces, the joyous smiles. The teenagers touched me the most. There must have been eight or ten of them. They seemed huge and awkward, even those that were only average size, because they all towered over their miniature great-grandparents. And they seemed not to have learned

SUE MILLER

yet the restraint of the formal embrace: they threw their arms with embarrassed and dangerous power around the elderly couple when their turns came, leaving them breathless and flustered in their wake.

When the line finally broke up, the grandparents were helped out to chairs on the back lawn, and people began finding beers or coffee or lemonade. They hailed each other, they slapped each other's shoulders, they embraced and wept. I was wearing several cameras slung around my neck, a sort of armor against intimacy, and it worked. By and large they ignored me. Occasionally someone would approach, eyebrows raised, drink in hand: "You're . . . ?"

I'd shake my head. "Just the photographer," I'd say, and gesture to my name tag.

The granddaughter found me on the back lawn. She had changed her mind. The big portrait would come before the meal. "Everyone's just going to spread out afterwards, and we'll never get them together again," she said. She was drinking beer now, and she seemed a little more relaxed. It took her twenty minutes or so to round everyone up. They gathered slowly on the wide front stairs of the house, and the old couple came and stood at the top.

I waited alone, in front of them on the lawn, while they discussed the arrangement they wanted, while teenage runners were dispatched for those who were obliviously chatting in the house or out back. Somewhere in the group on the stairs, a child started crying, in rising hysteria.

Finally the granddaughter in charge and one of the seventyish sons came and stood next to me. He had a bullhorn, and he translated her instructions in his amplified baritone. The family all fell obediently into the desired shape, a widening triangle, with the grandparents at its peak, the immediate children on the first step down, then the spouses and grandchildren beginning and tumbling down the stairs. The second and third cousins were asked to form a kind of border at the edges. In three long rows on the lawn at the bottom of the triangle, standing, kneeling, and then sitting, were the great-grandchildren. As I was photographing at last, one tiny member of the last generation crawled forward and sat back in the grass on his rubbery legs, sat back as though to look with amazement on all the other generations that had labored and suffered and loved to produce him.

It wasn't a good picture in any sense. There was hardly a way it could be. The best pictures, from my point of view, would be the ones the family didn't even want: Shots of a wailing child, clinging in lonely misery to the leg of his happily talking mother. Of two sisters, side by side, claimed by their genes in spite of wildly varied hairstyles, clothes, makeup. Of the elderly couple, sitting for a moment unattended and speechless in their lawn chairs, each of their faces sunk in isolation and exhaustion.

This, the family portrait, was simply a picture of almost reasonless increase, the instinctual pressure of greedy life wanting more, and then more. But when I looked at it later in my apartment, it seemed connected somehow with that strange assortment of images i'd chosen to remember my family by. And so, oddly, I stuck a copy of it up with them. A picture of perfect strangers. And though for a while it drew me anew to that corner of the room—it seemed to bring to life some question I still couldn't answer—finally it, too, became familiar as wallpaper; I rarely saw it either, though my eyes moved over it every day.

It wasn't until just recently, pregnant again myself and moving to a larger apartment in the city, that I looked clearly at these things once more. We were packing. My husband was doing the books and the heavy stuff. He had the ball game on the radio, and from time to time the announcer's excited voice or the rising cheers of the crowd would float in to me. I was in charge of the small things—dishes from the kitchen shelves, the pictures on the walls, the funny collections of stuff sitting around: a bowl of bright marbles and a shoe box full of Matchbox cars that my stepson played with when he came to stay with us on weekends. Some seashells and a striated, perfectly egg-shaped stone my husband had found for me on the beach before we were even sure I was pregnant.

I moved finally to the corner of the room where I'd stuck up my peculiar arrangement and looked again at all the images. And as I scanned them this time, I realized I was seeing them differently: not as alternative explanations of my family's meaning, competing with each other for dominance; but as one of those puzzles in which you are given different elements and asked to guess their connection, how they all fit together. And out of the blue I understood that the family photograph held the answer. That it was really a portrait of a kind of reckless courage, a testament to the great loving carelessness at the heart of every family's life, even ours. That each child represented such risk, such blind daring on its parents' parts—such possibility for anguish and pain—that each one's existence was a kind of miracle.

But almost simultaneously I realized that if I'd chosen three or four other items from my mother's magic trunks—as Mack would have, or Mary or Sarah—the puzzle itself would have changed shape, would have been different, the mysteries and preoccupations. This was the puzzle I had chosen to try to solve. And the exact nature of this puzzle, the way I had tried to solve it, had as much to do with the puzzle of who I was, the puzzle of what I wished to make of my life, as it did with the mystery of my family. My very choices, *how I saw them,* were part of the puzzle itself. The Virgin Mary who at first tries to flee her fate, the Mary who waits; the boy who is healthy, the boy who is ill; the understanding that comes from faith, the one that comes from a brave new science—they were all just possibilities. And the story they told me now as they came together was as different from what Mack's story might be—or Liddie's, or Mary's—as I am from them.

And, of course, the ending then is different too. Here is mine.

Lainey is pregnant, pregnant with her third child. She's "as big as a country barn," she says, as big as Mary in the pictures I took. As big as I am now. It's July, a hot day. The sun is invisible, directly overhead. She's walking slowly down Fifty-seventh Street, east, in the direction of the lake. Her feet are so swollen that she's put on my father's sandals to make herself comfortable. It's Tony walking next to her, that slightly rolling, dancer's walk. Lainey is trying to amuse her, this new friend, trying to be charming. "Mack was the hard one," she's saying. "My memory is he cried nonstop for the first three months. The most reluctant baby I ever saw." She makes her voice small. " 'Wait a minute,' " she says. " 'I take it all back. I've changed my mind.' "

Ahead of them, Mack and Allie, Tony's little boy, have run into the dark echo chamber of the viaduct. Now they're hooting to hear their own voices call back, and their sandals slap noisily in the cool air under there. The husbands are with them, a hundred feet or so ahead of the women. My father has Liddie on his shoulders. You can't see his head from back here, just her slender body rising out of his. Harold is turned to him, gesturing, talking. They're all going on a picnic.

When she enters the viaduct, Lainey welcomes

the cool air, thinks of it as a benediction—it puffs her hair, it makes her cotton maternity dress ruffle against her. Then she feels a pain, a little contraction, and she rests her hands on herself. She's been having these pains for the last few days, but she's tried to ignore them. The baby isn't due for two weeks yet, and she had these same convulsions nearly every day for a full month before Mack was born. She hasn't even mentioned them to my father.

When they come out into the sun again, Lainey blinks, the world is so bright, the colors so intense after the damp twilight of the viaduct. They pass the artists' studios, strange, ornate wooden storefronts left over from the 1893 world's fair. She remembers, looking into their musty interiors as she walks by now, how she yearned after the life she imagined in them when she first came to Chicago—the messy, unmade beds you could see in the back room behind the studios, the tables like still lifes: fruit, bottles of whiskey, books. They'd be gathered in there at any time of day, three or four of them, bearded men, slatternly looking women. Lainey had thought it wonderfully romantic. Now they all seem lost to her: their paintings and sculpture gathering dust in the streaked display windows, their childless, safe lives tawdry, without meaning. One of them, a woman with bored, empty eyes, stands in an open doorway and watches her wordlessly as she lumbers slowly past.

They cross Stony Island Avenue and enter the park. Tony is pushing a carriage, with her baby, Susan, lying asleep in it. They can see, as they start down the bridle path toward the lagoon, that the parking lot at the museum is full. A shimmer of heat rises over it, making the trees beyond vibrate oddly. The brightly colored cars in the sunshine look like miniatures from here, like so many of Mack's Matchbox toys.

They move through an opening in the thicket at

the bridle path's edge, and they are suddenly out on the lawn. It slopes slowly down toward the lagoon behind the museum, toward the spot that Liddie has told them is her favorite in the whole world, where an old tree stretches its thick trunk horizontally over the stagnant water. She likes to sit on it and dangle her feet in the murky green soup, watching the ducks squabble over crumbs she throws them. The trees arch thickly over them as they cross the grass; the sun is dappled, it loses its scorching power. Everything smells new. Ahead of them the husbands are spreading the blankets, and Lainey watches the flutter of their old blue bedspread. It sinks with incredible slow, billowing grace to the ground.

As soon as they are there, Lainey falls onto it and takes David's sandals off. Huge as they ought to be on her, they've left indented pink stripes in her shapeless feet.

My father has brought a camera, and over the long afternoon, he takes a roll of pictures, mostly of the children perched on the tree trunk. But there are also several of Lainey, even though she doesn't like him to photograph her pregnant. (Later, when we try to linger over these shots in the album, she will cry out, "Those ghastly pictures! Turn the page, turn the page!") One is of her lying down with Liddie astride her thighs, the little girl's hands resting on the drum of her mother's belly. And there's one of her alone that always fascinated me. Her mouth and eyes are peculiarly rounded, like a Kewpie doll's. She's feeling a contraction, a sharp one that almost makes her groan, that makes her think perhaps this baby means business after all.

The sun's shadows grow longer over the thick grass. They've finished all the food. Tony and Lainey lie side by side, smoking indolently in the murky sunlight, while the sweaty children make a game, screaming and running, of gathering the creased, salty wax paper, the napkins, the soggy paper plates, and throwing them away.

On their way home they walk into the setting sun, holding their hands up to shield their eyes when they speak to each other. Mack and Liddie sit turned in opposite directions in the carriage my father pushes. Liddie's singing quietly to herself, he's sucking his thumb, and his eyes are empty in his fatigue. The grownups are tired too, but they don't want the day to stop. My father asks Tony and Harold in for a drink, and while he mixes them, Lainey runs a tepid bath for the children, and she and Tony put them down to bed—all together to keep them happy—in her and my father's room.

Then the two couples sit together in the darkening living room. David has opened a can of almonds. They're sipping the strong martinis and talking. It doesn't matter what about—perhaps the political conventions coming up, maybe hospital stories: Harold is an M.D. too, a surgeon. It could be just gossip about the other couples on the street, or their personal histories: they barely know each other, after all; there's everything to discover, and it will all seem fascinating and complex at first. At any rate, they're happy. From outside come the excited shouts of other people's children at play in the square, and the twilight in here has grown so deep that Lainey can't tell until she tilts her glass against her lips whether it's empty or full.

But Allie has been up now twice, worried about where he is in this new house. First they heard his bare feet lightly smacking the second-floor hallway, and then his shy voice calling from the top of the stairs. Tony went up to him, put him back in bed with the other children. But when Susan begins to wail in her carriage in the front hall, they laughingly decide it's time to give up. Harold goes to the second floor and gets Allie, my father helps Tony lift the baby carriage down the porch stairs, and the Bakers leave, ambling along the shadowed path under the lemony sky, stopping to call back good night before they turn down the block to their own house.

Lainey goes up and rouses the children out of their bed. Liddie has been asleep, and she's cranky about having to get up again. She stumbles to the bathroom by herself and then into her room. My father goes in to her, to sing, to tuck her in.

Lainey flips the toilet seat up for Mack, crouches next to him as he lifts his stubby penis over the edge of the porcelain bowl. She bends her face for a moment into his damp neck.

"I pee standing up," he says hoarsely.

"What a smartie you are," she agrees.

"Not like Liddie," he says. He pulls the toilet handle, and together they watch the water swirl and gurgle.

"Well, she's a girl, like me. We're smart to sit," Lainey says.

He walks ahead of her to his bed and climbs in. Nearly instantly his breathing thickens. She peels back the blanket—it is still hot at ten o'clock—and pushes his hair off his forehead.

"Want a song, sweetie?" she asks.

He stares up at her fixedly as though trying to remember who she is. Then his eyelids lower.

Lainey sits on the edge of his bed and sings softly, just slightly out of tune, all the verses of "Ragtime Cowboy Joe."

When she moves back to the bathroom she's still humming. She bends over the tub, picks up the toys strewn across its bottom, and rinses away the thin layer of grit left by the children's bathwater. On the way to her room, she checks Liddie. The little girl has fallen quickly asleep again, crumpled uncomfortably into a corner against the wall. Lainey straightens her out, pulls the sheet gently over her.

David is in bed, reading by the bedside lamp when she comes in. He's wearing his glasses. They're horn-rimmed, severe, and she smiles at how peculiarly they go with the animal grace of his naked body. He takes them off as she undresses, and she feels his pale eyes steady on her. She lies down next to him. He turns the light off.

The sheets smell of the children, a sweet soapy odor. For a while my parents lie still, side by side. The window is open, and when the air blows in, the curtains rise like little flags and the bedroom brightens; then dims again as they fall back. Lainey can hear the stir of the silver maple leaves outside each time they flutter. Somewhere out on the street, conversing voices slowly fade. A solitary walker goes by. She thinks of how happy she is. She thinks of what she will say to her children when they ask her how she and my father fell in love—she has it planned. Her voice will be careless. "Oh, love," she'll say dismissively. "Oh, yes, we fell in love. But we didn't even know what love was until years after that."

"Are you awake?" he whispers.

"Yes," she says.

He moves down on the bed then and kneels naked at her feet. He begins to massage them.

She watches him, watches his body in the light her eyes have almost grown accustomed to. He is so white, so beautifully shaped. "I can't wait to make love again," she says.

"Needless to say . . ." He slides his fingers between her toes. His touch feels intimate and sexual, even there.

After a moment she says, "Tony's gorgeous, isn't

she?" It's true, but Lainey is asking, too, for David's admiration for herself.

"She laughs too much," David says.

"Well, you make her nervous. She told me so."

Now he grips her ankles, pulls her feet up onto his thighs. She can feel his electric springy hair under her soles. His penis lies, heavy and warm, between her feet. She presses them lightly against it.

"I'd like to make *you* nervous again," he whispers.

"Mmm," she answers. Her legs have pulled slightly apart when he lifted them, and he's looking down at her. She has the sense of being open to him, a sense that's more than sexual, that has to do also with the baby that moves now, hard, inside her.

His hands, cool and dry, move up and down her legs, pushing them apart. "Wouldn't you like it, to be just a little nervous tonight?" he asks. They've gotten so good at pleasing each other, even when they can't make love.

She can feel him stiffening under her feet. "I am, already, a *little* nervous," she whispers. But then his hand moving back over her foot hits a sensitive spot, and her whole leg jerks involuntarily. "Ah!" she says. "Tickle!"

"I thought you didn't indulge," he says.

She's told him this, that she can choose not to be ticklish. She learned it as a child, when her brothers tormented her. You could will insensitivity. You could make your body go away. "I *certainly* don't," she says, and she starts to concentrate on reaching that state. But now he touches her again—she's not ready yet—and she whoops with laughter, she turns her body sharply sideways, her legs swinging together.

"You're in my power now," he says. He's reaching over her, his hands are everywhere on her. She gives herself over to it, to him, to her body. She's laughing now, out of control, delirious with a happiness that feels like being a child and being a woman, all at once—that is both sex and play—when she feels the explosive burst of warm liquid flood from her body. Instantly she's motionless.

"David!" she cries. The leaves sigh outside the window and the curtains billow again, the faint light washes into the room. They find each other's eager faces in the few moments of light, they hold each other's gaze; until the curtains fall back again, and the room is dark, and the great adventure of their life begins.

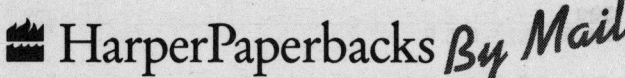